I0672024

THE
INSURRECTION PROTOCOL

A JAKE ANKYER ADVENTURE

BY D K HARRIS

ISBN-13: 979-8-9859767-0-0 (Paperback Edition)
ISBN-13: 979-8-9859767-1-7 (Hardback Edition)
ISBN-13: 979-8-9859767-2-2 (Ebook)
LCCN: 2022905258

Printed in the United States of America

Cover and Interior Design by Tami Boyce
www.tamiboyce.com

IN MEMORY OF JON SCHLICHTING
SEMPER FI

ACKNOWLEDGEMENTS

A NUMBER OF FRIENDS AND COLLEAGUES were immensely helpful to me in the creation of *The Resurrection Protocol*. When asked to help again with the sequel, *The Insurrection Protocol*, they all, unreservedly, agreed to step into the breach once more. In particular, I am indebted to Egil Fosslein, MD, and Marjorie Eskay-Auerbach MD, JD for their medical insights and editorial assistance, Michael Johnson for his editorial and military insights, John Louis Larsen (FBI Retired) for his manuscript review and suggestions, and to Jim Walthour for his firsthand Middle East knowledge. Finally, and most importantly, neither *The Resurrection Protocol* nor *The Insurrection Protocol* would have been written without my wife's direct editorial involvement, support, and encouragement. Thank you, Karen, ... And thank you all!

AUTHOR'S NOTES

THE RED PROTOCOL GROUP MEMBERS are able to communicate with each other with a device in their ear referred to as a "mastoid implant". When they are communicating this way, the text is italicized to distinguish dialogue from normal conversation.

George Makin, a Red Protocol Group operator is periodically undercover as Winston White. When he is communicating with other members of the Red Protocol Group he is referred to as "George". When he is using his undercover persona, he is referred to as "Winston", or "Winston White".

OTHER BOOKS BY D K HARRIS

The Resurrection Protocol

PART ONE

And I looked, and behold a pale horse:
and his name that sat on him was Death,
and Hell followed with him.

PREFACE

THE EIGHT CAPTIVES, FIVE CHILDREN AND THREE ADULTS, were huddled in a corner of the room. The room started out with two captives, and more were added over several days after interrogation. Thin grey soup in a dirty pot was brought in every other day along with a goatskin of water. The water was the source of the diarrhea and the stench increased with each additional arrival.

The room's door, which only unlocked from the outside, opened revealing two guards. One guard held an AK47. The other guard pushed a cart into the room loaded with fruit, bread, and bottled water.

"Stand up!" exclaimed the guard with the rifle. All but one adult captive stood up. The guard who had pushed the cart in dragged the prone captive to the corner of the room opposite the standing captives. The guard then led the children to the cart. He turned to the two adult captives standing in the corner and said, "Each of you is responsible for seeing to it that these children eat and drink their fill. You may have any leftover water and food. More food and water will be given each day. But if a child dies, his death will be upon each of you, and you will receive this punishment."

The guard with the AK47 walked over to the adult captive lying on the floor, emptying the gun's magazine into him, converting the captive into a flesh bag of smoking, unrecognizable organs. "This will be your fate if death visits any of these children. We will leave this body as a reminder of what awaits you."

The guards exited the room and the door swung shut, a lock clicking in place.

The smell of cordite and lingering smoke joined the human stench of the room. One of the remaining adult captives started towards the food cart. Another adult grabbed him. "The children eat and drink first!" he said, shoving the captive to one side.

MAY 1, 2017
LIBYAN DESERT

115 Degrees F
87 miles inland from the Fortress of Ghat
Ghat Libya

SAND.
LIEUTENANT COLONEL ABDUL SALAM SHENNIB
CONTEMPLATED SAND. Not just any sand. Libyan sand. It found its way into your eyes, mouth, throat, nose and up your ass. 3.3 million square miles of sand. Shennib had been posted in the cities of Tripoli and Misratah, the former on the Mediterranean Sea and the latter on the Gulf of Sidra. Shennib knew what water looked like and this did not qualify. On the other hand, he was still alive and carried a firearm, a distinct advantage in his current circumstances. He was a survivor. Prior to Muammar Gaddafi being overthrown, Shennib, through some distant uncle, was awarded a commission in the Libyan Army and sent to an American training

facility in Coronado, California run by the Navy SEAL training command. While there, one of his instructors befriended him... "What the hell is a Libyan soldier doing here?" his new friend asked. "Let's get a drink and you can tell me all about it."

Upon Shennib's return to Libya, Gaddafi was overthrown, and all hell broke loose. Numerous Libyan factions, including the beginnings of various terrorist enclaves, ultimately morphed into offshoots of the Islamic State, al-Qaeda...you name it, and were all staking out territory. Shennib traveled to Benghazi and dodged a bullet...literally. Fortunately, the Libyan army was still intact and was providing a semblance of order in the country at the request of the Libyan "Provisional Guard". Shennib's commanding officer, out of a sense of desperation to get an army presence throughout the country, posted Shennib to the city of Ghat, the capital of the Ghat District in the Fezzan region of southwestern Libya adjacent to the Algerian border. Apart from a few buildings of archaeological interest Ghat was of little consequence to the various militant factions. Shennib's life was uncomplicated if not boring. Which was about to change.

Shennib's Commandant called him into his office. "Abdul, have some tea. Make yourself comfortable."

"How can I be of service Commandant?" Shennib asked, while pouring a cup of particularly excellent tea the Commandant favored.

"We have had a somewhat unusual directive from Central Command in Benghazi," replied the Commandant. Are you familiar with the palace formerly occupied by Mutassim Gaddafi about 75 kilometers from here?"

"I've heard that the area was occupied by a loose band of soldiers, but I have not had a reason to travel there," replied Shennib.

"Well, you do now, Abdul," continued the Commandant. "Central Command has been contacted through a back channel by a high-level American counterterrorism unit and this counter terrorism unit has alerted them that there exists a Libyan terror cell that generates its money by kidnapping Libyan nationals from wealthy families and is presently holding a number of them for ransom. If they can't extract a ransom, they will sell the kidnap victims into the African slave trade."

"I know the slave trade is active in parts of Libya and that we periodically encounter slavers when we round up various antigovernment factions. But why is this of interest to the Americans?" asked Shennib.

"That's what makes this unusual," replied the Commandant. "It appears that this terrorism cell has inadvertently kidnapped a non-Libyan child the Americans are very interested in retrieving."

"An American child?" asked Shennib.

"That's not clear. There is also a rumor that this terror cell was involved in the death of the American ambassador in Benghazi awhile back and that the Americans want vengeance. It's speculation in my opinion. But what is not speculation is that the Americans have asked that one of our units meet them at Gadhafi's palace in the early morning to rescue the Libyan kidnap victims along with any Americans. They also want us there as a means of sanctioning their incursion into Libya. There is one more thing."

"And that would be sir?"

"They have asked specifically for you to be at the rendezvous."

"Me?" said Shennib.

"Yes. They want someone there that they recognize. They said this is very important and that you should be the one there."

"How would they recognize me? asked Shennib.

"I have no idea, said the Commandant. I recall that you attended an American training course, in California, I believe. Maybe that's it. In any event, my instructions are simply to send you and a four-man team to Mutassim Gaddafi's former palace to arrive at 7:30 PM on May 4th, exactly. There is an oasis nine kilometers North from the palace. They will meet you at that location. They also said, that under no circumstances, and I mean under no circumstances, are you to go any nearer to the palace than the oasis."

"And that would be because...?"

"They did not say except that your life and that of your unit could be in danger."

"Is this an active shooting situation?" asked Shennib. "If it is, I will need more than four men and will have to have appropriate armaments."

"The instructions are light arms only and no more than four men and yourself," said the commandant. "They have also requested that you bring two covered military trucks suitable for transporting up to twenty individuals."

"This sounds very dangerous and highly irregular," said Shennib.

"As much as I hate to say it, we have to trust the Americans," said the Commandant.

"But sir..."

"Shennib, you have your orders," said the Commandant. "Also keep in mind that when something does not make sense it's usually because you are missing information, which is highly likely in this situation. You have your orders. Report back to me upon your return. Dismissed."

Shennib stood up, saluted, did an about face and left the room.

HOLY INNOCENTS
TRAPPIST MONASTERY

Gila National Forest
New Mexico
May 1, 2017

THE HOLY INNOCENTS MONASTERY (REFERRED TO AS THE "ABBEY" BY ITS OCCUPANTS) sat as a large, carved stone edifice originally sited on 3,000 acres at the center of the Gila National Forest, which occupied 3.3 million acres in New Mexico. A recent security intrusion from a terrorist cell in the employ of the late Saddam Hussein was a close call which had resulted in a 27,000-foot expansion to accommodate the Trappist monks residing there. In addition, the acreage surrounding the Abbey was enlarged by 100,000 acres of forest to provide an enhanced security buffer. Asher Finkel, MD, PhD, the head of the Red Protocol Group, was determined to eliminate any future incursions to the Abbey in the interest of the safety of the Trappist monks as well as the security of the personnel which was the operational nucleus of the Red Protocol Group.

The Red Protocol Group, a unique component of the United States National Security Agency (N.S.A.), exists to neutralize events, that place the United States in a serious and potentially destructive situation, either physically, politically, or both, and operated outside the mission portfolio of other government agencies, including the military. An exception is a Navy SEAL team, which operates "off the books" as a military enhancement to the Red Protocol Group providing combat leverage as necessary to mission operators. The latter operators are in possession of skill sets and certain neurological enhancements, both physically and intellectually, and are exceptionally effective in eliminating a target threat in active combat situations.

The only government official able to initiate the Red Protocol process is the President of the United States. It is general knowledge that the first day of office involves the newly elected President reading a letter left by his predecessor. What is not widely known is that there is a second letter, which advises the new President of the existence of the Red Protocol Group and its purpose. The reaction of current President to this new information has caused an unscheduled meeting in the library of Holy Innocents Abbey, which will result in a chain of events shaking the United States to its core.

———————————

Jake Ankyer emerged from the wing back chair in one fluid motion as Asher Finkel entered the Monastery library. Ankyer was well groomed with black hair and stood at 6 feet 4 inches, weighing 235 pounds. Ankyer would have been just another unremarkable, large man, except for one green and one blue eye, the result of a condition called heterochromia, a genetic anomaly from a differing amount of melanin in each iris. He also had particularly thick wrists, exceptionally well-developed triceps muscles, and a posture not unlike that of a coiled spring. As he approached Finkel, Ankyer's gait was more of a gliding motion than a walk. His angular face and prominent brow conveyed high intelligence designed for the acquisition of complex information developing rapidly in real time. One was left with the impression that Ankyer did not possess the "sameness" of an ordinary large man. Different, but not different. Best described as "Other".

"Jake, good to see you. How was your flight from London?" asked Finkel.

"Unremarkable," replied Ankyer. "My neurological enhancements tend to mitigate jet lag for some reason... an added benefit. By the way, Brother Arlot reviewed the results of last week's neurological exam with me. There is virtually no change from the results six months ago. He is of the opinion that I may have stabilized at the enhanced levels. Something to do with the space between my synapsis remaining closed due to the declining distance between neurons.

"Excellent!" replied Finkel. "When we started the program, we thought that your mental and physical enhancements would tend to remain at heightened levels over time. If the data remain the same at your next evaluation, we may decide to dispense with the enhancement therapy all together. You will be able to stay in the field much longer. The deployment difference between a conventional submarine and a nuclear version!"

"You told him Dr. Finkel! I wanted to. You stole my thunder!" The exclamation came from a diminutive Asian female appearing to weigh slightly over 100 pounds walking over to Ankyer.

"Honey Pi! You're keeping secrets from me," said Ankyer. Honey Pi, MD DVM. Ankyer's personal physician and veterinarian to the Abbey's security wolf pack.

"Hey Jake. Where would the fun be if I told you everything?" replied Honey Pi.

"You tell him Honey!" came a voice from the entrance to the library. Everyone in the room turned towards the voice in the doorway. A 5-foot 10 inch, well formed, statuesque female, weighing in at 132 pounds looked back. Medium length dark blond hair and bangs accentuating slightly oval, dark brown eyes and a mouth terminating with a hint of a pout completed the vision. Margie Tallon MD, a pathologist formerly with the FBI Evidence Recovery Team, and now an integral component of the Red Protocol Group, walked in. Electrocuted in a Saddam Hussein swimming pool and rescued by Jake Ankyer from an enraged mesomorph, she was now recovering from PTSD and had bonded emotionally to Ankyer. After entering the room Dr. Tallon stood next to Ankyer.

Following Tallon into the library walked Master Chief Neil Groton and a very large Master Chief Fred Bell, both assigned to the Navy SEAL Team tasked with providing military support to the Red Protocol Group. Bell walked with a slight limp, having been crucified next to the pool in which Tallon was being electrocuted. Trailing Bell was another group consisting of Martin Asbury, MD, PhD, physician, and biochemist; Lester Arlot, MD, clinical anatomist; and Augustus Carter, PhD, clinical psychologist.

"Hey guys," said Ankyer. Bell walked over and gave Ankyer a fist bump. "I hear your genes now make you a badass forever," said Bell. Turning to Honey Pi, Anker said, "Is there no one who doesn't know my medical history?"

"Hard to say" replied Honey Pi." "By the way, how's Varna doing?" asked Ankyer.

"See for yourself," a voice replied. Standing in the doorway was a large, bald, head attached to a Grand Master martial arts body.

"William!" exclaimed Ankyer. Good to see you. Before he could answer, he was pushed aside by a 385-pound Mackenzie Valley Canadian Timber Wolf with activated Dire Wolf genes that bounded across the room and skidded to a halt in front of Ankyer. "Varna my friend!" exclaimed Ankyer. "Has Brother William been taking good care of you?"

"Of course, he has!" said William. Varna stood up over 6 feet on his back legs and snatched a very large dog biscuit in midair launched by William.

"Varna is going to get fat with all these dog biscuits," said Tallon.

"Ordinarily, I would agree with you," said Finkel. "But circumstances have arisen concerning Varna. We need to talk about him at the end of the briefing."

Dr. Finkel coughed slightly. "Now that everyone is here and Varna has had his dog biscuit, please join me at the conference table so we can begin." The group followed Finkel towards the center of the room to a large rectangular, polished rosewood table with swivel seats integrated into the base. The room itself was forty feet by sixty feet with large, stone walls interrupted by bookcases and a large HD TV monitor on the wall opposite the table. Lighting in the room was medium dim, emanating from wall sconces. Additional lighting was from a crystal chandelier suspended over the conference table. After everyone was seated, Finkel folded his hands in front of him, scanning the others at the table.

"I have two agenda items for our meeting today" said Finkel. "The first is administrative in nature. The second is operational.

THE INSURRECTION PROTOCOL

I'll address the administrative item first. As most of you are aware, the first time a newly elected U.S. president enters his White House office and sits at his desk he will see an envelope left for him by his immediate predecessor. The contents of the envelope will usually be a letter with various comments regarding the predecessor's time in office, including suggestions, and so on. In the case of our current President, Stephen Luis Gatling, he received a second 'For Your Eyes Only' letter. The second letter advised President Gatling of the existence of the Red Protocol Group, its mission, and a summary of its activities. Our new President was further advised to only utilize the Red Protocol Group in circumstances of dire emergency requiring highly selective intervention using our skill sets. Shortly thereafter, I received a call from the White House summoning me to a meeting with the President. Because of that meeting, my counterpart at the National Security Agency and I have initiated certain adjustments to our relationship with the N.S.A. Before going into those, I want to review a portion of a recording of my conversation with the President. Several people have met with the President only to have their conversation subsequently misrepresented. To memorialize the conversation accurately, I utilized a recording device integrated into my person as one of the dots on my polka doted bow tie. I have inserted "POTUS" to identify Gatling out of respect for the Office of the President. Please turn your attention to the monitor opposite our table."

The monitors flickered to life and text appeared on each.

POTUS: Stephen Luis Gatling, President of the United States
FINKEL: Asher Finkel, MD, PhD
Location: President's private library, White House.

----recording----

POTUS

"Dr. Finkel, I will get directly to the point. I don't trust many of the senior officials of the FBI and CIA. A number of my supporters have advised me that there could even be violent intent involved."

FINKEL

"I can't imagine…"

POTUS

"Well…imagine it. What's more, I'm not sure about the Secret Service. Considering various lapses brought to my attention by my Chief of Staff, the Treasury Department and more to the point, the protective services unit of the Secret Service may not be serving me well."

FINKEL

"I am astounded Mr. President. The Secret Service has always served without question. I know there have been infrequent lapses with incursions onto White House grounds, but with the recent upgrades to supervisory staff I would think the presidential Secret Service protective services would be substantially improved."

POTUS

"I am aware of the Secret Service staff changes. But when it comes to my security, I require unquestioned loyalty in addition to professional competence."

FINKEL

"Mr. President, a key requirement of a Secret Service agent is his or her willingness to take a bullet for you or others in their charge. That's their job. 'Loyalty' doesn't enter into it. In my opinion…"

THE INSURRECTION PROTOCOL

POTUS
"Dr. Finkel, we can debate the job requirements of Secret Service agents some other time. Loyalty is important to me, and I expect it from anyone who works for me, including you. What I need...no what I want, is the equivalent of the Roman Praetorian Guard."

FINKEL
"Mr. President, the Praetorian Guard were soldiers loyal to their commanders and to the extent it served their purposes, supportive of the Emperor. There are numerous examples of an Emperor being overthrown by the Praetorian Guard when it suited the Guard's objectives. I am not sure it's a good analogy.

POTUS
"Nevertheless, this brings me to the reason for my asking you in. I need protection I can count on. The letter concerning the Red Protocol Group indicates that the group is attached to the N.S.A. The letter also provides some detail on the recent Saddam Hussein affair, including general comments concerning a Red Protocol operator responsible for the affair's successful conclusion. The letter does not identify the operator, however. I am thinking of establishing a new group charged with my personal protection. From what I've read, your unnamed operator may be just the person I need to run it. As a matter of fact, if he is as capable as is inferred in the letter, he may be all I need."

FINKEL
"Mr. President, the Red Protocol Group is a unique, military response unit, which is highly surgical in nature and is deployed

only in extreme situations requiring the unusual skill sets of its operators. The person you are thinking of is a very highly, trained combat warrior, whose skills are unique and require continuous tuning. What he is not sir, is a guard."

POTUS
"He sounds like just what I am looking for. Since he works for the N.S.A, I could just have him transferred over to the White House. But I thought I would go by the books so to speak and discuss the matter with you first. Think it over. Discuss it with your operator. Don't take too long though."

"By the way, a friend of mine has an acquaintance who has a problem I'd like you to look into," said Gatling, handing Finkel an envelope marked TOP SECRET. It's self-explanatory. "

---low chime sounds---

POTUS
"That's the signal for my next meeting."

----recording ended----

The monitors flickered and went blank. Finkel paused, letting the POTUS/Finkel conversation sink in. Finkel then said: "We need to stop referring to Stephen Luis Gatling as 'president' in the unlikely event some part of our group's discussion is conveyed to unauthorized parties. We have come up with a code name we will use going forward. It's an acronym for the President's name." The monitors again flickered, and the President's name was displayed with specific letters in bold type.

THE INSURRECTION PROTOCOL

Stephen **Lu**is Gatling
SLUG

"Excellent" exclaimed Dr. Honey Pi. "It's perfect!"

"Simple linguistic cross manipulation," replied Finkel. "We needed a code word that is easily remembered, and which conveys the underlying essence of the individual."

"We'll have no trouble remembering this," observed Ankyer with a chuckle.

"I'm glad" said Finkel. "Because SLUG has caused the initiation of a rather dramatic change in our organization. But before I get into that, Augustus, I would like your professional opinion of SLUG in the conversation you have just reviewed."

Dr. Augustus Carter sat back in his chair sucking on a pipe, which was never observed being lit. Carter's rheumy eyes, shock of white hair and slight build belied a razor-sharp mind. "Disturbing," replied Carter. "Without examining him myself, its speculation, but in a nutshell, SLUG appears to suffer from what we call malignant narcissism syndrome, a collection of signs and symptoms which includes narcissistic personality disorder, antisocial personality disorder, paranoid traits and a number of schizoid personality disorders. It's not surprising that SLUG has managed to rise to the level of President as the malignant narcissist tends to derive higher levels of psychological gratification from successes over time, which also tends to self-feed and worsen the disorder. An individual with this malignant form of narcissism tends to develop substantial paranoia, which in this case, supports his desire to be protected by his vision of a Praetorian Guard. Considering all of this in context, what we have here with SLUG is a very sick puppy."

"Do you see his illness impacting the activities of our group?" asked Finkel.

"Absolutely," replied Carter. "SLUG's paranoia has already begun to damage his perception of the Secret Service protection he receives. Since he is aware of the Red Protocol Group and its capabilities, his paranoia could easily turn on the Group, either causing it to be disbanded or changed, making it ineffective, or worse, causing a counterproductive mission to be initiated."

"Any ideas as to how we might prevent that from occurring?" asked Finkel.

"Buy into his fantasy," replied Carter. "Provide SLUG the protection he perceives as being necessary. This would serve to dilute SLUG's paranoia regarding the Red Protocol Group should his paranoia increase which is highly likely. It would also provide an opportunity to keep track of him."

"Keep track of him?" queried Finkel.

"Absolutely," replied Carter. "The malignant form of narcissism afflicting SLUG, considering the powers invested in him, makes SLUG a clear and present danger to the United States."

"After my meeting with SLUG, I reviewed the conversation with my counterpart at the N.S.A. Our analysis of the President tracks directly with the view Dr. Carter just expressed. Placing someone from the Red Protocol Group in proximity to SLUG would serve to provide us with advance warning should SLUG's behavior become increasingly erratic. While outside the normal mission parameters of our group, we agreed that inserting a Red Protocol operator to keep an eye on SLUG makes sense."

"Surely you are not suggesting I become SLUG's bodyguard," said Ankyer.

"Not at all," replied Finkel. "He doesn't know who you are so we can insert a substitute. As a matter of fact, we have just the person."

THE INSURRECTION PROTOCOL

As if on cue, a tall, slightly limping figure appeared as a black silhouette in the entrance to the library. The figure walked in and was immediately recognized by the group.

SOMEWHERE IN BALTIMORE MARYLAND

May 1, 2017
9:00 PM Eastern Time

THE ROOM CONSISTED OF TWO LEATHER CHAIRS, A COFFEE TABLE upon which rested a carafe of water, and two crystal glasses. The entire room was painted in non-reflective light grey with soft light emanating from an unseen source. The room held no pictures or other adornments. A pneumatic pocket door opened and closed as each of two occupants entered. Unseen was a sound-deadening material lining the ceiling, walls, and door. The room had been scanned moments prior to their arrival for audio and video transmission devices or any electronic waves. On the coffee table was a small radio-like device which generated 'white noise' to provide additional privacy to the otherwise protected conversation.

The taller of the two men had an air of command presence. The second occupant, showing deference to the tall man, remained standing until the tall man was seated.

"I'm not comfortable meeting like this. I don't care what the security is," said Stephen Luis Gatling.

"We should not have to do this very often. What is it you require?" replied Mallory Tensale, Gatling's Chief of Staff.

"Are you familiar with the 25th Amendment to the Constitution?" asked Gatling.

"Generally, it has to do with removing the President from office, doesn't it?" said Tensale.

"Yes," said Gatling. "If the President is determined to be unable to fulfill the duties of the Office for any reason the 25th Amendment can be invoked, and the Vice President steps in. Most people think this is just a function of the Congress. In fact, it can be initiated by the Cabinet and the Vice President. A sitting Vice President and most of the Executive Branch's Cabinet can, on their own, agree to transfer power out of the hands of a sitting president to the vice president and then notify the Congress."

"And you're bringing this up because...?"

Gatling leaned forward in his chair. "I'm bringing this up because these bastards in my Cabinet, starting with Vice President Penelope fucking Bartlett, plan on invoking the 25th Amendment and throwing my ass out of office." Gatling's face had turned red and the arteries in his neck were pulsing noticeably.

"They can't just do it for Christ's sake," Tensale replied.

"They have come up with some bullshit that I'm paranoid because I want to start carrying the nuclear briefcase around myself. Hell. You never know when you might have to use it! They also are objecting to my plan to add my head to Mount Rushmore."

"What do you want me to do?" asked Tensale.

D K HARRIS

"I want you to get rid of them," said Gatling, his voice lowered and seething. The rims of his eyes were red now and some drool emerged from the corner of his mouth. Gatling had also started to hyperventilate completing the transformation.

"Get rid of them? All of them?"

"I thought about just a few of them. The ringleaders for sure, including the Vice President, the Attorney General, the Secretary of Education, and the Secretary of Defense. They're the ones who started it and some others jumped on board. They may not be the only ones though. The whole damn Cabinet may be infected. Better safe than sorry. I want to clean house."

"How did you find all this out?" asked the man.

"The wife of the Secretary of the Treasury spilled the beans to me at a dinner party. She said that her husband had been approached and that he was thinking about it. She also wanted to know if I would appoint her as Secretary of Education after the present one was fired. She said that the Vice President might be in on it since she wants to run in the next election. If she was moved into the Presidency after my removal, she could run as an incumbent."

"You're shitting me," said Tensale.

"I know what you're thinking. This woman is dumb as a rock, which would ordinarily be a gross understatement. But in this case, maybe not so much. She also gave me a copy of a draft menu from the White House chef. On the top was scribbled 'favorite meals of the vice p'. I had it checked out and they are in fact the bitch's favorite meals. These people are so confident of getting rid of me they are coordinating with the goddam kitchen!"

"Ok. I'm convinced" said Tensale. "Get rid of them how?"

"I don't care how as long as it doesn't get traced to me," replied Gatling. "One thing though. I don't want to just put a scare into them and get them gone for just a few weeks. I want them gone.

Period. How it's done is up to you. I must leave now. Are you clear on this?"

"Crystal," replied Tensale.

As the men rose from their chairs the pneumatic pocket door opened silently. President Gatling exited first, and the door closed. A few moments later the door reopened and Tensale exited. The carafe of water and two crystal glasses remained untouched.

HOLY INNOCENTS
TRAPPIST MONASTERY

Gila National Forest
New Mexico
May 1, 2017

GEORGE MAKIN, AKA PHILLIP BLACK, FORMER FBI SPECIAL AGENT undercover operative and now a member of the Red Protocol Group entered the library.

"Nice to see you in one piece, George ...pun intended," said Ankyer.

Finkel gestured to Makin inviting him to sit in a seat at the table Finkel had conveniently left empty. "George, why don't you give our colleagues a quick summary of the circumstances enabling you to rise from the dead."

"Thanks Dr. Finkel," said Makin. "As you all can see I have returned to the living, so to speak. Quite a trick after being blown up courtesy of Saddam Hussein."

"Hey" exclaimed Chief Fred Bell. "Hussein had me crucified on a floor!"

"We all have our crosses to bear," retorted Makin generating chuckles around the table.

"All right gentlemen," said Finkel. "We have a full agenda. Press on George."

"As I was saying, my part in the Saddam Hussein affair was to contact Saddam's banker, Hans Greffen at the INF Banque Nationale in Switzerland and persuade him that it would be in his interest to freeze all of Hussein's accounts and transfer the funds to our control. I accomplished this with the proviso that I would relocate Mr. Greffen and his family to a secure location out of the country. I arrived at Mr. Greffen's residence to collect him and his family and proceeded to Apartment 5 on the fourth floor. Once inside I told Greffen, his wife, son, and daughter to quickly pack one bag each with medications and other essentials and that we were leaving immediately. At that point there was a knock on the door. Greffen's wife Frieda said that she had invited a neighbor, Mrs. Blumquist to come and say goodbye. Greffen's daughter, Heidi, ran to open the door. The moment the door opened, Mrs. Blumquist somehow had been transformed into a black bearded, Saddam terrorist who rushed into the room and ignited an exploding vest."

"We know. That's why we all thought you were dead", said Margie Tallon.

"Ah, but what you did not know was that there were actually two explosions. The first was a small explosion resulting from the vest's detonator misfire. It was at that point I flattened myself on the floor. Immediately thereafter, the second, main explosion occurred incinerating Heidi and, it was assumed me, while blowing Greffen, Frieda and Rolf into small bits. However, as luck would have it, the terrorist's exploding vest had a Claymore mine incorporated into it. As you may know Claymore mines are convex shaped, anti- personnel mines which when activated, explode outward with great force. The first, smaller explosion pitched the terrorist forward in a downward angle position. Accordingly, when the Claymore mine exploded, not only was the Greffen family killed, the blast's additional downward angle also collapsed a large portion of the apartment's floor dropping it down to the third floor...and me with it. I was buried by debris for two days, dehydrated but still alive. Since the devastation in the Greffen apartment was extensive, it was assumed by first responders that all the inhabitants of the Greffen apartment were blown up. Of course, none of the first responders even knew I was there. Dr. Finkel immediately sent a recovery team under diplomatic immunity to secure and evaluate the crime scene. They eventually discovered me covered by debris on the third floor."

"When we got George back to the Abbey, his medical evaluation revealed a slight fracture of his left ankle, some dehydration, and that was it," said Dr. Honey Pi.

"You knew about this?" said Ankyer, his eyebrows raised.

"Hey, I'm the team doctor and doctors can keep secrets," replied Honey Pi.

"And what's more, George no longer officially exists which makes him perfect for keeping track of our friend SLUG, which is George's next undercover assignment," said Finkel. "Considering SLUG's erratic behavior and increasing paranoia, George will function as the new level of protection the President has requested and will, for the most part, be at his side constantly including in Cabinet meetings. SLUG is insisting on this, and it will work out nicely. George's operational name will be Winston White. We have developed a complete pedigree for him."

"But how will I be able to communicate all the information in real time?" asked Makin.

"Ah. Good question and a solution is at hand," said Finkel. "A micro, two-way communications device constructed from your cartilage to prevent rejection will be installed in a cavity in your mastoid process and it will be attached to your auditory nerve to facilitate communication. You and I can communicate via geo-synchronous satellite telecommunications, simply by you talking or whispering to yourself. You can hear my responses as if I were talking in your ear, all in real time. We used it with Jake during the Saddam affair, and it functioned so well we've implemented it with all Red Protocol operators. More importantly, any conversation within your hearing or out of your hearing in the physical space you occupy is automatically transmitted to recording devices here at the Abbey. We will be able to quickly analyze any information we receive and communicate back to you as necessary."

"You're converting me to a human bugging device!" exclaimed Makin. "There goes my privacy."

"Not true," replied Finkel. "You will be able to press a spot at the base of your right ear to turn the system off. We would like you to keep it on whenever you are with SLUG or are present at a conversation related to SLUG or any other matter you think we may be interested in."

"It takes some getting used to, having Dr. Finkel inside your head, but Dr. Finkel uses it judiciously," said Ankyer.

"After our meeting here, you can go to medical where they will be waiting for you," interjected Finkel.

During the conversation Varna had trotted over to Makin, sniffed him, and rubbed against Makin's leg. "Well, that's it, George," said Brother William. "You're officially on the team, or as Varna would growl, 'back in the pack'."

"Before we proceed to a discussion of our latest mission, I have a few administrative items for you," said Finkel. "As I mentioned earlier, my counterpart at the N.S.A. and I reached the conclusion that SLUG's behavior has been erratic to say the least. Additionally, SLUG's evident paranoia, along with a complete lack of Congressional oversight, has caused us to adjust the relationship between the N.S.A. and the Red Protocol Group. I have discussed elements of these changes with each of you individually and wanted to spend a few minutes today summarizing the total picture. In a nutshell, the Red Protocol Group is removing itself from the direct administration of the N.S.A. Instead, we will become a separate, independent organization, which will provide contractual services, primarily to the N.S.A. The N.S.A will continue to provide critical intelligence resources and mission support as now. The N.S.A. will request assistance for specific missions and provide us with mission details. Acceptance of the mission will, however, ultimately be our decision and will be dependent on mission parameters, our resource availability, and most importantly, consistent with our operational requirement of protecting the people of the United States. Significantly, missions will come through the N.S.A., not SLUG. Should SLUG request a mission it will be communicated to the N.S.A and then through them to the Red Protocol Group for us to accept or reject as appropriate.

"How will the new arrangement be supported financially?" asked Ankyer. ("Appropriate question from the most lethal PhD analytical economist on the planet," thought Margie Tallon.)

"An important question Dr. Ankyer," replied Finkel, who was in the habit of referring to Ankyer's academic credential paid for by the Red Protocol Group via the London School of Economics when the conversations shifted periodically to certain non-mission topics. "Our new status will be facilitated by approximately 15 billion euros and ongoing investment income, which have been transferred to Red Protocol Group accounts at different banking locations around the world. This has been accomplished courtesy of Saddam Hussein's funds and other assets transferred to our control. In addition, the Red Protocol Group will be compensated by fees from the N.S.A. for mission expenses as well as expenses associated with mission readiness activities including such items as our aircraft, laboratories, and security systems like Varna's wolf pack, for example. In addition, compensation for all Red Protocol staff will be very substantially increased including large separation bonuses and long-term retirement plans designed to fund all the needs of each staff member and at least two generations of their family members. The Red Protocol Group is highly demanding and financial security will be guaranteed for everyone. The Group has removed itself from a government entity subject to the increasing vagaries of Congressional oversight and the unpredictable behavior of SLUG. It has morphed into a tightly knit, extended family of professionals designed to protect the interests of the United States when other means are unavailable. The Red Protocol Group has become the last line of defense between chaos and the Homeland."

"Varna will expect a raise!" exclaimed Brother William as Varna's ears pricked up at his name.

"What about our Navy Seal team friends?" asked Honey Pi.

"Master Chief Groton, would you like to respond?" asked Finkel.

"Certainly, Dr. Finkel," replied Neil Groton. "Effective immediately, members of the entire Navy SEAL team have submitted their retirement papers and are pleased to commit their expertise and resources as part of the Red Protocol Group. Periodic additions to the group will be required to meet the exacting standards of Navy SEAL recruitment and training."

"Thank you Master Chief. It is an honor to have you and your colleagues with us," said Finkel.

"I can't complete my summary without mentioning Brother William, our grand martial arts master and keeper of Varna and the wolf pack. I have spoken to the Abbey's abbot, Father Bruno, and he has given Brother William a dispensation to work with us as a layperson, with his permission of course, until such time as Brother William retires or returns to the monastic life if he so chooses.

"I am absolutely committed to the program you suggest," said Brother William as he palmed a biscuit to Varna.

"So much for the administrative summary. I have already spoken with each of you regarding specific elements of the next Red Protocol mission. Now it's time to bring everyone into the complete picture," said Finkel.

The lights in the library dimmed. A walnut paneled wall opposite the conference table dissolved, becoming a translucent screen revealing a large map of Libya. A blinking red dot appeared on the map. "That blinking red dot is the city of Ghat, an unexceptional location in southwestern Libya close to the Algerian border. Apart from some minor, archeological significance, Ghat is generally invisible on everyone's radar. That is until recently. SLUG's predecessor was contacted by Emir Salazar bin Hamad bin Kartoon Al Sallazon on behalf of his son, Crown Prince Bamin bin Hamad Sallazon, the presumptive heir and likely the next Emir of Qatar."

THE INSURRECTION PROTOCOL

Finkel took a sip of water and continued. "It seems that a 184-foot Qatar yacht, the Flying Carpet, was on a pleasure cruise in the Mediterranean Sea two miles off the coast of Libya. What the ship was doing so close to Libya is anyone's guess. In any event, the Flying Carpet was approached by a boat and told to stop all engines. Ordinarily a ship the size of the Flying Carpet would ignore such a demand, fire up its dual 2000 horsepower engines, and leave them in its dust, metaphorically speaking. In this case however, the boat was not the usual 20-foot Somali pirate skiff with a 20-horsepower motor. It was a fifty-foot gunboat with a single cannon mounted in the forecastle. When the Flying Carpet failed to heave to, the gunboat promptly fired its cannon and blew a large hole slightly above the Flying Carpet's waterline. "

"I gather we are not talking about your normal "Blackbeard" type pirates at this juncture," remarked Ankyer.

"Definitely not," replied Finkel. "In fact, it turns out that the 'pirates' are a Libyan militant subgroup component of al-Qaeda. But I'm getting ahead of myself. Once the Flying Carpet was boarded by members of the gunboat crew, four Qatari security personnel were disarmed of their weapons and were secured with plastic cuffs along with the remainder of the crew. Five children, ages eleven through twelve along with three adult minders were led to the aft of the ship and down two flights of stairs to the Ski-doo personal watercraft launch platform and led over to the waiting gun boat. The captain asked that he and his crew be uncuffed to navigate the Flying Carpet to a port in Libya as the ship was starting to take on water. The request was ignored by the gunboat crew, which started the gunboat engines moving approximately fifty yards off the port side of the Flying Carpet. The gunboat then proceeded to fire its main cannon blowing a hole on the starboard side of the Flying Carpet below the water line. A second shot destroyed the flying bridge and a third the helicopter on the stern landing deck. A fourth shot hit just below the assembled crew blowing them apart. The fifth and final shot hit the engine room causing the yacht to explode. A security camera DVD was found floating in the debris, which is why we know what happened with the precision I just described."

"So far it looks like murder and kidnapping for ransom," said Margie Tallon.

"Ordinarily I would agree," replied Finkel. "But there is more. It turns out that the purpose of the voyage was a twelfth birthday celebration for Salud bin Hamad Sallazon, the son and heir of Crown Prince Bamin bin Hamad Sallazon, who is next in line in succession as the Qatar Emir.

What's more, N.S.A. intelligence intercepts indicate the pirates knew there were high value Qatar targets on board the Flying Carpet but did not know the Crown Prince's son was one of them. They evidently think they are just children of wealthy Qatar parents. They don't know they have the Crown Prince's son. The Qataris are particularly concerned that under interrogation one of the children or a minder might reveal that the Crown Prince's son is one of the captives. Such knowledge could escalate the situation and cause the pirates to kill one or more of the captives to demonstrate power in a ratcheted-up attempt to increase leverage of ransom or other demands."

Augustus Carter cleared his throat. "I think it's probably worse than that," said Carter. "The psychological stress of the capture itself might engender an accelerated Stockholm syndrome causing one or more of the captives to reveal the boy. Should this occur and considering the captors may be a faction of Al-Qaeda, which has a particularly violent psychological profile, they may immediately start carving pieces off the boy and sending them to the

Crown Prince sooner than later. This situation must be resolved as quickly as possible."

"I agree one hundred percent Dr. Carter," said Finkel. "As soon as the Qataris discovered what happened they contacted the C.I.A., which contacted the N.S.A., which contacted us. Qatar does not have a positive diplomatic relationship with Libya. The U.S. State Department is reluctant to ask for a SEAL team rescue given the political damage around the US ambassador killing a few years back. An inquiry was made to SLUG whose response, I understand, was to comment: 'What's in it for me? Maybe they will think twice again when they refuse to put my name on a Qatar golf course.' Taking all this into consideration, the N.S.A. has concluded that the Red Protocol Group is best positioned to respond to the situation and deploy its unique level of resources the problem requires. I will be directing mission information to my counterpart at the N.S.A. as appropriate. Any questions so far? Hearing none, let's review our mission's operational elements. An unusually interesting and challenging assignment if I do say so."

RESIDENCE OF
ANASTASIA MOON

Eagle River Ranch
Eagle River Ranch Colorado
May 2, 2017

ARKANSAS CONGRESSMAN PHILLIP MERKLIN STOOD BEFORE THE 60 by 45 foot, 1-inch-thick window and was struck by the view as always. Mountain peaks dusted with snow, a mountain pass 100 feet below, eagles soaring above on thermals with their forest home off in the distance. Merklin could stand and drink in the view all day from this window in the great room of the 40,000 square foot lodge. Outside the window was a stone deck cantilevered over a gorge that seemed to be cut from crystal, with a river of moving glass flowing towards broad plains in the distance. A herd of buffalo meandered in a distant plain. The view was but a small part of the 130,000 contiguous acres known as the Eagle River Ranch. Merklin always caught his breath in front of the window. "Phil, would you like to join the rest of us? The conference call will begin shortly."

The voice, soft but firm, emanated from behind Merklin and belonged to Anastasia Moon, the female scion of the Alfernon Corporation, a holding company which owned Eagle River Ranch, and controlled several billion dollars in corporate investments. The crown jewel of these was Sandstone Pharmaceuticals, the manufacturer and distributor of vitamin supplements consumed by over 40 percent of the inhabitants of planet earth. Moon's antecedent relatives, notably her great grandfather who founded the company, her grandfather and father all had what appeared to be a genetic predisposition for generating massive amounts of money and atherosclerosis. When Anastasia's father died suddenly of an aortic blockage at age 47, 25-year-old Anastasia, an only child whose mother's demise preceded her fathers', inherited the considerable family fortune including 100% of all the stock of every one of the companies in the family's corporate empire. Now, 10 years later, she was the financial centerpiece of a plan to take over control of the United States.

Merklin turned from the window and walked over to a spacious seating area with a three-quarter arc of leather chairs, each chair with a side table on which rested a glass of water. All the chairs were occupied. Anastasia Moon was curled in the middle of a red leather love seat in the open space at the top of the arc. A thick, beamed ceiling included numerous multihorned, buck deer, multiple light chandeliers spaced the length of the room, casting light on her and the other room's occupants. At either end of the room were two mounted bison heads. Across from the window was a two-story bookcase traversing the length of the room, the center of which included an open double door into a dimly lit hallway. As Merklin took his seat he was impressed by a serpent-like quality exuded by Moon, enhanced by her 5-foot 11-inch frame, jet black hair and black full length body suit. For a moment Merklin thought of the possibilities, but only briefly. Moon might look like a woman but was closer to a black widow spider.

Moon held a small remote control and pressed a center button. A small light on the remote flashed once.

The voice of Mallory Tensale, President Gatling's Chief of Staff's voice filled the room from a hidden speaker phone, "Good afternoon. Thank you for your attendance. Who is with us today?"

"Congressman Phillip Merklin, Buster Hornsbee from the Pentagon, and my assistants Mr. Sten, Mr. Bent and Mr. Blue," replied Moon.

"And our other Congressional colleagues?" asked Tensale

"With Congress in recess, a variety of Congressional duties prevented their attendance today. Congressman Merklin was able to fly in today on our corporate jet giving 'personal reasons' for his absence. He can update the others upon his return."

"Excellent," replied Tensale. "I will get to the point of our call. We have been given a green light for a second project. Our primary project of undermining Congress continues as scheduled without change. Our new project is the removal of President Gatling's Cabinet at his request. Our President is under the impression that the Cabinet is conspiring to invoke the Constitution's 25th Amendment to remove him from office. A plan he obviously neither supports nor intends to let occur."

"How 'removed' does he want them?" asked Moon.

"Not removed from the planet," replied Tensale. "That would not serve our interests regarding the first project. No. The Cabinet members must be incapacitated to the point they cannot function. This will cause the public to engage in conspiracy theories but not to coalesce around the idea of an act of war from an outside force.

THE INSURRECTION PROTOCOL

Acting Cabinet officers can be appointed until replacements are nominated and vetted by Congress. Before the replacements are in office however, the primary project will be executed leaving the country in chaos and providing the means for us to gain complete control. By then a Cabinet will have no functional purpose. President Gatling has in effect, provided us with the means to confuse the entire US population while our true purpose and mission will go forward unimpeded. Destroying the Cabinet will provide an elegant distraction, while the primary project eliminates the United States Congress's ability to function thereby providing a vacuum for us to fill and giving us the time and ability to emerge in control of the Country."

"I continue to remain concerned about the military," said Buster Hornsbee, the Pentagon congressional liaison. "There will be a natural inclination to take over. The Joint Chiefs of Staff will probably be accused of considering a military coup!"

"That will not be a problem," said Tensale. "The Joint Chiefs will be eliminated along with the Congressmen. They will be immediately replaced with our own people by Presidential directive."

"Brilliant!" replied Hornsbee. "I apologize for my momentary lapse."

"So how do we incapacitate the Cabinet?" asked Merklin.

"Remember the incidents in Cuba and China where U.S. diplomatic personnel were taken sick," said Tensale. "It's called the Havana Syndrome. The illness was induced as part of a test by the Chinese to determine if it was possible to disable U.S. embassy personnel. They have come up with a device that causes the symptoms of Meniere's disease."

"Meniere's disease? What's that?" Merklin asked.

"It's a medical condition of the middle ear that results in dizziness, loss of hearing, loss of balance and severe headaches. When an attack occurs it's very disabling and can last for 24 hours. The Chinese have improved on mother nature. Their version magnifies the disease symptoms dramatically. They utilize a transducer to generate high amplitude ultrasound waves, which cause the symptoms. The version we received from them increases the sound waves by a magnitude of two hundred times over the initial model and effectively destroys the middle ear and its balancing systems. We tried it out on a human subject a few days ago."

"What happened?" asked Merklin.

"The moment the device was turned on the subject fell to the floor, curled up in a ball and started screaming," replied Tensale.

"How long did the effects last?" replied Merklin.

"It's still going on three days later. It's a one-way ticket to hell. The only thing the Chinese have requested is that we provide them with a report of the effects, ideally with audio and video. Of course, we are not telling them we are using the device on the Cabinet. They may be tempted to mount a preemptive strike if they deduce our plan," said Tensale.

"How big is the device?" asked Moon.

"Not big. It's in capsule form can be inserted into one of the expensive pastries the Cabinet has become accustomed to eating at their meetings. The device itself is powered by an extremely small plutonium power source designed by the Japanese," said Tensale. "There is an activator switch on the side. The device is inserted into the pastry after the switch is pressed. It is timed to activate two minutes later."

"It would be interesting to be there when it happens," said Hornsbee.

"Glad you mentioned that" said Tensale. "You will be there to insert the device into the pastry and activate it."

"But……"

"Don't worry," said Tensale with a light chuckle. "The Chinese have also designed a hearing apparatus, which you will wear to generate white noise and cancel out the effects of the device."

"When will this take place?" asked Moon

"The next Cabinet meeting is scheduled for two months from now. That will provide us with ample time to complete preparations for our principal initiative. Our discussion is concluded," said Tensale "Anastasia will contact you with the time and date for our next conversation. Anastasia, please stay a moment."

Mr. Sten escorted the meeting participants from the room leaving Mr. Bent and Mr. Blue in the shadow of a corner of the room. When they had gone, Moon said: "You did not mention the suitcase bombs."

"For a reason," said Tensale. "As you know, the primary plan calls for the destruction of the Congressional representatives at strategic locations throughout the country. The nuclear devices provided by Russia are particularly dirty and will leave a half-life of radiation for over 150 years. That would work well into the Russian world dominance model, but not ours. We want to emerge as controlling the United States, not destroy it. Using dirty bombs was not a good strategy from the beginning. It was the best we had at the time. Now however, we have an alternative thanks to the Chinese. It turns out, that it is now possible to increase the power of what is now being called the 'Meniere device' way beyond the original test model. We've received several devices of varying power. At the highest power exposure will cause massive strokes or death to anyone in range. In fact, a video we received shows a test subject's head exploding. The power of the device for the Cabinet meeting will be lower causing permanent disability, but not being lethal as Gatling does not want them killed outright."

"A gruesome result, nevertheless," said Moon. "What about our associates carrying the Meniere device?" asked Moon.

"Merklin and Hornsbee will be provided the white noise hearing equipment. Unfortunately, the Meniere device will overwhelm the effectiveness of the white noise appliance causing our colleagues to suffer the same fate as the Cabinet."

"Collateral damage with the added benefit of sealing off the ability to identify us," said Moon. "When will we receive the devices?" asked Moon.

"We already have," replied Tensale. "The Chinese do not of course, know the device's true purpose, but they are quite pleased with the payment they have received."

"And the Russians?" said Moon.

"We have also taken delivery of dirty bombs from them and sent our agreed upon payment. They think we will cause devastation of the United States. We may have some future use for the bombs. Who knows? Maybe the bombs will find their way back to Russia...unexpectedly."

A chime sounded and the connection was broken.

Moon uncoiled from the couch and walked over to the wall of windows. She looked out at the mountains and smiled at her own reflection in the glass. A black widow spider, in her mind's eye complimented by the large red hourglass she had had tattooed on her back between her shoulder blades, blood drops descending down her back and into her gluteal cleft.

HOLY INNOCENTS
TRAPPIST MONASTERY

Gila National Forest
New Mexico
May 1, 2017

FINKEL WALKED OVER TO THE TELEVISION MONITOR AND CONTINUED SPEAKING. "As I mentioned, this mission has a number of challenging aspects. Qatar is considered by the United Nations as the wealthiest country on the planet. Out of a population of roughly 2.5 million, slightly over 12% are Qataris, with the balance 25% Indian, 4.8% Pakistani and 1.5% Iranian. The Qatari wealth is massive and is generated by the world's largest supply of liquid natural gas exports as well as substantial revenue from oil. Except for the 12% Qatari nationals, the balance of the population are imported workers receiving a minimum wage and are the source of some unrest. On the other hand, the Qatari national per capita income is $124,930 per year. We think

Al-Qaeda sympathizers within the Iranian Qatari population communicated the particulars of the Flying Carpet's voyage to the Libyan Al-Qaeda pirates. Importantly, as I mentioned earlier, the pirates know they have wealthy Qatari children captive, but they don't realize that Crown Prince Bamin's son is one of them.

"What about sending Neil and his team in to rescue the hostages?" asked Makin.

"Good question," replied Finkel. "Which brings up one of the mission challenges. The Qatari secret service has located an Iranian working in the Emir's palace who, through various interrogations, revealed the location of the Al-Qaeda pirate cell. It turns out that the pirates have occupied a residence 75 kilometers from a Libyan town called Ghat. No, that would be incorrect. It's not a residence. It's more of a large palace occupied at one time by Mutassim Gaddafi, the son of the late Muammar Gaddafi. It is a three-story rectangular stone structure with an interior courtyard. The size estimate is 60,000 square feet not including any basement or sub basements we can't visualize. In addition, infra-red satellite imagery of the occupants gives us a population of between 50 and 70 occupants. Any attempt at rescue by an assault force would likely result in a pitched battle possibly killing the captives. The only feasible way to accomplish this mission is to infiltrate the pirates from the inside, neutralize them and then find and extricate the hostages."

"That would be me," said Ankyer. "But neutralizing 50 to 70 pirates seems like a stretch."

"I agree," replied Finkel. Two red dots started blinking in the upper righthand corners of the room monitor. The images of Lori Jean-Mallory, PhD, a botanist formerly with the Smithsonian Institution, and Miles Zastovich, PhD, a plant biologist appeared on the screens. "We have been monitoring your discussion and perhaps can be of some assistance," said Dr. Jean-Mallory.

"Excellent," said Finkel. "Please proceed."

"This might be a little tricky, but if you can get it into the pirates' food supply...." said Dr. Zastovich.

"Get what into the food supply?" asked Ankyer.

"A combination of Amanita bisporigera and Amanita phalloides," replied Zastovich. "Also referred to as the 'white mushrooms of death'."

"What's it do, get them sick?" asked Ankyer.

"No," said Jean-Mallory. "It gets them dead! They are called the 'destroying angel' and 'death cap' mushrooms. They produce an amatoxin which causes vomiting, cramps, delirium, convulsions and diarrhea, destruction of all the liver and kidney tissue and, within 5 to 24 hours, death. A small piece of a mushroom cap is fatal."

"Show them the molecular diagrams!" said Zastovich. Two molecular diagrams filled one screen. "The diagram on the left is the combined molecules of the destroying angel and death cap mushrooms. The diagram on the right is the enhanced version. We were concerned that the elapsed time of 5 to 24 hours to death was too long, so we adjusted the molecule so that death results within minutes. We also increased the molecule's toxicity by a factor of 300%. In its enhanced state, the emulsion also destroys part of the stomach, which is then forcefully expelled in chunks in the vomit. It is as effective on a human as on the rat models. If someone ingests just a small amount of the enhanced molecule you had better get out of the way. Things will get messy fast! It took a while to clean up after the rats we tried it out on."

"What is the impact of dilution?" asked Finkel.

"In its emulsified form, a pint of the enhanced molecule will maintain its toxicity in up to 4 gallons of liquid. After that its potency will decline with every additional gallon of liquid," replied Jean-Mallory.

"Well, what do you think?" Doctors Jean-Mallory and Zastovich chimed together, beaming.

"I'm giving you guys a wide berth in the cafeteria," said Chief Fred Bell.

"Please stand by in case there are any questions," said Finkel.

"Will do!" as the images of Dr. Jean-Mallory and Dr. Zastovich and the molecular diagrams faded from the monitors.

Finkel turned to the group and raised his hand. "I know what you are thinking..."

"... how do I get this mushroom concoction into the pirates?" said Ankyer finishing Finkel's sentence. "Neil, would you like to enlighten everyone?" said Finkel.

SEAL Master Chief Neil Groton got up from his chair and stood before the group. "I have always heard that Dr. Finkel was crafty, but this time he has exceeded his reputation. A week ago, I was instructed to fly a team into Illizi Algeria and intercept one Alhar Mustafa who was trying to negotiate a nighttime crossing of the Libyan border. His Algerian location and destination was provided by our 'new best friends', in the Qatar Secret Service. It seems that the head chef...no let's be realistic, the short order cook...of the Al-Qaeda pirate cell located in the Mutassim Gaddafi palace where our captives are held was out at a small farm a short distance from the palace collecting produce for dinner. Apparently, it is customary for these Al-Qaeda pirates to wear a locked exploding vest to prevent defections when outside the premises of the palace. In any event, something went amiss. The cook's exploding vest did exactly what it was designed to do and exploded. Who knows why. A short circuit or maybe a call to the cell phone triggered from a wrong number. Whatever the reason, the cook's parts were mixed with the fruit and veggies and a piece of date palm. Panic from hungry pirates ensued at the palace and a replacement cook, namely Mustafa, was dispatched from an Algerian Al-Qaeda cell. We arrived at the crossover location provided by the Qataris and scooped him up in transit and are holding him in a secure 'black site' back in Algeria. The three Al-Qaeda fighters with him were dispatched. Under 'soft interrogation' we were able to ascertain from Mustafa that he is due at the palace in three days. May 4th. Mustafa also told us that none of the pirates, who are from Libya know him as he was recruited into Al-Qaeda in Iraq. The likelihood of a Libyan pirate recognizing Jake is therefore highly remote."

"The idea is to have Jake replace Mustafa and introduce the mushroom emulsion into the pirates' food supply," said Finkel. "That should place a dent in the pirate population. We also have an improved transponder aboard a geosynchronous satellite over the pirate stronghold. Instead of Jake having to trigger the exploding vests attached to any guards left over from the mushroom poisoning, Jake can tell us to activate the satellite transponder and we will trigger the exploding vests remotely by linking to Jake's internal mastoid communications device. The transponder will generate a cone of effectiveness of a mile in circumference from Jake's location.

"What about guards watching the captives?" asked Ankyer.

"Good point," replied Finkel. "You will have to engage guards close to the captives to prevent any exploding guards from causing collateral damage to captives before you tell us to activate the transponder."

"Ok. That should not be a problem. Finding the captives might be an issue. The size of the building will make it difficult for me to rapidly assess the captives' location, particularly if there are subbasements in this building."

"You will have Varna with you. The Qatar Secret Service has provided us with articles of clothing from each of the captives. Varna will absorb each captives' scent. Tracking the captives' location in the building with Varna's olfactory abilities should be possible. The Qataris also provided current photos of each of the captives for you to memorize for rapid identification." Hearing his name, Varna pricked his ears up, came to alert, and padded over to Ankyer. He placed his large head on Ankyer's lap expecting another dog biscuit or at least an ear rub, the latter of which he received.

"It's always good to have Varna on board. But how do I explain him?" asked Ankyer.

"That's a question we struggled with," said Finkel. "Honey Pi came to the rescue. Honey Pi?"

"Jake, one of our assumptions for this mission is that you will be operating for the most part in a low light environment. Our optometrist has provided light adjusting, infrared contact lenses, which will allow you to see as well in the dark as in the daylight. The lenses appear cloudy, and you can explain Varna by saying you have cataracts, and that Varna assists in guiding you to help compensate for your poor vision. A bonus is that the lenses will cover your blue and green eyes since heterochromia does not exist as a condition in the Middle East genome. As none of the pirates will have seen the chef before...we think...you should be able to convincingly deceive them."

"The 'we think' part is a little iffy, but nothing's perfect," said Ankyer. "What about weapons?"

"We have a solution there as well," said Finkel. We expect that you will be searched so we've come up with a way to get weapons in with Varna even if he has to go through a metal detector."

"What kind of weapons?" asked Ankyer.

"Our armorer has replicated your tactical crossbow and combat knife with a 3D computer printing process called stereo lithography which produces plastic-like polymers instead of metal parts. The crossbow has been expanded to two magazines. One magazine has ten armor piercing bolts and the second has ten AN-M14 TH3 incendiary bolts. The incendiary bolts burn at over nine thousand degrees Fahrenheit. He used the same technique to produce one inch thick, two inch wide and five inch long, highly concentrated white phosphorous grenades. You will have ten of those. Your contact lenses will automatically black out for five seconds to protect your corneas from damage, so make sure you are in a protected area until your contacts readjust."

"Ok, but how does Varna get the weapons in?" asked Anker

"Dr. Asbury, would you explain please?" asked Finkel.

"I've created a short film that illustrates the approach," said Asbury. Finkel handed Asbury the remote. He pressed a button and the film started up on the monitor and continued silently for four minutes.

"You're shitting me!" exclaimed Bell.

"Not withstanding your professional assessment Chief Bell, no... I am not 'shitting' you. Some thought has gone into this," replied Asbury, somewhat in a huff.

"And Varna is ok with this?" added Ankyer.

"We've been working with him," said Asbury. We are not quite there yet, but Varna should be ready in another day or so.

Finkel turned to the monitor, pressed a button on the remote, and the image of a large man with shaggy white hair and eyebrows appeared on the screen. "One of our continuing concerns has been the forty or more pirates you may have to contend with. Even with the use of the mushroom emulsion, you are going to need an edge.

THE INSURRECTION PROTOCOL

We thought of impregnating your tactical body wrap with a substance called Vantablack which reduces visibility in low light environments by as much as ninety five percent. However, one of our physicists has developed a blackening camouflage much more effective." said Finkel. "You know him. Dr. Ambrose Blackthorne. 'Blackie' to his friends. The material is basically made up of nanotubes which capture photons when light hits them. The National Institute of Standards and Technology has produced a version of black, called Ultra Black, which is 99.5 percent light absorbing. Blackie's version which we call Ultrablack IV after four developmental iterations, absorbs 99.995% of the light photons into nanotubes the walls of which are a billionth of a nanotube thick. We have impregnated your tactical body wrap under your outer clothes with Ultrablack IV so you will be effectively invisible in the dark.

Once you have removed your desert robes, you would need to engage the dynamic part of your mission in the dark, but between your infrared contact lenses and the Ultrablack IV tactical body wrap you should have a significant advantage engaging any remaining pirates after the food poisoning and exploding vest transponder phases of the operation," added Finkel. "We will also provide Ultrablack IV camo paste for your hands and face to complete the effect. Blackie, would you give your colleagues a demo please?" asked Finkel. as the image of Blackthorne walked over to a table.

"Hello everyone. Dr. Finkel just made my job easier with his excellent explanation. So, I'll cut to the chase." Blackthorne picked up a remote and the lights in the room were dimmed enough that he could just be seen. He then picked up a coat from the table and put it on. Blackthorn's body disappeared leaving only his head and hands showing. Everyone in the room, including Finkel applauded. Blackthorne then picked up a jar and rubbed the soft paste in the jar on his hands which disappeared, and on his face and neck which also disappeared leaving just his shock of white hair and mouth visible. "There's also a mouthwash available now which hides the mouth. Its flavor is black cherry." Blackthorne removed the coat and wiped his hands, face and neck again becoming visible.

"The military value of this is incredible!" exclaimed Neil.

"Quite right," replied Finkel. "On the other hand, with SLUG's obvious psychiatric challenges we are keeping this 'under our hat' so to speak, for the moment."

"A couple of questions," said Ankyer.

"Fire away," replied Finkel.

"Ultrablack IV is so black won't I appear as a black silhouette no matter how dark my surroundings may be?" asked Ankyer.

"Good question Jake," replied Finkel. "One thing we can do is to fire an electromagnetic pulse from the geosynchronous satellite shorting out the lights in the Gaddafi compound. That should help."

"Still, almost any background light from emergency lights could be a problem" said Ankyer.

"Jake, you have arrived at what may be the most exciting part of Blackie's research. Blackie, you want to tell him?" asked Finkel.

"We incorporated photonic crystals into the Ultrablack IV," said Blackthorne. "These are nano crystals with periodic dielectric structures that have a band gap that prevents propagation of certain frequency ranges of light. In other words, the Ultra Black IV with the imbedded photonic crystals causes the Ultra Black IV to adjust its 'blackness' to the area's ambient light, effectively eliminating the silhouette effect of the Ultra Black IV."

"It's a Star Trek Romulan cloaking device!" exclaimed Honey Pi.

"Almost, Dr. Pi," replied Blackthorne. "I'm a Trekkie myself. It does have its limitations as you get into the higher light ranges, but it should suffice for Jake's purposes."

"How about my eyes?" asked Ankyer. "The pirates may not be able to see most of me, but they may focus on the red glow of my infrared contacts."

"Excellent question," replied Blackthorne. "We designed your infrared contact lenses so that they are like light sensitive glasses. In normal light they look white and cloudy enhancing the story-line that your sight is diminished. They will darken as the light dims so that once the ambient light goes dark, they darken to the point they become as dark as the Ultra Black rest of you."

"One last question. What about Varna?" asked Ankyer.

"We've developed a spray version of Ultrablack IV which you can apply to Varna's head and coat. It should work for a while although you can't apply it to his mouth like the mouthwash developed for you. Something to do with his saliva and gag reflex. On the other hand, if he's attacking a target and the only thing visible are his jaws, fangs, and eyes, it should scare the shit out of the target disrupting their reflexes, so to speak," replied Blackthorne.

"Excellent'" said Ankyer. 'I assume you have figured out a way to deliver all of this."

"We have some logistical options," said Finkel. Since this will be a night mission, we need to come up with a way to deliver the materials and the mushroom emulsion after your insertion into the Al-Qaeda pirate nest. We did not want to try to bring the mushroom emulsion in with Varna since it's so toxic and could kill him if it leaked or the vessel it is in is damaged. We are still working on it. We will give you the details before you leave in three days, since that's when our chef is due to arrive at the pirate's location. I think that covers the essential elements of the mission."

VARNA

"DR. FINKEL, YOU WERE GOING TO MENTION VARNA," said Honey Pi.

"Oh yes. Varna. Let me give you some context. When we located the Red Protocol Group to the Abbey, we thought it would be useful to add military canines, war dogs if you will, to our offensive compliment. Neil agreed noting that war dogs are considered an integral component of Navy SEAL teams. We tried several dogs and could not achieve what we believed to be the ideal intelligence and aggression combination. The issue was exacerbated by the fact that the war dog would be attached primarily to one operator such as Jake. Since war dogs have handlers, we did not think it would be feasible for Jake to have to worry about controlling a war dog at the same time he was neutralizing an objective.

What was needed was a tactical animal that combined high intelligence and aggression along with the independence of action associated with a kinetic weapons team. In other words, an active compliment to Jake that did not require hands-on control. After some investigation, it was concluded that the ideal war dog would not be a dog at all, but a wolf. And the ideal wolf with the characteristics we wanted was a Mackenzie Valley Canadian Timber Wolf. And not just one but a breeding pair. Which brings us to Brother William. William, please proceed."

"Thank you Dr. Finkel." Brother William walked over to Varna who immediately nuzzled him. (Prior to joining the Trappists, Brother William Spear was a grand master in combat karate, teaching offensive combat skills to Navy SEAL trainees at the Coronado Naval Base SEAL training facility in San Diego California. At the request of Finkel and with his and the Abbot's agreement, Brother William temporarily transferred over to the Red Protocol Group when the Group took up residence at the Abbey to assist with refinement of Ankyer's martial arts skills. Before becoming a Trappist monk, Brother William also spent time as a fur trapper in Canada.)

"When I joined the Trappists, I was looking forward to a life of solitude and contemplation. Instead, I somehow found myself freezing my ass off in northern Canada tracking a wolf pack. Who said God doesn't have a sense of humor! Anyway, I picked up the track of a small wolf pack, came around a bend, and found myself thirty-five yards away from a large, enraged, male grizzly bear. It seems the bear and wolf pack had collided. Two wolves were down, the bear swiped at a third decapitating it, and proceeded to eviscerate a fourth. The bear saw me, let out an enraged scream, and charged. Fortunately, I was armed with a Smith & Wesson Model 500 pistol, with a 6.5-inch barrel and loaded with .500 S&W cartridges...best to be armed when hunting wolves. The bear got within 10 yards and reared up on its back legs, becoming a twelve-foot-high snarling visage of death!"

"Brother William......"

"Sorry Dr. Finkel. I get carried away. I fired my Smith & Wesson four times into the chest of the grizzly bear dropping it within four feet of me. A close call indeed! After my ears stopped ringing, I heard mewling from under a bush and, as luck would have it, discovered two wolf cubs. I promptly stuffed the cubs in my ruck sack and got out of there as fast as my snowshoes would take me. I did not want to be there if the blood scent attracted more wolves or bears. Four miles later I was at my lake base camp and was transported by a bush pilot to a private runway and a jet back to the Abbey. I then deposited the wolf cubs with Dr. Finkel.

"My God," exclaimed Honey Pi. "We did not realize we had an 'Indiana Jones' in our midst."

"Consideration should be given to making Brother William a field operative," said Ankyer

"You are too kind Jake," replied Brother William. "I am now, however, a practitioner of peace and love."

"Hard to believe when you beat me up in combat martial arts training," replied Ankyer.

"Thank you, Brother William," said Finkel. "Now it would be helpful if Dr. Mars, our geneticist, could give us a quick science review."

Finkel tapped the remote control and the next thing the group saw was an image on the teleprompter of a very large, ferocious canine. A bespectacled, Adrian Mars MD, PhD entered the video picture and stepped to the side of the image. "Thank you Dr. Finkel. It's a pleasure as always. When Brother William delivered the wolf pups the first order of business was to do an evaluation of each wolf's genome to determine exactly what kind of wolves we were dealing with. We used a technique referred to as archaic introgression mapping. It's been used to assess the extent to which archaic Neanderthal genes have been introduced into the current human genome. The theory is that the Neanderthal genetic structure is useful in avoiding several human infections. Using a similar technique, we evaluated the genetic structure of the wolves Brother William delivered. The female pup turned out to be a pure bred, Mackenzie Valley, Canadian Timber Wolf. The male pup, our friend Varna here, was more interesting. The genetic evaluation revealed a dormant Dire wolf gene."

"But Dire wolves have been extinct for over 10,000 years," remarked Honey Pi.

"You are absolutely correct Dr. Pi," said Mars. "It is not unusual to see dormant extinct genes in the genetic 'caravan' so to speak. For example, genetic assessment of humans with European lineage often have dormant Neanderthal genes which archaic introgression mapping has demonstrated."

"That goes a long way towards explaining Chief Bell," said Ankyer.

"Hey!" exclaimed Bell as the rest of the group laughed.

"Now, now gentlemen and gentle women," said Finkel. "Please continue Dr. Mars."

"Since we had not previously had access to the Dire wolf gene before, we thought it would be interesting to try using biochemical gene splitting technology, which we developed for another application, to try an activate the Dire wolf gene."

"Sort of like Jurassic Park," said Chief Neal Groton.

"Not quite," replied Mars. "In Jurassic Park, the dinosaurs were cloned from DNA pulled from mosquitoes encased in amber which had sucked blood from its dinosaur victim. To use a scientific term, the Jurassic Park science is 'bullshit'. Our approach is the real thing. Our process of gene regulation activates the dormant gene...turning it on so to speak... and the result was Varna, or so we thought. However, it turned out that when Varna's dormant Dire wolf gene was activated, our science team inadvertently activated another dormant, recessive gene. We became suspicious when Varna started adding large amounts of muscle and increased bone density with a significant jump in metabolism. We are now giving him specially formulated high protein dog biscuits to accommodate his heightened caloric burn rate. We recently did a further deep DNA evaluation and discovered Varna now has an additional activated gene of an Epycion Haydini, an extinct prehistoric canine that lived about 5,000,000 years ago in the late Miocene period. What's more, these animals averaged 7 feet in length and weighed in at 400 to 550 pounds...about the size of a large adult lion. They were ferocious apex predators with a bite force beyond that of a present-day jaguar, which is greater than that of a lion. We are not certain how all this will play out since Varna is not a purebred Epycion. However, his combined genetic architecture of Epycion, Dire wolf and contemporary Canadian Timber wolf make Varna a particularly lethal and aggressive combination. He has an exceedingly powerful bite force and high intelligence as well." The teleprompter had two-way video and Mars looked directly at Ankyer. "Jake, Varna is still evolving, and you will have to be especially careful with him. It's like having a grenade with explosive characteristics which keep changing.

"Thank you, Dr. Mars. I will use the care you suggest," replied Ankyer.

"One other thing," said Mars. "When Varna is not occupied with Jake on a mission, being the alpha male of the pack, Varna is busy making more wolfs. We have checked the wolf cubs sired by Varna and have discovered that the Dire wolf/ Epycion Haydini genes are being transmitted to Varna's progeny. We have had to relocate normal Abbey wolves without the activated genes to other packs outside the Abbey to prevent the new strain from destroying their smaller and less aggressive pack mates. We have also been tracking food source populations to determine food chain changes resulting from the new, combined wolf strain, as the new strain has a higher metabolism and requires a substantial caloric uptake, resulting in increased prey consumption."

"Thank you, Dr. Mars," said Finkel.

"Jake, you and Varna will be inserted in Libya in three days to coincide with the pirates' expectation of the chef's arrival. George, you have been cleared by White House security to join SLUG two days from now and will meet with him at that time. SLUG's increased psychological instability is cause for concern and we will need to start your monitoring sooner than we anticipated. Your portfolio is described as a "presidential advisor-at-large," which will give you access to all SLUG's meetings and trips. That should deflect any questions from inquisitive Cabinet members or staff. We are unsure as to how SLUG will react to your being "glued to his hip" as it were. If SLUG's paranoia fulminates in your direction we may have to pull you prematurely. Short of that, we will be analyzing all of SLUG's interactions in real time courtesy of your mastoid implant. That will provide us with an ongoing psychological assessment. If we assess that SLUG is becoming a threat to you, himself or others we can adjust your mission as necessary."

Finkel stood up. "Thank you everyone. Our briefing is concluded." The room's occupants started walking out, including Varna busily nuzzling Brother William's pocket containing another biscuit. As they were leaving, Makin caught up with Ankyer. "Jake, give me a minute, will you?" "Sure. What's up?" They walked over to two wing back chairs and sat down.

"After getting nearly blown up and rescued by our colleagues, I was transported back to the Abbey for what was called "assessment and rehabilitation," said Makin. "I was given several treatments in a machine similar to a positron emission scanner. I am familiar with PET scanners as diagnostic tools, but this was not that. After the treatments, I felt different, as if I could anticipate what was going to happen, but not quite. It's continued to this day. It's weird."

"Stop right there'" said Ankyer. "Welcome to the admission to what I call 'Dr. Finkel's science experiment'. You're right. It was not a PET scanner. It's a device like a PET scanner, but it doesn't do imaging...or it does but also does something else. It closes the micro distance of the synaptic gaps of your neurotransmitters' electricity crossing over to transmit information in your brain. It doesn't make you smarter, or physically improved. However, it does accelerate the movement of electrons across the synaptic gaps much faster and more efficiently. Put another way, your body operates as it did before but is enhanced as if you were always performing at peak efficiency, which you are not. In my case, for example, I was in peak physical condition before the treatment and could run a mile flat out in about 5.5 minutes. After the treatment, my mile time improved to under 4 minutes. But that's not all. My thinking changed. I can see relationships developing in real time as events unfold. I mentioned this to Dr. Finkel, and he promptly enrolled me in the London School of Economics' PhD program in analytical, macroeconomics. Ten months later I had a PhD.

"Clarity." They turned to see Dr. Finkel standing there. "Jake was not smarter. He was...and is...able to process information more quickly and with great precision. That's why Jake and the others in training in the group can rapidly redefine and reconstruct mission parameters in highly volatile situations. The reduction in the micro distances between synapses makes Jake, and now you George, exceptionally efficient both mentally and physically."

"I knew something was different," said Makin. "I felt it."

"As Jake mentioned earlier, Brother Arlot, our neuroanatomist, has become of the opinion that while we thought the synaptic gap reduction was temporarily due to the elasticity of the neurons, it now appears with Jake at least, that repeated treatments have reduced synapse elasticity and eliminated the tendency of the neurons to return to their normal state."

"No more treatments," said Ankyer.

"We entered you in the treatment program, George, because we assessed that placing you in SLUG's environment would benefit from having you in an enhanced state. And it's not just SLUG's psychological degeneration we are concerned about. As usual, SLUG himself selected his Cabinet and many of the members tend to mirror SLUG's negative tendencies. As a result, a number of Cabinet appointees and high-level operatives have had to resign in disgrace for a variety of reasons.

Having you co-located with SLUG provides access to core senior decision makers so we can accurately assess in real time the nature and velocity with which members of the group are damaging the government. N.S.A. has also noted a 'whisper' in its intercepts that various Cabinet officials are voicing personal concerns about SLUG. The snake eating its tail. If possible, George, an ancillary part of your mission will be to help us refine our understanding of any coordinated Cabinet unrest and potential consequences. Well, there it is. Your missions will be activated on schedule. Excuse me gentlemen. I have some other matters to attend to," said Finkel as he exited the library.

"That was helpful, Jake," said Makin. "I had another question. Or more like an observation."

"Shoot," said Ankyer.

"I was wondering about Honey Pi. I know that she's responsible for medical care for you and Varna, and now me. I get the impression that she also gets close to actual operations. I guess from an operational point of view I'm not quite sure how to interact with her."

"Honey Pi is complex. She is exceedingly intelligent and committed to our organization. I had a chance to observe her during the terrorist incursion at the Abbey when we were dealing with Saddam Hussein. It turns out that a Hussein terrorist actually got as far as the Abbey building. Honey Pi put a hole the size of a watermelon in his chest with a military shotgun without hesitation. She didn't even blink. Let me put it this way with an analogy. If Honey Pi was a cat, you would expect her to purr if you stroked her. You would be wrong. The only time Honey Pi would purr is if she were a lioness after a kill. On the other hand, she is fiercely protective of her friends and colleagues whether they are a patient or not."

"Humm. Good to know," said Makin. "I'll keep that in mind," as he and Ankyer left the room.

LIBYAN DESERT
Nine kilometers northeast of Motassim Gaddafi palace
Libya
May 4, 2017

THE HELICOPTER GUNSHIP DROPPED THEM OFF IN THE DESERT AT EXACTLY 4:00 AM Eastern European Time. The desert temperature was 63 degrees Fahrenheit. It would climb to 112 degrees later. The man, although tall, had a crooked back, and the large, obese dog had fur best described as disgusting and probably infested with insects. They had been walking down the dusty road for two hours, covering three miles faster than their bedraggled condition would suggest possible. The horizon was turning a light purple, sunrise having occurred at 6:15 AM.

As they followed a bend in the road, the man saw what appeared to be a large building shimmering in the far distance. He estimated the building to be three or four miles away. He opened a canteen and took a small sip of water. He was preparing to pour water into his hand to give to the dog when the sand three feet away suddenly erupted as if by a small object landing. Then another. And another. The man said to the dog, "Under fire. Down!" He dropped to his knees waving his arms. The eruptions multiplied rapidly. There was no cover. The man saw a cloud of dust rapidly approaching. As it came close, he saw two open bed trucks with machine guns mounted in the back firing in their direction. The trucks came to an abrupt stop in front of the man and the dog, and four ragged men jumped out each holding AK-47s.

"Who are you? What are you doing here?" exclaimed one of the men.

"Don't shoot! Don't shoot!" replied the ragged man spitting sand as he placed one arm over the back of the quivering dog. The man opened the palm of his raised hand in supplication. "Praise Allah. I am Alhar Mustafa sent by the brothers in Algeria to cook for the esteemed Libyan brothers here and their excellent leader, Sheikh Masta bin al-Zara."

"You don't look like a cook," said the gunman. "What is this disgusting fat animal?" he continued. "I think I will shoot it."

"No, no!" the man on the ground exclaimed. "Please! Don't! I found this animal to help me as my eyesight is very poor."

"What did you do before you were a cook?" asked the man as he charged his AK-47 preparing to fire.

"I was a maker of IED bombs to kill Americans in Libya. A bomb exploded damaging my eyes. They became cloudy making it difficult to see. I learned to cook in a village to support myself. Please don't hurt me or my animal," whimpered the man.

The man lowered his gun. "I heard about this one," the man said. "We have been expecting a cook since our last one blew himself up. Put him and his beast in the back of my truck. We will take him to al-Zara and let him decide what to do with them. I hope he is the cook. I'm losing weight from the crap we've been eating over the past weeks." A man walked over and lowered the gate of one of the flatbed trucks. The filthy, bedraggled man struggled to his feet and climbed into the back of the truck bed. The fat dog jumped in the back of the truck. One of the pirates thought to himself, "How can a dog that fat jump into the truck that easily?" But he shrugged and let the thought pass.

LIBYAN DESERT
Motassim Gaddafi Palace
Libya
May 4, 2017

SHEIKH MASTA BIN AL-ZARA STOOD ON THE THIRD-FLOOR BALCONY of the 60,000 square foot palace and looked down upon the rectangular sand courtyard. He was a large man who had fought his way to the top of the al-Qaeda cell, testified to by the many scars he carried. The most prominent one traveled across his forehead and down his cheek, terminating at his jaw. The man who wielded the knife had his head blown off by another brother, Barka, a huge man almost 7 feet tall and 400 pounds. Barka became the Sheikh's personal bodyguard after saving his life.

Twenty brothers were engaged in target practice shooting at targets 100 feet distant, their AK-47s set on automatic fire. Al-Zara was not happy. Using up ammunition at this rate was expensive and the al-Qaeda pirate budget was stingy. Not only was the ammunition budget under pressure, but money was tight for everything. Fire fights with Libyan militia were breaking out causing pirate casualties, and he had lost two boats in attempted ship boardings. One to a freighter crew armed with a World War II bazooka, and another to an American patrol boat while attempting to overcome a large cruise ship.

If it was not for the gunboat capturing the Qatari pleasure ship with the children and minders, the month would have been a complete waste. Even at that, attempts to ransom the captives from the Qataris had resulted in nothing but silence. Nothing! Now, instead of millions of euros, he would have to be satisfied with whatever he could get for the captives at the slave market. Still, children in particular should bring a decent price at auction. As he was contemplating the burdens of leadership, Barka called him from behind.

"Sheikh, a patrol has brought someone here for you."

The Sheikh turned and walked into a very large rectangular room furnished with Persian carpets, a variety of dusty sofas and chairs strewn about, and a table with dirty dishes, reflecting a lack of a cleaning service and general male sloppiness. The room was forty yards long and twenty yards wide and had been a "great room" for its former occupant. Life sized marble statues of Roman emperors and gods were alternately spaced twenty feet apart making a corridor from the room's entrance three quarters of the way into the room. There were fifteen crystal chandeliers spaced from one end of the room to the other. The center of the room was open flooring with pillows arranged in a large circle used for infrequent meetings of the pirate brothers and occasional higher up al-Qaida visitors. Four brothers stood in the circle around a grizzled man on his knees dressed in filthy desert robes. Next to the man was a large, fat, drooling dog with a matted, shaggy coat. "What the hell is this?" asked al-Zara.

"A man we found in the desert walking towards the compound," replied one of the men.

"No, you fool. I can see the man. What is this disgusting creature?"

"It was with the man when we found him."

"Barka. Shoot this thing!' said al-Zara.

Barka immediately pulled a pistol from his robes and aimed it at the dog.

"No, no, effendi!" exclaimed the man. This is a dog I found that helps me see where I am going to do my work."

"Work? What work?"

"My name is Alhar Mustafa, effendi. I am the cook you sent for."

"Wait Barka," said al-Zara. "A cook you say. I have been expecting you. You're late."

"Apologies, effendi. I was moved across the border by the Algerian brothers two nights ago, but we were lost in the desert which caused our delay. I was left many miles away on the road that leads to your castle. I was walking here when the brothers found me."

"How is it you can cook if you are blind?" asked al-Zara.

"I was a bomb maker for the brothers in Iraq. Unfortunately, a bomb I was making exploded and left my eyes clouded. I learned to cook for the brothers to support myself. I can see to cook but need help walking around. I found this ugly dog and use it to guide me. Please, my lord. Do not kill it."

The Sheikh stood looking at the man. They sure as hell needed a cook. The food Marfa al-Sarfa, the cook's assistant made, was almost inedible. Decent food should boost morale, which needed boosting considering the pirates' recent defeats. "Alright. Your dog stays. Just keep it away from me. Barka, take Mustafa to the kitchen. Oh, by the way. Was he checked for weapons?"

"Yes, Sheikh," replied one of the pirates. "He has just the clothes on his back."

"Oh, and Mustafa, you better be a good cook. We are partial to stews for my men and Barka and I eat steaks. If you cannot cook these for us, we will have no use for you, or your beast."

Mustafa was helped to his feet by Barka, who loomed over him. Standing up Mustafa had a crooked back and limped when he walked; he was aided by holding a rope around the dog's neck. "This Mustafa may not last long enough to cook the first meal," thought al-Zara. "If he can actually cook, at least one of my problems will be solved." He turned and walked back out to the balcony and resumed watching the target practice. It occurred to him that he should have the pirates' exploding vests removed before coming into the building in case another one blew up as had happened to the former cook. Something to think about. Making up new rules was tedious. If he remembered, he would talk to Barka about it next week.

Barka led Mustafa out of the room followed by the other pirates. "The kitchen is the next floor down. You'll also sleep down there," said Barka. Mustafa shuffled along next to the dog, which farted frequently as they moved along. "If it was up to me, I'd kill this beast. Your Arabic is unusually good. High end for a cook or bomb maker," noted Barka.

"Before becoming a bomb maker, I taught Arabic at a madrassa school in Pakistan."

"Harrumph," replied Barka.

Mustafa followed Barka to the second floor with a balcony similar to that of the third floor. They then walked through a door opening to a large kitchen area. Pots and pans were strewn over several preparation tables. Food stuffs way past their 'sell by' dates were piled on other tables. One table had various cans and bottles of what appeared to be spices. A short, fat man with long stringy black hair stood over a pile of gray beef cutting it into chunks. Along one wall were three large stoves, and along another wall two large ovens. A walk-in refrigeration room was located on another wall, with the door open.

Barka walked over to the man and said: "al-Safa, this is the new cook that has just arrived." Barka then turned to Mustafa. "This is Marfa al-Safa the cook's helper who will help you prepare meals." Looking around Barka added: "I don't know how this will be accomplished, but you can see why we badly need a cook." While he was speaking, the fat dog waddled over to a chunk of meat that had fallen on the floor. He sniffed it and turned away. "Even the dog will not eat this shit," said Barka, turning to Mustafa. "You better know what the hell you are doing. Another bad meal and the Sheikh will kill you and your dog himself." With that Barka turned and walked out.

"Was he serious when he said the Sheikh would kill us?" Mustafa asked al-Safa. Al-Safa responded. "I am glad you are here to save our lives... I hope."

"Why is the refrigeration room door open?" asked Mustafa.

"It gets hot in here and leaving the door open helps keep the kitchen cool," replied al-Safa.

"I heard there were some captives here. Do we need to feed them as well?" asked Mustafa.

"The cook used to make a platter of fruits and bread but that stopped when he was blown up.:

"Where was the food delivered?"

"Somewhere in the basement. Is the Sheikh going to shoot us?"

"Hopefully not, but we have to work fast," replied Mustafa. "Go around the kitchen and collect all the meat. Take it outside and bury it in the sand. What time do they eat here?"

"Usually after dark. Many of the brothers are out at sea looking for boats to attack. They usually return after dark and eat together outdoors in the courtyard. The Sheikh and Barka eat at the same time with the Sheikh in the great hall on the third floor."

"What do you usually feed the brothers?"

"They like to eat beef stew."

"Good. Where do you get your food?"

"There is a large market about four miles away. Since the brothers like meat, the market always has much on hand."

"Ok. After you bury the garbage, call this market, and tell them to deliver enough beef for 50 people along with 30 pounds of assorted vegetables, two gallons of beef gravy and four large steaks. Also, and this is very important. Have them send 10 pounds of mushrooms. I don't care what kind. Be sure and tell the guards about the delivery so they don't shoot the truck driver on the way in. Finally, tell Barka that we will have the meal ready at 8:30 PM tonight. Can you remember all that?"

"Yes. I will start right away," replied al-Safa. "Will they shoot us?"

"No, but we must hurry," replied Mustafa.

Al-Safa collected all the rotting food in a wheeled cart and rapidly pushed it out the door.

———————————

Ankyer heard Finkel's voice over his mastoid implant. *"Jake, we heard everything. Feeding them beef stew fits perfectly."*

"I thought the Sheikh was going to shoot Varna. It was a close call," replied Ankyer. *"Our plan is intact, but I hadn't counted on actually cooking for 50 or so pirates. I can do the steaks but feeding beef stew to 50 pirates is above my pay grade."*

"As soon as I heard that you were going to have to cook, I called in our executive chef, Mike Blastow," said Finkel.

"Jake, this is Mike. Do you have any spices around there?" Ankyer read off the labels on the cans and bottles on the table.

"Not great but it will have to do," said Blastow. *"How much time do we have?"*

"I am serving the meal at 8:30 PM," said Ankyer.

"Ok. You will need about 90 minutes to put this together. Dr. Finkel said that you have to do steaks as well?"

"Correct. The Sheikh and his bodyguard eat separately from everyone else."

"Ok. You will need about 10 minutes on the grill for the four 14-ounce steaks done medium rare. One steak each is usual. Two each since we don't now if they are big eaters."

"One guy is a giant so two steaks sounds right," said Ankyer.

"Put them on the grill 12 minutes before you serve the gruel... sorry beef stew," said Blastow.

"What about the mushroom emulsion?" asked Ankyer.

"Add the emulsion to the pot just before you send the beef stew to the eating area. You don't have to stir it. It will diffuse into the pots automatically," said Finkel. *"Expect the delivery of the emulsion and the other items we discussed at the Northeast corner of the second-floor balcony at 7:30 PM. Monitoring of the building indicates no infrared activity until around 10:00 PM which suggests the area is used for sleeping quarters."*

"Ok," said Ankyer. *"How do I make the beef stew?"*

"It's easy enough," said Blastow. *"Here's what you do..."*

MOTASSIM GADDAFI PALACE
Kitchen
5:30 PM

AL-SAFA RETURNED WITH A CART LOADED WITH THE FOOD STUFFS as Mustafa had directed. They unpacked the food, cleared off a table of dirty dishes, and arranged the food by type. Mustafa picked up a meat cleaver and chopped the rounds of beef into bite sized chunks while al-Safa cleaned the vegetables. Mustafa tossed a large chunk of beef to the dog, which reared up, caught the beef, and swallowed it without chewing. "Your dog seems very energetic for its size," observed al-Safa.

"The dog is quick to eat which is why it's so fat," replied Mustafa as he chopped up the remaining beef. He secreted the cleaver in his robes when he had finished. "Al-Safa, I must take the dog out to relieve itself. While I'm gone chop up the vegetables and throw some in each of the three large kettles over there. Then put the beef in trays and roast them in the ovens at 450 degrees for 20 minutes. Turn the beef and roast it for ten more minutes and put the beef in the three kettles and add the gravy. I will do the seasoning and add it to the gravy when I return and then grill the steaks. Can you keep all that straight?"

"Yes," replied al-Safa. "But I have a question. Why not just let the dog shit in the kitchen and save yourself the trouble of taking it out?" said al-Safa as he turned to start unpacking the food containers.

"Al-Safa, let's do it my way. That's why I am the chef, and you are the helper," replied Mustafa walking out the kitchen door followed by the dog.

———————

Ankyer opened a door across from the kitchen entrance. Ankyer and Varna descended steps, which opened into a dimly lit subbasement. Appearing to be talking to himself Ankyer said: *"If you want my opinion, we could just have let the cook's helper cook for the pirates for a few more days and he would have killed them all."*

"Not a bad idea," replied Finkel. *"But as long as we have gone to this trouble..."*

As Ankyer and Varna walked down the corridor, Varna moved his head slightly from side to side, his nostril opening and closing. He partially opened his mouth and bared his teeth. *"It looks like Varna has picked up a scent,"* said Ankyer.

The corridor was long and wide and evidently used for storage. There were five evenly spaced doors on the right and three sets of double doors on the left. Ankyer opened the first door on the right and peered in. The room was piled with furniture, rugs, and various sized lamps. He closed the door and walked to the second door. Varna became increasingly agitated, and saliva dripped from his jaws. He started a low guttural growl. *"Dr.*

Finkel, Varna has picked up a strong scent from a room we are approaching." Ankyer and Varna entered the room and were confronted by an overpowering odor of rotting flesh. The scene was remarkable even in Ankyer's experience.

WHITE HOUSE
Washington DC
President's private library

WINSTON WHITE (AKA GEORGE MAKIN) WAS ESCORTED INTO THE ROOM by a Secret Service agent. "The President will be with you shortly," said the agent.

White surveyed the room. Smaller than he would have expected, the room was furnished with a leather love seat, two wing back chairs and a coffee table. In one corner of the room there was a small desk with a computer monitor. In another was a small liquor cabinet with an adjacent sink. White heard a rustling behind him. Stephen Louis Gatling walked into the room closing the door behind him. "Mr. White. Thank you for coming. I assume you have been briefed by Dr. Finkel."

"Yes, Mr. President," replied White.

Gatling sat in one of the chairs. "Have a seat. Please."

White sat down across from Gatling.

"The Secret Service is not enamored with your being armed I must tell you. On the other hand, your security clearance was approved with the speed of light. Even I was surprised. Let me get right to it. I have reason to believe that various people in my administration, including members of my Cabinet, are untrustworthy. The press is also methodically poisoning the public's mind with fake news and untruths regarding my approaches to governing the country."

"Why are you telling me this, sir?"

"Things are becoming so toxic that I am not sure I'm safe," replied Gatling. "That's why I have directed the Red Protocol Group to serve as a kind of Praetorian Guard, loyal to me, and available to protect me at all costs."

"Mr. President, the Secret Service is tasked to protect you," said White.

"There are some issues there," replied Gatling. "A Secret Service agent was overheard to remark that my idea to place festive balloons on the Tomb of the Unknown Soldier on Veterans Day was not appropriate. Another agent was rumored to disagree with my thought to have a Gatling Day parade in Washington DC on the Fourth of July. The latest snub was the Director of the Secret Service refusing to guarantee the security of the President of Russia during an address to a joint session of Congress, prior to our next election. And it's getting worse. People are giving me strange looks. I need protection and the Red Protocol Group can give it to me."

"Mr. President, I can see why you may be concerned, but protecting you is not my job."

"If not that, what is your job then?" exclaimed Gatling.

"My job, simply put, is to keep you alive. Period. Should circumstances develop where your life is in danger, the Red Protocol

Group will activate and eliminate the threat. Normal protective services must continue to be the purview of the Secret Service. If issues arise within the Secret Service protection unit, we will of course address them. Think of me as the 'tip of the spear,' tasked with synchronous threat assessment and authorized to activate appropriate countermeasures. To do that I will have to be in your presence at all public and private meetings, without exception. Your private time with your family would, of course not require my physical presence."

"Ok. Whatever you need. I will instruct Mallory Tensale, my Chief of Staff, to provide you access to all of my scheduled meetings."

"And your unscheduled ones as well," said White. "All of them. As well as security access to any location you happen to be at the time."

"You drive a hard bargain Mr. White."

"You can carry me on the White House staff as your personal security consultant should questions arise. Also, please wear this watch at all times," said White handing Gatling what appeared to be an Apple watch. "It performs all the functions of a normal watch and, most importantly, provides me your exact location and vital signs. Please put it on now." Gatling placed the watch on his wrist.

"Ouch."

"Sorry about that," said White. "There is a nano needle that taps into your wrist and stream's location data to this," said White holding out his wrist with a similar watch. White pressed the front of his watch and numbers started appearing on the watch face. "See. Easy. You can now go about your daily business secure in the knowledge that I will be there when you need me."

"Perfect," said Gatling. "I feel better already."

Gatling got up from the chair and walked to the door.

"See you around Mr. President," said White to Gatling's back as Gatling left the room.

"Did you get all of that?" said Makin to himself.

"We did," replied Finkel. *"It's worse than we thought. The good news is when the injector went into SLUG's wrist it also inserted a nano transponder allowing us to monitor all his conversations even when you are not close by."*

MOTASSIM GADDAFI PALACE
Subbasement

ONCE IN THE ROOM, ANKYER OBSERVED TWO NAKED MEN GUTTED, with entrails hanging out. They were dangling a foot from the floor on meat hooks inserted under their chins and extending out of their mouths. The eyeholes of the hooks were connected to short cables attached to the ceiling. Large pools of blood had collected beneath each of the men, their cut off toes lying in a pile along with their burned and severed feet. Their eyes had been gouged out, skin flayed from their faces and genitals burned off. Varna walked over and sat in front of the dangling corpses.

"It appears that Varna has identified two of the Qatari party's minders," said Ankyer. *"They have been tortured extensively, and not too long ago considering the uncongealed blood. It's possible the pirates know about the Crown prince's son but considering the level of torture it does not appear that the minders gave him up. The third minder must be around here somewhere. I'll check the other rooms in the subbasement and then go to the package drop point."*

"Agreed. It is even more important we keep to our schedule now," the voice of Finkel said in Ankyer's head. *"Let me know when you want the package,"* continued Finkel.

"Will do," said Ankyer.

Ankyer and Varna exited the room and opened the next door down the hall. They entered the room, walking towards the room's center. Quickly surveying the room, Ankyer noticed a pile of rags and a partially decomposed corpse in a corner. There was a tipped over cart with rotted fruit and bread strewn around in the center of the room. Varna walked over to the corpse and growled.

"I've just found what's left of another corpse," said Ankyer. *"I'm guessing it's the third minder,"* said Ankyer.

Just then, Varna turned and let out a guttural growl.

"Who the fuck are you?" a voice behind Ankyer exclaimed in Arabic.

Ankyer turned and was confronted by a thin man dressed in a soiled white gown covered in blotches of blood.

"I am Alhar Mustafa, the new cook," said Ankyer.

"Bullshit," replied the man. "I know Alhar Mustafa from Iraq and you are not him. Who are you?" he asked as he advanced on Ankyer holding an automatic pistol.

"Wait!" exclaimed Ankyer. "I'll tell you!" The meat cleaver Ankyer had taken from the kitchen appeared from his robes and flew in one motion towards the man with mind numbing speed and turned once over the fifteen-foot distance. Before the man could pull the trigger, the cleaver hit him in the center of his forehead, continuing through his skull, and bisecting the man's brain, separating both hemi spheres, and butterflying the brain and skull wide open, The cleaver ended up lodged at the top of the man's spine. The man crumpled to the floor, spinal fluid, and blood pooling around the parted head.

"Close call?" asked Finkel in Ankyer's head.

"Not really, but he will need a new hat size," replied Ankyer. *"This guy said he knew Mustafa from Iraq. It would be wise to accelerate things on the chance that more of the other pirates may have also run into Mustafa. I have one more room down here to check and then I will make my way to the drop point on the second-floor balcony."*

"We have checked that location with satellite infrared and there is no activity there now. I'll let you know if that changes," replied Finkel. *"Before I forget, check the pirate to see if he's wearing an exploding vest,"* added Finkel. *"We don't want him exploding if any captives happen to be around."*

Ankyer pulled open the pirate's robes. *"No vest,"* said Ankyer.

"Excellent," replied Finkel.

Ankyer and Varna walked out of the room and down the hall to a double set of doors. Anker kicked the doors open and entered a large room with twelve men and women cowering in a corner. One of the men stood up wobbling and walked unsteadily over to Ankyer.

"Please. Please help us. We will do whatever you say. We cannot last much longer," said the man in broken Arabic."

"I am not a pirate," replied Ankyer. "Where are you people from?"

"We were captured from a cruise ship a week ago. There were three men and five children from another ship added to our group, but the pirates separated us from them as soon as we arrived. Do you know where they are?" he asked as he reached out towards Ankyer's arm, eliciting barred fangs and a deep growl from Varna.

"Don't come any closer to me. He may not look like it, but this is a highly protective combat animal that will tear you apart. The three men are dead, and I don't know where the children are. As a matter of fact, I'm looking for children the pirates have taken myself. There is a rescue mission underway, but you and the others will have to last awhile longer. It is likely you will hear gunfire and explosions in a few hours. Whatever you do, do not leave this room. I will give your location to the others who will be coming. They will identify themselves with the word 'freedom' when they arrive at the room." Ankyer noticed a metal cabinet adjacent to the door. "When I leave, move that cabinet in front of the door. Remember, do not leave the room under any circumstances. I'm sorry I cannot help you more right now. The situation in this compound is very dangerous." With that Ankyer and Varna left the room, closing the doors behind them.

"Did you hear all that Dr. Finkel?"

"I did. We will free the people as soon as you advise us the situation in the compound is under control, and we can enter the area. You need to go to the balcony of the second floor outside the area the pirates sleep in so we can deliver your material. Satellite monitoring currently indicates no infrared activity and it is starting to get dark. I'll let you know if we see any infrared images while you are in transit."

Ankyer ran down the corridor with Varna loping behind him. They entered a stairwell that connected each floor of the compound and was designed for servants moving between floors. They rapidly climbed the stairs and exited at the second floor into a very large room with cots, bunk beds and dirty clothes and food strewn about. The walls of the room were decorated with seascape scenes, and crystal chandeliers hung from the ceiling. Possibly once used as a ballroom, the room now had the appearance of a badly used cave dwelling with a faint odor of feces in the air. Ankyer and Varna made their way to a sliding window and out an adjacent door to the balcony. The balcony was in the shadows, with the sun setting on the opposite side of the compound.

"We've arrived at the balcony," said Ankyer. "Considering the living conditions in the sleeping quarters, the morale of the pirates must be pretty low."

"Our intelligence would tend to confirm that based on interrogation of pirates captured over several months. Once you start the operation, casualties will probably diminish the will to fight. Don't take any chances though," said Finkel.

"Roger that," replied Ankyer. "On the other hand, with what we have planned I doubt there will be many pirates left anyway. I'm ready for the package."

"Stand back from the edge of the balcony," replied Finkel.

A military drone, painted in Ultrablack IV and on station 4,000 feet above the Gaddafi compound, adjusted its silenced four-corner, rotary electric engines and dropped under power towards the balcony, homing in on the signal emanating from Ankyer's mastoid communications device. The drone came to rest on a ledge two feet from Ankyer. Two compartments, one on each side of the drone's fuselage opened upwards into the body.

"The drone's amazing. It's right in front of me and I can hardly see it. In fact, I wouldn't see it if I didn't know it was there. Even so, it was just an impression until the side bays opened up."

"It's painted in Ultrablack IV, the same substance we used for your tactical body wrap," said Finkel.

As Ankyer removed the payload, Finkel listed off the contents: "One tactical body wrap with integrated combat harness; one tube of Ultrablack IV camo cream; one aerosol cannister with Ultrablack spray, for Varna; four five-ounce tubes of mushroom emulsion; ten concentrated white phosphorous grenades with adhesive backing, and a container carrying a capsule for Varna to swallow, which will detach the faux fur and ribs bonded by bio adhesive to Varna's sides. In addition to the drone payload, Varna is also carrying one polymer combat knife, one polymer tactical pneumatic crossbow, four crossbow magazines...two with ten armor piercing bolts each and two magazines with ten AN-M14 TH3 incendiary bolts. We have also added a DNA detector pen loaded with a sample of the Crown Prince son's DNA. Place it on the arm, push, and it will extract a blood sample and compare it immediately to the Qatar prince's preloaded DNA. Light in pen turns green equal's a match. Red is no match.

"Got it," said Ankyer

"Let me know when you are ready to initiate the active component of the mission," said Finkel.

"I noticed the pods on either side of the drone," remarked Ankyer.

"Very observant," replied Finkel. "We integrated two micro missiles with nuclear war heads. They are available to sanitize the Gaddafi site if you think its warranted. It would be a very small detonation with a circumference of two miles and a radiation half-life of one hundred years. We would, of course, covertly advise the responsible Libyan government assuming we could identify one."

"Excellent," replied Ankyer. "I'll let you know."

The drone pulled back and rapidly accelerated vertically to its "on station" position over the Gaddafi complex.

Ankyer removed his dirty white robes and put on the tactical body wrap. He then stored the drone's inventory in the receptacles on the body wrap combat harness and covered himself again with the dirty robes.

"I can still see myself in the body wrap," said Anker.

"That's because of the infrared optics in your contact lenses are picking up your body heat. You are effectively invisible to anyone else," replied Finkel.

"All set," said Ankyer. "I have to get back to the kitchen."

"Confirmed. Let me know when we should emit the satellite's electromagnetic pulse and the transponder signals," said Finkel.

"*Will do,*" replied Ankyer as he and Varna headed back to the kitchen.

"Where have you been!" exclaimed al-Safa. "It's dark and they have turned on the lights in the courtyard. A Brother came up here, yelled at me and said they would feed us our balls if their dinner was not ready in thirty minutes, and that was five minutes ago! If we don't feed them, they will come here and kill us!"

"Calm yourself, al-Safa. Look at the size of my dog. It takes him a long time to pee. Where are the steaks for Sheikh al-Zara and Barka?"

"They are next to the grill. "The kettles of beef stew are on the cart," said al-Safa.

"Go get the knives and forks from the far table over there," directed Mustafa as he walked to the grill, sprinkled some seasoning on the steaks, and put them on the hot grill. Thirteen minutes later the steaks were plated along with potatoes and salad and placed on the cart.

While al-Safa retrieved the knives and forks, Mustafa walked over to the food cart, removed three mushroom emulsion tubes from his robes and added the contents of each tube to the three kettles. He then reached back into his robe, pulled out the fourth emulsion tube and added it equally to each kettle.

Al-Safa came up behind Ankyer, placed the knives and forks on the cart and asked, "What did you put in the kettles, Chef?"

"Just some extra seasoning I found in the pantry," replied Mustafa as he placed the plated steaks onto the cart. "Now go to the great hall first and serve al-Zara and Barka their steaks. And then go to the courtyard and serve your Brothers the beef stew.

You may as well eat with them. I will find something for myself here. Now hurry!"

Al-Safa pushed the cart out the door and disappeared down the hall. Ankyer removed his robes, retrieved Varna's capsule from a pocket of his combat body wrap and carefully pushed it into the side of Varna's mouth. Varna immediately crunched down on the capsule, swallowed, and padded over to a corner of the kitchen. Meanwhile, Ankyer applied the Ultra Black IV camo cream to his exposed skin. Varna, shaking slightly, walked back to Ankyer and lay at his feet.

"Dr. Finkel. When can Varna's faux fur be removed?" asked Ankyer

"If Varna is shaking his temperature has spiked and the heat will have loosened the bio adhesive. Grab the fur on his flanks and pull," replied Finkel.

Ankyer did as instructed, and the faux fur and ribs pulled off revealing Varna's true anatomy. Varna stood up, stretched, and emitted a low growl while rubbing against Ankyer's leg. The concave faux sides contained the cross bow and other items in the combat inventory which had been secreted in Varna's body as he walked into the entrance of the pirate stronghold. Ankyer placed the items in the combat suit receptacles designed for each item except for the crossbow. He then sprayed the polymer crossbow with Ultra Black IV and loaded the crossbow with both AN-M14 TH3 incendiary bolt magazines, attaching it to a diagonal strap on his combat harness. Finally, Ankyer sprayed Varna with Ultra Black IV being careful not to spray his head, which had two fangs now protruding from the lips of his upper jaw. Ankyer sprayed the Ultra Black IV on his hands and rubbed Varna's head avoiding his eyes. Now coated in Ultra Black IV, Varna disappeared, except for his eyes and the tips of his fangs. Ankyer was able to see Varna with the infrared, light adjustable contact lenses he was wearing. For his part Varna could not see Ankyer except for the contacts on his eyes, but Varna's acute sense of smell located Ankyer's precise position. Varna let out a double sneeze, shook his massive body once again, and sat next Ankyer.

"Ok Varna, my friend. It's time for us to go to work." Ankyer, with Varna at his side, walked to a patio window overlooking the building's rectangular, interior courtyard. The large courtyard had three, long tables set up in one corner twenty yards from a building entrance. Each table had fifteen chairs along with fifteen place settings of cups and large spoons. Pirates were seated at each table; the first two tables being completely occupied. The third table had five occupants along with ten empty chairs and place settings.

"Dr. Finkel, we may have a problem. It looks like there are ten pirates not accounted for. There are ten empty chairs with place settings. Some number of pirates will not be exposed to the adulterated beef stew," said Ankyer.

"Probably pirates on guard duty or out on a kidnapping run. We'll start a count of infrared images and try to find them. How much time do we have?" asked Finkel.

"It looks like time's up," replied Ankyer. *"Marfa al-Safa, my cook's helper, just showed up running and pushing the food cart. The pirates are banging their cups on the table and raising hell. He's unloading the food cart now. He will be serving the beef stew momentarily. How much time do I have after they start eating?"*

"Five, maybe ten minutes max. When the white mushroom emulsion was made it was infused with glutamates which generate a savory taste called 'umami'. The taste enhances flavor and causes a strong desire to eat rapidly. It is especially effective with meat. We wanted the effect of the emulsion to occur rapidly to eliminate as many pirates as quickly as possible."

"OK. I'll deal with the missing pirates. Let me know if you spot them," said Ankyer

"We are scanning infrared images in the area of the citadel now," replied Finkel.

Marfa al-Safa finished distributing the beef stew, served himself and sat down at one of the empty spaces in the third table.

"Damn it, al-Safa, this beef stew is terrific!" exclaimed a pirate at the first table. "Did you cook it?

Al-Safa, wanting to take credit for the dinner replied: "I did cook it. I know how to cook. I am a great cook!" as he started to eat the beef stew.

Another pirate at the second table finished his first bowl of stew and wiped up the remaining gravy with a large chunk of bread. "This shit is great!" he exclaimed as he went to the pot to get some more.

"Take as much as you want!" al-Safa yelled out. "I made extra for everybody!" rising to the praise of his fellow pirates.

The pirates quieted down and ate as fast as they could so they could get extra portions. "I can't believe how good this tastes," said another pirate as he refilled his cup with water from a jug on the table.

The pirates had been eating for about ten minutes when a pirate from the first table stood up with his hands on his stomach and vomited on the head of the pirate next to him. The first pirate let out with a screech as grey matter from his partially dissolved stomach was expelled from his mouth. A pirate from the second table made a guttural sound, vomited, and started hemorrhaging blood from his mouth.

"What the fuck have you done!' screamed a pirate at the third table at al-Safa.

"I don't know! I don't understand it!" exclaimed al-Safa "I did everything the cook told me to do!" said al-Safa as he stood up. A pirate from the second table started vomiting, turned toward al-Safa, pulled his gun and shot al-Safa in the head

Ankyer observed the mayhem as it started to take over. *"Dr. Finkel, game on. The mushroom emulsion is working exactly as expected. Give me ten minutes and activate the electromagnetic pulse to shut down the lights. I'm moving out."*

"Copy. We're also activating the transponder for the exploding vests. Over and Out." replied Finkel

WASHINGTON D.C.
Luba's Congressional Café

GEORGE MAKIN, AKA WINSTON WHITE, SAT AT A SMALL TABLE IN LUBA'S Congressional Café sipping a cup of black coffee. A waitress came over and set a bowl of what appeared to be gruel in front of him.

"Here's the hummus you ordered sir."

"Is it good today?" asked Makin.

"I don't know sir. I haven't served it in three or four months. The last person who ordered it said something about it being brown and congealing whatever that means."

"Thank you," replied Makin. "I'll do my best with it."

With that the waitress left, Makin stuck a spoon in the hummus and pushed it aside.

Finkel spoke, his voice being captured in Makin's mastoid implant. *"I didn't think you liked hummus," said Finkel.*

"I don't," replied Makin as he turned slightly to shield his lips from the few patrons in Luba's, not wanting to give others the

impression he was talking to himself. *"The White House executive dining room menu does not include hummus and I needed an excuse to leave the building and exit SLUG's reach."*

"Hummus is not something I particularly care for either," replied Finkel.

"Dr. Finkel, I overheard a conversation between SLUG and Mallory Tensale, SLUG's Chief of Staff. Normally SLUG has me in attendance in all meetings, even on a back bench in Cabinet meetings. In this case, however, the pattern was interrupted. We traveled in an unmarked Lincoln Town Car to a three-story brownstone in Baltimore Maryland. After we entered SLUG instructed me to wait outside of what appeared to be a secure, first floor room. Before the door to the room closed, I observed Tensale standing in the center of the room waiting for SLUG to enter. A pocket door then slid closed. I sat in a chair about 15 feet from the entrance to the room. Because of the Abbey's neurological treatment, my enhanced hearing permitted me to overhear a conversation which was fragmented, indicating a sound deadening technology was used. I was able to hear enough, however, to cause me to initiate this conversation. It appears that SLUG is involved in a conspiracy to somehow physically harm the Cabinet as well as the Vice President."

"Physically harm?" repeated Finkel.

"I heard fragments. There was mention of a person named Moon as well as someone named Hornsbee. SLUG also mentioned '25th Amendment' and 'it looks like the Cabinet is out to get me and that has to be stopped.' He also said that the Vice President is the ringleader. From snatches of comments, it appears that SLUG is involved in some plan to eliminate the Cabinet, and Tensale is somehow involved in executing the plan."

"How did you deduce that?" asked Finkel.

"Then Tensale said to SLUG: 'Ok, I can handle that.' He also asked SLUG how he was going to replace the Cabinet members. SLUG replied

that he would appoint each Cabinet Member's immediate deputy as 'Acting Head' of the Department. 'What about the VP?' asked Tensale. SLUG replied that he was thinking about Moon. Then Tensale replied that Moon would be a good choice. SLUG replied '... and she's also got a great ass.' Tensale also noted that SLUG could replace him and appoint Merklin as Chief of Staff saying Merklin is loyal and that it would make Tensale more available to do the other things."

"I can see why you are concerned," said Finkel. Particularly with 'the other things' comment. "Did SLUG mention a time frame?"

"Not as such, although he said that as soon as he could get the VP and the cabinet in a meeting; and then the voices started getting blurred."

"Anything else?" asked Finkel.

"Two additional items of note. As they were walking towards the door, I think Tensale said 'Chinese technology' and Cuba. I also think SLUG said something like 'maybe will work on the Congress, at least the Democrats.' Tensale sounded like he said: 'Logistics more complicated but I don't see why not.' That's it."

"Ok. We'll investigate it. You better get back. Bring some hummus back to the White House with you in case someone asks where you were."

As Makin was leaving Luba's a boy about eleven walked out behind him stopped and said: "Hey mister. You were talking to yourself. Sometimes I talk to myself."

Makin replied "You noticed? The thing is if you talk to yourself there's a pretty good chance you will agree with what you're saying."

"Didn't think of that. I'll keep it in mind. Hey, You must like hummus too. My dad always sends me here to get some for him. My name's Tim."

"Hi Tim. My name's George. Nice to meet you although it's not a good idea to talk to strangers you know."

"I know. But we both have hummus, so we have something in common."

"There is that. Ok. Maybe I'll see you around when I make my next hummus run. Take care of yourself Tim."

"Will do. Nice to meet you, George."

"Same here Tim."

MOTASSIM GADDAFI PALACE
Libya
Third Floor Great Room

SHEIKH MASTA BIN AL-ZARA AND HIS BODYGUARD, BARKA, sat at a long, black onyx table at the far end of the Great Room. Al-Safa, the cooks assistant had moments earlier delivered their dinner consisting of two strip steaks each, along with plates of fresh salad and fruit. Large crystal chandeliers were strategically placed down the center of the Great Room with the last one centered over the two men at the onyx table.

"God damn!" exclaimed Sheikh Masta bin al-Zara. "This is the best fucking steak I have ever eaten. How's yours Barka?"

"Best I've ever had," replied Barka. "That fucking cook must know what he's doing. Not only that, al-Safa brought three large pots of beef stew down to the men and they are jumping all over it. Al-Safa said he did the cooking but he's bullshitting. He can't boil water. Has to be the work of the new cook. For an ex-bomb maker this cook knows his shit."

"Too bad his eyesight is shot," said al-Zara. "We could have had him making bombs when he wasn't cooking," added al-Zara laughing.

"What's going on with him?' asked Barka looking at a young teenage boy who was seated on the floor, naked and glassy eyed, tethered by a chain and leather dog collar to a heavy chair.

"Ah, he's used up," replied al-Zara. "He looked like the best of the lot from that Qatar pleasure ship we captured, but it turned out he was a dud. I'm going to give him to the brothers and when they're done, they can bury him in the desert. Those cheap bastard Qataris never answered our ransom demands for this kid and his friends. This one is too far gone, but at least we will get money from the traders at the slave market. That reminds me, have the minders in the basement shot tomorrow if they are still alive after their torture. They are of no use to us now."

"As you wish, Sheikh," replied Barka.

At that moment the chandeliers in the Great Room dimmed and went out. Two security lights at the ends of the ceiling flickered on casting a dim orange light in the room's corners but otherwise leaving the rest of the room in darkness. A moment later the sound of a gunshot and two large explosions coming from the direction of the courtyard filled the Great Room.

"What the fuck was that?" exclaimed al-Zara as he leapt to his feet.

"I will find out," said Barka running towards the balcony.

A third explosion shook the building. Al-Zara joined Barka on the balcony overlooking the courtyard just in time to see a pirate at the second table expel grey tissue from his stomach in a gush of blood. The pirate next to him ignited his exploding vest, blowing himself into various sized chunks of flesh.

"God fucking damn it!" exclaimed al-Zara. "What the hell is going on?"

By this time the courtyard was chaotic with pirates running around holding their stomachs. Some seemed to be blowing themselves up to avoid the fate of their comrades.

'It's got to be the food," said Barka. "Look. Someone shot Marfa al-Safa in the head.

"It can't be him," said al-Zara. "He's too fucking stupid to do something like this. It's got to be that goddamn cook! Where the fuck is he?"

Just then an open bed truck pulled into the courtyard containing 22 pirates.

"Where the hell did they come from?" asked al-Zara.

"They were on a raid off the coast and must have picked up the other brothers on the way in," replied Barka.

"Hey, you in the courtyard!' exclaimed al-Zara. The newly arrived pirates looked up towards the third floor. "Get your asses up here...now!" screamed al-Zara. "Barka, you find that fucking cook and drag him in here. Don't kill him. We have to find out what the fuck is going on!"

"As you wish Sheikh," as Barka turned and ran off the balcony.

––––––––––––

As Ankyer observed the courtyard chaos, he noted the arrival of the truck with the additional pirates.

"It looks like we underestimated the pirate count," said Ankyer. *"There are 22 new arrivals, not the ten we expected."*

"Our infrared count tallies with that," replied Finkel.

"When I say 'transponder' signal the geosynchronous satellite to activate their vests. Maybe I can improve the odds."

"Check," replied Finkel.

Ankyer and Varna quickly moved up the back stairs to the third floor. They emerged outside two partially open massive double doors. Ankyer entered the Great Room and attached five of his ten white phosphorous grenades onto the back of one of the partially open double doors. Ankyer and Varna then moved rapidly down the center to the midpoint of the room. Ankyer turned and knelt patting the floor causing Varna to drop down as well.

The herd of pirates al-Zara had summoned entered the room through the open double doors and started running down the middle of the room. Ankyer fired an AN-M14 TH3 incendiary bolt into the half of the double door affixed with the five white phosphorus grenades. The bolt exploded causing the first grenade to explode; each of the remaining four grenades detonating sequentially, effecting one immense explosion. The ensuing fireball engulfed the entryway as well as the back half of the room. Flaming body parts of the pirates who had entered the room were followed by screaming pirates with white phosphorus fire eating through various areas of their bodies. Others were firing their AKs as the phosphorus flames consumed them. Seven remaining pirates entered the room, blinded by smoke from the grenades and trying to avoid the scattered remains of their companions. Ankyer, followed by Varna, got up and ran towards the location of a screaming al-Zara.

"God dammit!" exclaimed al-Zara. "Get up here with me," he yelled to however many pirates were still standing.

"Transponder," said Ankyer under his breath.

With all the screaming and yelling, three of the seven pirates did not hear the beeping under their shirts nor see the wisp of smoke before their vests detonated. They blew apart, spraying ball bearings and shrapnel that tore off pieces of the remaining four pirates. Multiple explosions also emanated from the courtyard generating large plumes of smoke and sand. Sheikh Masta bin al-Zara loudly exclaimed, "Shit!" as flames and acrid smoke started filling the room.

Another pirate from the courtyard managed to stagger into the Great Room holding an AK-47 in one hand and holding part of his stomach tissue in the other. He made his way around the dismembered pirates and the invisible Ankyer and Varna to stand in front of the Sheikh. As he said, "I am here my Sheikh" he vomited blood over the front of the Sheikh's body. The Sheikh pulled a 45 automatic from his waist and shot the pirate in the eye, dropping him in a heap. "Barka!" exclaimed the Sheikh. "Where are you?"

"Here!" yelled Barka while he was running through the smoke to al-Zara and picking up the AK-47 dropped by the pirate.

"Goddamn it," said a-Zara. "All our brothers are either blowing up or holding onto their stomachs."

"It's got to be that fucking cook!" exclaimed Barka.

"Where is the bastard?" asked the Sheikh.

"Right here," said a disembodied voice.

Barka turned and leveled the AK-47 in the direction of the voice, setting the selector to automatic. Just as he was getting ready to fire, a set of jaws connected to teeth and two long fangs came out of nowhere, and clamped down on Barka's forearm, amputating it as Barka's finger pulled the trigger and the weapon sprayed 7.62 mm bullets into the floor. The jaws, connected to nothing else Barka could see picked up the arm and hand still clutching the AK-47, and flung them in the air. While Barka was tracking the flight of his bloody arm and weapon, he noticed the front of his shirt was open, exposing a long, bloody gash through which his intestines protruded.

While Varna was biting through Barka's arm, Ankyer had opened up Barka's stomach with his combat knife and shoved in an armed, white phosphorous grenade. Ankyer spun Barka around facing the Sheikh and executed a front kick to Barka's lower back propelling him towards the Sheikh and dropping Barka to his knees. What happened next was not part of the plan. Barka lurched towards the Sheikh, Barka's abdominal cavity spraying white phosphorous and flaming organs on the Sheikh. The white phosphorous burned through both Sheikh's legs above the knee and damaged both arms. The Sheikh screamed and passed out. Ankyer then leveled his combat crossbow towards the entrance of the Great Room and sprayed it with the remaining explosive bolts causing the room to become a cauldron of fire and eliminating access should any straggling pirates try to get in.

Ankyer moved over to the naked boy with the dog collar and checked his pulse. Dead. Ankyer then applied the DNA pen to the boy's shoulder. Red light.

"Dr. Finkel, there is a dead boy here that just tested negative with the DNA pen. It appears that the pirate Sheikh is the only one still alive who knows where the Qatari kids are, including the heir. The pirate is badly wounded. A white phosphorous grenade burned parts of his legs off and damaged his arms. It looks like the phosphorous may have cauterized major blood vessels, but there still appears to be substantial blood loss from bleeders. I have to move him quickly or he may not survive interrogation. Any thoughts?" asked Ankyer.

"Jake let me link in Honey Pi and see what she thinks."

"Jake, its Honey Pi. I've been monitoring the conversation. Do you have tourniquets in your med pack?"

"Yes, but this is still an active situation. I may need them for me or Varna."

"Ok. Is there any ammunition around?"

"Yes. Ammunition I have lots of."

"Ok. Pull the bullet heads off and sprinkle gunpowder on the areas of the pirate's arms and leg stumps where he's bleeding and light it. It will temporarily cauterize the bleeders. Get him to the extraction site as fast as possible. He probably will not last long."

"Will do. Thanks!"

Honey Pi's suggestion stopped the Sheikh's bleeding. Four more explosions came from the courtyard and Ankyer ran to the third-floor balcony with Varna. Smoking bodies and body parts lay everywhere. Three pirates without exploding vests, who had entered the courtyard after the beef stew had been eaten by the others, had piled into a small pickup truck, and were attempting to leave the compound. Anker dropped the incendiary bolt magazine from the crossbow, inserted the armor piercing bolt magazine, and fired off five bolts into the rear of the pickup. The truck coasted to a stop fifty feet from the building.

Ankyer dragged the Sheikh's body to the edge of the third-floor balcony and looked down at a pile of bodies and body parts extending several feet from the building. He hoisted the Sheikh over the balcony and dropped the body down onto the body pile below. Ankyer turned and saw that the Great Room was consumed with flames preventing an exit out the front. He turned back towards the wall and yelled "Varna". Ankyer then leapt over the third-floor balcony wall, followed by Varna, both landing on the pile of bodies and joining the smoldering Sheikh.

Ankyer then ran up to the pickup truck, pulled the three bodies from the truck cab, got in and backed it up to the body pile topped off with the Sheikh. He lowered the rear gate, placed the Sheikh's body in the back along with some additional anatomical items he picked up in the area. Varna jumped aboard causing the truck to groan from the additional weight. Ankyer then slammed the truck's gate shut.

THE INSURRECTION PROTOCOL

"Dr. Finkel I'm self-extracting now," said Ankyer, communicating through his mastoid implant. *"I will be driving to the oasis in a brown, rusted pickup truck with the pirate chief and Varna in the back. The pirate is unconscious, and it is critical that a medical unit be on hand to treat him as soon as we arrive. He is the only one who knows the location of the Qatari boy. I'm not sure how long the pirate will survive."*

"Honey Pi is assembling the medical unit as we speak. Can you give me a situation report?" asked Finkel.

"The entire pirate cadre is dead as far as I can tell. There may be Qatari captives and possibly some Iraqi captives in a barricaded room in a subbasement. They will be waiting for someone to yell 'freedom' so they can remove the barricade. The rescue unit should bring water. The captives are in poor condition. The third-floor Great Room is burning and likely to engulf the rest of the building so time is of the essence for the rescue team."

"Our infrared satellite scan indicates fifty-seven dead bodies in the courtyard and in various other building locations not including any captives we can't see in the subbasement," replied Finkel.

"I'm about five miles out from the oasis," said Ankyer.

"We'll be ready for you," replied Finkel.

OASIS
Nine kilometers from Mutassim Gaddafi's Palace
Libya
May 4, 2017

LIEUTENANT COLONEL ABDUL SALAM SHENNIB AND THREE SOLDIERS in a camouflaged, military transport vehicle pulled into the oasis, about nine kilometers from the Mutassim Gaddafi palace, at exactly 7:30 PM, as instructed by Shennib's Commandant. The transport was followed by a fourth soldier driving another similar sized covered army truck painted in desert camouflage. Darkness was beginning to cover the area, but Shennib could still make out various features. The oasis encompassed eight acres, incorporating several large palm trees, fruit trees, five medium sized concrete outbuildings, and a large vegetable garden, not well maintained. The center of the oasis was relatively flat, covered in concrete and windblown sand.

The transports pulled into an area next to a palm tree at the edge of a small lake, covering the aquifer which was the source of the oasis water supply. Four 6-inch water pipes, each connected to an outlet valve, emerged from a corner of the lake and disappeared back underground. This was clearly the water source for the large palace shimmering in the hot air in the distance.

What got Shennib's immediate attention was the Blackhawk helicopter parked in the center of the oasis, as well as seven men in desert camouflage fatigues with battle harnesses, standing next to the aircraft. The men were holding rifles and fragmentary grenades. One of the men detached from the group and walked out of the gloom over to Shennib and his men, who by that time had exited their vehicles.

"Abdul!" exclaimed the man as he approached. "Welcome to the party. We asked that they send you."

"Neil Groton is that you?" asked Shennib. "You're a long way from Navy SEAL Command in Coronado California. How good to see you, my friend. Is this a SEAL operation? I really don't know much other than my instructions to be here with a small team. I didn't even know Americans were operating in this area."

"I'm really sorry to spring this on you," replied Groton. "To give you the short version, this is a sensitive rescue operation of ten or so Libyans and Qataris who were on a Qatari yacht that was captured by some al Qaeda pirates. They have been held for ransom. Some of the captives might be Americans and are thought to be diplomats, which is why we are involved. To be honest, intelligence is not quite up to standard on this one. Long story short, since the U.S. is not authorized to operate in Libya, my unit got tagged to rescue the whole bunch of them, including any Qataris who were running the boat, mixing cocktails and so on. You're here to give us cover in case the diplomatic shit hits the fan."

"So, what you're saying is, that if the rescue mission fails, you're not here and we take the blame," said Shennib.

"Now don't get all twisted up, Abdul, but yeah, that's the gist of it.

"Shit," muttered Shennib.

"There's some good news in all of this," said Groton. "First, this is not the first time we've done something like this, and we've always come out on top. Second, you and your team will go in and rescue the captives in Gaddafi's palace and, need I say, get all the credit!"

"Now you're talking," replied Shennib.

"Oh, and there's one last piece of good news," said Groton

"Which is?"

"You get promoted to full Colonel, assuming we pull this off," replied Groton. "The paperwork is already headed to your Commandant."

"I'm your man!" said Shennib. "By the way, how many pirates are we talking about?"

"Now there's the rub. Glad you asked. Our intel indicates around 50 or 60 infrared images. We don't have eyes on the captives since they are being kept in a subbasement."

"Between me and my four men and your group, the odds seem to be in the pirates' favor," observed Shennib.

Shennib guided Groton away from his men and said in a lowered voice: "Neil, there's no way this can be pulled off with this unit's strength. What the hell is really going on?"

"Ok. On a need-to-know basis, we have an edge. We have an operator in the Gaddafi palace. Our job here is as a resource back-up. Our operator will handle the pirates."

"No way," replied Shennib. "Unless.... There's been a rumor around for a few years that there is a U.S. commando unit that includes some Navy SEALs and has the capability to engage in extremely complicated and sensitive missions. Apparently, there's an operator who blew away just about every military training protocol in the SEALs, British SAS and every special ops group there is. It's just a rumor. Lots of special ops' gossip. No. It can't be... can it?"

"Abdul, you're a smart guy which is why we asked for you specifically," Groton replied, his voice turning to ice. "Remember, I said 'need to know'."

"God damnit, Neal, I do need to know. I am responsible for my troops.

Just as Groton was about to reply, two silenced Sikorsky UH-60M Black Hawk helicopters dropped down landing next to the one already on the ground.

"That would be the medical team," said Groton. "Look Abdul. You are part of something you probably didn't anticipate. Follow my lead and go with the flow. This will work out and you'll have a story for your grandkids."

"Ok," replied Lieutenant Colonel Abdul Salam Shennib. "I'm on board. What is it exactly you want us to do?"

"In a few minutes...."

Suddenly, multiple explosions emanated from the direction of the Gaddafi palace. The palace started to glow with more explosions following.

"Looks like we are off and running," said Groton. "As soon as our operator arrives, he will advise us as to the location of the captives in the palace. You and your team will take your trucks as fast as possible to the palace, go to the location, collect the captives. We will assess the condition of the captives and, assuming they are in a condition to travel, load them into your trucks except the Americans, if there are any. You and your team will drive the captives to your barracks in Ghat. The captives will be delivered to your Commandant who will turn them over to representatives of the captives' countries. That's it. We will provision your trucks with food and water for the captives before you leave here and will fuel the trucks before you take off." Groton was again interrupted by explosions from the direction of the palace. As Groton finished, he and Shennib were approached by three figures who had walked over from the direction of the newly arrived helicopters.

"Colonel Shennib, this is our medical team. Doctors Pi and Walthour, assisted by Mr. Bell."

"Mr. Bell and I met once at Coronado. Good to see you again Master Chief.

"Same here Colonel."

"We are setting up in that building next to the helicopters, Neil," said Honey Pi. What's the status at the palace?"

"I'll check," replied Groton as he walked a short distance, turning away from the group.

"*Neil, sitrep please,*" said Finkel's voice through Groton's mastoid implant.

"*We have linked up with Libyan team and briefed the officer. Honey Pi, Dr. Walthour and Fred Bell have arrived. The medical component is being set up.*

"*From what we can see Jake has completed the kinetic part of the mission and is in a truck traveling at high speed towards your location. We have Apache Guardian attack copters above and behind him, but there does not appear to be any pursuit. He should be there in fifteen minutes or less,*" said Finkel.

"*We'll be ready for him,*" replied Groton as he turned and walked back to the group.

"He's about fifteen minutes out," said Groton to Honey Pi.

"Ok. We'll head over to the medical setup," replied Honey Pi, as she, Walthour, and Bell turned and walked towards the helicopters.

"Let's get your trucks and men over to the helicopters and we can get you fueled up for the trip to the palace," said Groton. "We've decided that Chief Bell and I will go with you to the palace to provide additional support."

"I was hoping you would," replied Shennib as they walked back to Shennib's men.

Groton and Shennib and his men jogged over to the helicopters and stopped in front of one with eleven boxes stacked together on the sand.

"This is the food and water for you and the captives' trip back to Ghat," said Groton to Shennib. Shennib's men loaded the boxes into their Libyan trucks which had been moved over to the helicopter.

"Once you're under way you can distribute the provisions to your 'guests'. We've provided high protein rations but distribute them judiciously since the captives' diet has likely been compromised since they've been in the palace."

As Groton was speaking, Fred Bell walked up and pointed towards the road coming into the oasis. In the dim light they could see an open bed truck traveling at high-speed, trailing a cloud of dust. The truck quickly decelerated and stopped 30 yards from the oasis perimeter.

The driver's side door opened, but Shennib could not see a figure. Honey Pi and Walthour joined the group and watched as the back gate of the truck opened. The truck bed rose several inches, as if a substantial weight had been removed. A large set of jaws carrying what looked like a detached human arm and hand appeared.

Shennib had trouble processing what he was seeing and turned to Groton who said: "That would be our operator and his combat assistant." As they watched, Ankyer stripped off his Ultra Black tactical body wrap and combat harness and replaced them with a flight suit handed to him by one of the men.

Another man walked over to the jaws that were visible holding the human arm spraying a substance from a can, revealing a huge combination Canadian Timber/Dire/Epycion animal. He then gave Varna a head-pat, removed the arm and hand from his jaws and placed it in a box containing additional appendages from the back of the truck.

Two men reached into the truck bed and pulled out a legless human torso and placed it on the ground. Ankyer grasped the human trunk by the hair on its head and dragged it over to the group by the helicopters. The body trunk bumped on the ground along the way.

Shennib turned to Groton and said, "This is getting really interesting."

Groton replied: "It gets better. Wait."

Ankyer stopped in front of the group letting the trunk fall to the ground "This is our chief pirate, Sheikh Masta bin al-Zara, or what's left of him," said Ankyer. We need to wake him up while he's still alive, since he's the only one who knows where the Qatari boy is.

Honey Pi bent over to examine the Sheikh.

"Looks like you stopped most of the hemorrhaging, Jake," she said.

"I used your suggestion of sprinkling the gun powder from the AK-47 bullets on his arms and leg stumps and lighting it. The way it flared up I thought he was going to burn to a crisp, but here we are."

"Varna looks a little the worse for wear," said Honey Pi.

"He took some shrapnel during the fire fight, but nothing looks too serious," replied Ankyer.

"Dr. Walthour, would you please take Varna over to the medical tent and check him out?" asked Honey Pi.

"Definitely," replied Walthour. Varna nosed Walthour's pants pocket, looking for a biscuit, as they detached from the group and walked towards a large, camouflaged tent.

"Ok, lets deal with the Sheikh," said Honey Pi. "I'll start saline and plasma drips on him." She pressed a stethoscope on several places on the trunk. "He's not in the greatest shape, but what the heck, he's still on the planet. Honey Pi turned to the four men: "Roll our friend onto the stretcher and put him on the operating table I had set up in that building." They moved the body onto the stretcher and Honey Pi followed them towards the building. "Give me ten minutes to get him hooked up and we'll go from there," said Honey Pi over her shoulder to Ankyer.

"Jake, this is Lt. Colonel Shennib," said Groton. "The Colonel and his team will be collecting the captives and taking them back to Ghat."

"Nice to meet you, Colonel," said Ankyer.

"And I, you, "replied Shennib. "You are a legend sir and it's a privilege to work with you."

"Would you guys do me a favor and help me move this box of body parts into the building with Dr. Pi? Thanks."

Groton and Bell picked up the box and walked it into the building led by Ankyer and followed by Shennib.

Honey Pi had the now naked Sheikh trunk on a two-part operating table with the back cranked up to 60 degrees. The Sheikh's leg stumps extended out and his shredded arms hung from his sides. Several plastic bags hung next to his body intubated to various locations on his trunk.

"Guys, place the box of parts diagonally from the Sheikh so it's in his line of sight," said Honey Pi. "Good."

Looking at Honey Pi, Anker asked: "So how are we doing?"

"I've got him on a saline drip, plasma, blood substitute and morphine. Your basic kitchen sink. I also mixed up a cocktail of aldosterone, cortisol, and noradrenaline, heavy on the adrenaline and a liberal dose of epinephrine. Honey Pi looked over at the box and said: "Jake you have a problem."

"Which is?"

"Look at the box. You have two right legs and two left arms."

"Oh boy," replied Ankyer. "I just grabbed what was handy. There were body parts all over the place."

"90% of his groin is also missing. I don't suppose you have a groin package in your box of goodies?" asked Honey Pi.

"Even if I'd seen one, I doubt I would have picked it up," said Ankyer

"Ok. He's going to be disoriented anyway and we'll put a sheet over what's left of his legs so he probably will not notice. What he will notice will be different shoes on the feet. Let's get the shoes and what's left of the clothes off the legs.

As Bell and Groton were stripping the clothes off the body parts, Ankyer asked Honey Pi: "So how do we wake him up?"

"My cocktail should do the trick. But we'll probably only get 5 or 10 minutes out of him. We are giving him an adrenaline rush to get him conscious, but I may have gone a little overboard. Bottom line, my job is to get him awake, not to save his life. The other problem we have is that he is leaking. The white phosphorous cauterized the leg stumps. Sprinkling and lighting off the bullets' gun powder on his arms sealed a lot of bleeders, but I'm guessing he has internal bleeding in several places. He's losing fluid as rapidly as we are pumping it in."

"Ok. Let's wake him up and see what happens," said Ankyer.

Off to the side Shennib tugged on Groton's sleeve. "Do you guys usually do interrogations with boxes of body parts?"

"Not usually," replied Groton. "It looks like Jake is making this up as he goes along."

"OK. Everyone put on these surgical masks except Jake. Ready?" Honey Pi turned the spigot to 'flow' on the bag containing the adrenaline cocktail. Almost immediately Sheikh Masta bin al-Zara's eyelids began to flutter. Honey Pi slapped him on the face once. Twice. The Sheikh's eyes opened the third time. Honey Pi stepped back and Ankyer stepped up to the table.

"Sheikh! Wake up!" exclaimed Ankyer.

The Sheikh's eyes focused and looked around. "I feel like shit," were his first works.

"Sheikh, remember me?" asked Ankyer

Looking at Ankyer, the Sheikh exclaimed: "You're the fucking cook! You killed all my men with your goddam beef stew! What am I doing here? I thought I was blown up." He tried to raise his arms and realized that they were shredded down to the bone."

"It wasn't me," replied Ankyer. "The cook assistant Marfa al-Safa must have put tainted meat in the stew."

"Bullshit. My arms. I can't feel my legs," said the Sheikh.

"I saved your legs when they were blown off and found some arms. Look in the box," said Ankyer.

The Sheikh looked over at the box. "I can get my arms and legs back? Those are my arms and legs?" he said groggily.

"100% Sheikh. These are famous transplant doctors that were brought here, and they specialize in arm and leg transplants. You are an important person to al-Qaida and a leader of pirates."

"I AM important," said the Sheikh with emphasis. "Have them put my arms and legs back on."

"One thing," said Ankyer. One of the boys you captured is a cousin of the Iraqi al-Qaida chief who sent me to cook for you. He wants his cousin back. Tell me where he is, and these doctors will replace your arms and legs."

At that moment, the Sheikh's eyes rolled up and his head fell forward.

"Shit," said Honey Pi and jabbed the Sheikh with a hypodermic. The Sheikh's eyes fluttered open.

"Are my arms and legs back on yet?" he asked

"As soon as you tell me where I can find this cousin of the al-Qaida chief," replied Ankyer.

"I don't give a shit about the kid. He can have him. I had him and the other kids shipped off to a slave trader for money."

"Where?" asked Ankyer

"The slave trader you fool."

"But where is this slave trader?"

"Somewhere," said the Sheikh groggily. "Oh...somewhere in the desert."

"Where in the desert," pressed Ankyer.

"Ah...yes...it's the Lost Oasis about 100 miles from the Palace. They are selling the lot of them in three days, I think. Now can I have my fucking arms and legs?" said the Sheikh as he eyed the box.

"Did you get that Dr. Finkel?" asked Ankyer through his mastoid transplant.

"Yes," replied Finkel. We've just repositioned the satellite and are checking. Ok we've found it. It's 109.04 miles from you. There are a number of tents and...yes there is even a platform in the center.

That's it. The name is actually 'Lost Palms' oasis. Very remote. You're good."

"Roger that," replied Ankyer.

At that moment, the Sheikh's trunk bucked on the operating table, and he started hemorrhaging from the mouth and ears. His head flopped forward.

"Oops," said Honey Pi as she checked the trunk with her stethoscope.

"What happened?" asked Ankyer.

"You lead a charmed life," replied Honey Pi. "Our pirate buddy's heart just stopped. Time to bury this jerk and the body parts somewhere in the desert."

Groton turned to Shennib. "It goes without saying that you can't tell anyone what you've seen here today."

"Tell anyone? Who would I tell? No one would believe me," replied Shennib.

"Atta boy. Enjoy your new promotion, Colonel."

"Jake, what's the condition of the palace when you left?" asked Groton

"The third floor was on fire with considerable smoke. The second and first floor was not involved yet. The subbasement with the room holding the captives should be ok but you had better get moving," said Ankyer.

"I am sending a map of the palace pinpointing the location of the captives to your iPad," said Finkel to Groton via Groton's mastoid implant.

"Got it," replied Groton. "Fred Bell and I will accompany Colonel Shennib and his team to the palace and retrieve the captives now."

"Excellent," said Finkel. "When you return you and Fred link up with Jake and we can discuss how to deal with this slave market and

the rescue of the Qatari boy. We need to move quickly to ensure the boy is there."

"*Will do,*" replied Groton as he and Shennib trotted out to the Libyan trucks and Shennib's team. Bell was behind the wheel of a Humvee parked next to the Libyan truck.

"Abdul, you and your men follow me and Chief Bell to the Palace." Shennib and his men got into the trucks and the vehicles drove off.

"*Dr. Finkel, regarding the slave market, I'm concerned that if we go in full throttle with helicopters they may panic and kill the children including the Qatari boy.*"

"That's definitely a concern," replied Finkel. "We have some ideas about that. What do you think of this approach...?"

After Finkel explained the idea, he said: "We are locating them now and should have them in position within 5 miles of the slavers by early tomorrow morning. We will also have the equipment and clothes ready."

"*I've never done this before. Should be interesting,*" replied Ankyer.

"*There's a first time for everything,*" replied Finkel.

MUTASSIM GADDAFI'S PALACE
Libya

THE LIBYAN TRUCKS AND THE HUMVEE WITH GROTON AND BELL entered the main gate and parked in the center of the courtyard. Shennib and his team stepped out of the truck, as did Groton and Bell from the Humvee and were greeted by a war zone. Body parts were strewn all about. Stomach parts lay in front of heads detached from bodies. Blood was splashed everywhere and AK-47s and twisted tables and chairs were strewn about. Smoke curled from blown out windows on the palace's floors with smoke and flames flaring.

"This is positively medieval. Almost like a plane crash. Ankyer did this?" said Shennib in a hushed voice. "Where are the rest of his men?"

"We don't have time to go into it, Shennib," replied Groton. "Fred and I will go in and retrieve the captives. Post your men at the entrance. If you see anyone other than us or the captives we have with us, shoot them," said Groton.

With that Bell and Groton ran into the building.

"Jake, this is Neal. Fred and I are in the building."

"Ok. There is a stairwell 30 feet to your right. Take the stairs down two flights to a subbasement. There are three doors on the right a double set of doors on he left. The captives are barricaded behind the double doors. Shout 'freedom'. The captives have been told to open the door when they hear that word," said Ankyer.

Groton and Bell did as they were instructed. The doors opened and twelve ragged men and women spilled out into the hall.

"Thank God," a man said. "They took the children. Do you have them?"

"No. but we are working on that. We must hurry. Follow me single file. When you leave the building, put your hands over your head and walk towards the trucks. Make no sudden moves. There are soldiers out there who will help you into the trucks. There is also food and water. They will take you to the city of Ghat and you will be turned over to your Embassy people," said Groton.

"But the children!" exclaimed the man.

"We are taking care of that and will communicate with the Embassy," replied Groton. "We must move quickly. This is a very dangerous area."

The captives formed a line with Groton at the head and Bell at the back and walked quickly up the stairs and out of the building. Shennib and his men loaded the captives into the Libyan military trucks and quickly distributed food and water. Three of the Libyan soldiers got in the front of one truck and the fourth soldier got behind the wheel of the second.

Groton said: "Shennib, it's been a pleasure."

"We will have to do this again sometime," replied Shennib.

"Works for me," replied Groton. "You never know. If you get a promotion every time you're on one of our missions, you will be running the Libyan military while still a young man!" With that they shook hands, Shennib got in the passenger side of the second idling Libyan truck; Groton and Bell got in the Humvee and started it up. The vehicles roared out of the Palace gate, the Libyan trucks turning left towards Ghat and the Humvee right, towards the oasis.

Ten minutes later, the Ultrablack IV camouflaged drone dropped from its 4,000 foot on-station altitude to 1,000 feet directly over the Gaddafi compound. The compound was infused with clouds of smoke from fires on the building's first second and third floors. Two pods opened on the underbelly of the drone and two, two foot, WS4 neutron bomb tipped missiles launched and exploded 300 feet above the compound. The down blast incinerated the compound and everything else within a half mile. The small, tactical, nuclear explosion turned the surrounding sand to glass with surprisingly little radiation. Another advance in nuclear missile delivery courtesy of the Abbey scientists.

On the way back from the compound, Groton said: *"Jake, we're done here."*

"Ok. Dr. Finkel wants us to meet at the extraction point. We are packing up here and will meet you there."

"What about the Humvee?" asked Groton.

"We'll blow it up and fly the Blackhawks out. We have a briefing with Dr. Finkel in a couple hours. He has another job for us."

"Interesting?" asked Groton.

"You won't believe it," replied Ankyer.

"10-4," said Groton.

WASHINGTON D.C.
May 2017

MALLORY TENSALE, FORMER SENATOR FROM WEST VIRGINIA AND CURRENTLY Chief of Staff to the President of the United States, reflected on his latest clandestine meeting with Stephen Louis Gatling in the secure room Baltimore. Tensale and Gatling went together all the way back to the Yale Skull and Bones Society. Their friendship extended over the years to the point that Gatling trusted Tensale as much as a malignant narcissist could trust anyone. Gatling was nuts then and even more nuts now.

For some odd reason Gatling's rampant paranoia did not extend to Tensale. Probably because Gatling was not smart enough to figure out how to become dictator of the United States but thought Tensale was. No matter. Tensale was ok with that. The big question was, could he count on the cabal of hard case right- wingers he had assembled to pull it off. The linchpin was Anastasia Moon. The others fawned over her, and she absorbed the attention like a sponge. Anastasia wanted to sit at the right hand of Gatling once he was dictator. It wasn't about money for her; she had a ton of that. It was all about power. And Tensale had spent quality time assuring her that power would be hers.

But on to the current business at hand. Tomorrow's Cabinet meeting agenda called for Vice President Penelope Bartlett to chair the meeting, as President Gatling had a personal emergency that would take him to Camp David accompanied by Tensale. Arkansas Congressman Phillip Merklin would be on hand to report on his State's initiative to eliminate its clean air regulations, bringing them into closer alignment with Gatling's anti climate change position.

If things went as planned, and assuming the Chinese device worked as advertised, Merklin's report would not happen. Merklin would hand off the Chinese device to Buster Hornsbee before the meeting started. A platter of jelly donuts, to which many Cabinet members were partial, would be on a table. Hornsbee would surreptitiously insert the device into a donut that would be placed at the bottom of the pile. The device was constructed of biochemical molecular components that would interact with the sugar in the donut and activate 15 minutes later. The device would then dissolve, to prevent its subsequent discovery.

Perfect. What could go wrong? Merklin would then take his seat at the conference table and wait for the fireworks. He would have an appliance in each ear generating white noise that would protect him from the effects of the device. Or so he thought. God, the Chinese were smart, thought Tensale. Fireworks, fortune cookies and now sonic weapons!

CABINET ROOM
Washington D.C.
May 2017

THE CABINET ROOM HAD BEEN PREPARED BY THE WHITE HOUSE ATTENDANTS ninety minutes before the meeting. Since President Gatling and Chief of Staff Tensale would not be present, the seating name plates had been rearranged to reflect Vice President Bartlett's position as meeting Chair. The agenda had been distributed, the audio-visual system checked, and presentation sequences confirmed with Cabinet members' staff. As it was a morning meeting, a light Continental breakfast was in order. The White House stewards had arranged the place settings and were busy hovering over plates of pastries, fruit, and various juices on tables just outside the Cabinet room along with urns of hot water for tea and coffee. Normally, the stewards would take orders from the Cabinet members and serve them once they were in the room. Cabinet member staff were seated in chairs behind their respective Secretaries.

One exception to the continental breakfast service was the Secretary of Education, Ernestine "Boopsie" McNulty. "Boopsie" McNulty had worn a body sculpting under garment since her mid-twenties to maintain an hour-glass figure. The result was a thin-waisted figure reminiscent of the Jazz Age cartoon character Betty Boop. This was fine, as she much preferred 'Boopsie' to her given name "Ernestine" which she felt her parents had given her during a drug-induced psychotic break.

Boopsie did whatever she wanted to, due in no small part to her husband's $10 million contribution to President Gatling's Super Pac prior to the election. In this regard, she insisted that for breakfast meetings she be presented with an oversized, custom, jelly donut stuffed with raspberry filling. which for some strange reason she felt was in keeping with her Betty Boop-like figure. A steward had placed the jelly donut apart from the other donuts with a small sign...'Secretary McNulty'.

Twenty minutes later, Buster Hornsbee, Pentagon liaison, walked by the Secretary's jelly donut, dropped a pen, and while bending over to pick it up inserted a gelatin capsule into the center via the jelly donut raspberry injection site. He picked up his pen and walked into the Cabinet room ostensibly to check his presentation laptop. While walking into the room Hornsbee inserted the white noise apparatus designed to counteract the sonic disrupter effects into his ears. Hornsbee then took his seat behind the Secretary of Defense's chair at the conference table and waited with anticipation.

The Cabinet room rapidly filled. The last people to arrive were Vice President Bartlett and her Chief of Staff. The stewards took orders from the luminaries around the large oblong conference table, quickly returning with the requested breakfast items, then exiting and closing the doors behind them. Boopsie McNulty's jelly donut appeared in front of her accompanied by a mug (she did not want to run out in the middle of the meeting) of Bellocq's Gypsy Caravan black tea, her favorite. Not one to wait on ceremony, Boopsie virtually inhaled the large jelly donut (next time she would order two, she thought) before her colleagues around the table had barely settled into their seats. Two minutes later Boopsie's stomach acid interacted with the sonic disrupter gelatin capsule activating the capsule's molecular computer.

"Yes, Congressman Merklin?" said Vice President Bartlett to Merklin who walked over to Bartlett's chair. Merklin bent over and said "Sorry, Madam Vice President, an unscheduled call of nature. Please start without me."

"As you wish, Congressman," replied Bartlett as Merklin left the room shutting the door behind him. Vice President Penelope Bartlett gaveled the meeting to order. "President Gatling sends his regrets," she said. "The President has an emergency extended conference call this morning and is at Camp David. However, we have several important agenda items and following his wishes, we will carry on with our meeting. Does anyone have a question before we start?" Boopsie McNulty's eyes bulged, and her complexion went from tan, to red, to purple and she raised her hand. "The chair recognizes Secretary of Education, Boopsie McNulty. Boopsie?"

Boopsie McNulty rose from her chair, waving her arms, opened her mouth emitting a loud, belch-like sound. She pitched forward on the table with her arms splayed out, a pool of blood enlarging under her head. The other occupants of the Cabinet room sat in shock...but not for long. An extremely high pitched, supersonic tone filled the room causing everyone to press their hands to their heads and scream, blood hemorrhaging from their mouths and ears.

The head steward, standing in the corridor just outside a closed Cabinet door heard the sounds of mayhem coming from the room and remarked to the steward standing next to him: "Man. That must be one hell of a presentation!".

"What did you say?" the other steward replied. "I can't hear you."

HOLY INNOCENTS
TRAPPIST MONASTERY

Gila National Forest
New Mexico

THE LARGE SCREEN MONITOR FLICKERED TO LIFE IN THE ABBEY LIBRARY. An image of Major General Marcus Boyd, MD, Chief of Pathology at Walter Reed Hospital filled the screen.

"Good afternoon, Dr. Finkel. Thank you for taking the time. I know that you are extremely busy."

"Not too busy to help out an old friend," replied Finkel.

"Did you receive Secretary McNulty's remains we flew into the Abbey yesterday?" asked Boyd.

"We received them, and an examination is underway," replied Finkel. "Thank you for not doing an autopsy. It made our examination easier."

"Well, once we performed a full body CAT scan it became obvious that we needed specialized expertise and you and your colleagues at the Abbey came immediately to mind."

"We also received Mr. Buster Hornsbee's head which has been processed for examination," said Finkel.

"Thank you. We were not sure what was going on with Hornsbee, but his injuries were not the same as the others and we thought we'd send it along with Boopsie".

"We have some results, but they are not as definitive as we would like. In that regard, we would like to keep the body and the head a little longer if that's agreeable with you," replied Finkel.

"That's fine with us. As you might expect, President Gatling wants answers, and the pressure is turned up. Any insight you can provide will be extremely valuable. I will leave you to it then. Let me know when you have concluded your review. By the way, we assembled a list of people in the Cabinet room at the time of the event. One participant, Congressman Philip Merklin evidently said something to the Vice President and left the room. Asked afterwards, he said it was a 'call of nature'."

"Lucky for him," replied Finkel. "We'll return Secretary McNulty's body and Mr. Hornsbee's head to you in a few days and contact you with our findings," said Finkel.

"Thanks again," said Boyd. And the screen went black.

After Boyd signed off, Dr. Margie Tallon and Dr. Lester Arlot entered the room and George Makin linked in remotely via his mastoid implant.

"Margie, please give us an overview," asked Finkel.

Tallon clicked the remote that she was holding, and a picture of a body cavity filled the bottom third of the screen. "As you can see, Secretary McNulty's heart and lungs have jellified. We believe that an exceptionally high frequency sound wave in the chest cavity was the cause of the extensive organ damage. We also discovered an intact portion of a partially eaten jelly donut with the remains of a gelatin capsule imbedded in it. Curiously, the molecular structure of human internal organs appear to be more susceptible to high frequency sound wave damage than do baked goods. Definitely something we would like to investigate further."

"Dr. Arlot, would you like to add to the discussion?" asked Finkel.

"Thank you Dr. Finkel. We placed the pieces of jelly donut along with the remains of the gelatin capsule under an electron microscope. I can tell you unequivocally, Dr. Finkel, that the capsule is the source of Ms. McNulty's demise. What we discovered is that the gelatin capsule is in fact the delivery system of an internal biocomputer which we believe generated the sound wave. Once the gelatin capsule encountered Boopsie's, sorry, Secretary McNulty's stomach, the acid started dissolving the capsule triggering the biocomputer."

"What's more," continued Arlot, "the device is like what we believe caused the employees in the Cuban and Chinese U.S. foreign embassies to exhibit significant hearing loss and vertigo consistent with Meniere's disease awhile back, also referred to as the Havana Syndrome. That's it in a nutshell."

"So you think it's the same technology that caused the Cuban and Chinese situations," said Finkel.

"Those situations could have been just tests," replied Arlot. This device was the Cuban and Chinese events on steroids. As I understand it from the event description sent along with Ms. McNulty's remains, except for Buster Hornsbee, the other people in the Cabinet room suffered massive auditory damage."

"That's true," replied Finkel. "Regarding Hornsbee, prior to our teleconference, Dr. Boyd indicated he found some kind of hearing aids that appeared to have melted into his ears and then into his brain. That is why they boxed up Hornsbee's head along with the so-called hearing aids and sent them along with Secretary McNulty."

"One could argue. that this could be construed as an assassination attempt on SLUG which failed because of a change in scheduling," interjected George Makin, aka Winston White communicating through his mastoid implant, his voice filling the room.

"That's definitely a possibility," replied Finkel. *"Boyd indicated that the FBI is looking into that."*

"George. Were you able to listen in on the entire call?"

"Yes, Dr. Finkel," replied Makin.

'Excellent. I would like to hear any observations, each of you may have," said Finkel. *"George, you first."*

"Concerning whether or not it was an assassination attempt on SLUG, I think not. His being absent from the meeting with his Chief of Staff is too convenient. Also, it appears that notwithstanding the two fatalities, the sound device was designed to injure, not to kill. Couple that with SLUG's suspicion that his Cabinet was discussing the 25th Amendment to force him from office, it's feasible that SLUG was behind it."

"I agree, George," said Finkel.

"Margie...your opinion?" continued Finkel.

"I think Boopsie McNulty was collateral damage. Someone secreted the device in the jelly donut expecting the donut to be brought into the room with the other pastries sometime between placing it on the credenza and it being delivered to Boopsie."

"To that point, Dr. Arlot, could you tell if the device had a timer on it? asked Finkel.

"Well, it was damaged, but from what I could see when we placed the device under the electron microscope, it appears to in fact have had timing software. When Boopsie ate the raspberry filled donut, her gastric acid set the device off prematurely."

"What about Buster Hornsbee," asked Finkel.

"He's interesting as well," Arlot said. "Hornsbee's temples were melted along with both ears. He had two devices, one in each ear, which might have been construed as hearing aids. In fact, under closer examination, they were white noise cancelling devices. However, it appears the devices were altered to increase the effects substantially, and as a result, melted into his head."

"I would say that establishes Hornsbee as the delivery person for the device. He probably inserted the device into the raspberry jelly donut just prior to the donut being brought into Boopsie," said Makin.

"...which eliminated Hornsbee from being interrogated," added Tallon.

"Excellent analysis," said Finkel. "I completely agree.

"So, it looks like President Gatling and possibly Chief of Staff Tensale may have been behind the attack on the Cabinet, in an effort to remove the threat of Gatling being eliminated from Office via the 25th Amendment. Agreed?

"Agreed," replied Makin, Arlot and Tallon in chorus.

"What about Congressman Merklin?" asked Finkel.

"I don't believe in coincidences," replied Makin.

"Neither do I," said Finkel. *"We'll take a deeper dive into that."*

"There's another possibility," said Makin.

"And that is...?" asked Finkel.

"In addition to eliminating the Cabinet, this could have been a trial run for a much larger operation," said Makin through his mastoid implant.

After a pause in the conversation Finkel said: *"That is worth considering George. Definitely worth considering."*

MAY 7, 2017
Lost Palms Oasis
Libyan Desert.

SHEIKH ALIM BIN AMIT AL-HEYDAR WAS PLEASED WITH HIMSELF. The slave business was booming. He had fifteen slaves for sale today. Six girls, five men and, best of all, four young boys. The boys had cost him dearly. The al-Qaeda pirate he bought them from was a tough negotiator and a bastard. What the pirate didn't know was that the Sheikh already had buyers for the boys from the Qatari pleasure boat.

The pirate must have thought the slaver lived under a rock. It was common knowledge that the boys and their minders were kidnapped from the boat. When the pirate called him, he said one of the boys had died, but he was prepared to sell the four remaining children. The pirate wanted to also sell the minders, but the Sheikh had buyers only for the boys and was not interested. The buyers he had were a group of wealthy pedophiles, Middle Eastern oil businessmen who had talked to one of the Sheikh's contacts in a

Thailand 'Red Light' district. They arrived the day before, and after a sumptuous dinner, looked the boys over and were eager to buy.

The bidding for the boys would open at $ 50,000 each, American. The group consisted of ten bidders, so the Sheikh expected competition and a big payday. The tents were set up and the bidders were enjoying their breakfasts. The boys were bathed and powdered. A few hours from now the Sheikh would be adding to his wealth substantially, even after paying his men.

Al-Heydar walked out of his tent as the glow of sunrise was visible; this was one of his favorite times of day. As he scanned the horizon, he noticed an animal standing on a sand dune far off in the distance. Desert heat waves had started to appear, so it was difficult for the Sheikh to see clearly. The animal seemed to be pacing back and forth, stopping to look in his direction. "A desert wolf," surmised the Sheikh, "but to see it from such a distance would mean it was very large. No matter," he thought. After the sale he might take a few of his men in a truck fitted with sand tires and drive out to get a better look. If it was still around, he would shoot it. A trophy befitting a wealthy Sheikh!

———

Ahmad Dayan Hamza, a tall Bedouin chieftain, walked up to Ankyer and bowed. "It is an honor to meet a warrior such as you, Sheikh Ankyer. Your reputation among the Bedouin tribes is spoken of around many campfires."

"The honor is mine, Sayyid Ahmad Dayan Hamza," replied Ankyer, using the Bedouin honorific 'Sayyid'. "My friends call me 'Jake'."

"And my friends call me Ahmad," said Hamza. "Dr. Finkel, an old and trusted friend, told me of your quest and need for transportation. I assume you and your men can ride?"

"Absolutely," replied Ankyer. "However, there is a significant difference between the average horse and a charger, amounting to a weight of 1500 pounds each," he said, as he looked at the corral. "They are magnificent."

"The white stallion is yours to command, Jake. The four black chargers are for your men. I will have the honor of riding by your side on Bakush, my black charger with the white forelock. Each horse is battle-tested. Their shoes have been honed to razor sharpness and each saddle has a cutlass attached for close-in fighting. The charger is a weapon by itself, my friend. Dr. Finkel told me that he was concerned that a helicopter attack could result in the slavers killing the captives. The ruse of desert folk riding towards the encampment will hopefully give the slavers pause, possibly thinking more buyers are on the way. Once we are among them, they will be ours," said Hamza.

Neil Groton, Chief Bell and two other SEALs walked up. Ankyer introduced them.

"I can't wait to ride a charger," said Bell. "I used to ride bulls in my younger, wilder youth."

"A bull rider!" exclaimed Hamza "Many in my tribe will want to hear of your exploits!"

"Exploits. He's definitely not short on exploits," said Ankyer.

"Dr. Finkel told me of a war dog in your company, a magnificent beast. I would be grateful to see him," said Hamza.

"Ah, you are referring to Varna," replied Ankyer. "He's not a dog, but a wolf. There is a Qatari princeling who is among the captives. Varna is now ranging ahead of us towards the encampment. When we ride in, Varna will seek out the boy and protect him if possible."

"A true adventure!" exclaimed Hamza. "Worthy of a retelling among my tribes' campfires!"

Ankyer turned, reached into a carton, withdrew a Heckler & Koch MP5 machine gun, and gave it to Hamza. "An excellent weapon, and one with which I am familiar," said Hamza. "There is a holster on your saddle opposite the sword which the MP5 should fit in nicely," said Ankyer.

"We need to leave now," said Ankyer as he stared out in the distance. *"We are leaving now Dr. Finkel."*

"Excellent Jake. We have active satellite download on the camp. They are assembling what looks like a platform for the auction. We can see that Varna is in position. Good luck. Hamza is a good man."

"He has been helpful already, Dr. Finkel."

"Good. The helicopter support will land in the camp when you are ready."

Hamza looked at Ankyer. "You talk to Dr. Finkel in the sky! A wonder."

"A wonder indeed," replied Ankyer. "We must leave now. I don't want Varna out there too long without water, and it looks like the slavers are preparing for the auction."

Ankyer, the SEALs and Hamza entered the corral and mounted the chargers.

The horses' muscles rippled, foam started to accumulate on the bits in their mouth, and they reared as they adjusted to the weight of the riders. Ankyer tightened his grip on the reins of the white stallion. He dug his heels in its side and the charger bolted forward into the desert, followed by Hamza and the rest of the company.

Alim bin Amit al-Heydar was not happy. He wanted the auction to proceed before noon, when the desert temperature would climb to its highest. It was now 11:00 AM and the presentation platform was not finished. Something to do with rotten wood. One of the workers promised the wood would be replaced shortly. He could still see the wolf, or whatever it was, pacing in the distance. The last thing al-Heydar needed was a wolf in the camp prior to the proceedings.

He pointed to one of his men walking by. "Ali, bring me my field glasses." The man returned shortly with military binoculars. He scanned the horizon in the direction of the wolf. "God damnit," he thought. The heat was causing the air to shimmer. He couldn't quite focus. The wolf was at least a mile or more off. He adjusted the focal distance, and the wolf came into view. "Holy shit," he thought. "The fucking animal is enormous!" The wolf continued to pace back and forth.

"What was that behind it? A dust cloud. Riders! Coming up behind the wolf." One rider was very tall. A Bedouin! If only he could get the Bedouins interested in his slaves. He would make a fortune. And it looked like they were riding in al-Heydar's direction.

He turned to a group of slavers. "Hurry, god damnit!" Get the slave boys out from the tent and line them up in front of the platform except for the boy with the red ribbon around his neck. Get him up on the platform and chain him to the pole. And call the buyers from breakfast and tell them the auction will start in twenty minutes. Hurry! We have new buyers riding in from the desert!"

Al-Heydar's men were scrambling around the encampment and the buyers started wandering over to the chairs, which had been set out in front of the platform. Al-Heydar beckoned Ali over. "Make sure all our men are armed. The riders coming into camp are probably buyers, but then again you never know what the desert brings." Ali scurried away to carry out his master's instructions.

Ankyer and his companions had been riding hard, their robes flapping, as clouds of sand rose from the horses' hooves. Each rider and his respective charger had goggles to protect their eyes from the sun's glare and sand particles. The horses and riders pulled up ten yards from Varna. The chargers started bucking and wheeling around, disturbed by what they scented as a large predator in their midst. Varna saw Ankyer, letting out a piercing howl. Ankyer pulled the reins to control his stallion as it reared.

The Bedouin Hamza, also controlling his charger exclaimed: "What a beast! He's magnificent!"

Ankyer replied: "Ahmad meet Varna. He started out as a wolf but is now what you behold. We think of him as our war dog, but as you can see, he is much more."

Ankyer dismounted, handing his charger's reins to Chief Bell, and taking a water bag from his saddle. He walked over to Varna with the water bag and squirted half the water into Varna's open mouth and the other half over Varna's head to cool him down. Varna rubbed against him.

"He must weigh at least 300 pounds," said Hamza.

"Closer to 385 now," replied Ankyer.

"What is that covering over him," asked Hamza.

"It's a specialized, light Kevlar covering to absorb the shock of bullets. It's like the coverings of our horses. We expect at least some of the people in the slaver camp will be armed, and while the Kevlar protection isn't perfect, it should be adequate."

Ankyer became silent for a moment. *"Yes, Dr. Finkel. We're set to go. Yes, Varna is in good condition, and ready. OK. Thank you,"* said Ankyer.

Ankyer took the reins of his charger from Chief Bell, remounted, and addressed his companions. "Dr. Finkel has just confirmed that the real time satellite imagery shows the slavers are assembling the slaves for the auction. I will give Varna the scent of the Qatari boy again, so he can find him. The imagery shows four boys which is consistent with our intel. Three of the boys are chained together off to one side of a large, rectangular platform, and one boy is chained to a pole on the platform. The other people in the camp are either slavers or bidders and are subject to a 'take no prisoners' protocol." Ankyer reached into his robe and withdrew a piece of cloth. He leaned over and let Varna smell it. Varna's muscles tensed as his snout wrinkled.

"Varna, seek," said Ankyer. Varna turned and raced towards the slavers' encampment. Ankyer exclaimed: "Gentlemen!" turned his white stallion towards the figure of Varna, growing smaller in the distance, and dug his heels into the charger's flanks. The charger reared up and bolted forward at a full gallop unleashing 1500 pounds of compressed fury. The chargers ridden by the Bedouin and the SEALs followed at full gallop.

Al-Heydar refocused the binoculars on the dust cloud rapidly approaching. The riders' robes flapped furiously in the wind and their faces were covered to protect from the sand blast. He saw that they were heavily armed, including the Bedouin. The wolf-beast was ahead of the riders and on a full run. Al-Heydar was having second thoughts. The riders looked more like attackers, not buyers. He trotted over to the platform, picked up an AK-47 and climbed the stairs. He walked over to the glassy-eyed boy chained to the pole; he was glad they had drugged the slaves. Easier to control them.

Just then one of the buyers yelled, "Get the auction started, god damnit. I don't have all day. Get the bidding going on the boy on the platform!" exclaimed another buyer.

"As you wish, sir," replied al-Heydar. "Bidding will start at $ 50,000 dollars. Do I hear $ 50,000?" All the bidders' hands shot up. "Do I hear $ 60,000?" Three bidders' hands were raised. Al-Heydar couldn't believe it.

"$ 80,000!" yelled a bidder. '$ 80,000," said al-Heydar. Do I hear $90,000?" asked. Al-Heydar. "$ 80,000 is the bid. $ 80,000 once, twice. Sold at $ 80,000!"

"Unchain the boy," yelled a large, dark skinned, sweating fat man. "How much for the other three? I'll buy them all," he said. As al-Heydar turned to reply, he saw a beast from hell launch itself from a sand berm 20 yards away. A shadow blotted out the sun in his eyes. Varna landed at the center of the platform on top of al-Heydar, bowling him over onto his back. Al-Heydar tried to reach for the AK-47, but the weight of Varna pinned him to the platform. Varna let out with a roar and ripped off al-Heydar's face from the nose down. He threw the piece of bloody flesh into the bidders' seated in front of the platform. Al-Heydar, still alive with eyes bulging like saucers, put his hand up to his face, and felt nothing but blood and mangled tissue. Varna bent his muzzle once again over al-Heydar and ripped down with his saber incisors decapitating the slaver.

Ankyer arrived, his legs gripping the stallion's flanks and guiding it as he held a MP-5 in one hand and the combat cross bow in the other. The successful bidder pulled a pistol out of his jacket and shot at Varna, only to be blown apart from an exploding bolt fired from the crossbow by Ankyer in midair, while his charger, steaming from exertion, vaulted over a table 80 feet away and reared up in front of the platform. The remaining bidders ran for their lives and were hit with a hail of bullets and white phosphorous grenades from the SEALS. Two slavers, aiming their AK-47's towards Ankyer were ridden over by the Bedouin Hamza. One slaver was torn to pieces by Hamza's charger's sharpened horseshoes; the other cut down by the Bedouin's scimitar.

Bell and Neal rode their horses into a group of slavers shooting their AKs in random directions. They were no match for Chief Bell's and Chief Neal's MP5s' withering fire. One slaver managed to get off a shot hitting Neal in the chest and knocking him off his horse. Bell dismounted his charger, shot the slaver in the shoulder, pulled his scimitar from the charger's saddle, and cut the slaver down with one stroke. Bell turned to Groton. "Neal, how bad is it?"

"Not too bad," replied Neal. "The bastard knocked me down, but the Kevlar saved me. Those guys at the Abbey sure know how to make vests! I'll have to buy them a beer when we get back."

"Hell," replied Bell. "With all our money you can buy them a brewery. I'll even chip in."

Ankyer vaulted off his horse, simultaneously spraying three more slavers with his MP5. He sprinted up to the platform. Varna was standing in front of the boy, shielding the boy's body and roaring, with his teeth barred, blood and flesh dripping and hanging from his sabers. Varna stopped when he saw Ankyer and wagged his tail. "How are you, my friend?" asked Ankyer as he quickly checked Varna over. "Oops. Looks like you lost the tip of an ear, buddy."

Bell walked up. "How are we doing?"

"Varna got clipped in the ear. The kids seem ok except they are all a little disoriented. I'm guessing the slavers drugged them. Do me a favor and check what's left of this guy for a key to unlock the chains on this kid," asked Ankyer. Ankyer pulled the DNA pen from his battle harness and pushed the tip into the boy's shoulder, without eliciting a reaction. Ankyer checked the reading. "Bingo. We got the Prince's boy," Ankyer said.

"And I've got the key," replied Bell. They unlocked the boy's chains as the boy sat holding onto Varna.

"Looks like Varna made a new friend," said Ankyer and bent over picking up a pointed piece of bloody fur. "And I'm guessing this is the tip of Varna's ear that got shot off."

Ankyer walked to the edge of the platform. Neal rode up. "Jake. We found six women and five men shackled in a tent. Looks like they were next up to be sold after the boys."

"Thanks, Neal," replied Ankyer. "How's everything else?"

"Under control," replied Groton. "Slaves are all accounted for. All the slavers and bidders are dead."

"How about us?" asked Ankyer.

"Everyone is ok including our Bedouin friend. No casualties except me. I was shot in the chest, but the Kevlar vest saved my ass."

"Getting shot in the chest and having your ass saved at the same time," is one for the books. I'll write it up in the log," replied Ankyer.

"Smart ass," said Groton as the Bedouin rode up.

"You guys sure know how to fight!" said Sheikh Hamza as he pulled up on his charger in a cloud of sand. We will make you honorary Bedouins!"

Ankyer gave Hamza a 'thumbs-up' and looked towards the horizon.

"Dr. Finkel. Sit Rep. Slaver camp site under control. All boys safe and secure. Qatari prince identified and safe. Freed an additional eleven adults. All slavers and bidders neutralized. Two casualties. Neal Groton shot in chest. Damage mitigated by Kevlar vest. Top of Varna's ear shot off. Ear tip recovered. Otherwise, no damage."

"Excellent," replied Finkel. "There are three helicopters inbound, one with the medical team. Should be there momentarily."

"I have some super glue I can put on Varna's ear if that would help," said Ankyer.

"Don't you dare touch that ear!"

"Honey Pi! Why am I not surprised?"

"I don't suppose you found the ear tip that got shot off?"

"As a matter of fact, I searched and found a chunk of fur that looks like a piece of Varna."

"Well at least you did something constructive," replied Honey Pi.

"Ok, you two. This is a combat channel," said Finkel.

At that moment three helicopters swooped in. Dr. Honey Pi, Brother William, and Dr. Walthour jumped out of one and started jogging towards the slave camp. Varna spied them, let out with a howl, jumped off the platform and bounded towards them. Brother William frantically dug into his pocket for some high protein biscuits just as Varna got to them in a licking frenzy. Brother William finally distracted him with three biscuits as Ankyer walked up.

"I don't get greetings like that," said Ankyer.

"That's because you don't feed him," said Honey Pi giving Ankyer an elbow. "Got the chunk of ear?" she asked. Ankyer pulled the ear tip from a pocket and handed it to Honey Pi.

Looking at Walthour, Honey Pi handed him the ear tip and asked, "What do you think Jim?" Walthour looked at the tip, walked over to Varna, held his head, and examined the wound. "Not a problem," he said. We'll clean up the edges, super glue the tip on and he will be good as new in a week or so."

"Ahem," said Ankyer looking at Honey Pi.

"Don't say a word, Jake. Is there a tent we can use to check out the children and the other captives?" she asked. "Also, it would be nice to know what kind of drugs they gave the kids."

"That tent over there is air conditioned. We did a quick survey of the camp and found a bottle of Rohypnol, which is likely what they used," Ankyer replied.

"You certainly are a full-service operation," said Honey Pi as they walked towards the tent the boys and other captives were being escorted to. "We will take Varna to the adjacent tent," said Walthour as he placed the ear tip in a small cold container.

"Ok," said Ankyer. We'll see you back at our camp.

"Dr. Finkel, we are secure here," said Ankyer. "The captives are being checked out by Honey Pi and will be transported to our camp. Varna is being attended to by Dr. Walthour. Neil, Bell, the other SEALs, Ahmad Dayan Hamza and I will mount up and ride back to the camp," said Ankyer.

"Excellent," replied Finkel. "We will convey the Bedouin's courage in battle to his tribe, who will honor him upon his return. We have also sent news of the rescue to the Qataris. Well done, as usual, Jake."

SOMEWHERE IN
BALTIMORE MARYLAND

PRESIDENT STEPHEN LOUIS GATLING PACED BACK AND FORTH IN THE ROOM. "What the fuck happened, damn it! I wanted the cabinet disabled. Not killed!"

Mallory Tensale held up a hand. "Hold on, Mr. President. You instructed me to eliminate the Cabinet Secretaries and the Vice President. That's what I did!"

"I didn't tell you to kill them, for Christ sakes," replied Gatling. "Boopsie McNulty's husband is a major campaign contributor. With Boopsie dead he might put his money somewhere else! I don't give a shit about her, but we're talking millions of dollars here!"

"Look, sir," replied Tensale. "There was no way to anticipate the dumb bitch would eat the device we used to disable the Cabinet. After all, she was the Secretary of Education."

"Oh, yeah," said Gatling. "She used up what brains she had snaring her billionaire husband. Whose bright idea was it to shove this thing of yours into her raspberry filled jelly donut? She inhales those things. She's famous for it!"

"Congressman Merklin gave the device to one of our people, Buster Hornsbee, a Pentagon congressional liaison. Hornsbee inserted the device into the jelly donut, assuming it would be carried into the conference room just before it went off."

"What happened to Hornsbee?" asked Gatling.

"He's dead," replied Tensale. "He was wearing ear plugs which he thought would generate white noise to dilute the sound waves from the device. Instead, they amplified the sound waves and burned his ears off along with a portion of his brain on each side of his head. We didn't want to chance his being discovered."

"How the hell do you explain that?" said Gatling.

"There was so much chaos it will be difficult to figure out what happened," said Tensale. "As a matter of fact, there were four people in the room wearing hearing aids. The hearing aids melted but didn't kill them."

"Well, that's something, anyway. The important thing is that this disaster can't be traced back to me," said Gatling.

"Not a chance," said Tensale. "The device self-destructed after it went off in Boopsie's stomach. Plus, there's a suspicion growing that what happened is related to the physical problems the embassy staff in Cuba and China experienced."

"And was it?" asked Gatling.

"Let's just say it was similar, sir.

"Ok. What's the likelihood of the Vice President and Cabinet Secretaries recovering from this thing?"

"Nil sir. The hearing loss is permanent and the ability to concentrate is dramatically reduced, as much as 60 percent in some cases."

"So, these traitorous bastards are gone," said Gatling

"Absolutely"

"Ok. I will appoint acting Cabinet Secretaries. The last thing I need is to have those morons in the Senate questioning my appointees."

"Do you have anyone specifically in mind?"

"Yes. I have a list of my golf club members. They are dumb as rocks and will be perfect for the jobs. You can start contacting them. I also like the idea of blaming the Chinese for the current Cabinets' loss. Afterall, my political base is a bunch of sheep and will buy into whatever I throw at them. Anything else, Mallory?"

"One other item. Where is this bodyguard you've had around?"

"Oh, Mr. White. I don't think I need him anymore. I'm uncomfortable with him being around where I am all the time. Besides, if I keep the Secret Service boys well fed and happy, Mr. White may not be necessary. I'll probably keep him at the White House just in case, but I didn't bring him with me today, for example."

"The reason I ask," said Tensale, "is that White comes from the Red Protocol Group. Correct?"

"Yes," replied Gatling. "So what?"

"It turns out that Boopsie's corpse was sent to Walter Reed Hospital for an autopsy. After they did a CAT scan and looked around, they sent the cadaver out for an independent evaluation to pathologists at the Red Protocol Group, who they evidently use in sensitive cases. There is a possibility that the autopsy results may be conveyed to White."

"OK. Is that a problem?"

"Not as far as I can see," said Tensale. "They won't find anything Walter Reed didn't."

"Even so, the head of the Red Protocol Group is Dr. Asher Finkel. He's smart. Not as smart as me, but smart, nevertheless. Can we find out the results of their evaluation?" asked Gatling.

"The Chief of Pathology at Walter Reed is General Marcus Boyd. If I pull out the 'national security' card he'll probably let me know if Finkel's operation finds anything we should be concerned about."

"And if they find something?" asked Gatling.

"They won't. But if they start asking questions, we can handle it," replied Tensale.

"Handle it how?" asked Gatling.

"Get rid of Finkel of course," replied Tensale.

"Makes sense. Also, there is one more thing we need to discuss," said Gatling.

THE CONSTABLE CLUB
Embassy Row
Washington DC

GEORGE MAKIN SAT IN THE LEATHER CHAIR IN THE CONSTABLE CLUB LIBRARY and placed his drink on the ebony side table next to him. He activated his mastoid implant.

"You know, Dr. Finkel, the first time I was here, I thought to myself, if I had not gone into the FBI but rather into investment banking or some other lucrative career, I might be able one day to afford to become a member in a place like this."

"And yet George, here you are. A full-fledged member of the Constable Club and the Red Protocol Group. Quite an achievement, especially as you also managed to return from the dead and to become the principal security person for the President of the United States," replied Finkel.

"Except that I'm no longer asked to attend Presidential meetings," said Makin.

"Well, we expected something like that to occur, given his volatility. At least you still have access to the White House. I think with the

attack that befell his Cabinet, SLUG's 25th Amendment issue was resolved, and his paranoia may have lessened somewhat," said Finkel.

"I also think he was getting twitchy about me being around when he met with Chief-of-Staff Tensale in the house in Baltimore," said Makin.

"Well, not all is lost. He continues to wear the tracking watch you gave him. For the moment at least, we can isolate his movements and listen in on him even when he's 'off the clock' so to speak," replied Finkel. "There is little doubt SLUG was somehow involved in the event that disabled the Cabinet. And Tensale would almost have to have been part of the plan."

"There's something else," said Makin. "As I mentioned during our conversation at Luba's Congressional Café, the last time I went to Baltimore with SLUG and Tensale, I overheard SLUG and Tensale discussing the new Cabinet. Considering what's happened, it looks like they are going forward with their plan. The Cabinet deputies will be installed as Acting Secretaries in the interest of insuring continuity of the principal Government Departments and avoiding the Senate confirmation process. And as you know, Tensale has been replaced with Phillip Merklin as Chief-of-Staff. As for making Anastasia Moon the Vice President, all hell broke loose in the House and Senate. Ms. Moon has no experience in Washington, and SLUG decided to make Aneal Mercastor, the Congressman from Illinois, the VP. Mercastor is extremely wealthy and a good friend of Tensale. Moon is still in the picture, though. She called a press conference during which she said she would be happy to support the President in any way she could and would be working with Tensale who now occupies the new position of 'Senior Policy Advisor to the President' to that end. Recall during our earlier conversation it was suggested that the Cabinet event might be a test of a larger operation. Considering all that's happened, it appears that in addition to relieving the 25th Amendment pressure on SLUG, *it was, in fact, designed as a test for a larger operation. The problem is that we don't know what the larger operation entails."*

"I'm with you 100%," replied Finkel. *"In fact, we've been working with our friends at the N.S.A. to develop more background information. We've also been tracking Tensale and Moon and have determined that they are planning something which we believe is related to the technology underlying the Cabinet event. We also know that Tensale has been in contact with the Chinese and that substantial funds have been transferred from Moon to a Chinese-controlled company located in Montserrat, in the Caribbean.*

Montserrat is a British overseas territory, and our British friends are helping to keep track of the money flow. So far, we don't know what the payment is for, but one could guess it has something to do with the Chinese technology we suspect was used in Cuba and possibly the Cabinet event."

"How much?" asked Makin

"$ 35,000,000," replied Finkel. *"We are also tracking Moon's bank accounts in case it was some kind of down payment. Now that you are no longer 'protecting' SLUG, I would like you to take over this little project and keep track of things. I have a feeling Mr. Tensale and Ms. Moon will be entering our orbit sooner than later."*

"Glad to do it," Dr. Finkel. *"By the way, how's Jake doing?"*

"After he and the team rescued the Qatari princeling from the slavers, the Qatari government contacted us and invited Jake to Qatar as the special guest of Salazar bin Hamad bin Kartoon Al Sallazon, the eighth Emir of Qatar. His son is Crown Prince Bamin, the father of Salud bin Hamad Sallazon, the rescued princeling. Jake is currently in London at the London School of Economics receiving an award for his paper on analytical macroeconomics, which has been instrumental in Jake being proposed for next year's Nobel prize in economics. It turns out his intellectual skills are on a par with his physical and military

skills. If he gets the prize, it will be awarded to an 'anonymous' recipient in absentia as the publicity might expose the Red Protocol Group to unwanted public scrutiny. Jake is fine with that and values his relationship with us to be more important than any publicity he might receive. It took some discussion with the Nobel committee, but they eventually appreciated our point of view.

Honey Pi is also in London because the Qataris very much want to see Varna after viewing a film clip of the rescue from the slavers, which shows Varna protecting the boy during the operation. Honey Pi insisted on going along to make sure Varna is not stressed by the proceedings, as if Varna could be stressed by anything," said Finkel. *"Jake and Honey Pi are staying at our London residence on Embassy Row and will fly to Qatar from there. Varna is being flown to Qatar from the Abbey along with Brother William at his request, to ensure that Varna is adequately cared for. I've learned over the years that giving Brother William what he requests is generally a good idea."*

LONDON ENGLAND
Antonio's Trattoria

"GOD, YOU LIVE WELL ON THE ROAD," SAID HONEY PI. "An evening of opera in a box at the Royal Albert Hall, dinner in a private dining room, in the best Italian restaurant I've ever been in, in my life. Hell, maybe the best restaurant I've ever been in period. And to top it off, I'm staying in a mansion on Embassy Row in London."

"Well, there are certain perks associated with being a master commando with the Red Protocol Group," said Ankyer.

"The mansion is definitely over the top," replied Honey Pi.

"It beats Motel 6, that's for sure," said Ankyer.

"No argument there," replied Honey Pi.

"Our residence here has some history, said Ankyer. 14 Prince's Gate was at one time the residence of Joseph P. Kennedy, U.S. Ambassador and father of our former president, Jack. It was sold a few times, the last sale being to our Dr. Finkel by the Royal College of General Practitioners. Turns out our illustrious Dr.

Finkel is an honorary member of the Royal College. The College, not unlike other not-for-profit organizations, had a budget short-fall and intended to put the residence up for sale. Dr. Finkel found out about it and purchased it for cash at twice the amount the College would get on the open market to bulk up its finances. He completely renovated the building to the original interior architectural specification. Of course, it has been upgraded several times since then. When I came here to live during my Ph.D. program at the London School of Economics, Dr. Finkel had the fifth floor converted into a full gym which comes in very handy."

"How many others live here?" asked Honey Pi.

"Just me, Miles Demarco, Ronald the French chef, and various housekeepers who appear and disappear," replied Ankyer.

"Miles, the valet I met?" asked Honey Pi

"Miles is much more than that," replied Ankyer. "He has a PhD in political science, is a Master practitioner in Krav Maga, developed for the Israeli Defense Force, and keeps me on the straight and narrow when I'm in London. He also impersonates the best butler on the planet for the benefit of the 'outside world'. Brother William spent a fair amount of time here keeping my physical and martial arts skills tuned. But ordinarily it's just me, Miles, Ronald, and the mysterious housekeepers... although Miles has a variety of female guests from time to time. Anytime you're in London this is where you will stay. There's lots of bedrooms."

"I was thinking of one in particular for tonight," said Honey Pi.

"Funny, so was I," replied Ankyer.

Just then Ankyer's and Honey Pi's mastoid implants activated.

"Good evening. How are you guys doing?"

"Great," replied Ankyer.

"Jake is a master of understatement," chimed in Honey Pi.

"How's my favorite Italian restaurant?" asked Finkel.

"Excellent as always," replied Ankyer.

"And your entre?" asked Finkel

"Kobe Chateaubriand Bouquetiere Italiano," said Ankyer.

"Ah. Excellent choice. We need to add a few pounds to Honey Pi's delicate frame."

"So far Jake has not complained about my frame," said Honey Pi.

"The wine?" asked Finkel.

"Tenuta dell 'Ornellaia' Vendemia d'Artista Special Edition Bolgheri Superiore," said Ankyer.

"From Tuscany?" asked Finkel.

"From Tuscany," said Ankyer.

"A perfect pairing! I knew the sommelier course we sent you to would pay off," said Finkel. *"Tell me Jake, how is Miles?"*

"He sends his regards. He said he needs a raise to save up to convert his E Type Jaguar's engine to electric. Although with your revised retirement program, Miles can afford to buy a fleet of them."

"Tell him his Jaguar will be picked up and taken to Marlborough Design over at Silverstone Technology Park. We will have another E Type delivered to keep him happy while his is being worked on. It will take about six months. By the way, have you had your dessert wine yet?" asked Finkel.

"We were just about to order it," replied Ankyer.

"Hold off," said Finkel. *"Our Qatari friends are sending a bottle of wine to the residence as a gift prior to your leaving for Qatar. It should be there when you return from dinner. Brother William and Varna are on the way on the Leer jet and should land at Heathrow General Aviation tomorrow at 10:00 AM.*

After refueling you should be on your way to Qatar by around 11:00 AM.

Enjoy the remainder of your evening."

"Thank you Dr. Finkel," Honey Pi and Ankyer said in unison.

"Dr. Finkel is really something," said Honey Pi

"You're right about that," replied Ankyer. Let's leave. It's a short walk back to the residence. Let's see what the Qatari's left us."

ON THE WAY TO THE RED PROTOCOL'S LONDON RESIDENCE

14 Prince's Gate

BETWEEN THE HOURS OF 7:00 PM AND 10:00 PM THE DAY'S LIGHT WAS WANING leaving enough twilight along with street-lights to navigate the narrow back streets of Knightsbridge. The pedestrian foot traffic was light with most people either home for dinner or attending to their needs in a private club or favorite pub. It was also the time when predators emerge looking for well-to-do prey who have not left with the larger herd due to working late or any of several other reasons.

This evening the predators were out and about on a street be-hind the massive and popular Harrod's store. Lions hunt in prides and a human pride was hunting. This particular pride was from the West End area of Westminster, a notorious high crime area in

London. Marco Balloni, 6 feet 6 inches and 260 pounds, was called "Lunchmeat" only by his closest friends. Alister Montcrief III was rumored to be a distant relation of a British Earl, which was dubious, as it wasn't clear who his parents were. Alister was called "Three;" the rest of his name being too difficult for his few acquaintances to remember. And Rooster Bilbo, five feet six and sporting a distended gut, had a large black protuberance on the side of his nose adorned with numerous black hairs, earning him the name "Mole". Of the three, Lunchmeat had an aggression quotient off the charts. He had been psychoanalyzed by the staff at Her Majesty's Prison Belmarsh and had spent extended time as a guest at HM Prison Wakefield. Three was passive aggressive and did whatever Lunchmeat wanted. Mole had an out-of-control sex drive for which he had been jailed at Wakefield, where he met Lunchmeat. All three had a cocaine habit that needed immediate refinancing, and which brought them to the street behind Harrod's.

"Lunchmeat, we need some fuckin' cash," said Three. "I haven't done a line of coke in four days."

"I need to get laid," added Mole.

"Yeah, yeah," replied Lunchmeat. "You fuckers always want something. Oops, do you see what I see?" asked Lunchmeat.

Three looked across the street and saw the answer to their cocaine problem. Mole felt a tingling in his groin.

Anker and Honey Pi were walking arm-in-arm across the street about 25 yards ahead of the trio looking at the contents of Harrod's display windows.

"I can't remember when, if ever, I've had such a pleasant evening," she said to Ankyer.

"'Ditto back at you," he replied.

Honey Pi squeezed Ankyer's arm and said: "...And I see numerous pleasant evenings in our future."

"You're my Doctor. Isn't that some kind of violation of medical ethics?"

"Possibly, but as of yesterday Dr. Finkel transferred your healthcare over to Commander Walthour. I'll still be responsible for Varna, but you my friend, will not feel my cold stethoscope again. Seems that Dr. Finkel wants me to get more involved in tactical operations."

"Well, that's an interesting development."

"Oi!" a voice behind them shouted. "Hold up there. We want to talk to you!" as the three caballeros crossed the street.

As the trio approached them, Ankyer remarked to Honey Pi: "This does not appear to be a social call."

"I will not let this ruin an otherwise lovely evening," replied Honey Pi. "You may have to protect me."

"Work, work, work. All I do is work," said Ankyer under his breath.

Lunchmeat, Three and Mole spread out as they approached the two.

Lunchmeat said: "Give me your wallet and watch and maybe I won't hurt you too much, boyo," looking at Ankyer.

"Yea...what he said!" exclaimed Three.

Mole yelled: "I'm going to fuck your girlfriend till she can't walk asshole."

Honey Pi observed: "Wow, it's so nice to be wanted. Do you promise to be gentle?" asked Honey Pi in a mocking tone.

As he approached Ankyer, Lunchmeat reached into his pocket. His hand emerged holding an Italian-made, pearl handled, 7-inch stiletto. "Snick" went the stiletto. The blade was pointed four inches from Ankyer's breastbone. Considering his size, Lunchmeat was used to intimidating his adversaries. He did not anticipate Ankyer's left hand as it covered his hand holding the knife. Ankyer stepped to the right and twisted Lunchmeat's wrist, fracturing several wrist bones, and dismantling his hand's tendons. Lunchmeat lost his grip on the knife, which Ankyer deftly caught with his other hand. He reached around and inserted the stiletto blade into Lunchmeat's left ear so hard, two inches emerged from his right ear. Meanwhile, Three let out a yell and charged Ankyer who pulled the stiletto from Lunchmeat's head and hurled it at Three, striking him between the eyes and burying the knife to the hilt. Ankyer then turned to save Honey Pi, who, as it turned out, did not require saving.

Mole had managed to get behind Honey Pi and had circled his arms around her back and chest. Honey Pi raised her right leg, brought her foot scraping down his chin, stamping on Mole's arch and causing excruciating pain forcing Mole to lose his grip. She pivoted as Mole bent partially over from pain. She then stepped back into a left front fighting stance. Slightly curling the fingers of her right hand, she struck Mole with her palm in an upswing. The blow drove the cartilage in Mole's nose into his brain, dropping him to the ground. Dead.

Total elapsed time of Ankyer and Honey Pi's encounter starting with demand for Ankyer's wallet to the demise of Lunchmeat, Three and Mole... 15.7 seconds.

Ankyer walked over to Honey Pi, stepping around the remains of Mole. "Nicely done," he said. "You're not even breathing hard."

"Thanks to Brother William," she replied. "You're not the only one who works out with him. He has been showing me some self-defense skills."

"You could not have a better teacher," replied Ankyer. At that moment a black Range Rover pulled up and the passenger window rolled down. "Get in you two," said Miles. "The Qatar guy showed up with the wine."

"How did you know to come get us?" asked Honey Pi as the Range Rover roared away.

"Dr. Finkel asked that I retrieve you from your little altercation. Each of your heart rates increased slightly and he checked to make sure you were ok."

"He may want to check with the Metro Police. We are probably on the highlight reel of their CCTV."

"Already done," replied Miles. "You know, sometimes it doesn't matter what your occupation in life is, shit happens."

"You've got that right Miles," said Honey Pi. "About our heart rates, Miles. They may get a little elevated, or maybe even a lot elevated, later." "It won't be necessary for Dr. Finkel to save us," said Honey Pi.

"Absolutely," replied Miles. "He is way ahead of you."

"That's usually the case," said Ankyer as the Range Rover pulled into 14 Prince's Gate.

14 PRINCE'S GATE
City of Westminster
London England

MILES LED ANKYER AND HONEY PI INTO A LARGE MAHOGANY PANELED LIBRARY. The panels were highly polished, the bookcases reaching to the top of the 15-foot ceiling with a ladder attached to horizontal runners. The room was furnished with red leather club furniture in several seating configurations. A large, lit, marble fireplace, the opening flanked by marble lions, occupied the center of one wall. At the end of the room stood a tall figure attired in black formal evening dress, next to a waist high antique bar table. On the table were two half-filled French crystal cut wine glasses and an opened bottle of wine.

"I would like to introduce you to Ambassador Dahame Najem Suleman from Qatar," said Miles.

"It is a pleasure to meet you both, Dr. Ankyer and Dr. Pi." said Ambassador Dahame Najem Suleman bowing slightly and shaking their hands. "I have been sent by His Excellency and Royal

Highness, the Emir of Qatar. His Royal Highness is looking forward to meeting you soon. He was informed that you would be passing through London and wanted to provide you a small gift prior to your journey to our country tomorrow. Dr. Finkel mentioned that you would be coming here after dinner tonight and we thought you might enjoy some wine as an after dinner libation."

"That is very considerate. Please extend our gratitude to the Emir," replied Ankyer.

"I will indeed. Now if you will excuse me, I have a plane to catch," Suleman said as he bowed to Ankyer and Honey Pi. He turned and walked towards the door of the library. Miles followed him and over his shoulder said, "Don't drink all that wine, you guys."

Ankyer picked up a glass and touched Honey' Pi's. "Here's to a beautiful and erudite companion," he said.

Miles returned to the room holding an empty wine glass.

"Hope you don't mind sharing," said Miles.

"Not at all," said Honey Pi. "Ambassador Suleman seems like a nice enough fellow."

"That he is," replied Miles. "The Ambassador is also the brother of the Emir and his closest confidant. He also let me in on a secret regarding the wine you guys are drinking," said Miles as he poured some wine into his glass. "This bottle of 1945 Romaine-Conti Burgundy was recently acquired from a Sotheby's wine auction for $ 558,000, making it the most expensive bottle of wine in the world."

"Not bad for a 'small gift'," said Ankyer.

"Not bad at all," added Honey Pi.

Later, Miles escorted Ankyer and Honey Pi to their rooms. He dropped Ankyer off at the Master suite and showed Honey Pi to an adjoining bedroom. "Sleep tight, Dr. Pi," said Miles. "Tomorrow will be the beginning of an interesting journey. "Thank you,

Miles. It seems like most journeys with the Red Protocol Group are interesting."

A short time later, Ankyer heard a soft knocking on the door to his suite.

Opening the door, Honey Pi stepped in with a stethoscope around her neck.

The flickering of the fireplace in the Master Bedroom caught her attention. "My bedroom doesn't have a fireplace. Can I stay here tonight?"

Ankyer's mouth opened, then closed, then opened again.

"That's ok, Jake," said Honey Pi as she got in the four-poster king sized bed. "Get over here. It's cold and that fireplace isn't hot enough!"

The following morning after Ankyer and Honey Pi finished one of Ronald's famous full English breakfasts in the solarium, Honey Pi got up from her chair and gave Ankyer a peck on the cheek.

"Getting a little familiar, aren't we?", asked Ankyer.

"After wearing ourselves out last night and this morning, 'getting familiar' seems to be somewhat of an understatement," said Honey Pi. "But the fact is that I fell in love the moment I saw you. But I was stuck being your doctor. Then Dr. Finkel took care of that problem and here I am."

"You always get what you want?" asked Ankyer

"Always," replied Honey Pi.

"Hmm. I'll have to think about that. Ok I thought about it. I'm all in," said Ankyer.

"Ok. That's taken care of. What's next on the agenda?" she asked.

"Anker started to mentally revisit the evenings and morning's activities and said: "Well, now that you mention it..."

He was interrupted by Miles who said, "You two have visitors."

"Varna!" exclaimed Honey Pi as the wolf bounded past Ankyer without giving him so much as a nod. Varna skidded to a stop in front of Honey Pi, stretching his neck and giving Honey Pi a sloppy kiss. "Whew! These guys haven't been brushing your teeth, sweetie!" She gave him a hug while scratching his ears and fed him a giant muffin from the breakfast table.

"Hey! Watch those muffins," said a robed figure with a large bald head. "He's on a high protein diet. Carbs not so much."

"Brother William! It's a good thing you're here to save Varna from the clutches of his vet," said Ankyer as Honey Pi gave Varna another giant muffin.

"Hey. I'm his doctor and I can give him treats when I want to."

"And what do you have to say about it, Jake?" asked Brother William.

"Honey Pi and I have come to a recent understanding that she's management and I'm labor," Jake replied.

"Welcome to the club," replied Brother William. "As a matter of fact, I watched the CCTV video of your latest adventure."

"You mean there's CCTV in here?" asked Ankyer.

"No, Jake. That's NOT what he means," said Honey Pi. "He's talking about the late departed thugs."

"What did you think I meant Jake?" asked Brother William.

"Never mind," retorted Honey Pi.

"The CCTV footage suggests that you could use some fine tuning on your situational awareness Honey Pi," said Brother

William. "The thug that tried to rape you flanked you when you were focused on Jake's attackers. On the positive side, stamping on his arch was well done and your upward palm hand thrust to his nose was particularly well executed."

"Your ability to criticize and praise your student at the same time is one of your many charms Brother William," replied Honey Pi.

While the discourse between Honey Pi and Brother William went on, Varna finished his giant muffin and lay down at Honey Pi's feet. He then rolled over on his back, soliciting a tummy rub, his fangs protruding from his substantial jaws.

"You do know that Varna is a combat animal, don't you," observed Ankyer.

"Yes, I do," replied Honey Pi. "I also know that Varna is my baby and that you are jealous."

Miles announced, "The pilots just called and advised me that the Gulfstream 700 is ready for the flight to Qatar.

"That's the lap of luxury," said Ankyer.

"As I understand it, the Qatar Emir wanted to fly you in his private Airbus380 which is described as a palace in the sky, but Dr. Finkel just received delivery of the Gulfstream at the Abbey and wanted to try it out," said Miles. "You guys need to get to General Aviation at Heathrow ASAP."

Honey Pi gave Varna a head rub with both hands causing him to get up and give her another sloppy kiss.

"I need to start carrying a towel, that's for sure," said Honey Pi. Brother William launched a large, protein biscuit and Varna rose on his back legs to his 12-foot height and gobbled the biscuit in mid-air. The group started for the door of the solarium leaving Ankyer standing in the middle of the room.

"Hey, wait for me?" said Ankyer.

GULFSTREAM 700
One mile into Qatar Air Space

ANKYER WAS HALF ASLEEP WHEN HE FELT THE GULFSTREAM PITCHING SLIGHTLY. Ankyer's voice was picked up by the passenger compartment speaker phone. "Hey Andy, what's up?" he asked.

"I'm acknowledging some visitors," the pilot replied. "Take a look out the starboard and port windows. You don't see this very often."

"Are my eyes deceiving me or are those fighters?"

"Actually, they are F-22 Raptors," said the pilot. "There's another one in front of us. We are being vectored to an 'off-the-grid' military base in Qatar. ETA 35 minutes."

"I didn't think this kind of hardware existed outside the American inventory," said Ankyer.

"Neither did I," replied the pilot.

"Not only that," the copilot chimed in. "Our missile detection software is going nuts. I'm guessing these guys are loaded with Sidewinders and air-to-air AMRAAMs."

"How do you suppose they got them?" asked Ankyer

"When they first showed up, I contacted Dr. Finkel," said the pilot. "He checked and it looks like they got them through a small American export company at the direction of our Department of Defense along with a parts and maintenance contract. Seems that one of SLUG's friends is the intermediary. The payment goes to his buddy and from there to 'who knows where'."

"Looks like SLUG is cashing in big time," replied Ankyer.

Honey Pi's eyes fluttered open. "What's up?"

"Look out the window," said Ankyer.

"Wow. An air show," she replied.

"By the way, it would be nice if we had some decent clothes when we meet up with the Emir. Honey Pi and I didn't manage to dodge all the blood from the thugs," said Ankyer.

"Actually, we loaded some suit bags and other stuff in the back at the direction of Dr. Finkel", said the copilot. "He said something like he didn't want anyone dressed like 'ragamuffins' representing the Red Protocol Group when you guys meet with the Emir. Everything is labeled. You probably want to change before we land. I'm not sure how much time you have before you meet with the Emir."

"I'm first!" exclaimed Honey Pi moving out of the seat, climbing over Varna, and heading towards the back of the plane.

"Hey, what about me?" asked Brother William.

"Got you covered Brother William," said the copilot. "Dr. Finkel sent a clean robe. Something about not wanting you to smell bad."

Honey Pi returned down the aisle dressed in a brilliant white pant suit, her jet-black hair normally in a ponytail, now loose at her shoulders.

"I may renounce my vocation," said Brother William. "You are a vision!" he continued. "That suit is really something!"

"'Really something' doesn't quite cover it," said Ankyer. "That's a Dormeiul Vanquish II vicuna suit," he added.

"Eat your hearts out boys," said Honey Pi.

"I am, I am," said Ankyer.

Andy tuned in from the cockpit and added: "Jake, Dr. Finkel asked me to tell you to try and not spill red wine on Honey Pi if at all possible."

"Don't get too grumpy Jake," Honey Pi said. "There's another suit bag with a Dormeiul label for you in the back."

Ankyer immediately got up from his seat, walked around Varna in the aisle and went back aft. Shortly thereafter he returned dressed in a black-on-black Vanquish II suit with a black silk, long sleeved crew neck shirt. "Wow, 007!" exclaimed Brother William.

"I can do things 007 can't," said Ankyer.

"Ok everyone," the pilot said over the intercom. "Enough with the fashion statements. Buckle up and make sure Varna is secured. We don't want a 385-pound animal rolling around the aisle screwing up our Gulfstream's trim." The Gulfstream then banked sharply to port as it rapidly descended. A few minutes later the pilot came back on the intercom. "Look outside. The F 22s are on either side of us and one is still in front. It looks like we will all be landing together. An air show in our honor!" The four jets landed in unison on three adjacent runways coming to a halt exactly next to each other in front of a very large, camouflaged aircraft hangar. The pilot opened the Gulfstream's main passenger hatch. On the way out Ankyer said: "Andy, you have to let me try one of those landings some time." The pilot replied: "Sure if you can carve out some training time from playing with the Super Hornet."

Ankyer looked out the hatch, turned to Honey Pi and said, "You're going to love this." Honey Pi looked out and saw a red carpet leading from the Gulfstream's stairs thirty-five yards to two dark maroon Rolls Royce limousines. There were two black Lincoln SUVs in the front and two more in the back. The Rolls' chauffeurs were dressed in livery. Standing next to the SUVs were several, very large men dressed in black, plain clothes. The red carpet was lined on both sides by soldiers in dress uniforms with rifles at parade rest. As Ankyer and Pi reached the bottom of the Gulfstream's stairs they were approached by a tall military officer and an older, white haired man in formal dress.

"Welcome to Qatar's Special Forces Emir Al Sallazon Airfield, Dr. Ankyer and Dr. Pi," said the white-haired man. "My name is Amid bin Albari al Sari. I serve as Minister to the Emir of Qatar and offer the Emir's personal greetings. This is Major General Ali bin Muhammid who serves as the General of the Qatar Armed Forces."

"Welcome to Qatar," said the General. "I trust our fighters did not startle you."

"Quite the contrary General," replied Ankyer. "We enjoyed the escort."

"I understand you are a fighter pilot yourself Dr. Ankyer," replied the General.

"I fly a F/A-18F Super Hornet every so often," replied Ankyer. "I haven't had an opportunity to fly an F 22," said Ankyer nodding towards one of the fighters."

"We can remedy that if you have enough time during your visit," said the General.

"I understand Dr. Pi that you are both a physician and a veterinarian," said the Minister.

"That's true," Honey Pi replied. "The Red Protocol Group and Varna manage to keep me busy."

A reinforced military pickup truck with an open truck bed pulled up several yards from the Gulfstream. "I hope you were able to bring Varna," said the Minister. "The Emir viewed a video and is excited to see him." Dr. Finkel indicated that he would be more comfortable in this kind of truck.

"No doubt about that," said Ankyer.

"Varna is accompanied by Brother William, his trainer and companion when Varna is not on a mission," said Honey Pi. "People can look at Varna but should not approach him unless Dr. Ankyer, Brother William or myself are present. Varna is a combat animal and can be high strung."

"Understood," said the Minister. "I should add that some of us have seen a film of Varna protecting Crown Prince Bamin's son at the slave camp. There is little doubt that Varna saved the boy's life."

A cargo door on the side of the Gulfstream opened and slid into the fuselage while a platform with two figures on it emerged. Brother William was dressed in a brown robe with a wide leather belt. The second figure dwarfed the first, as it flexed its massive shoulder muscles and roared.

The General's jaw dropped. "My god, what a magnificent creature!" he exclaimed. "And it has saber tooth fangs!" Turning to Ankyer, he continued: "I understand that you've been in battle with him?"

"Many times," replied Ankyer.

"I don't know what could stand before him in battle," said the General still in awe.

"Nothing I have seen so far," said Ankyer.

The Gulfstream platform completed its descent and Brother William walked off followed by Varna. The back gate of the pickup truck was lowered by two soldiers exposing the truck bed. Brother William spoke to Varna, who bounded over to the truck, leapt over the truck ramp, and landed in the middle of the truck bed causing the truck's shock absorbers to flex. Brother William then threw a protein biscuit towards the truck and Varna reared up on his hind legs and snagged the biscuit on the fly. Varna looked towards the soldiers lined up along the red carpet...and roared again, his muscles flexing under his glistening coat. Soldiers attached a canvas canopy to the truck bed while lifting the ramp and locking it in place.

"The Emir would like to see Varna close up. Will the Emir be safe?" asked the Minister, as he watched Varna with trepidation.

"Definitely. But no one should make a sudden movement towards me or others in our party," replied Ankyer echoing Honey Pi's admonition.

The Minister led the way to the beginning of the red carpet. "There is someone who would like to greet you," he said to Ankyer. A tall, slender figure in flowing robes approached Ankyer. "I am sure you remember Sheikh Hamza," said the Minister.

"Ahmad!" exclaimed Ankyer. "It's good to see you, my friend!"

"And you and Dr. Pi," replied Hamza. "It seems we have all been invited to the same party." Hamza extended his hand to Honey Pi who stepped inside his arm, stood on her tip toes, and gave him a hug.

"You better be careful, Honey," said Ankyer. "Bedouin sheikhs are known to throw beautiful women on the backs of their camels and ride off into the desert."

"As it turns out, I happen to like camels," retorted Honey Pi while Ahamad grinned."

"We need to make haste," said the Minister. "We have about a thirty-minute journey and the Emir is expecting us. General!"

General Muhammid called out: "Attention! Present arms!" causing the soldiers to come to attention. The party then walked down the red carpet to the waiting limousines. The General turned to the group and saluted. He turned back to the soldiers and with the command "Prepare salute." The soldiers did an 'about face,' raised their rifles to their shoulders and fired three volleys into the air, then returning to 'attention'. The General turned back to the group by the limousines and saluted again.

The Minister and Hamza entered one of the Rolls limousines and Ankyer and Honey Pi entered the other. The vehicle drove off with one black SUV leading and another following. The truck with Varna and Brother William, brought up the rear, with Varna letting out another roar as they passed the General and the soldiers.

ROYAL PALACE
Emir of Qatar
Sheikh Salazar bin Hamad bin Kartoon Al Sallazon

THERE ARE PALACES...AND THEN THERE ARE PALACES. The palace of the Emir of Qatar was the latter. With a footprint of 2500 square acres, the palace was a series of white granite-connected buildings arranged in a hexagon. A road of grey granite lined with palm trees extended two miles from the outside boulevard into an immense courtyard formed by white and pink marble geometric patterns. Waterfalls cascaded from the roofs of several buildings and a variety of desert flora was artfully placed in various locations throughout.

A two-story white marble, manned, guard house was situated just outside two massive, gilded iron gates. Additional guard houses were spaced every quarter mile ending at the courtyard. The Rolls Royce caravan stopped briefly at each guard station before continuing. The truck containing Varna was positioned thirty yards back and did not stop at the guard stations. The caravan stopped in front of the five-story main entrance which consisted of two massive inset polished mahogany doors. Fifteen-foot interior pivot doors were incorporated into the larger ones. The party exited the Rolls limousines. The Minister spoke to a military officer who had walked out of the building. He then turned to Anker, Pi and Hamza and said: "Well, what do you think?"

"I'm speechless," said Honey Pi.

"An understatement," added Ankyer.

"I'd heard of this palace, but never imagined...," said Hamza.

"It's a working palace," said the Minister. "The Emir stays here periodically. This Palace also is used to host dignitaries from other countries in addition to being used for some administrative functions. We will be meeting the Emir in the private residence section and a luncheon will be served. Jake, after lunch the Emir would like to have a private audience with you while Dr. Pi and Sheikh Hamza are provided a tour of some of the more interesting parts of the palace, if that is acceptable."

"That's fine with me," said Honey Pi.

"I can't wait," echoed Hamza.

"Lead on," said Ankyer, "Oh, what about Varna and Brother William?"

"They will go in a separate side entrance. We were concerned that Varna's appearance might be somewhat disruptive and frighten the staff."

"Probably not a bad idea. We generally like to keep Varna back from the public view," said Anker.

With that, they walked through the main entrance. The truck with Varna and Brother William drove through a side portico off the main entrance.

Once inside, the Minister escorted Ankyer, Hamza and Honey Pi into the main hall. Honey Pi's mouth opened, as she looked around. "There are no words," she said.

"We have entered the palace's Grand Reception Hall designed to impress our visitors," said the Minister. "The floor to ceiling height is seventy-five feet, ten inches," continued the Minister. "The interior is constructed from polished white and black granite, and the entire floor is Lux Touch marble, the most expensive marble in the world, costing $ 1,000,000 per square meter. As you can see, the interior space of the hall is quite large, 40,000 square feet."

The Minister led the group down the center of the Hall continuing with his commentary. "The lighting in the palace is a subdued bluish tint traveling from the sides, up through flying buttresses to the peak in the center. A five-ton chandelier from Baccarat is the centerpiece, with two additional 3-ton Baccarat chandeliers centered in the remaining ceiling space. There are conference rooms on either side of us hidden from public view.

The architect for this building and the rest of the complex was the world renowned I.M. Pei who, alas, has passed on." As the minister ended his commentary, they stopped in front of a tall figure in white robes. "It is my honor to present to you Crown Prince Sheikh Bamin bin Hamid Sallazon, the father of Sheikh Salud bin Hamad Sallazon, the young man you recently rescued."

"On behalf of the Emir, welcome to Qatar," said the Crown Prince.

"Your Highness, this is Dr. Jake Ankyer, Dr. Honey Pi and Sheikh Ahmad Dayan Hamza," said the Minister. The Crown Prince shook hands with everyone as he was introduced.

"Thank you for visiting our country. I hope you had a comfortable flight. I trust the wine we had delivered to your London residence was acceptable."

"The wine was superb," replied Ankyer.

"Excellent. I was saving it for a special occasion, and I could not think of anything more special than saving my son's life. The Emir is anxious to meet each of you. Sheikh Hamza, our tent is your tent."

"And ours is yours, Excellency," said Hamza, bowing.

The Crown Prince led them up to twelve-foot, rosewood double doors. "This may seem a little formal, my friends. However, the Emir prefers informal gatherings. Once the formalities are completed, the 'ties are loosened' so to speak." With that the Crown Prince nodded to a large man dressed in a tuxedo who pressed a button on the side of the doors.

The doors opened and the party walked into a large room constructed completely from Calacatta marble. At the far end of the room, seated on a throne-like chair and flanked by two large male cheetahs chained on either side, was a fiftyish figure with a short salt and pepper beard. He was dressed in a long white kandura with a purple sash and a Ghutra headdress held in place by a dark purple circular band or Agal. Halfway into the room a side pocket door whooshed open, and Brother William walked into the room with Varna at his side. Varna padded over to Ankyer and Honey Pi and stood between them rubbing his massive flanks against each. As the group approached the dais, the Crown Prince said: "Your Excellency, may I present the warriors from the West and our Bedouin brother, Sheikh Ahmad Dayan Hamza. It is my honor to introduce you to His Excellency and Royal Highness, Sheikh Salazar Bin Hamad Bin Kartoon Al-Sallazon, The Emir of Qatar.

The Emir said: "Welcome to our country. Our house is your house under the providence of Allah. I am pleased you brought this magnificent animal that saved my grandson from the slavers in the heat of battle." As the Emir was speaking, the two cheetahs hissed and folded their ears back. Varna opened his jaws and bared his large fangs. He uttered a low growl causing the two cheetahs to start shaking and urinate in place. Two aids appeared, unhooked the cheetahs from the dais and led them out of the room with their tails between their legs while a third aid quickly mopped up the urine.

"I apologize," said Ankyer. "Varna is very protective and was just sending a gentle warning to your cheetahs." The Emir chuckled. "No apology is necessary. The cheetahs are just pets. Varna is a battle tested warrior. A life-sized bronze statue of him guarding my grandson is to be displayed in our courtyard for all to see!" With that the Emir descended the dais and shook everyone's hand. Brother William gave the Emir a large protein biscuit, which Varna immediately took from the Emir. Varna permitted the Emir to tentatively pat him on the head.

"I hope your journey has not been too arduous," said the Emir.

"Indeed not," replied Ankyer. "We are most thankful for your welcome and your hospitality."

"I understand we have a light luncheon prepared for you," said the Emir. "Before partaking of that, however, there is someone you should meet." The Emir nodded to an aid and a thin, young boy entered the room with an elegantly dressed woman. "This is Sheikh Salud Bin Hamad Sallazon, my grandson, accompanied by his mother. You recently met him under different circumstances."

"Nice to see you again. That was quite an adventure we had," said Ankyer. Varna padded over to the boy, sniffed him, and then nuzzled him almost knocking him over. "You'll have to forgive Varna," said Ankyer. "He now considers you part of his pack and doesn't know his own strength." As he said that, the boy leaned over, put his arms around Varna's neck and gave him a hug. Varna in turn gave the boy a lick leaving a trail of saliva. The boy wiped it off with the sleeve of his tunic and wandered back to his mother who was joined by Crown Prince Bamin. Ankyer noticed that the woman had dried tears on her cheeks.

"It is our custom," said the Emir, "that when the life of one of our children is saved, the child becomes the property of the savior. Accordingly, Salud now belongs to you."

Without missing a beat, Ankyer replied: "Thank you for your generous gift and I accept Salud in the spirit in which he is offered." Salud's mother gasped and held the boy tightly. "Is it permissible to give a gift in return?" asked Ankyer.

The Emir looked puzzled and said: "It is not necessary, but what do you have in mind?"

Ankyer replied; "Since Salud is now my property, I return him as a gift to your family in return for your generosity." The parents of Salud put their arms around him and the mother cried softly.

"You are a most considerate man, Jake Ankyer," said the Emir. "We accept your gift with our deepest gratitude." A man in a white coat whispered in the Emir's ear. "Our lunch is served," said the Emir, at which point a section of a wall slid open revealing another paneled room. There was a table piled high with a large variety of food. A maître d' led the group to a round table. As they approached the table, the Emir touched Ankyer's arm. "After lunch, a tour of the residence has been arranged for your party. While that is underway, I would like to talk to you alone, if you don't mind."

"I will look forward to it, your Excellency," replied Ankyer.

As they were sitting down, Honey Pi whispered to Ankyer, "Ankyer, you're an old softy."

"I don't know what I'd do with a kid anyway," replied Ankyer.

"There is that" said Honey Pi. "I'm so hungry I could eat a horse."

"Be careful what you wish for. There's probably barbequed palomino somewhere in all this food."

As lunch started, the Emir said: "Welcome to our guests. If there is something you don't see on the table, please let our maitre d' know." Servers with plates approached each person at the table. Ankyer looked at Honey Pi with a slight smile.

"Don't even think about it," she whispered.

The lunch proceeded with Ankyer and Honey Pi complementing the Emir on their reception at the military base as well as the spectacular palace. The Emir insisted that Varna stay at the lunch. Varna sat next to Brother William, who fed him a steady supply of biscuits to prevent him from drooling.

SOMEWHERE IN BALTIMORE MARYLAND (CONTINUED)

GATLING LEANED BACK IN HIS CHAIR, FOLDED HIS HANDS in tent fashion and said: "You know Mallory, you were so successful dealing with our Cabinet problem, it occurs to me that we should think bigger."

"How so sir?"

"Our problem with the Cabinet was that they could band together and hit me with the 25th Amendment. But there's a bigger problem. If members of the House and Senate got sufficiently pissed off at me, the House could impeach me on some trumped-up charge and the Senate could find me guilty. That would be the ball game. On the other hand, if what happened to the Cabinet also happened to the congressmen and senators...?"

"That is thinking big, Sir. But eliminating one hundred senators and four hundred and thirty-five congressmen would be very difficult, if not impossible to pull off."

"They all would not have to go. Just the heads of the two hundred and fifty congressional committees and the Majority and Minority leaders in the House and Senate. All we need to do is cut off the fucking head. The rest of them are sheep. Now that I'm thinking about it, if we got rid of all the leadership, I could invoke martial law and keep it going indefinitely!"

"Brilliant!" exclaimed Tensale. "Let's do it!"

"Based on the Cabinet crisis, I will call for a Zoom security briefing in a secure location in each State. The Senators and Congressional leaders in the State will be required to attend. If you can place your device in each location and figure out a way to set it off..."

"I'll need to check, but there may be a way. Give me the exact locations when you have them and a few weeks after that we should be ready to implement your plan!"

"You've got to be shitting me," Moon exclaimed.

"I know. Its wild," said Tensale

"It's a fucking coup!" replied Moon. "Is it even possible?"

"It is," said Tensale. "I've checked with some of my contacts."

"Here's how it would work."

Moon sat in the chair in her Great Room and looked out the 30 by 45-foot window in her lodge as Tensale described the plan. When he'd finished, she stood up and started pacing back and forth. "My god. You're right. It could work. There is one problem though."

"Which is?" asked Tensale.

"Gatling is nuts," Moon said.

ROYAL PALACE
Emir of Qatar
Sheikh Salazar bin Hamad bin Kartoon Al Sallazon

WHEN LUNCH CONCLUDED, THE EMIR SAID TO THE GUESTS: "I would like to steal Jake and Varna away from you for a short time, if you don't mind. Minister Sari will provide you a guided tour of the palace including our private museum, which is not available for viewing by the general public."

With that, the group separated. Honey Pi, Brother William and Sheikh Hamza followed the Minister, and Ankyer and Varna followed the Emir and Crown Prince Sallazon through a door held open by an orderly. The door led to a medium sized study with a crackling fireplace, and a large video screen surrounded by polished bookcases of African blackwood. The Emir motioned Ankyer to leather chairs in the center of the room, each chair with a side table on which a crystal goblet of water with lemon garnish was placed. "Please make yourself comfortable, Jake." Ankyer sat down followed by Varna who lay down next to him on semi alert.

Ankyer gave Varna a protein biscuit, one of several provided by Brother William. The Emir and Crown Prince sat down across from Ankyer.

The Emir took a drink from his crystal water goblet and looked pensively at Ankyer. "Jake, I would like to show you a short video provided to me by your Dr. Finkel, a longstanding friend of mine. The Crown Prince has not seen this and, at Dr. Finkel's request, no one else will other than my closest advisors."

The Emir pressed a button on the remote and the video screen flickered and came to life showing a still image of the slaver's platform with the Crown Prince's son chained to a post and the slaver Sheikh al-Haydar next to the boy, grabbing the boy's hair on his head with one hand and holding a long knife with the other. The slaver appeared to be yelling something with the arteries in his neck bulging.

"This is a satellite recording in real time of the recent events surrounding the rescue of my grandson."

The Crown Prince edged forward in his chair in rapt attention. The Emir pressed the button again and the video started playing with sound. The entire sequence of events played out starting with Varna hurtling onto the platform and ripping into the slaver, followed by Ankyer's arrival blowing a bidder apart with exploding bolts from the combat crossbow. Varna sat up next to Ankyer, growling with his fangs barred and Ankyer placed his hand on Varna's neck. Mayhem, punctuated by screams and flying bodies, filled the screen. The video showed the Bedouin Hamza riding down several slavers swinging his bloody sword connecting with each of them; and Bell and Groton engaging another group of slavers, firing their MP5s on automatic as they went. The video continued following the battle, including Ankyer killing three more slavers and sprinting up the platform to Varna and the chained boy, firing both his MP5 and crossbow as he went. The video also showed Ankyer inserting the needle from the DNA pen into the boy's shoulder and saying, "Ok. We got the prince kid."

The video concluded by panning the area littered with slaver and buyers' bodies, some blown apart, with billowing smoke and random explosions. The video screen then flickered off. The Crown Prince turned and looked at Ankyer with his mouth open.

"Dr. Finkel also informed me that prior to rescuing Crown Prince Sallazon's son, you single handedly overcame and killed the 57 al-Qaeda, pedophile pirates who destroyed our yacht, and captured my grandson, forcing the pirate chief to reveal the slave auction location where the boy was being held," the Emir continued.

"I had some help," interjected Ankyer, as he gave Varna another protein biscuit to calm him down. "Dr. Pi, Sheikh Hamza, and the members of the combat team all contributed significantly to rescuing the boy, as did Dr. Finkel's technical support, which I can not emphasize enough."

"I understand that" replied the Emir. "And everyone involved in the rescue will be amply rewarded as it is within our power to do so. But you, sir, are exceptional. Never in the history of our country has someone demonstrated such courage in battle. You have respected our customs by returning the boy as a gift to his mother, which is nothing the Crown Prince or myself could have anticipated. You may not realize it. but your courage and generosity have preserved the succession in the Qatar dynasty. We are a small country of 2.6 million souls. Of that, 313,000 are Qatari citizens. The rest are expatriates and other contract workers providing necessary services. Within our citizen population, there are 6,000 citizens of royal linage in Qatar, starting with myself and continuing with the Crown Prince, followed by his son, who you rescued. What you have accomplished. Jake, has saved our country from the potential strife of an internal conflict of succession which, worst case, could have badly damaged our country.

Ankyer, not often at a loss for words replied: "Glad to have been of help your Highness."

The Emir and Crown prince laughed. "In addition to your extraordinary abilities, you are also a master of understatement Jake. Not everyone can save a country," replied the Emir, smiling. "Qatar may be small, but thanks to the will of Allah, we are among the wealthiest countries on Earth. Qatar exists atop 26 billion barrels of oil and 858 trillion cubic feet of natural gas and is the world's largest exporter of liquid natural gas. We are also building a 1,000 solar panel array not unlike the 500 Noor solar energy panel array in Morocco. When completed our solar power program will provide clean energy to the entire Arabian Peninsula providing even more revenue to Qatar. To place our country's wealth in perspective, the average per capita income for a Qatari citizen is over $ 200,000 per year. Qatar may not be large, but its financial reserves allow us to provide financial security for all our citizens as well as import any services we may need. Which brings me to a decision I have made. I have decided to officially appoint you a Qatari sheikh, a member of the Qatari royal lineage and a full citizen of Qatar."

"That is quite an honor, your Highness. And I accept the title in the spirit of your generosity," said Ankyer

"It's more than just a title, Jake. A sheikhdom in Qatar is associated with an annual stipend. While we do not wish to cheapen what you have done in rescuing my grandson, it is our custom and one which I want to extend to you."

"The Red Protocol Group's compensation is quite substantial your highness. I'm not sure... Dr. Finkel."

"I have discussed this with Dr. Finkel, and he fully supports this arrangement, as long as it does not in any way interfere with your U.S. citizenship or Red Protocol Group responsibilities, which it does not."

"In that case, your Highness, I accept your generous offer," said Ankyer.

"Excellent. We have opened an account for you, in the bank we maintain for our sheikhs, in the amount of 85 million euros. We will continue to add the equivalent of 85 million euros each year. We also would like to encourage you visit us from time to time and to that end we have deeded a residence in Qatar for your use along with an appropriate staff." The video screen flickered to life showing a four story, stone, seaside building with multiple wings, terraces, gardens, and water features.

"That's a palace!" remarked Ankyer.

"Its modest by our standards but we wanted you to be comfortable when you visit," replied the Emir.

"Welcome to the brotherhood of Qatari sheikhs!" said the Crown Prince.

"There is one additional item we need to discuss, Jake," said the Emir. As I mentioned before. The Middle East is a conglomeration of countries of various sizes, wealth, and populations. Some, like Qatar and Saudi Arabia are quite wealthy while others, such as Syria, are self-destructive and influenced by very large military powers such as Russia. Qatar, to survive during all this military and political turbulence has, unknown to many, developed an exceptionally sophisticated and far-reaching intelligence apparatus. We believe that knowledge is leverage which, judiciously applied, can make up for our small size. We highly value our relationship with the United States and periodically offer ourselves as intermediaries to facilitate interactions with countries having strained relations with the U.S. such as Iran, and now, more recently Afghanistan, for example. However, it's not our policy or desire to interfere with your country's internal activities. Nevertheless, several months ago one of our operatives became aware of a plan involving your President, who intended to somehow disable his Cabinet, because there were discussions underway regarding his removal from office. We chose not to interfere in an internal U.S. struggle because we didn't want to inadvertently damage any relationships with our contacts. As you know, the President's Cabinet was eliminated through some kind of attack and subsequently replaced by President Gatling's hand-picked people. Moving to the present day, the same contacts have again approached our operative. It now appears that another attack of some kind is being planned, but this time it is not clear who the targets are. The contacts also indicated that the plot is being designed within the U.S."

"You must tell someone," said Ankyer.

"I am telling you," replied the Emir. "We dare not communicate this to anyone in the American government as we have no idea who in the government may be involved."

"And you trust these contacts?" asked Ankyer.

"They have worked for us off and on for years and have provided accurate information without exception."

"What are you asking of me?" asked Ankyer

"I have known about the Red Protocol Group for some time, and I know and trust Dr. Finkel. Also, as you are now a sheikh in our royal family, I trust you as well. I understand that the Red Protocol Group is an organization independent from the U.S.

Government, but also maintains a strong interest in protecting American citizens. We would like you to discuss this with Dr. Finkel and decide whether to pursue this matter. I will consider this a favor to Dr. Finkel for having engaged the Red Protocol Group to save my grandson."

"I will convey the situation to Dr. Finkel immediately."

"There is something else that may be helpful," said the Emir. "We have a name. Anastasia Moon. She is a wealthy woman who, as we understand, has some relationships with high up U.S. Government officials. We cannot confirm who they are or even if she is involved. Our contact also provided our operative with a copy of a list of numbers. We are told the numbers were ordered by your President's Chief of Staff. We had a computer engineer in our employ examine them. She said that they appear to be some kind of code developed using advanced number theory, but they are too complex for her skills to decipher them. Unfortunately, we can't just hand over this information because if it was somehow discovered we gave you coded information, our intelligence organization would be severely compromised."

"Then how?" asked Ankyer. The Emir turned to the Crown Prince who motioned to an orderly to open the door to an outside courtyard.

"Let me show you something," said the Crown Prince. They all stood up and walked to the open door with Varna padding along with Ankyer.

"Have you ever driven a race car, Jake?" asked the Crown Prince.

"No, but it's on my list of things to do some time."

"Well, your ship has come in my friend," said the Crown Prince.

They walked into a courtyard enclosed by high concrete walls. In the middle of the paved encloser sat a gleaming, black Porsche 918 Spyder.

"Are you familiar with this car, Jake?" asked the Crown Prince.

"Yes, I am. It's a 918 Porsche Spyder. Notably, it broke the record at the Nurburgring Nordschleife racing test track with a time of 6:57 minutes. It exceeded the previous record by 14 minutes. I've always been a fan of the Spyder but have not been this close to one."

"Well, Jake, you can get as close to this one as you like. You now own it."

"You are kidding!"

"Crown Princes don't 'kid' as you say," replied the Crown Prince with a smile. "This car also has a Weissach Package. The same racing enhancement that Marc Lieb had on his 918 when he smashed the Nurburgring record September 4th, 2013."

"Impressive," said Ankyer walking up to the Porsche, opening the driver's door and peering inside."

"You will be driving this on the Nordschleife track very shortly," said the Crown Prince.

"How's that?" asked Ankyer.

"As my father said, we are a small country with imported expertise and an extensive intelligence service. We are in possession of coded information which unfortunately we cannot decipher, even with our available experts, but which appears to possibly endanger the United States. To protect our intelligence resources, we have conceived of a plan which involves the Red Protocol Group, and which we have reviewed with Dr. Finkel."

"He didn't mention it to me," said Ankyer.

"Dr. Finkel wanted you to evaluate the plan directly from us, independent of any preconceived bias," said the Emir.

"Ok. Sounds like Dr. Finkel. What's the plan?"

Turning to his son the Emir said: "Please explain."

"It's fairly simple," said the Crown Prince. "We are giving the Porsche to you as a gift for rescuing my son. Part of the gift is providing you the opportunity to drive the 918 on the Nurburgring Nordschleife course. We will ship the car in a cargo plane to Nürburg, Rhineland-Palatinate, Germany, tomorrow. You and I will follow in a separate plane.

The course has been rented for the day. The Germans objected to closing public access for an entire day, but we can be very persuasive. Once there, you will drive the course to become acquainted with both the course and the car. After that you will drive a timed lap. Once you have completed the lap, the system will then upload the coded data via a secure transponder linked to the car's infotainment system to a Red Protocol geosynchronous satellite. The data will then be downloaded to a secure Red Protocol server located at the Red Protocol Abbey location. After the transmission, all traces of the data will be erased from the car's infotainment system."

"Seems a little convoluted to me," said Ankyer. "Why don't you just have someone with experience driving the course go around and upload the data at the finish?"

"Well, there's a little wrinkle there," said the Crown Prince.

"Ah. There usually is," replied Ankyer.

"You mentioned before that a 918 Porsche Spyder broke the record at the racing test track," said the Crown Prince. The subterfuge we could think of to protect the data in the infotainment system from hacking or someone otherwise getting access to it, is to release the data by actually exceeding the previous 6:57 minute record. The infotainment system has been engineered to monitor the lap time and upload the data to the satellite only when the lap time beats the record. The course is exceedingly difficult with several drivers having been killed attempting records. You are the only one in our opinion who has a chance to pull this off."

"And Dr. Finkel is ok with this?"

"He is if you are," replied the Emir.

"Alright. As a newly minted Qatari sheikh, I'm in."

"Excellent," said the Emir. "Your colleagues have probably finished the tour and we need to move on this quickly."

"We have several course maps you can review on the flight to Germany," said the Crown Prince. "And since we have private access to the track all day, you can have as many practice laps as you want."

"One should be enough," said Ankyer.

"I've been there to watch races," said the Crown Prince. "It is similar to the Le Mans France course. Numerous twists and turns. Extremely challenging requiring split second responses to turns. How are your reflexes?"

"You wouldn't believe them," replied Ankyer.

"I asked Dr. Finkel the same question and his reply was the same," said the Emir.

As they exited the courtyard and re-entered the study, Ankyer noticed three empty picture frames on a wall. "That's a little unusual," remarked Ankyer.

"There's a story there", said the Emir. "The empty frames are meant to hold three paintings. A triptych if you will. It reflects the essence of Arabian history during three periods of time. The triptych is called 'Three Seas'. The first painting is titled the 'Sea of Sand'. The second, the 'Sea of Oil'. And the third, the 'Sea of Plenty'. Each is connected to the other in a timeline from the past to the present day. The Three Seas represent the progression of the Arabian people from a wasteland, through the discovery of vast petroleum deposits of oil and gas, to the cultural and economic expansion of the present day in the countries in the Arabian Peninsula and ultimately connecting to the Arab diaspora throughout the world."

"No one knows where the paintings are, or even who the artist is," continued the Emir. "But there are rumors. Because of the paintings' potential cultural importance to the Arab people, many individuals and countries in the Middle East are searching for them, including Qatar and Saudi Arabia. Not to mention the Sultanate of Brunei, the UAE, Morocco, and Egypt. Virtually every Arab country has some kind of initiative underway to find them."

"They must be very valuable," said Ankyer

"Priceless," replied the Emir. "It is also rumored that the artist came out of retirement to execute the paintings and does not intend to paint again, making them truly unique. We believe the paintings may actually be located somewhere in North America. But that again, is speculation."

"An interesting mystery, indeed," said Ankyer.

Returning to the luncheon area, Honey Pi walked up to Ankyer.

"Have a good tour?" Ankyer asked.

"Great. I'll tell you all about it," she replied. "How about you?"

"You won't believe it," he replied.

RESIDENCE OF ANASTASIA MOON

Eagle River Ranch
Eagle River Ranch Colorado

MALLORY TENSALE STOOD BY THE GREAT ROOM'S MASSIVE FIREPLACE watching the Chinese technicians through the open double doors of the large, paneled library.

"You sure know how to live well, Anastasia," said Tensale.

"I've been at it since I was born," replied Moon. "How much longer will the technicians be working in the library?"

"Probably for another few hours. These computers are more advanced than your run-of-the-mill Macbook Pro."

"Don't be an asshole, Mallory. Just give me the Cliff's Notes version of how all this is going to work."

"Ok. The two computers being installed in your library are state-of-the-art high-performance units. They are military grade and will operate flawlessly even if there is an earthquake, explosion, etc. They are 6 feet high and 4 feet wide."

"Why so big?" interrupted Moon.

"Because there is considerable circuitry in each unit, they generate substantial heat which is handled by two cooling units in each cabinet."

"Why two cooling units?" asked Moon.

"Redundancy in case a cooling unit breaks down. One box, the one with "A" on the side, houses the software which generates the subsonic, auditory signal. The second box, with "B" on the side is a multiplexing computer which will transmit the signal from the "A" machine to the secure laptops issued to each of the Congressional committee chairpersons, 284 in all, at various locations around the country. This will be accomplished using a 2000 megabits per second hyper modem. There will be multiple transmissions.

"So how does this weapon work?" asked Moon.

"At first, we thought a low intensity, subsonic, acoustic beacon would suffice to disable each of the target congressmen for an extended period," said Tensale. "However, we were concerned that he or she might recover and reassume the leadership position on the committee. So, we decided to increase the amplitude of the subsonic sound wave. Now, it will fry the auditory nerve and will simultaneously cause a high intensity electrical pulse damaging the brain and killing the target instantly. Kind of like what happened to Boopsie McNulty except no one will have to eat the transmitter," said Tensale as he chuckled.

"And Gatling is ok with this?" asked Moon.

"We haven't told him. Why bother him with details? Anyway, once the congressmen and congress women start dying, all he has to do is declare martial law and take over the country. Game, set, match!"

"So, all these congress people are sitting somewhere in front of their computers. Why would they be doing that?"

"Gatling will have called the equivalent of an emergency Federal Zoom meeting to announce the results of the investigation into the previous Cabinet attack."

"Ok. But how does this sonic computer, Computer A, figure out where all these congressmen's laptops are?"

"Ah. Good question. Each congressmen's laptop has a unique IP address. One of my last projects prior to leaving the White House was to have the Congressional IT director send me a file of all the congressionally issued laptop IP addresses using a security concern as the rationale. We then had the addresses encoded by a Chinese cryptographer who is a mathematical genius. He used number theory to produce an unbreakable code for each IP address. Computer A decodes the address and computer B sends the subsonic signal to the target computer, wherever it is!"

"What if the computer is in the congressman's family room and his wife and kids are somewhere around? Will the signal hit them?"

"Collateral damage," replied Tensale. "Makes everything more poignant."

"You are a diabolical fucker, you know that?" said Moon.

"Whatever it takes," replied Tensale.

"Are you sure Gatling is up to this? He is nuts after all," said Moon.

"I will be there with him every step of the way. Also, the B computer is programmed to transmit the signal to the congressional computers in groups of 25 every few minutes until the job is finished. This sequencing is designed to create chaos but happens fast enough so that no one will be able to figure out what's going on until it's too late."

"You know, this might just work," said Moon. "Two things. First, what happens if this math genius somehow gets grabbed by the FBI or someone?"

"That could be a problem except that he's located in China.

"Ok. Second, after all this happens, these computers are still in my library. I'm not happy with that."

"The same team in your library now will be here during the operation. When it's complete, they will pull everything out. One hour, tops. The next day you will be on your way to Washington to meet with Gatling and graciously accept the job of Vice President."

"It seems that there are a fair number of people involved in this. Is the operation secure?" asked Moon.

"I have worked with everyone involved in this for years. Plus, no one knows the whole picture except you and me."

"And Gatling," said Moon.

"Well, there is that. He doesn't know about increasing the amplitude of the sound waves. We may have to have a conversation about that downstream."

"When is liftoff? asked Moon

"Week after next," said Tensale.

Moon walked over to the window of her great room, looked out. Paused and turned to Tensale. "Let's do it," she said.

QATAR BOEING 777-9X
38,000 feet
Flight Plan: Qatar to Frankfurt Germany

WALKING TOWARDS THE MAIN SALON OF THE 777, Crown Prince Bamin asked Ankyer: "What did you think of the flight deck?"

"Very impressive, as is the rest of the aircraft. I'm not use to this much space."

"It is expansive to say the least," replied the Crown Prince. "By the way, please call me Bamin. My friends do and I hope that we are friends."

"We definitely are, Bamin. One thing, your pilot mentioned that the Rolls Royce engines are beyond standard on the power curve. Why's that?"

"Well, as you probably noticed, all the decking is made of Carrera marble, the same type used in the Emir's palace. My father is partial to Carrera marble as a building material and uses it extensively. The marble added so much weight to the 777 that it altered the aerodynamics and we had to redesign the engines to increase the power."

"That must have set you back," said Ankyer.

"It added another twenty million. The "out the door" price was $ 425.8 million before engine mods plus another $ 225 million in upgrades including the marble. Not too bad actually even when considering the other four."

"The other four what?"

"The other four 777s. We have five in the fleet. The four others are laid out like this. Since we're talking planes, we have also ordered a Gulfstream g700 for your exclusive use. It should be ready in two months or so. We mentioned it to Dr. Pi, and she offered to work with our aircraft interior designer. Something about you being interior design challenged and she did not want to be embarrassed flying around with you."

As they entered the main salon of the 777, Ankyer noticed a waterfall separating the end of the salon from the next section of the plane. "A waterfall? How did you manage that?" he asked as they sat down at a round, marble inlaid crystal table. Bamin said "Jeneene, would you please bring Jake and me iced teas?" A few moments later Anker watched as a stately attendant emerged from the waterfall and placed two iced teas on the crystal table.

"Will there be anything else Highness?" she asked.

"Not at the moment, Jeneene. Thank you," replied Bamin.

The attendant then withdrew, once again walking through the waterfall.

"It has to be a hologram," said Ankyer.

"Right on," replied Bamin. "The Emir is partial to water and likes to have water features around him. Originally, he wanted actual water for the waterfall, but the engineering proved to be too difficult."

"I did notice several waterfalls at his palace," said Ankyer.

"You should see them on his yacht the 'Lady Azure.',' said Bamin.

"It is a 398-foot vessel built by Lürssen. It took four years to complete and was delivered just this year. It is available for use by the Qatar Family sheikhs, which now includes you, should you desire."

"I could get used to being a Qatari sheikh," said Ankyer.

"Part of our 'evil plan'" replied Bamin with a smile. With that Bamin picked up a remote control from the table and pressed a button. A television monitor lowered from the ceiling, flickered on, and showed the outlines of a Le Mans style closed circuit road annotated with what appeared to be names of towns.

"This is the Nurburgring Nordschleife circuit. It is 12.8 miles long and has 33 left turns and 40 right turns. It has numerous steep elevation changes, blind corners, and no runoff areas. Last year there were 81 officially logged accidents involving amateur drivers, two deaths and numerous serious injuries. As we discussed, the lap record is 6 minutes 57 seconds achieved by Porsche factory racer Marc Lieb. His fastest lap was 111.53 mph. Lieb's record is what you will need to beat to download the coded information on the 918's infotainment system. Think you're up to it?"

As he studied the diagram on the screen, Ankyer replied: "Shouldn't be a problem as long as the car is properly tuned, and a tire doesn't blow."

"The car's onboard Weissach package is the same as was used by Lieb when he broke the record. You're essentially driving the same car."

"What was Lieb's top speed on the circuit again?" asked Ankyer.

"111.53 mph," said Bamin. "You seem pretty confident my friend," added Bamin.

"I periodically fly a F/A-18F Super Hornet in the Navy's Top Gun combat school. I also hold instructor status in the school. While I have not actually driven a 918, I think I can manage."

The television monitor changed the display to a picture of a 918 Porsche Spyder with specifications underneath. "As you can see the 918's main motor is a MR6 4.6-liter, 4,593 cc V8 with an output of 875 horsepower. The engine is synchronized with two additional electric motors, one on each axle, for an additional output of 282 horsepower. It has a seven speed, dual-clutch automatic transmission which can be converted to manual with paddle shifters. The car has five operating modes. The main engine and the electric motors operate independently except when the Racing mode is selected, and the Hot Lap button is pushed. This engages all engines at a combined output of 1002 horsepower. There is an RS Spyder which has a more aggressive power configuration, but that was not used in Lieb's record run. That's pretty much it. The car has a top speed of 214 miles per hour according to Porsche, but that speed is not possible on the Nordschleife course.

"Hmm," said Ankyer. "Is the Hot Lap feature always available on demand?" he asked.

"As far as I know," replied Bamin.

"What about tires?" asked Ankyer

"The Weissach Package requires special tires. 265/35 ZR 20s in the front and 325/30 ZR 21s in the rear. We are having four complete sets of tires delivered with the car along with a team of Porsche-trained, Qatari mechanics."

"Ok. I think I have all the information I need. I've spoken with Dr. Finkel. He asked that I do this as quickly as possible so that our associates can begin analyzing the codes. I'll do two runs. One for course familiarization, and the second for speed."

"You seem quite confident my friend."

"Confident yes. Overconfident, never.

"You are a remarkable person, Jake Ankyer," said Bamin. "I am looking forward to your run on the Nordschleife circuit."

The 777 started to descend and executed a shallow bank. "We are ten minutes out of Frankfurt Hahn airport gentlemen," the pilot said over the intercom. "Please fasten your seatbelts."

"On to Nurburgring!" said Ankyer.

"I can't wait!" exclaimed Bamin.

NURBURG GERMANY
Nurburgring Nordschleife Circuit
6:00 AM Greenwich Mean Time (GMT)

THE EARLY MORNING FOG WAS LIFTING AS THE HELICOPTER LANDED 200 yards from the Nordschleife circuit car paddock. Oskar Weiner, the managing director of the Nurburgring Nordschleife Circuit, greeted Bamin as he alighted from the helicopter. The plan was for Ankyer to remain in the helicopter until after Bamin and the Course Director left.

"On behalf of our Board of Directors, it is my pleasure to welcome you to the Nurburgring Nordschleife Circuit, Prince Sallazon. We have two cars ready as you requested. One car will take us to our central, course tracking building, and the other will take your driver to the paddock location where your car is parked with your mechanics."

"I appreciate you accommodating us," replied Bamin.

"On the contrary, it is we who appreciate you," said Weiner. "It is generally not our policy to close down the whole circuit for an entire day, but your minister was very persuasive."

"I'm glad you came to an agreement," said Bamin.

"Let's just say our budget is balanced for the remainder of the year," replied Weiner. The driver of one of the Mercedes 500 limousines opened the back door for Bamin, who was joined in the back seat by Weiner.

"The fog should lift shortly," said Weiner. "We generally prefer to wait 30 minutes or so to give the circuit a chance to dry out after the fog lifts. It looks like a light fog so the circuit should be in good condition. When would you like to start?"

"Our driver will ride over in the car you've provided to the paddock shortly. We plan on two trips around the circuit, the first for familiarization since our driver has not been here before, and the second trip for speed."

"Trying to break Marc Lieb's Porsche record, are you?" said Weiner jokingly.

"Mr. Weiner let me be direct. Our purpose here today is to test certain new features of the Porsche 918 which are confidential. I will need all copies of video taken during the runs as per the agreement with our Minister. Have you and everyone on you staff signed and returned the nondisclosure agreements our Minister sent?"

"Of course, Prince Sallazon. You can rely on us," said Weiner rather stiffly.

"Excellent," said Bamin. "We want to see your budget remain in balance."

The car pulled into the driveway of course tracking building and Bamin and Weiner entered the circuit tracking room.

"As you can see, we have monitors focused on the entire circuit. This is to ensure emergency help is available should there be an accident, which may befall your driver since he has not driven here before. The circuit has numerous sharp turns and requires better than average driving ability at any speed over 90 miles per hour. A Lamborghini was totaled here yesterday by a driver who has driven the track numerous times."

"I'll keep that in mind," said Bamin.

"Is that your driver down there?" asked Weiner.

"It appears so," replied Bamin looking towards the paddock.

Ankyer walked around the black 918 Spyder with two Qatari mechanics. He pointed to the rear wheels while walking around the car. He put on a crash helmet provided by one of the mechanics, opened the driver's side door and got in. Ankyer nodded as a mechanic knelt by his side and pointed to several things in the 918's cockpit. The mechanic stood up and closed the driver's door. He stood back saying something to another mechanic. Ankyer started the car, let it idle for a few minutes to warm up, and drove out to the circuit starting line. He pulled out slowly and gradually increased his speed down the course.

"He doesn't seem to be in a hurry," said Weiner as the Porsche entered the Castrol-S curve.

"As I mentioned earlier, the first run is for familiarization," replied Bamin.

"At this rate he will take around 20 minutes to complete the circuit," said Weiner. We can monitor his speed on the indicator dial above the teleprompter. The dial next to it projects the total lap time considering speed changes over the course. I was wrong. His completion projection is 23.6 minutes and climbing." Bamin and Weiner continued watching as the Porsche traversed the course and crossed the finish line in front of the tracking building.

"25.8 minutes. Qatar paid a lot of money to drive to the grocery store!" remarked Weiner.

Ankyer drove over to the paddock, shut the Porsche down, got out, took off his helmet and started talking to the mechanics. He pointed to the right front tire and the left rear tire. The mechanics rolled out an air compressor and did something to each tire.

"It looks like they are adjusting tire pressures," said Weiner. "Porsche 918 tire pressures are sacred. They should never be adjusted from factory standard. They could blow up at high speed. Of course, with your driver's last performance not much chance of that!"

"Mr. Weiner, I came here to observe my driver on your track. Not to listen to your insulting commentary. Kindly shut the fuck up."

Weiner's eyes opened wide. He paused and said: "Apologies Prince. I thought you were here to test the Porsche. I didn't know..."

"That's the point," said Bamin. "You don't know. He's getting ready for his next run."

Ankyer got back in the Porsche, made some comments to the mechanics, started the car, and drove back to the starting line. He switched the transmission from automatic to manual. He revved the engine up to 7000 RPM and hit the Hot Lap button. The Porsche screamed off the line, swerved slightly, and shot down the track.

Weiner watched the speed indicator dial above the monitors as the needle passed 180 miles per hour. "He won't make the turn," said Weiner as Ankyer made the turn, then another turn, then another.

Ankyer down shifted for the next straightaway and hit the Hot Lap button increasing speed to 205 miles per hour. He continued to hit the Hot Lap button going into the bottom of the succeeding curves, followed by downshifting to reduce speed and then increasing speed coming out of the top of each curve. He hit the downhill

Kottenborn straight at 215 mph and was up to 235 mph going into a fast curve called Schwedenkreuz hitting 243 mph before dropping speed. He crossed the finish line at 248 mph and pulled next to the paddock with three of the four tires on fire. The technicians raced to the car dousing the tires with fire extinguishers.

Weiner looked at the dials with his mouth open. Ankyer's average speed was 194 mph with a top speed of 253 mph. The elapsed circuit time was clocked at 5.85 minutes start to finish. "Impossible!" exclaimed Weiner. "This can't be," he sputtered. "There must be something wrong with the tracking calibration!"

A technician came running into the room. "There is nothing wrong with the calibration," said the technician in German. "We checked the computers. Everything is in order. The speeds and times are accurate," said the technician.

Weiner turned to Bamin and asked, "What is going on here?"

Prince Sallazon replied, "What's going on here is that you and every one of your employees today is restricted by the NDA you all signed from communicating to anyone that you have witnessed here. As I mentioned earlier, all videos and images, digital or otherwise, are to be given to me."

The technician handed Bamin a briefcase. "The briefcase contains all the recorded videos and images of the runs as you required," said Weiner.

"They have been deleted from your system?" asked Bamin.

Weiner looked at the technician and repeated the question in German.

The technician replied that the system had been swept clean of all still and video images. Weiner repeated the technician's reply to Bamin in English.

"In that case our business here is concluded," said Bamin as he turned and walked out the door.

Weiner turned to the technician and asked in German if there were any recordings.

"Of course," the technician replied.

"Good. Put them in the safe in my office and do not discuss this with anyone."

"As you wish sir," replied the technician.

"Nice run," one of the Qatari mechanics said to Ankyer as he exited the Porsche.

"Thanks. I had a little left on the last straightaway, but didn't want to push it," replied Ankyer, laughing.

"We'll check the car out, but other than trashing the tires, it appears ok. We are supposed to deliver it to your residence in Qatar after servicing, if that's ok with you."

"Works for me," replied Ankyer as he walked away.

"Did the codes upload from the Porsche's infotainment system Dr. Finkel?" asked Ankyer through his mastoid implant.

"They uploaded perfectly Jake. You didn't take any chances when you broke the Nurburgring record though."

"I didn't want to chance the car's infotainment system activating for the record, so I decided to press it. The Porsche 918 is certified for 218 miles per hour. I got it up to 253 miles per hour but backed off not wanting to blow a gasket."

"Talk about blowing a gasket, we were all watching your run and we were thrilled to say the least."

"What about the codes?" asked Ankyer

"We're not sure what to make of them. Brother Arlot is running them on the N.S.A. quantum computers now. He is hoping to have the codes deciphered in a few days."

"Here comes Bamin," said Ankyer

"Bamin?" replied Finkel

"The Crown Prince. We are close friends now that I am a sheikh."

"Ok," said Finkel. *"I talked with the Emir about this new development concerning you. I am supportive of it since the Emir, and I go back a way. He understands the parameters of your relationship with Qatar and the Red Protocol Group. He even has agreed to let us maintain an active presence in Qatar with our operatives and technology should Middle East issues need our involvement. You are now our Ambassador along with everything else."*

"Ok. Have to go," said Ankyer.

"Jake!" exclaimed Bamin. "Is there anything you do not do? Riding war horses to rescue Qatari nobility, racing cars with flaming tires, conducting advanced research at the London School of Economics. I'm in awe!"

"I spoke with my father a few moments ago. He said to tell you Dr. Pi wants to have a chat with you when you get back to Qatar. Something about your trip in the Porsche. I can hardly wait to see the greeting you receive."

"You and me both," replied Ankyer as they walked over to the helicopter. At the same time the 918 Porsche was being loaded onto a flatbed truck.

"The car will be delivered to your Palace in Qatar before we arrive," said Bamin.

"With new tires?" asked Ankyer

"With new tires," said Bamin slapping Ankyer on the back as they entered the helicopter.

ROLLS ROYCE PHANTOM VIII LIMOUSINE

Ankyer Palace
Qatar

THE ROLLS ROYCE LIMOUSINE PULLED UP TO THE STONE GATEHOUSE where three Qatari soldiers stood at attention. The Qatari Crown prince turned to Ankyer and said: "Jake, you are a precious commodity to our country and as such, have security on a 24/7 basis. The gatehouse to your residence has military security. Our national security service is for the most part invisible and non-intrusive. Will this be a problem for you?"

"Generally, security is not a problem for me. I understand your concern, however, and appreciate your efforts on my behalf."

"Excellent. If the security arrangement becomes burdensome let me know and we will figure something out. In the meantime, your residence is in the middle of a five-square mile, private seaside location so we will be a few minutes getting there."

The limousine continued down the road flanked by lush gardens and palm trees. It finally pulled up to a large, granite stone car parking area with a magnificent, three-story marble building flanked by rectangular wings, turrets, and several tiers of marble steps with large urns containing palm trees.

"Welcome home, Jake Ankyer"

"Bamin, you've got to be kidding."

"Well, it is a little ostentatious, but we like to make a statement when someone comes to visit one of our family sheikhs," said the Crown Prince laughing.

Ankyer looked out the window to see Honey Pi walking down the six tiers of marble steps towards the limo. Bamin lowered the back window and said: "See Dr. Pi, I told you I would bring him back in one piece."

"Lucky for you Bamin."

"I thought you were mad at me," said Ankyer.

"Pure theatrics," replied Honey Pi.

"Turns out that the Emir and I have lots of similar interests. He even wants to make me a shaykhah, which is the female equivalent of 'sheikh'."

"I figured you would get along with the Emir. You didn't waste any time. You get a palace too?"

"He offered me one, but I told him one is plenty. By the way, that run of yours in the Porsche was something else."

As they walked into the main reception hall, Ankyer said: "How big is this place?"

"Actually, I asked the Emir. He said he wasn't sure but thought it was around 60,000 square feet. Seems bigger though."

"When does the tour start?" asked Ankyer.

"The Emir gave me a short tour the other day," said Honey Pi. "There are reception rooms for reception rooms! Chief Bell would like the kitchen. It's incredible. It has appliances I don't even recognize. The Emir said the kitchen comes with a professional staff including a world-renowned chef."

"I bet they don't know how to make a Wally burger," said Ankyer.

"You would lose. I had one for lunch yesterday," said Pi.

After that they wandered from one room to another and wound up sitting on a veranda overlooking lush gardens and fountains.

"By the way, there is a butler who will give us the grand tour. All you have to say is 'butler' and he shows up. He's about as big as you are, and I think he's packing."

"Probably part of their security set up,' said Ankyer.

"The Emir also showed me the library. It has just about every medical text known to man. It even has a few economics books."

"Just a few?" asked Ankyer

"A few. Like around 4000 few. The library is three stories high with an escalator."

"How do you find anything? They have a computer catalogue?"

"They do, but you don't have to worry about that. There is a resident librarian."

"God," said Ankyer.

"Wait until you see the gym. Plus, there is a running path in and around the estate including an obstacle course. Plus, there are numerous other buildings, including a guest residence that, believe it or not, has a guest residence. It will take a while to get all this figured out. Seems like they want you around and to be happy."

"No problem there," replied Ankyer.

With that both their mastoid implants activated. *"Before you two get too comfortable, there is a tele conference call we have to have."*

"Dr. Finkel! I thought we'd be hearing from you but not so soon."

"Ordinarily you'd be correct except the preliminary analysis of the uploaded Qatari codes has been completed. We have a problem. Or should I say the United States has a problem."

"Honey Pi and I are in a Qatar building," said Ankyer. *"I'm not sure how secure it is."*

"I spoke to the Emir about your security needs and a secure room is in the building," said Finkel.

"Ok. When is the teleconference?"

"Thirty minutes," replied Finkel.

"See you then," said Ankyer

SECURE PHONE CALL
Presidential Top Secret/Digital Limited
Washington DC

GATLING: "I PREFER TO USE OUR BALTIMORE LOCATION for these conversations."

Tensale: "I agree Mr. President. This will be short, and I thought a secure call would be sufficient."

Gatling: "Ok. Go ahead.

Tensale: "The computer equipment has been installed at Moon's location. During testing a slight coding malfunction caused one of the secure, test laptops to go offline. We are checking into it and should have it resolved shortly. However, since we will only have one shot at this, we are checking the IP addresses of all the secure laptops. Bottom line, we want to extend the execution of the operation out one week in an abundance of caution."

Gatling: "It's a damn good thing you called. I was just getting ready to have a directive sent out scheduling the tele-conference. What date are we talking about now?"

Tensale: "It is now September 15th. Unless we find another problem. But I'm 98% sure."

Gatling: "Ok. By the way, I've decided to bring Winston White back as my special security person. When this thing happens, I'll need all the security I can get. Martial law is a big step and I expect there will be push back from the opposition."

Tensale: "Whatever you want to do. But be careful. His involvement with the Red Protocol Group makes me uncomfortable."

Gatling: "That may be, but I need a 'Plan B' if the Secret Service turns on me. What about Moon?"

Tensale: "When the balloon goes up, she will be on her way here. I want her in my sights to make sure she doesn't get any big ideas."

Gatling: "Such as?"

Tensale: "Can't say. But let's not take any chances."

Gatling: "Another thing I've been thinking about. The whole idea is to eliminate Congressional and other officials by deploying the sound weapon. I am worried that they may recover and assume their former duties. After all, they are elected officials. What can we do to prevent this from happening?"

Tensale: "You make a good point. We can always increase the amplitude of the sound wave to cause permanent hearing damage."

Gatling: "That may work up to a point. But there is always lip reading. I've also heard of digital hearing appliances that use bone conductivity. We need to come up with something."

Tensale: "Let me think about it."

Gatling: "Well think fast. September 15th is approaching quickly."

Gatling disconnected and Tensale dialed Moon using a burner phone they both had.

Tensale: "I just got off the phone with Gatling. He wants all the targets stopped from ever resuming their Congressional duties. Ever."

Moon: "Kill them?"

Tensale: "He didn't say that exactly but there is no doubt about the inference."

Moon: "Excellent. Things have a way of working out."

Tensale: "He is also bringing back Winston White from the Red Protocol Group as personal protection. This is not good. The Red Protocol Group has a reputation as a counter terrorist organization. White could cause us problems potentially. Any ideas?"

Moon: "I'll have my Mr. Sten and Mr. Blue take care of him just before commencement of the operation. Just get me a picture of him and let me know where he will be. I'll send them out."

Tensale: "Good plan. Just make sure it's a permanent solution," and hung up.

ANKYER'S PALACE
Qatar

HONEY PI REAPPEARED DRESSED IN BLACK SLACKS, A BEIGE BLOUSE, and a white lab coat.

Ankyer looked at his watch and asked, "how did you do that so fast?"

"It's not hard if you know what you're doing."

"Ok, let's try this 'Butler' thing," said Ankyer

"Butler."

A large figure entered the open doorway. "Yes sir. How may I be of assistance?"

"Do you have a name?" asked Ankyer

"Yes sir. You may call me Claude if you wish, or just 'Butler'. There are five of us scattered around the grounds to assist as you may require. You can call us all 'Claude'."

"Ok. Well, let's stick with Claude for the moment."

"Claude, we need to go to the 'Secure Room' at once," said Ankyer.

"As you wish, sir. Please follow me." They followed Claude out into the paneled hall. A pocket door opened in the wall with a "woosh", and they entered an elevator. The door closed after them.

"Where does this elevator take us?" asked Ankyer.

"The main residence has four floors, sir. There is a fifth, underground floor to park the cars and under that, a sixth floor which incorporates the Secure Room." A few moments later the elevator opened.

"That was fast," said Ankyer.

"The elevator operates with artificial intelligence software and automatically stops at the floor you request. It also ascends and descends in a gravity neutral, vertical tunnel which cancels out the sense of movement."

Ankyer and Pi exited the elevator and walked through an opening of massive double oak doors. After entering, a metal door closed behind them. The room had the ambience of a private club library. There was a large screen on one wall. The rest of the room was furnished with red leather chairs and couches, polished rosewood tables, and a side table with cold beverages and several chafing dishes, plates, and bowls of fruit. Two chairs faced the screen. They had side tables with glasses and carafes of water, pads of paper and pens.

"I could get use to this," said Ankyer

"I'm beginning to think that's the idea," replied Honey Pi.

The screen came to life with an image of Dr. Finkel in the center and numerous other images.

"Good morning or afternoon depending on where you are," said Finkel as he acknowledged everyone on the teleconference. "I apologize for this hurried conference call, but information has come to light which requires our collective and immediate attention. Let's lead off with Dr. Tallon. Margie?"

"Thank you, Dr. Finkel. Many of you may recall, a short time ago Ernestine McNulty, President Gatling's Secretary of Education died abruptly in a Cabinet meeting. Known to her friends and associates as "Boopsie", she was the victim of an explosion in her torso. The body was shipped to our location at the Abbey along with the head of Buster Hornsbee, a Pentagon congressional liaison, and we did an autopsy on each. What remained of Boopsie's stomach was of interest. We discovered the remains of a jelly donut, which when examined under an electron microscope, revealed part of a minute biocomputer. Dr. Arlot..."

"After Dr. Tallon extracted the biocomputer from the jelly donut remains, we discovered that a portion of it was wrapped in a gelatin capsule. We concluded that only three countries currently have the technology to manufacture a biocomputer of the type we discovered: The United States, Russia, and China. We focused the electron microscope on the remains of the gelatin capsule and imaged part of a Chinese character on the capsule's interior wall. As far as I'm concerned, that's close enough to eliminate the U.S. and Russia as possible sources. Moving on, we analyzed the biocomputer remains as best we could and concluded that it was designed to emit a very high, hypersonic sound wave which likely caused the demise of Ms. McNulty and affected the others in the room."

"And how did you divine the intensity of the soundwave?" asked Finkel.

"Ah, we got lucky there," replied Arlot. "Hornsbee was wearing what appeared to be noise cancelling ear buds which has led us to believe he was the one who brought the jelly donut into the Cabinet room. When the sonic weapon was activated, it overwhelmed the ear buds and partially melted them into the sides of Hornsbee's head killing him. Analyzing the white noise capacity of the ear buds, we inferred that the soundwave overpowering the white noise cancellation capacity of the ear buds would have had to be extremely powerful."

"Excellent analysis, Doctor Arlot," said Finkel. "Which brings us to our two new additions to the Red Protocol Group: Doctor Juno Su and Doctor Wen Lee. Professor Su is a leading Chinese acoustics scientist who has recently escaped to the U.S. from China's Uyghur genocide. He is also a winner of the Abel prize for applied computer science. Doctor Wen Lee, also from China, is the youngest winner of the Fields Medal in mathematics with additional expertise in numbers theory and is an acknowledged international expert in computer science. Doctor Lee came to the U.S. to escape Chinese repression and to avoid being forced to emigrate to North Korea to work on their nuclear weapons program. Welcome to the Red Protocol Group gentlemen."

"Thank you, Dr. Finkel," said Drs. Su and Lee in unison.

"Based on your briefing by Drs. Arlot and Tallon, have you any conclusions to share with the group? Dr. Lee?"

"Thank you Dr. Finkel. Before I start, Honey Pi, is that really you?"

"You bet it is," replied Honey Pi.

"You know each other?" asked Finkel.

"Definitely," said Honey Pi. "Dr. Lee and I were on a panel at a medical informatics symposium several years back. Glad to see you Wen!" said Honey Pi.

"Same here," replied Lee. "Honey Pi absolutely trounced me at a Chinese Go game in a bar after the meeting. Of course, she didn't bother to tell me that she holds the rank of 'Professional 8th Dan', about as high as you can achieve."

"I had to do something to pass the time in med school," said Honey Pi.

"You mean pay your way through med school. I found out she is so good that people were betting on her in tournaments and giving her a piece of their winnings, which were substantial."

"I knew that Brother Augustus is a card shark but didn't realize we also had a 'Go shark' in our midst. We need to discuss that further Dr. Pi," said Finkel laughing. "But for the moment, can we return to the matter at hand, Dr. Lee?"

"Sorry, Dr. Finkel. I've had an opportunity to review several of the Qatari codes that were downloaded. First off, no Qatari mathematician came up with these codes. They are elegant almost beyond comprehension. Heavy stuff. It's a combination of applied number theory, Fibonacci series computations, and fractal geometry. Without dropping into hyper math nerd mode, a cryptographic model which uses all three is theoretically unbreakable. On the other hand, all is not lost. It turns out that a group of mathematicians named Frieden, Ilstrum, Dunlop and Osterkamp came up with something called the FIDO algorithm. It operates on three-dimensional line fragments which exist in the form of lattices, and which include fractals which are seen often in nature such as in flowers and the like. Add Fibonacci series numbers and it's a new ballgame. Conventional cryptography relies on prime numbers and results in codes which can usually be cracked using conventional computers. But this other type adds a level of complexity which even exceeds the computing power of super computers."

"So even with the FIDO Algorithm we can't crack it," said Brother Arlot.

"Right. Up to a point," replied Lee. "Except maybe."

"It has to be quantum computers," said Su.

"You are 100% correct Dr. Su," said Lee. Dr. Su is referring to a new technology which is referred to as quantum computing. It basically takes a math problem which would require 10,000 years, if ever, to solve and solves it in a few hours. It is disruptive technology which will fundamentally change computer science. It's rumored that the Chinese have designed a Quantum computer, but just a rumor. The United States, however, has in fact designed one. Actually, two of them, both currently housed at the N.S.A.. Dr. Finkel, using his contacts got me some time on one of them. I used the FIDO algorithm on a few of the codes. It took thirty minutes, but it looks like the quantum computers may have cracked the codes! Let me show you."

A document appeared in the center of the Zoom screen.

Qatar Code:	37877##&900871000&$00998
Quantum Decoded:	3001:df9:00:6789:07:5532:1:99
Qatar Code:	49877##&977546000*$00334
Quantum Decoded:	5001:df3:00:7896:032:6626:8:10

"Those look like Internet Protocol addresses, but not like any I've ever seen," said Brother Arlot."

"You are almost correct," said Finkel. They are IP version 6 addresses modified for Top Secret use by the U.S. Government. My N.S.A. colleague has informed me that these are the IP addresses of the secure laptop computers of the Chairman of the House Agriculture Committee and the Vice Chairman of the Senate Committee on Homeland Security. There are 252 additional codes on the list. We won't know for sure...the computers are still processing, but it's beginning to appear that we are dealing with IP addresses of top-secret government computers, issued for use by members of Congress and other senior government officials."

"Do we know how Qatar got access to the codes?" asked Augustus Carter.

"I may be able to help there," said Ankyer. "I had a conversation with the Emir. He indicated that Qatar has contacts in the U.S. and one of them gave the list to a Qatari intelligence operative. The contact said the list was a duplicate of another list prepared by Gatling's former chief of staff. The contacts also came up with a name. Anastasia Moon. It may not mean anything, but the name was provided within the context of the codes. We probably should investigate both Moon and the ex-chief of staff."

"That would be Mallory Tensale," said Finkel. "What's more, Tensale and Moon know each other. And SLUG at one point was focused on her as a Vice Presidential replacement for Penelope Bartlett who was a victim of the Cabinet attack. If Tensale directed the list of Top-Secret codes be developed and he was transitioning out of the White House, the question becomes why now? And for what reason? Anything else for us Dr. Lee?"

"Yes. I think I know who developed the codes," said Lee. "You said the fragment of the device which caused Boopsie to explode had Chinese markings on it?"

"Correct," replied Finkel.

"My educated guess is the creator of the codes is a Chinese mathematician named Bao Lo."

"You're kidding," said Ankyer stifling a laugh.

"I know. With a name like that you should sue your parents. Bao Lo had a tough childhood, although it turned out he is smart. He is also a real jerk. He was even up for a Field's Medal but didn't get any votes. I happened to run into someone on the Field's Medal review committee at a meeting and asked what happened to Bao Lo. He said, 'I'm not in the habit of voting for assholes.' Lo eventually wound up working for the Guoanbu, the Chinese Ministry of State Security in their cryptographic division. He's like the rumored antisocial super techies IBM kept in the basement of their buildings and trotted out to solve extremely difficult computer software problems, after which they were returned to the murky depths. This is Bao Lo in spades."

"Ok. But where does this get us?" asked Ankyer.

"Remember I said that the codes we were trying to figure out are the intersection of applied number theory, Fibonacci series computations, and fractal geometry. In a Fibonacci sequence, each number equals the sum of the previous two numbers: 0, 1, 1, 2, 3, 5, 8, 13, 21, 34, and so on. Now add fractal geometry to the equation. For example, if you break off a floret on a cauliflower, the floret will look like an exact duplicate of the larger cauliflower. Break off a floret from that and it will also look the same. You'll see a spiral emanating from the center point, along which all the smaller florets are arranged. This is a Fibonacci spiral, a series of arcs whose radii follow the Fibonacci sequence. If you count the number of spirals in one direction, and then count the number of spirals in the other direction, they will be — without fail — consecutive Fibonacci numbers. Every time. In theory, this continues into infinity except of course you will eventually run out of florets. However, and this is important, the number sequence based on the cauliflower florets can continue, leading to an exceedingly large array of numbers. A skilled cryptographer can then apply the resulting number structure to a code which is almost unbreakable. Using the Quantum computers, we were able to analyze the coding structure and compare it to fractal Fibonacci sequences. A process which could theoretically take tens of thousands of years. But it worked. Believe it or not, we discovered that the fractal/Fibonacci sequence used on the Qatari codes was that of a Romanesco broccoli. Now this is where it gets wild. Virtually all mathematicians who do advanced fractal analysis like to use examples of fractal occurrences in nature as reference points. Examples include branches of trees, animal circulatory systems, snowflakes, lightning and electricity, plants and leaves, geographic terrain and river systems, clouds, and crystals. A Bao Lo paper on advanced fractal analysis, which was used in part to evaluate his Field's medal candidacy used, here it comes, Romanesco broccoli as the core fractal example of his analysis. Bao Lo's and by extension, the Chinese Ministry of State Security's fingerprints are all over these codes."

"The smoking veggie!" exclaimed Honey Pi.

"Exactly," said Lee.

"To summarize, connecting the dots we have a Chinese mathematician / cryptologist working for the Chinese Secret Service who has constructed an unbreakable coding system which he has applied to a Top-Secret list of Internet Protocol addresses supplied by SLUG's immediate past Chief of Staff, and all of which are associated with U.S. Congressional committee chairperson's government issued computers," said Finkel. "Except that the unbreakable coding system has been broken by Dr. Lee and the N.S.A.'s Quantum computer. Is that the gist of it Dr. Lee?"

"A perfect summary, Dr. Finkel," replied Lee

"Well, that's one shoe that's dropped. What about the other one?" asked Finkel. "What do you have to say about all this, Dr. Su?"

"Thank you Dr. Finkel," said Su. "Dr. Lee's analysis is correct in my opinion. But the question remains, 'Why go to all the trouble?'. Clearly inserting the Chinese sound weapon in Ms. Boopsie McNulty's jelly donut worked. She died. But wait. Did it really work? I suggest no, it did not. In fact, it was a calamity. After all, we are here discussing the revelation of the Chinese sound weapon device. No. The objective was to disable all the people in the Cabinet room by hiding the device in the jelly donut, not hiding it in Boopsie McNulty. That she ate the jelly donut was completely unforeseen. It gave the wrong impression that Boopsie was the target and everyone else was collateral damage. In fact, everyone in the room including Boopsie McNulty was the target. To be clear, if Boopsie McNulty was in fact the target, why not send a sonic weapon device imbedded in a jelly donut to each of the people on the coded list? Why? Because it wouldn't work. A significant percentage of the people on the list would not eat the jelly donut!

"Your logic is sublime, Dr. Su," said Finkel, chuckling.

"Thank you Dr. Finkel. No, in my opinion the Chinese are smarter than that. In fact, the Chinese role in this escapade was just to develop and deliver the device. Another actor was responsible for placing the device in the Cabinet room. Someone else was directing Buster Hornsbee who could have simply walked into the Cabinet room with the device, dropped it on the floor or placed it behind a piece of furniture, and let the device operate as intended. But Hornsbee decided to be creative and placed it in the jelly donut with the results we know occurred. In my opinion, the Chinese found out about the jelly donut debacle and when asked by the actor in the U.S. to expand the victims of the technology, came up with a different approach from the biodegradable capsule ingested by Ms. McNulty."

"And the different approach?" asked Finkel.

"I'll get to that but please indulge me for a moment," said Su. "As I mentioned, the intent of the Cabinet event was to damage all the occupants of the room. That did in fact occur, despite Ms. McNulty's ingestion of the sonic weapon capsule, not because of it. In terms of damage to human hearing, a sound wave with a third harmonic amplitude is extremely dangerous to the human hearing system. Using the decibel as the common measure of sound, 30 decibels might be about right for a quiet bedroom. At the other end, a chain saw operates at around 120 decibels. 150 decibels is high enough to burst human ear drums. Between 185 and 200 decibels is lethal. I've evaluated the remains of the device found in Ms. McNulty and have concluded it could operate at 300 decibels. Coupled with an amplitude of 3rd harmonics, why then was everyone in the room not killed? If the device was placed on the floor or even in a jelly donut death would be almost instantaneous. But that did not occur. Instead, virtually all the people in the room were afflicted with what appeared to be a form of Meniere's disease which causes hearing loss, loss of balance and projectile vomiting. Why then? The solution lies with Boopsie McNulty. Once activated, a significant percentage of the weapon's energy was dissipated by the dissolving of Ms. McNulty's soft tissue internal organs such as the heart, liver, lungs, and brain as the sound tried to exit her body. The result was a 3rd harmonic sound of somewhere between 140 and 150 decibels. As I understand it, several victim's eardrums were burst."

"Actually, nearly all of them," said Brother Arlot

"There you go," said Su. "Ms. McNulty's internal organs being turned to mush absorbed sufficient sound energy to reduce the decibel count from 300 decibels to about 150 decibels. There are two basic conclusions to be drawn. First, the intent of the assault was to kill, not injure everyone in the room. The second conclusion is that the power of the sonic weapon is so substantial to be lethal."

"I think I know the answer but will ask anyway. How in your opinion does this relate to the list of Internet Protocol addresses, Dr. Su?" asked Finkel.

"As I understand it from Brother Arlot, each of the IP addresses corresponds to a military grade MacBook Pro computer with advanced communications and audio systems."

"Good Lord," interjected Augustus Carter.

"You are right there with me, Dr. Carter," said Su. "Rather than building the weapon to function as a small individual device, in theory at least, the Chinese have devised a system to transmit a lethal 3rd harmonic, 300 plus decibel sound over the Internet to the IP addresses on the list. Anyone within range of one of the target MacBook computers will die. The good news is they probably will not die instantly. A protracted sound wave of 5 to 10 minutes will probably be necessary to achieve the desired effect."

"Brother Arlot," started Finkel.

"I'm ahead of you," said Arlot. "We have several MacBook Pro computers and are reverse engineering the device extracted from Boopsie and testing Dr. Su's theory as we speak. We should have results within the hour."

"Excellent," replied Finkel. "We'll wait. Everyone please stay where you are."

The monitor in front of Honey Pi and Ankyer went blank.

PART TWO

Behold a white horse.
And he that sat upon him was called
Faithful and True,
And in righteousness he doth judge and make war.

ANKYER PALACE
Qatar

ANKYER LOOKED AT HONEY PI.

"Well, what do you think?" he asked.

"This whole thing is diabolical. We haven't gotten there yet, but it looks like SLUG is willing to kill hundreds of people to stay in office."

"Maybe. Or Tensale is willing to kill hundreds of people to keep SLUG in office," replied Ankyer.

"Worse yet, if this Chinese technology is demonstrated to work it could be used to kill anyone who has their computer turned on. Tens of millions of people!" said Honey Pi.

"Which is why Dr. Finkel has us sitting in neutral waiting for the screen to start up again," replied Ankyer.

"On a completely different subject, has it occurred to you why the Emir is shoveling all this money in your direction?" asked Honey Pi."

"Well, I was involved in saving his grandson," replied Ankyer.

"Maybe," said Honey Pi. "But come on. Millions of dollars a year. A palace. Making you a Qatari sheikh, in his family no less."

"I get your point. Maybe my good looks and light repartee?"

"Ok. Stop stuffing yourself with golf ball sized raspberries. I don't want you to choke when you hear this," said Honey Pi.

"When you were on your latest adventure in Germany, I was in the company of the Emir. He dropped by our humble abode here to watch you drive the Porsche Spyder. When you came to the end of the second run with the flaming tires and that incredible time, our favorite Emir was beside himself. He then got serious. He asked me what I thought of you. I said 'Well, Jake is incredibly handsome, and extremely smart. A Ph.D. world-class economist who people want to be awarded the Nobel Prize for his contributions to analytical macroeconomics is also an attention-getter. The Emir looked at me for a few minutes and then asked 'How does he do what he does militarily? Eliminating over 50 pirates, rescuing my grandson from all those slavers, and even rescuing you from those thugs in London...I saw the CCTV footage. He does things that even above average people can't do. How does he do them?' I replied that I also helped in my rescue, and he said that had not escaped his attention. I told him in the most general terms that you benefited from some advanced training at the Abbey but could not say more than that."

"Hey, you're pretty ok yourself," said Ankyer.

"Boy, you sure know how to return a compliment," said Honey Pi somewhat exasperatedly. "But that's not the big news."

"Big news?' said Ankyer.

"Fasten your seat belt," said Honey Pi. "After the Emir had finished contemplating, he said that he was concerned about his son and your friend, the Crown Prince. He allowed that the Crown Prince was not as serious about being head of state as the Emir thought he should be. The Emir then said… are you ready?… that he thought you would make a better successor to the Qatar throne than the Crown Prince and that he was thinking of adopting you to place you in the position of direct succession. He also said that he had discussed it with the Crown Prince, and it looks like the Crown Prince is on board."

"What about his grandson? He's next in line to the throne," said Ankyer

"Looks like the kid is more interested in upping his score in Mario," replied Honey Pi.

"Yeah, but he's still a kid," said Ankyer.

"I thought of that," said Honey Pi. "And then it occurred to me that the Emir might know something we don't. We should check out his medical records. And then he said he liked the idea of me being your consort, and he would make me a Qatari sheikha which is the female equivalent of one of your sheikh bigshots. And he wanted my opinion of all this."

"And you said?" replied Ankyer.

"I said I would talk to you about it, but I liked the idea of being a sheikha consort."

"What! You said what? I…you…he what? How…."

Honey Pi got up, went over to Ankyer, put her arms around him and said "Aw come on. Being a sheikha consort to a hot Emir like you would be fun!"

"What…how…us…running Qatar! sputtered Ankyer.

At that moment the monitor sprang to life with Finkel at the center surrounded with images of Ankyer, Honey Pi, Dr. Su, Dr. Lee, Brother Arlot, Brother Carter, Brother McCabe, Neal Groton, Margie Tallon, and Dr. Asbury. George Makin participated in audio via his mastoid implant.

"Is everyone ready to continue?" asked Finkel. "Jake, you look a little flustered. Everything ok?"

"Absolutely, Dr. Finkel. Honey Pi and I were just discussing all of this," as Honey Pi returned to her chair with a slight, mischievous smile.

"Excellent. Brother Arlot what do you have for us?"

"Thank you Dr. Finkel. We successfully reverse engineered the remains of the sonic device found in Boopsie McNulty. Running acoustic checks, the device was rated at an amplitude of level three harmonics. Regarding the decibel rating itself, Dr. Su's estimate of 300 decibels was incorrect. The rating is in fact 450 decibels, well beyond lethal range. We then tested three military grade Apple MacBook Pros of the type issued to Congress, in three acoustic chambers each containing a laboratory rat. You can see the results."

The television monitor showed three images of rats, each in a large transparent cube. A timer in the corner of the screen counted down from 5. By the time it arrived at 1 each of the three rats' heads had exploded. "We then tried it on several different, lower-level computers with the same results. The bottom line is even a rudimentary computer sound system can accommodate the sound produced by the sonic weapon. At the lower end of the computers, the decibel output degraded slightly, but in no case lower than 400 decibels. Finally, we tested the effective range of the device. Our conclusion is that any mammal within 150 feet of a computer emitting the sound would die. Outside that range, animals, including humans, would suffer significant degrees of hearing loss, up to a range of 500 feet. A survey of U.S. households in the United States in 2019 indicated that 86.6 percent of those households have Internet access. If someone somehow acquired the IP addresses for all U.S. household computers, this technology could potentially wipe out a large percentage of the U.S. population." Arlot paused. "Actually, it's worse than that. Smart phones are computers and aircraft operate using computers. All with Internet access and all with sound systems. For that matter, virtually the entire U.S. technical infrastructure is operated by computers with imbedded IP addresses. This could theoretically cause more damage than nuclear weapons. It would be cataclysmic."

"What if a computer is turned off?" asked Finkel.

"We tried that. The amount of energy generated by the decibel level of the weapon activates the computer."

"Thank you, Brother Arlot," said Finkel. "Comments anyone?"

Makin said: *"I have some thoughts, Dr. Finkel."*

"Go ahead George."

"Considering that we are of the opinion that SLUG conspired to eliminate his Cabinet with technology like what we just witnessed, I think it's a fair assumption that he is involved in this somehow. I'm pretty sure after the analysis of the list we will discover that most if not all the Congressional leadership is represented. He may in fact be "firing for effect" to eliminate any Congressional opposition to whatever plan he may have. The question is however, is SLUG smart enough to pull it off? The answer is probably not. However, Mallory Tensale is. And he's the one who had the IP list prepared," said Makin pausing.

"That's solid thinking George. Please continue," said Finkel.

"I also don't think that they can use raw IP addresses to do this. If they were somehow discovered the game would be up. However, if they left the IP addresses encoded and decoded them in real time..."

"They would need a Quantum computer!" interjected Lee. "Actually, maybe two. One to decode the addresses, and the other to transmit the codes and lethal sound to the target IP locations and serve as backup if the first one goes haywire. These computers are very new and do not have a long maintainability history."

"Also, in my latest involvement with SLUG, I've gone everywhere with him except for when he goes to the Baltimore location where he

met with Tensale the only time I was present. It might be a stretch, but I've been told to stay back six times when SLUG has gone to Baltimore which we've confirmed with our tracking device he still wears for some reason. I also cross checked that with his Top-Secret itinerary log he must keep if there's a national emergency. There's no doubt he was going to Baltimore, probably to meet with Tensale."

"The issue in my mind is where are the Quantum computers?" said Su. "They would have to be in a secure location to protect against discovery and very hard to find."

"Communications," said Lee. "If what we think is going on here is in fact what's going on, then there has to be very high-speed communications to transmit to the IP addresses to prevent discovery."

"They'd have to test it," said Su. The U.S. has developed 100 gigabyte per second transmission technology. It's 10,000 times faster than an iPhone transmission."

"I bet the Chinese have it too," said Lee

"Probably stolen," said Su. "They may be using something like that with the Quantum computers they supplied," he added.

"Is there some way we can check locations for a transmission rate that high?" asked Lee.

"There's something that might help us," said Makin. "When Tensale was SLUG's Chief of Staff, White House trip logs indicate he made a number of trips out to Colorado to meet with Anastasia Moon. She was being considered as Vice President after the then Vice President was disabled during the Cabinet attack. Moon lives in a very large estate situated in the center of tens of thousands of remote acres she also owns. It's a long shot, but maybe Tensale has placed the Quantum computers there."

"Would Moon go along with something like this?" asked Finkel.

"Possibly," said Makin. "Moon is extremely wealthy and word around the White House is that she is also into power. That might

be enough to pull her into a plan like this. If we keep Tensale as the center piece linked to SLUG, then anyone else Tensale meets with has to be suspect."

"I'll talk to my friend at N.S.A. and see if they may have detected any ultra-high data transmissions emanating from Moon's residence," said Finkel.

"I'm still concerned about this scenario in which the United States is obliterated by this technology," said Margie Tallon

"GNP," said Ankyer.

"GNP?" asked Tallon

"Gross National Product. Putting my economics hat on for a moment, a substantial part of the Chinese GNP is generated by the United States. A huge amount of their revenue comes from us. If the Chinese obliterated the U.S., the U.S. part of their revenue would drop to zero placing their economy into a tailspin from which they might not recover. Self-interest would probably stop them from pulling the trigger on the weapon."

"What about Russia?" retorted Arlot.

"Same answer but for a different reason," said Ankyer. "Putin's core interest is maintaining as much power as he can, economic or otherwise. Russia has an enormous investment in military tech-nology on the premise of "mutual assured destruction" with the United States. Putin and his oligarchs generate billions in revenue for their bank accounts. Eliminating the United States kills the golden goose. No, for the moment at least, this looks like a SLUG power grab being orchestrated by Tensale."

"I agree with your thesis, Jake," said Finkel. "However, if Tensale and SLUG manage to pull this off, they may use the tech-nology to obliterate a smaller country, say Scotland, and threaten to do the same to other countries to line their pockets. I would not put anything past these people, especially SLUG."

"Ransomware taken to the extreme," said Lee.

"Exactly," replied Finkel. "But first things first. Let's see if we can determine if Ms. Moon's estate is a high-speed data center.

RESIDENCE OF ANASTASIA MOON

Eagle River Ranch
Eagle River Ranch Colorado
"Burner" Phone Call

MOON: "WHAT THE HELL IS GOING ON? I've got more Chinese running around here than in a fortune cookie factory!"

Tensale: "The refrigeration units for the computers are inadequate. They had to swap in higher BTU units. They should be installed and tested by the end of the week."

Moon: "What about all these other guys who showed up today. What are they doing?"

Tensale: "Communications. The Chinese want to be sure that the computers can't be detected communicating with each other while one is transmitting decoded IP address to the other."

Moon: "Bullshit. The goddamn things are standing right next to each other."

Tensale: "That's the problem. For the computer doing the decoding to be secure from detection or interference, the communications must be routed to a Chinese node on an island in the South China Sea and from there to a number of nodes around the world before connecting with the computer sending the sound signal to the IP addresses. And that computer must go through the same routing process as the first one."

Moon: "So what's this do to our timeline?"

Tensale: "The communications piece was already built into the timeline. But the refrigeration issue means that everything must be retested. We're looking at another two weeks. Three weeks total since Gatling has to reschedule the Congressional Zoom call."

Moon: "Ok. Now listen carefully. If something else gets fucked up and I get my tits caught in a wringer with all this equipment and Chinese assholes running around my Great Room, you and Gatling are going to be the first on my list when I spill my guts to the U.S. Justice Department."

Tensale: Trying to visualize turning the crank on the wringer. "This is it. Everything is under control. We will be good to go."

Moon: "You better be."

Tensale: "Don't forget about Winston White."

Moon: "It's on my list." And hung up.

After she hung up on Tensale, Moon raised her hand and beckoned to Mr. Sten, Mr. Bent and Mr. Blue. "Follow me out to the deck." They did as directed and sat around an oval table with Moon.

"Tensale is concerned about a guy President Gatling brought in as his special bodyguard. His name is Winston White. Ordinarily, I would not be concerned, but White is associated with something called the Red Protocol Group which has a history of taking down terrorist organizations. Since our project is nearing activation, Tensale considers White to be a possible threat. Since White is close to the President, Tensale has asked that White be eliminated."

"Permanently?" asked Sten.

"Tensale did not specifically request that, but I don't want to take any chances. Yes. Permanently. You and Mr. Blue can take the Bombardier to Washington DC. today. If you can make it look like an accident all the better. If not, just make sure he disappears. It will look like he was involved with the elimination of the Congressmen, or at least that's the spin we'll put on it. Mr. Bent, you stay back here with me. I don't like all these Chinese running around here. If they decide to start something, I may need protection."

"No problem," replied Mr. Bent.

"What does this Winston White look like?" asked Sten.

"Tensale is sending me a picture. I'll upload it to the jet as soon as I get it. Tensale is also sending us the location of a restaurant, where we might find him. Obviously, he can't be dealt with inside the White House, so you may have to get creative."

"Not a problem," replied Sten. "We can be very creative."

"Alright then. Get going," said Moon as she stood up from the table and walked back into the Great Room.

MOON'S BOMBARDIER
CHALLENGER 650
37,000 feet headed to Washington DC

STEN WALKED DOWN THE AISLE TO THE FOLD-OUT TABLE AND SAT OPPOSITE BLUE.

"That didn't take long," Sten said handing the picture to Blue.

"So, this is the hotshot who protects Gatling," said Blue. "He doesn't look like that big a deal."

"Who knows? If he's guarding Gatling, he must have some background. It doesn't make any difference. If Moon wants him dead, he's dead," said Sten.

"Which brings up the question of how we kill him," said Blue. "She said to make it look like an accident."

"Bullshit," replied Sten. "She also said to make him disappear. I don't want to screw around with this. We grab him, kill him, and dump him."

"Dump him where?" asked Blue.

"Hell, we have the plane. We take off, head out to the Atlantic, slow the plane down, descend to 1,000 feet, dump him and turn around and head back to Colorado."

"I wonder what Moon's up to with all those Chinese?" asked Blue. "I don't like all those guys around there. It makes it harder to guard her."

"Beats me," said Sten. "That's above our pay grade. What I don't like is having Tensale around. I don't trust him. If it was up to me, I'd get rid of him along with White."

"How do we want to take White out?" asked Blue.

"We can catch up with him at this restaurant he supposedly hangs out at," replied Sten. "This was faxed along with the picture of him," handing a piece of paper to Blue. We can follow him from there, grab him and force him into the car. I've got the silenced 22. I'll take him out as soon as he's in the car and we'll head to the airport. They don't check anything at General Aviation where the plane is. We can load him and take off. Piece of cake from there."

"Sounds like a plan. "Good idea. That's why Moon pays you the big bucks."

"Stick with me and she might promote you," replied Sten.

ANKYER PALACE
Qatar

ANKYER CALLED FOR CLAUDE THE BUTLER AND ASKED THAT HE AND HONEY PI be taken to the library. Once there, Ankyer instructed Claude that they should not be disturbed. Claude walked out of the library closing the double doors behind him.

Ankyer walked over to a table, noting, "There seems to be iced tea everywhere we go in the palace," said Ankyer. He filled two glasses and brought them over to where Honey Pi had seated herself. He set the glasses on the table and sat across from her.

"They know you like iced tea and there is a standing order for it to be present in every room you enter," "The Emir pays great attention to detail. It's going to take some getting used to. By the way, you must have said something about the floor in the Emir's palace. He's having us relocated to the guest building while they replace the teak floor in this building with the same white, Lux Touch marble he has."

"You're kidding," said Ankyer.

"I don't kid about marble. You must be careful what you say around him. After all, he's grooming you to be the next Emir."

"I'm going to have to have a talk about that with him," said Ankyer.

"Talk away, but don't screw up my sheikha deal," replied Honey Pi as she leaned over and squeezed Ankyer's arm.

"Ok. On to important things," said Ankyer. "I think Dr. Finkel has a real problem here. If this crazy plan is real, it will be almost impossible to stop. All they have to do is hit 'return' on a computer keyboard and hundreds of congress people and innocent bystanders are dead and the country is in chaos."

"Better start thinking millions of people," replied Honey Pi. "I'm not sure even SLUG is crazy enough to do that. But Tensale might be."

"Tensale?" asked Ankyer.

"Tensale seems to be at the center of all of this. For sure, SLUG is not smart enough to pull this off. But all the technical linkages with the Chinese, the coded list, the Boopsie situation, the link with Moon... all of it... could have been coordinated by Tensale from his Chief of Staff position. Its circumstantial at this point but connecting all the dots it's certainly possible."

"But what's in it for him?" asked Ankyer.

"Power, revenge. He may be as nuts as SLUG. But he needs SLUG to step in when this all happens to control the country."

"Maybe," said Ankyer. "But what if SLUG turns on him?"

"He may," replied Honey Pi. "He has turned on a lot of people in the past. But I'd bet Tensale would eliminate SLUG in a heartbeat if he even thought SLUG was turning on him. Getting rid of SLUG may even be part of the plan."

"Ok. I'm with you. But how do we stop it?" said Ankyer.

"Well, we managed to stop the Saddam Hussein madness," replied Honey Pi.

"Yes, we did. But that was different," said Ankyer.

"How so?" asked Honey Pi.

"While it's true Hussein's plan involved numerous locations, this plan may involve hundreds or thousands of locations across the country. Even millions if you include anyone with a personal computer or a smart phone. I don't think SLUG would do it because he's a politician and needs a country to control. Tensale on the other hand...We don't know what the hell is driving him. Even worse, if some 'ransomware' organization were to get hold of IP addresses, the sound weapon software, and the Quantum computers, they could demand billions of dollars. They might even kill a few hundred thousand people as a demonstration."

"I could see possibly getting the software and the computers, but the IP addresses? That's a stretch."

"That would be the easy part," said Ankyer. They could hack into Apple, Microsoft, credit bureaus, or virtually any commercial organization that has an online customer data base. Think Amazon. Billions of IP addresses. Keep in mind what Brother Arlot said earlier. It would be cataclysmic. A disaster."

"When you put it that way you're scaring the hell out of me," said Honey Pi. "On the other hand, the actual sound would have to be transmitted from some source to computers, etc. So, if we could identify the transmission source, we could prevent the sound transmission."

"Good point," said Ankyer. "So, we're back to identifying the location of the communication. And if it's a Quantum computer as Dr. Lee suggests, it is unlikely there would be many of them."

"Correct," said Honey Pi.

At that moment Ankyer's and Honey Pi's mastoid implants fired off.

"Jake, Honey Pi...are you by yourselves?" asked Dr. Finkel.

"Yes, we are Dr. Finkel," said Ankyer.

"Good," said Finkel. *"I've just heard from Brother Arlot who spoke with his contact at the N.S.A. They have detected an exceptionally high energy communications signal. Wait, I have another a signal from George Makin."*

LUBA'S
CONGRESSIONAL CAFÉ
Washington DC

A YOUNG PRETEEN WALKED INTO LUBA'S AND HEADED down the aisle towards George Makin. He stopped at Makin's table and said: "Hi George. Picking up your hummus?"

"Hi Tim. You're right on time as usual."

"You sure eat a lot of hummus George. You must really like it."

"I hate the stuff, Tim. I pick it up for a friend of mine from work who can't get out of the office."

"I know what you mean," replied Tim. "I get it for my dad who also can't get away from work."

"By the way, how did you do on your math test last week?" asked Makin.

"I got an A+," said Tim. "My teacher said they were thinking of promoting me to an advanced math class if it is ok with my parents. What do you think George?"

"Go for it, Tim. Math is a hard subject. If you're good at it, it may help you get a good job when you finish your studies."

"That's what my mom said, too."

"Great minds think alike," replied Tim. "I'd better get going. Dad likes hummus for a snack when he gets home from work. By the way, when I got here, I noticed two big guys up by the front door who had what looked like a picture of you on their table and one of them said 'There he is.' as I walked by. Are they friends of yours?" Makin glanced around Tim's shoulder at Sten and Blue.

"Listen carefully, Tim. They are not friends of mine and, in fact, could be bad people. Take my package of hummus, my treat, and walk slowly out of the store and don't look at them when you go out."

"Is something wrong? Can I help?" asked Tim.

"You have been a big help already. Now leave the store. I'll see you next week. Good news about your math test."

Tim turned and did as Makin instructed.

Makin activated his mastoid implant and briefed Finkel as to the situation.

"Are they still there George?"

"Yes. I think they are waiting for me to leave. They will probably either intercept me or follow me."

"Ok. As it happens Neil and Chef Bell are at the Constable Club which is close by. Are you with us gentlemen?"

"We are in the SUV and on the way," said Groton entering the conversation. "ETA roughly five minutes. Can you hang out there that long, George?"

"No problem," replied Makin as he waived the waitress over and asked for an iced tea.

"I'll let you know when we arrive," said Groton.

"If it comes to it, try not to kill them both," said Finkel. "This situation is unanticipated, and we need to keep at least one alive to get clarification."

"*Roger that Dr. Finkel,*" replied Bell.

Groton's and Bell's SUV pulled up just past the door to Luba's Congressional Café five minutes later.

"*We're here George. Walk out and turn left. Walk about six yards past the SUV and keep going. Chief Bell and I will intercept your friends.*"

"*Will do,*" replied Makin getting up from his table, walking past Sten and Blue while exiting Luba's. Sten and Blue followed Makin out. As Makin walked past a black SUV, Groton and Bell stepped between Makin and Sten and Blue, stopping them.

"Hey, assholes. Get out of our way," said Blue.

"Not today, pardner," said Bell.

Blue reached into his sport coat, his hand emerging with a snub-nosed revolver. Bell seemed to magically obtain a black combat knife and inserted it through two of Blue's ribs and into his heart, pulling it out quickly to minimize bleeding. Blue's eyes opened wide, and he said: "Whaaaa" and fell into Bell's arms who directed his body into the back seat of the SUV. Sten reached into his sport coat, prompting Groton to deliver a Dim Mak finger strike to Sten's carotid sinus, which caused him to pass out. Groton pushed Sten into the SUV on top of Blue and slammed the door.

"He won't be out long, so we have to move," said Groton.

"No problem. I'll get in the back with him and put him back to sleep if he comes to," said Bell.

"*Dr. Finkel, we have the two subjects. One resisted and is deceased and the other is unconscious. We should be back at the Constable Club in five minutes.*"

"*Excellent. I alerted the staff there to be ready to interrogate the subject when you arrive. It shouldn't take too long to find out what's going on.*"

ANKYER PALACE
Qatar

ANKYER'S AND HONEY PI'S MASTOID IMPLANTS ACTIVATED.

"I apologize for abruptly signing off before. It seems that two assassins attempted to kidnap and kill George Makin," said Finkel. "Fortunately, Neil Groton and Chief Bell were in the area and neutralized the threat. DNA comparisons of the two individuals revealed that both are convicted felons. One, Horatio Blue, was incarcerated for eleven years for attempted murder during an armed robbery and the other, Arnold Sten, was convicted of armed mayhem, but the sentence was reduced to time served due to a legal technicality. Neil and Chief Bell intercepted them before they could attack George, so George is not implicated in the event and continues in his role of protecting SLUG. Blue did not survive the altercation, but Sten did and has been interrogated. Under chemical interrogation, Sten indicated both he and Blue were employees of the Alfernon Corporation which is solely owned by Anastasia Moon.

THE INSURRECTION PROTOCOL

As I mentioned earlier, Brother Arlot has informed me that his contact at the N.S.A. told him that they had just detected a very high energy transmission. It was extremely short, probably a test of some kind, but they were nevertheless able to pinpoint its location. Its source was within five miles of the Eagle River Ranch. The property covers thousands of square miles. It is so large that it has its own postal address. Eagle River Ranch is owned by the Alfernon Corporation and..."

"...Anastasia Moon," said Ankyer finishing Finkel's sentence.

"And she has the Quantum computers," interjected Honey Pi.

"We now know that is the case," said Finkel. *"Once N.S.A. located the communication module, they also isolated the IP addresses of two linked Quantum computers at the same location. One computer evidently has the sonic weapon software and the other the IP code algorithms. Brother Arlot's contact indicated that the N.S.A. would be installing a Quantum computer at the Abbey along with an exceptionally high-speed communications module."*

"Why at the Abbey?" asked Ankyer. *"We already have access to a Quantum computer at their location."*

"Plausible deniability," replied Finkel. *"They want us to hack into Moon's Quantum computers and steal the sound weapon software assuming it's there to steal along with the IP code algorithms. The NSA wants to be able to say they had nothing to do with it in case we are caught."*

"No surprise there," said Ankyer.

"There's more," said Finkel. *"Assuming we successfully acquire the sound weapon software and the IP code algorithms, N.S.A. wants us to disable both of Moon's Quantum computers and the communication's module."*

"Disable?" asked Ankyer.

"Destroy," said Finkel. *"It has to look like an accident. We have to keep the Chinese guessing in case they are thinking about trying something else."*

"Ok. Let me think about that," said Ankyer. "But let's go back to the hacking. How do we do that?"

"Ah, there we may have caught a break. Leonard the Mouse," replied Finkel. "Leonard has savant-level skill in computer hacking."

"Leonard the Mouse!" exclaimed Ankyer. "He lives on the edge of reality as well as in the basement of the Abbey."

"I will grant that Leonard is somewhat unusual. But he is also among the most skilled hackers in the United States."

"Did you mention the Quantum computers to Leonard?" asked Ankyer.

"I did," replied Finkel.

"He started drooling, didn't he?" asked Ankyer

"Well... yes he did," replied Finkel. "But I plan to have Dr. Lee monitor Leonard to keep him focused on the task."

"God," said Ankyer.

"Jake, given our time constraints, Leonard is the shortest distance between two points, Dr. Lee says he has never seen anyone with Leonard's level of skill. I'm not sure we could find someone with Leonard's capabilities in time."

"Ok. I'll buy into Leonard. But why not have him hack the computers, acquire the software, and then wipe it off the systems."

"We thought of that. Right after we captured the coordinates of the communications signal, Leonard hacked into the computer housing the sound weapon software and confirmed that the software is actually present at Moon's complex. Leonard informed us that the software is linked to a security kernel which will probably set off the weapon if the module is breached. However, Leonard also said that he thinks he can mimic the security kernel and swap it into the Quantum computer for the original security kernel without any initiation of the software. It doesn't eliminate the ability of the computer to activate the weapon, but it will leave a security module which would not activate the sonic weapon if Leonard managed to download it."

"What's Dr. Lee's take on this?" asked Ankyer

"Dr. Lee said he thinks it is theoretically possible," said Finkel. "He also said that the act of swapping our security kernel for the real one could set the real one off. We won't know until we try it. The trick will be to switch the security kernels and disable the Quantum computers as fast as possible before they have time to transmit the sound weapon to the IP addresses."

"So, we have to assume the Quantum computers will be destroyed as soon as the security kernels are swapped and the weapon software in downloaded," repeated Ankyer.

"That's exactly what Dr. Lee said," replied Finkel.

"So, you want me to come up with a way, using your word, to 'disable' Moon's Quantum computers at the same time they are activated by Leonard downloading the sonic weapon software."

"That's pretty much it," replied Finkel.

"Time frame?" asked Ankyer.

"Well, it looks like they tested the communications part of the plan. They must be getting close. If we assume SLUG is somehow involved, he may be able to give us a clue. I've asked George Makin in his persona as Winston White to see if he can find anything out from SLUG."

"Do you think SLUG was in on the attempt on George?" asked Ankyer.

"Probably not," replied Finkel. "SLUG sees Winston White as his protector. This sounds more like Tensale and Moon trying to cover their bases."

"Ok. Let me think about all this and I'll get back to you," said Ankyer.

"Thanks Jake," replied Finkel.

"What's your take on all of this?" asked Ankyer turning to Honey Pi.

RESIDENCE OF ANASTASIA MOON

Eagle River Ranch
Eagle River Ranch Colorado
"Burner" Phone Call

TENSALE: "ANASTASIA, ITS TENSALE."

Moon: "I know who it is. Who else has this burner phone number? What do you want now?"

Tensale: "I was at the White House today and I saw Winston White come out of the Oval Office."

Moon: "Wait. Mr. Bent is here." Mr. Bent said that Mr. Sten missed his last two check-ins. He just tried him again now and no response. Sten and Blue are MIA."

Tensale: "I'm assuming they are missing in action permanently. We can't have White interacting with Gatling at this point. My guess is that with Sten and Blue missing, White is a larger threat than I first thought."

Moon: "Ok. I'll send Mr. Bent. I probably should have sent him first. He is very skilled at handling these kinds of matters. It might be useful for Mr. Bent to have a talk with White and see what, if anything, is going on. I hope no one is keeping track of White. There won't be many pieces left. Mr. Bent enjoys his work."

Tensale: "We have just under two weeks now. It would be helpful if Mr. Bent moves right along."

Moon: "I'll have the plane come back and pick him up today. Fax another picture of White to the plane."

Tensale: "Mr. Bent must really be something."

Moon: "Believe me. Of all the people on this planet, Mr. Bent is the last person you would want to come after you."

ANKYER PALACE
Qatar

"WELL, WITH THE WORLD POTENTIALLY AT RISK, Dr. Finkel isn't asking much of you. You certainly don't get involved in small missions do you," said Honey Pi.

"Turns out that the Abbey's little science experiment on me makes me a real-time strategic thinker when it comes to combat-related things. Dr. Finkel asks my opinion periodically, which is fine with me, since I usually wind up in the thick of things."

"I noticed," said Honey Pi.

"But this one is a puzzler. If the computers are sitting in Moon's rumpus room, how do you destroy them and make it look like an accident. I thought about trying to sneak Dr. Lee in there so he could deactivate them, but they would spot him in an instant," said Ankyer.

"I have a couple thoughts," said Honey Pi. "Someone said earlier that Moon's Eagle River Ranch complex sat in the mountains in the middle of several thousand acres."

"Right. Tens of thousands," replied Ankyer.

"Ok. What's the likelihood of Colorado Gas running a gas line through those mountains and up to Moon's enclave?"

"Zero," replied Ankyer.

"Alright, so what's Moon using to power her toaster?" asked Honey Pi.

"A generator connected to......" said Ankyer.

"What?" finished Honey Pi.

Ankyer activated his mastoid complex. *"Dr. Finkel, Honey Pi and I have a question for you. How does Moon power her Eagle River Ranch?"*

"We have construction blueprints. Let me check and get back to you."

"Thanks Dr. Finkel."

"By the way, while we're waiting for Dr. Finkel to get back to us, I have news for you," said Honey Pi.

"Which is?" asked Ankyer

"The Emir told me he had a surprise for you. Something to do with cars but he wanted to tell you himself."

"This is getting out of hand," said Ankyer.

"It certainly is," replied Honey Pi.

Just then......

"I'm back," said Finkel. *Miss Moon gets her power supply from LPG gas. There are four 30,000-gallon LPG tanks buried around the property."*

"How close to the building," asked Ankyer

"According to the blueprints, the gas lines run about 50 feet from the tanks to the building."

"Thanks Dr. Finkel. I'll get back to you."

"There's your solution," said Honey Pi. "Blow up the tanks. It would be a hell of an accident!"

"LPG tanks that big going up would melt the whole place," replied Ankyer. That's brilliant!"

"I'd better tell Dr. Finkel the plan. We don't want to unnecessarily worry him."

Ankyer activated his mastoid implant again.

"Dr. Finkel…Honey Pi and I may have a solution to our Quantum computer problem at Moon's ranch."

"Excellent," said Finkel. *"Let's hear it."*

"Actually, it was Honey Pi's idea," said Ankyer as he described the LPG strategy."

"Brilliant!" said Finkel. *"I knew you and Honey Pi would make an excellent team."*

"It seems to be working out," replied Ankyer.

"But how do you propose to ignite the LPG tanks?" asked Finkel.

"Well, I had a thought on that," said Ankyer explaining his idea.

"I like it," said Finkel. *"Except our F-18 is in our hangar getting a major annual overhaul. I don't think we have enough time to reassemble, and flight test it."*

"The Qatari's have one here. I'll talk to the Emir. I'll also need Carl. Can you get him here?"

"No problem," said Finkel. *"We'll fly him there with mechanics by late tomorrow. They will also bring the additional instrumentation and upgrades you mentioned. Carl wants to see your palace anyway. Everyone wants to see the palace for that matter. The 'word' has gotten out."*

"I hope he's not disappointed," replied Ankyer. *"They are moving me to a visitor's palace on my grounds,"* telling Finkel about the new Lux marble floor.

"This is getting out of hand," said Finkel.

"That's what I said to Honey Pi," said Ankyer.

WHITE HOUSE
Washington D.C.

GEORGE MAKIN, AKA WINSTON WHITE, SAT ACROSS from the President in the small dining room adjacent to the Oval Office.

"These are difficult times we are in, Winston," said the President.

"Indeed, they are Mr. President," replied White.

"Twelve days from now, at 12 Noon Eastern Time, September 15th to be exact, I will be on a secure Zoom call with all the Congressional leaders and selected other officials in my administration. The purpose of the call is to inform them that I will be declaring martial law across the entire country."

"Martial law, sir. Is that called for, Mr. President?"

"Ordinarily, I would not consider such a thing, but there are cross currents, Winston. Cross currents of treachery that even reach up to the Secret Service who are supposedly protecting me. There are enemies everywhere. I cannot risk exposing Americans to a lawless revolution of anarchists. Look at what happened to my Cabinet for God's sake. Poor Boopsie McNulty, whose husband donated millions to my campaign. Gone in an instant. The addition of my likeness to Mount Rushmore mocked by the far left. And let's not forget my nomination for the Nobel Peace Prize. Not even submitted! No, Winston, there are cross currents of evil directed towards me which cannot be allowed to stand! The reason I asked you here today is to make sure that you are on my team, loyal to me and to me alone. That's important, especially now. I have grave suspicions that agents of the Secret Service do not have my well-being as a top priority. Since you have been here, I have felt safer and want it kept that way especially with my martial law announcement."

"Mr. President, I had no idea. Insurrection! You can rest assured that I will be by your side during this tumult."

"Mallory Tensale will also be here on the 15th. He may no longer be my Chief of Staff, but he will be valuable should problems arise when martial law is invoked."

"This is certainly a dire situation, Mr. President. You can count on me."

Makin left the White House and took several cab rides, switching three times to elude anyone following him. Dr. Finkel believed there could possibly be another attempt on George's life, particularly since the first two men were connected to Anastasia Moon. Makin finally arrived at Bertha's Hamburger & Chili Emporium a block from the National Zoo. The hamburgers did not come close to the Wally Burger chili-cheese-bacon combination special, but then there was really no comparison. Honey Pi was in the habit of ordering them regularly at the Abbey. Chief Bell held the record, having consumed three double Wally-burgers at one sitting and lived, a testament to his constitution. Makin had concluded that Honey Pi's medical credentials should be re-evaluated.

"Dr. Finkel, George here," said Makin as he activated his mastoid implant.

"What do you have George?" asked Finkel.

"I left SLUG about twenty minutes ago. I used several different cabs to evade anyone following me. I agree with you that we can't be too careful. To that point, SLUG advised me that a secure Zoom meeting has been scheduled for 12:00 PM EST on September 15th. The entire Congressional Committee leadership will be online for the call. He also said that selected other officials will be involved but did not say who. I'm guessing Pentagon and Homeland Security senior staff. Maybe the Supreme Court Justices. But I don't know that to be a fact. I'm guessing that as soon as all the parties to the call are online, the sonic weapon will be deployed. He also said that he intended to implement martial law. He wants me to be there, and by extension the Red Protocol Group, to protect him should the Secret Service go after him. He said that Tensale would be there to assist him if complications arise from his announcement of martial law. Finally, SLUG said that evil was being directed at him ... his words not mine, based on him not being nominated for the Nobel Peace Prize and not having his likeness added to Mount Rushmore. He is clearly deranged, but we already knew that."

"You had quite a meeting," replied Finkel. *"September 15th gives us a little time but not much. Jake and Honey Pi have come up with a plan to take care of the Quantum computers at the Eagle River Ranch in Colorado. Now that we have a firm time and date, we can start working on that.*

Of equal concern is SLUG's mental condition. August Carter is of the opinion that should SLUG have a shock, such as the sonic weapon plan not working, he may very well have a psychotic break. Ordinarily that could be contained, but SLUG still has access to the President's emergency satchel or 'nuclear football', and could conceivably launch nuclear weapons at Russia, China or even U.S. cities. Dr. Carter does think the latter possibility is not out of the question and strongly suggests we develop a plan to mitigate that.

Tensale being with SLUG is also a concern. He is very capable of manipulating SLUG and that must be considered, particularly since we now believe Tensale is coordinating the sonic weapon event. He will have to be factored into any plan for SLUG."

"What can I do?" asked Makin.

"We will have to assess that at the Abbey. However, since you will be physically present with SLUG and Tensale, you will definitely be the point person in whatever plan we develop."

"Whatever I can do," replied Makin. "By the way, SLUG gave no indication that he was aware of my attempted abduction. So that leaves Tensale behind it."

"Excellent point, George," replied Finkel. "We will incorporate that consideration into our plan."

Having completed his conversation with Dr. Finkel, Makin finished what he considered to be a sub-par chili cheese bacon burger compared to a Wally burger and paid the cashier. He stepped into the street and hailed a cab. As the cab pulled away from Bertha's Hamburger & Chili Emporium, a non-descript, grey Chevrolet sedan pulled out from the curb and followed Makin's cab.

MR. BENT GOES TO WASHINGTON

Washington D.C.

HERMAN BENT WAS DISARMINGLY NON-DESCRIPT. Not of slight stature but also not overly muscular, Herman Bent was just another man in a crowd. Except he wasn't. He delighted as a child pulling wings off insects and burning ants with a magnifying glass. He graduated to vivisecting animals when he could catch them and had his first orgasm dismantling a living squirrel.

When he reached seventeen, he joined the Army with the express purpose of killing as many people as he could for the thrill of it. Sent to Iraq, he was attached to a reconnaissance unit where it was discovered that he a had a talent for getting captives to confess to just about anything. Bent had early on come to realize that rather than causing a subject to provide information to avoid pain and death, Bent's animating principle was to cause so much pain and mayhem to the subject's body that the subject would provide

Bent information so that Bent would kill the subject to stop it. Within six months he was promoted to sergeant and loaned out to other units who had recalcitrant captives. The problem was that after a visit from Sergeant Bent the captive was in no condition for further interrogation.

A special operations first sergeant advised his company commander that after Sergeant Bent physically dismembered a 70-year-old Iraqi insurgent, it was clear that Bent was in fact 'bent' and probably psychotic. The company commander's response was "great, let's send him to Afghanistan. A friend of mine is the CO of an intelligence unit there and they're having a hell of a time getting intel out of Taliban prisoners. Bent would fit right in."

And so, Sergeant Bent was transferred to the 3rd Intelligence Battalion in Afghanistan where his life's ambition as a serial killer/torturer was fulfilled. So much so in fact, that he was told he would be promoted to Sergeant First Class if he would re-up when his enlistment expired...which he did. In one instance, he was given a particularly difficult Taliban insurgent to interrogate. It was customary to record all interrogations and between the screaming and keening of the captive, intelligence officers were able to discern actionable intelligence. Afterwards, one intelligence officer told Bent that no one had been able to break the insurgent and Bent had in fact gotten great information. But suddenly Bent had stopped the interrogation. Why had Bent stopped the interrogation asked the officer. "Because the bastard ran out of blood," said Sergeant Bent.

By then the CIA operatives in Afghanistan had heard about Sergeant Bent and they pulled rank and had Sergeant Bent moved over to a CIA "Black Ops" information gathering program. After a year even the CIA realized that they had a monster on their hands, to the point where no one was willing to be alone in the same room with him. It was decided that Bent would be given a medical discharge for the "convenience of the Government". Herman Bent was 24 years old at the time. In consideration of Bent's singular contribution to the U.S. Army and the CIA, Bent's medical discharge had attached to it a substantial monthly stipend which gave him a reasonable livelihood and freedom of movement.

It was then rumored that Bent plied his unusual talents in Syria, Iran, South America, and several African countries. He left each location with a generous severance package with the understanding he would not return. Even mercenary groups became wary of bringing him in. Finally, his unique talents resulted in diminishing returns and work dried up...until Anastasia Moon.

One of Moon's "talent scouts" had brought Bent to her attention. She hired him through the Alfernon Corporation, not so much for protection, but rather as an implied threat to anyone who thought about doing anything that might displease her. Bent took the job, which was basically to hang around Moon, because it paid exceptionally well, and was the only employment he could find. Now, this Winston White person. Moon should have sent him out to eliminate White instead of dispatching Sten and Blue. They were not up to it. He was. The tingling in his groin was back. Let the good times roll!

Bent had no problem following White from the White House to Bertha's Hamburger & Chili Emporium. White's subterfuge of changing cabs several times was child's play. White's assumption that he had eluded any trackers the first time applied to his next trip made Bent's tail that much easier. Bent pulled over across the street from a large stone building called the Constable Club and watched White walk in. Nice place, Bent thought. Too bad White's stay there, and on planet Earth for that matter, would be shorter than White anticipated. It was 4:00 PM. With any luck White would leave the Constable Club and it would be game time.

Bent sat back in the non-descript Chevrolet, thought about his impending time with White, and got an erection. Meanwhile, George Makin, aka Winston White, was having a sherry in the Constable Club lounge accompanied by Brother William and Varna. Brother William was having a lemonade and Varna was munching on a protein biscuit.

"You know William, Varna seems to get bigger every time I see him. What's he weigh these days?"

"I'm guessing it's around 390 pounds give or take. Hard to know because I see him all the time except when he's with Jake or getting checked over by Honey Pi."

"Looks like all muscle to me," said Makin.

"It is," replied Brother William. "The only problem is that Chief Bell insists on teaching Varna tricks, like 'roll over', and 'sit up'. I've told him that Varna is trained as a war animal. If Jake runs into trouble out in the field the last thing he needs is having Varna rolling over. Varna absolutely loves Bell since the Chief is always giving Varna treats."

"Add in Honey Pi's belly rubs and Varna might decide to retire," said Makin. "Look, I have to run out to the pharmacy to pick up a prescription. You guys want to watch a movie when I get back?"

"Sure," replied Brother William.

"How about King Kong? Varna likes to snarl at the gorilla."

"You got it," said Makin standing up. "I'll meet you in the media room in twenty minutes."

———————————

Herman Bent was a strong proponent of patience. He was rewarded by the sight of Winston White exiting the front of the Constable Club. White turned left and walked down the street with a complete absence of other foot traffic. Bent pulled the car out and drove 20 yards past Makin. He then stopped the car, got out, and approached his target.

"Excuse me sir, this is my first time in Washington, and I seem to be lost."

"Be happy to help," replied Makin. "Where is it you are trying…" and felt a pin prick in his neck. The next thing Makin new, he was tied naked and spread-eagled on a double bed with absolutely no recollection how he got there. The other curiosity was that the only things he could move were his eyes and mouth.

"Ah, Mr. White. You're back with us. Let me introduce myself. My name is Herman Bent, and I work for Anastasia Moon. You may be wondering why I'm telling you this. Well, two hours from now you will be in small pieces, flushed into the Washington DC sanitary system, and as a courtesy I, think it only fair to tell you who I am and who sent me."

"How…Why?" responded White.

"Ah, 'how' is easy. A quick needle jab with a syringe of a narcotic that induces a physical state letting me guide you into my low-end rental car and from there into this flea bag motel. The 'why' is more complicated. Miss Moon sent two amateurs to take care of you, and for some reason they disappeared leaving you to continue guarding President Gatling, or whatever it is you are doing. Seems Anastasia and her friends see you as some kind of threat. Well, not for much longer."

Bent jabbed Makin in the shoulder with a syringe. "It will take about thirty minutes to return feeling to your body. I wouldn't want you to miss any of the fun. I have duct tape in my little toolbox which I will apply to your mouth so you can't scream. We don't want to disturb the neighbors. I bet you're wondering why I don't have any clothes on. Simple. This room will have blood spatter all over and it is much easier for me to shower rather than change clothes afterwards."

Bent walked over to a chair and sat down. "Well Mr. White, enjoy the tingling as feeling returns to your body. It will be the last tingling you will feel on this earth." Bent reached into a bag at his feet and removed a pair of handheld garden pruners. "You are probably wondering how I'm going to invoke all this mayhem on your body. Well, here it is, a professional hand pruner. Japanese steel, And very sharp. This instrument will take you apart in a flash. But I'm going to take my time. I could have just shot you in the head, but lucky for me, I'm given flexibility in my work," said Bent tittering.

Makin tried to activate his mastoid implant to communicate with Finkel but to no avail.

Meanwhile however, Brother William did activate his mastoid implant.

"Dr. Finkel, Brother William here."

"Yes, Brother William," replied Finkel.

"Dr. Finkel, we may have a problem. George Makin is staying here and left for a short errand and said he would return in twenty minutes. That was an hour ago. I'm concerned."

"Let me check his mastoid implant," said Finkel. After a moment, "It's not operating. This is highly unusual. We may be looking at a second attempt to kidnap and possibly kill George. Finding him may be a problem."

"I've got an idea," said Brother William. A short time later, Brother William re activated his mastoid implant. "I'm in George's room with Varna, here at the Club. Varna has been sniffing George's *clothing. As you know, Varna's sense of smell is very acute and can pick up a scent for miles."*

"*Chief Bell, we have a problem,*" said Finkel explaining the situation.

"*Brother William, I'll be in front of the Constable Club in ten minutes,*" said Bell. "*Meet you and Varna out in front.*"

Ten minutes later Brother William and Varna piled into the back of a large black SUV.

"I brought additional items of George's clothing to reinforce the scent for Varna. I hope we are not too late."

"We'll do our best," replied Bell

"He said he was walking to the pharmacy down the street. Let's go in that direction and see if Varna starts reacting," said Brother William.

Herman Bent was excited. Looking at the bedside clock he said: "Well Winston, looks like time's about up. Let's see if your body is back with us." Bent walked over to Makin and ran the handle of the Japanese pruner along the bottom of Makin's foot eliciting a strong neurological flexion response. "Wow. You ARE back with us. I think I will start with your toes and work my way up. Oops I forgot. Let's get that mouth covered. Don't want any screaming, do we? By the way, if you, no... when you pass out, I have another drug that will bring you back. Better dying through chemistry."

Bent removed a roll of grey duct tape from his bag and tore off a piece. "In case you're wondering, I've done this before." Bent climbed on top of Makin's chest. As he leaned over to apply the duct tape, the door exploded inward followed by a huge snarling head. Varna swiveled his head surveying the room, then focusing on the bed. Varna leapt hitting Bent and knocking him off Makin. Bent held his arms in front of him yelling 'NO! Please!' as Varna sunk his fangs into Bent's chest crushing his sternum and three ribs while at the same time pulverizing Bent's heart, and then continuing to tear Bent apart.

"Varna!" exclaimed Bell as Varna turned his head, his jaws dripping gore. "Here!" Varna sat up and looked at Bell; the blood lust shutting down instantly.

Brother William entered the room, untied Makin who appeared stunned saying, "I have to get a new line of work."

"*Dr. Finkel, we arrived just as some maniac was about to start taking George apart. You wouldn't believe what was going on here.*"

"*Is this person still alive?*" asked Finkel.

"*Unfortunately, Varna got to him first,*" replied Brother William.

"*Too bad. It would be nice to know who sent this person,*" said Finkel.

"*We do know,*" chimed in Makin, his mastoid implant functioning again. "*This guy said his name was Herman Bent and that he was sent by Anastasia Moon. He told me that out of a sense of fairness if you can believe it; figuring I wouldn't survive to tell anyone else.*"

"*I've heard of Herman Bent,*" said Bell. "*When I was deployed with the SEALs in South America, the CIA brought an interrogator in to question a drug lord. Bent had quite a reputation.*"

"*Not anymore,*" said Makin as Varna rubbed against him still dripping pieces of Bent.

"*Ok. That eliminates any possible question about Ms. Moon. You should leave now, and I will have the remains of Mr. Bent disposed of,*" said Finkel. *George are you still able to function at the White House?*"

"*Definitely,*" replied Makin. "*I want to see this through now more than ever.*"

"Good. A medical team will be on hand when you return to the Constable Club. You're going to get a thorough medical and psychological evaluation," said Finkel."

"Ok but..."

"No 'buts'," George.

"I was going to say "Ok. But could someone find me a pair of pants?"

EAGLE RIVER RANCH
Eagle River Ranch Colorado

ANASTASIA MOON'S PRIVATE SMART PHONE BUZZED IN HER POCKET. She looked at the incoming number which was from her contact in the District of Columbia Metropolitan Police Department. Strange. There was no reason she could think of why her contact should be calling her on her private number.

"Yes," Moon answered.

"Ms. Moon. You know who this is?"

"I do," replied Moon.

"A situation has occurred that I wanted to give you a heads-up on. I assume our usual arrangement is in effect?" referring to the retainer Moon paid her contact for information.

"Yes, of course. What's happened?" asked Moon.

"Last night one of our patrol officers on second shift was driving by a cheap motel in the seamier part of the city when he noticed an unmarked ambulance pulling in front of a unit at the end of the building. The officer entered the parking lot to provide assistance, as well as to investigate any other issues since the motel had a history of drug ODs etc.," said the contact pausing.

"Go on," said Moon starting to get tense.

"The officer followed three attendants into the motel room and immediately observed blood spatters all over the place. Walls, ceiling, everywhere. The officer also observed pieces of a naked body thrown about the room. Upon closer inspection he observed that the body's chest had been ripped apart. The heart, entrails, several ribs, an arm and a leg were lying several feet away."

"I appreciate the information, but why the gory details?"

"To give you context. Before becoming a police officer, our guy was an Army medical corpsman which enabled him to rapidly assess injuries. He is convinced that a wild animal of some kind inflicted the damage he observed. The officer told the ambulance attendants to stand outside while he surveyed the room. The officer noticed a pair of pants in a corner of the room. He pulled a thin wallet out from the back pants pocket and identified the individual."

"Who was it?" asked Moon.

"The driver's license said, 'Herman Bent'. I would have called you for that reason alone since I recalled a person named Bent was on your security detail. But there is something else."

"Which is?" asked Moon, now in shock.

"When the officer was about to call the incident in, one of the so-called ambulance attendants walked up to him and handed him a smart phone. The officer was informed that the ambulance people were from Homeland Security, that his presence was a breach of national security, and that he was to leave the premises immediately. The officer declined to leave. The voice on the phone was replaced by our Chief, who also ordered the officer to leave immediately.

Since I'm the Watch Commander, the officer's Sergeant brought this to my attention. I mentioned it to the Chief, who informed me that the events I've just described to you never happened. End of story.

To satisfy my own curiosity, I went to the motel the following day and had the desk clerk let me into the room in question. It was in pristine condition. Literally spotless. Not the normal cleaning of a motel maid. I asked the clerk if anything happened the evening before and he said that the night clerk reported nothing unusual. Now I don't know what this Bent fellow was up to, or if he was in Washington on business for you, but if he was there on your busines, you may have a hell of a problem on your hands. The Sergeant mentioned that the officer was shaken by what he saw. The Sergeant also said that the officer indicated that there were pieces of duct tape lying on the floor in the vicinity of the bed which led him to believe that there was another person in the room at some point, possibly secured to the bed. It's not rocket science or a leap of faith to infer from the crime scene that Bent may have had another person immobilized on the bed. Why Bent was naked is, of course, another point of interest. Had the crime scene remained intact we may have been able to pull DNA off the duct tape. But that's not possible since the duct tape disappeared along with all the other evidence. That's it."

"I can tell you that I have absolutely no idea why Mr. Bent was there or what he was doing," said Moon.

"I understand," the contact said. "As far as my department is concerned that matter is closed. When my Chief says, 'something never happened' then it never happened."

"Thank you for your call," said Moon and disconnected.

Moon retrieved the 'burner' phone from a side table drawer and called Tensale. Tensale picked up immediately.

"Yes," Tensale said.

"Now listen very carefully. I want all these fucking Chinese techies and their fucking equipment out of my fucking house by the end of the fucking day. I am done with this bullshit and your plan to take over the World."

"Hold on," replied Tensale. "What's happened?"

"I sent Mr. Bent to Washington DC to take care of Winston White as I said I would. I've just found out that Bent is dead. And not just dead, but ripped apart by some fucking wild animal in a goddamn sleazy motel room."

"I'll look into it," replied Tensale.

"No, you won't," said Moon. "The motel room was apparently sanitized and that as far as the cops are concerned, nothing ever happened. I send three highly skilled people to get rid of some security guy and they all either disappear or wind up eaten by some goddamn wild animal. There's something going on here and its way above your pay grade. And I don't want anything more to do with it. I'm out! Are you listening?"

"Ok. Now you listen," said Tensale. "First, the people at your location are not just Chinese techies but highly trained computer science people. What's more, they are not all computer scientists. Some are Chinese security agents and are there to protect China's property and, importantly, to make sure nothing stops the plan from being implemented...including you."

"Are you threatening me, Tensale?"

"Not at all. If they even think you might screw this up, they will kill you. That's not a threat. It's a certainty. But look. We are only a few days from the plan being implemented. And it's going to work. I will be with Gatling when he makes the Zoom call on the 15th. By 12 Noon Eastern time or shortly thereafter, every single person on that Zoom call will be dead. Period. And you will be Gatling's Vice President. And if something should happen to Gatling, you become the first woman president in the history of this country. Wouldn't you want that instead of being dead?"

"Fuck... Ok but this thing doesn't kill everyone right away?"

"Not instantly. Within five minutes or so. It takes a few minutes of concentrated sound to overwhelm a person's auditory system. But by the time someone realizes what's happening it's all over. Now as far as Winston White is concerned, it may be that I underestimated him and this Red Protocol Group he works for. Gatling did say that they were an anti-terrorism organization, but frankly all I was interested in then was to give Gatling a sense of wellbeing to calm down his paranoia. Look, you sent three guys after White. Two are missing and one is dead. It could be a coincidence. Although I'm guessing it isn't. The two missing guys...who knows? They may have just decided to stop working for you and bailed. The dead guy is weird. But I don't give a damn if it was a werewolf or a zombie that got him. He's out of the picture. As for White, he will be glued to Gatling on the 15th. After that, Gatling will probably feel more secure and get rid of White. Send him back to the Red Protocol Group. Hell, I'll be there with Gatling on the 15th anyway. What's White going to do? I'll tell you what. Nothing. And he doesn't know anything anyway. He's only there because Gatling is paranoid and thinks White can protect him from some kind of fantasy coup."

"What do you know about the Red Protocol Group?" asked Moon.

"Not much is known about them," said Tensale. "They are run by some old scientist and were somehow involved with an alleged commando operation concerning Saddam Hussein.

There is a rumor that Gatling's predecessor left a note concerning them and told Gatling to destroy the note after he read it, which Gatling did as far as I know. I've seen White several times and believe me, he is no commando. He looks more like a law professor. Anyway, what can he do? Our operation is too sophisticated and far along to stop."

"Alright. I'm still in but the second the operation is complete I want all these Chinese types and their computer junk out of here."

"Not a problem," replied Tensale.

"One more thing," said Moon. When we were looking for information on White, we ran into another guy named Ankyer. He's also involved with this Red Protocol Group."

"I'm aware of him although I didn't mention Ankyer because he's irrelevant. It looks like he may be a kind of monk in an Abbey out west. As far as we know he's an economist and hangs out with a dog named 'Varnish'. Even if he was a threat, what's he going to do from a monastery? Have his dog bite us?"

"Alright. Let me know if anything else weird happens."

"Will do," replied Tensale and disconnected.

ANKYER PALACE
Qatar

THERE WAS A KNOCK ON THE LIBRARY DOOR.

"Come in," said Ankyer

Claude the Butler walked in. "The Emir is here and would like to see you if you're not busy," he said.

"I'm never too busy to see the Emir," replied Ankyer.

"Jake! I hope you and Dr. Pi are comfortable in your residence," said the Emir as he walked in the room.

"'Comfortable' is an understatement your Excellency. I was going to ask to see you if you have time," said Ankyer.

"Of course," said the Emir. "But first I have a little surprise for you. Follow me."

Ankyer and Honey Pi followed the Emir through the Palace's maze of hallways into the car display garage. An attendant bowed towards the Emir and pushed a button which opened double doors.

"Jake, your course record with the 918 Porsche at the Nurburgring Ring in Germany was incredible. And the flaming tires at the end. What a finish! We have the Porsche permanently on display in the Great Hall in my palace museum, including the burnt-up tires. It's now the most popular exhibit!"

"I'm glad things worked out the way they did," replied Ankyer.

"I wanted to give you a remembrance of your magnificent accomplishment. As I mentioned, the original car is now on display, so I had an identical Porsche 918 Spyder brought here for you as a gift, with new tires of course!" said the Emir as he chuckled.

Two spotlights illuminated a black, gleaming 918 Porsche Spyder, causing Honey Pi's jaw to drop."

"It's beautiful your Highness," said Ankyer. "A magnificent example. Thank you!"

"As a new sheikh in our family, you bring us great honor with your feats. You deserve to be rewarded. But there's more!" said the Emir laughing. More ceiling spotlights went on. A Pagani Zonda HP Barchetta appeared, followed by a McLaren P1. A Ferrari SF90 Stradale. A Bugatti La Voiture Noire. And a Rolls-Royce Boat Tail.

"My favorite is the Pagani," said the Emir. "Supposedly only two Pagani Barchettas were built. There was a third which you see here. I imposed upon Mr. Pagani and after seeing the video of your performance at Nurburgring he agreed to make the third Barchetta available to, in his words, 'the greatest race car driver in the World'. The display garage accommodates 50 cars. Someone with your skills deserves to have a first-class car collection so I am starting you off with these. As you add to the collection, have the bills sent to me."

"This is overwhelming," said Ankyer.

They walked around the cars noting how remarkable each car was. The Emir beamed with satisfaction. Ankyer said: "I don't want to take advantage of your generosity your Highness, but I do have a favor to ask."

"Of course," said the Emir. "What is it?"

"Can I borrow your F-18 Super Hornet?"

"My Super Hornet? Really? We just got it delivered. None of our pilots are even trained on it yet. I don't suppose you…?"

"I'd be happy to train your pilots," said Ankyer.

The Emir pulled a smart phone out of his pocket.

"General Muhammid, Sheikh Ankyer would like to borrow our F-18 fighter. Would you please meet us at the entrance of his palace in say, the next 15 minutes? Excellent. We'll see you then."

"We're all set," said the Emir. This is exciting!"

"Believe me your Highness, 'exciting' is Jake's middle name," said Honey Pi.

A short time later Qatari General Ali bin Muhammid joined the Emir, Ankyer and Honey Pi on a private, first floor veranda at Ankyer's palace.

"I understand you would like to borrow our F-18 Super Hornet," said Muhammid.

"Yes General. That is correct."

"You would be flying it yourself I presume?"

"I would fly it along with my usual copilot who is on his way here as we speak. He should arrive tomorrow morning."

"You would use it for a training flight perhaps?" said the General.

"No. It would be for a mission. The F-18 I usually fly is dismantled for annual maintenance and cannot be made ready in time."

"Where would you fly it? Somewhere in Qatar?" asked the General.

"I would be flying it across the Atlantic to the United States," replied Ankyer.

"Across the Atlantic!" exclaimed the General. "There is not enough fuel. It cannot be done."

"The reason I am asking to use your aircraft is that the F-18 Super Hornet has standard outsized fuel tanks."

"Even so, the distance is too great," replied the General looking at the Emir.

"Ordinarily I would agree with you. However, my copilot is bringing conformal fuel tanks, or CFTs, that are attached semi-permanently to the Hornet and extend its range considerably. The CFTs are attached to the fuselage on both sides of the engine air intakes. After the mission, the F-18 Hornet will be returned to Qatar with the CFTs installed for your use."

"Most generous Sheikh Jake, but even with auxiliary fuel tanks you would still run out of fuel," said the General.

"That's where the aircraft carrier comes in," said Ankyer.

"The aircraft carrier!" repeated General Muhammid.

"I will be refueling the Hornet on a U.S. aircraft carrier," said Ankyer. "To facilitate a carrier landing, my copilot will be bringing mechanics with him to install a tailhook on the Hornet as well as additional instrumentation, as I will be flying at night."

"This is incredible," said Muhammid turning to the Emir. "Even someone as skilled as Sheikh Ankyer would be hard pressed to succeed on this adventure! Still, even with a carrier landing to refuel, if you encounter headwinds over the Atlantic, which you most assuredly will, your fuel capacity may still not be enough."

"One additional thing in our favor is that the Super Hornet carries 33% more internal fuel, increasing mission range by 41% and endurance by 50% over the original "Legacy" Hornet. And I will have an additional advantage once I get close to the United States. The U.S. Airforce has recently deployed what's called a MQ-25 Stingray jet refueling drone, which carries 15,000 pounds of fuel. I will intercept the MQ-25 just before I enter the East coast of the U.S., and execute an airborne refueling. That should get me halfway to my destination at which point I will link up with a second MQ-25 drone and another refueling will take place. That will get me to my destination with fuel to spare."

"How could we not do this!" exclaimed the Emir. This is amazing. Surely an adventure to go in the history books brought about by a Qatari sheikh no less!"

"And our F-18 is returned how?" asked the General.

"By conventional military transport," replied Ankyer. "I wouldn't want to push my luck," replied Ankyer. "Oh, and one more thing. My copilot and the mechanics will be installing two AGM-84H/K SLAM-ER Standoff Land Attack Harpoon Missiles."

"Ah. Now you have my attention!" said the General. Our friends in Saudi Arabia and the United Arab Emirates already have such weapons."

"We will likely use the weapons on the mission, but will replace them for your use afterwards," said Ankyer.

"We would be honored to have the weapons in our arsenal," said General Muhammid. When do your friends arrive?"

"They are already on their way and should be here sometime tomorrow."

"See Ali, I told you Jake would be an excellent addition to our sheikh family," said the Emir.

"You are wise as always your Highness," replied the General. "What then are you planning to do with our F-18 Jake," asked the General.

"I can't be specific," said Ankyer. "But what I can tell you is that it has to do with the codes you supplied, and that it is a matter of United States national security."

"Excellent," said the Emir. "Anything my country can do to support our friends in the United States we will do."

"Thank you, your Highness," replied Ankyer.

As they walked back into Jake's Palace, the Emir said: "Jake, I would like to speak privately with you and Dr. Honey Pi for a few minutes."

"Of course," said Ankyer. "Lead the way."

The Emir escorted Ankyer and Honey Pi to a reception room on a side of the entrance hall and closed the door. They sat down in soft leather chairs.

"I'll come right to the point," said the Emir. "I've been diagnosed with Stage II prostate cancer. A British oncologist was flown in and did a biopsy. I was told that there was a chance I could die from it. Amid, my minister, has counseled me that I should plan for succession to the throne if the worst happens, or if I become incapacitated."

"Excuse me your Highness," said Honey Pi. "If I may ask, how long ago were you advised of your condition."

"Two months ago."

"And how old are you?"

"Fifty-seven."

"Did the doctor indicate the type of stage II cancer, and if so A or B?

"A."

"Ok. May I make a few observations?" asked Honey Pi.

"Please do Doctor," said the Emir.

"First, assuming the British doctor's diagnosis is correct, your cancer has been caught at an early stage. Phase II A cancer involves only one part of your prostate and generally grows very slowly. Second, your cancer is very treatable by either surgery, radiation, or both."

"I will not die?"

"No, you will not. At least not from this. And the Red Protocol Group has an advanced medical facility at the Abbey as well as access to the finest cancer specialists in the United States. I would have to check with Dr. Finkel, but I see no reason why you could not fly to our facility at the Abbey, be treated, and be back here within a week. You would, of course, have to go back periodically for monitoring, or our physicians could coordinate with your doctors here, which ever you desire."

"Could you handle my care?" asked the Emir.

"I'm not a cancer specialist but could certainly coordinate with my colleagues back at the Abbey as necessary. I'd be happy to help," replied Honey Pi.

Turning to Jake, the Emir said: "I thought I was a dead man. I was going to propose adopting you so you could be named Emir. The Crown Prince has no interest, and my grandson is too young. But now..."

"Your Highness, you will probably out last me," said Ankyer. "However, I would be happy to provide any counsel you may request, as long as it does not conflict with my responsibilities at the Red Protocol Group or with the United States."

"You'll have no conflict with us, I can assure you. And your counsel will be most gratifying," said the Emir as he stood up. "I feel better already!" he said. "Dr. Pi, I would appreciate it if you would speak with Dr. Finkel so I can make plans for my trip to the Abbey!"

"I'll speak with him right away," said Honey Pi.

With that, the Emir shook their hands and left the room. Honey Pi said: "You almost became an Emir."

"Not even close," said Ankyer. "I'd have to give up my U.S. citizenship and that I couldn't do."

"I didn't think so," said Honey Pi. She then said "Clyde."

"Yes Dr. Pi" as Clyde walked in.

"We're ready for dinner Clyde."

"Would you be dining in the grand dining room or a smaller dining venue. There are several."

"Well, I..." started Ankyer.

"The veranda outside the master bedroom would be perfect," interrupted Honey Pi.

"Dinner will be served on the master bedroom veranda in twenty minutes, with an appropriate wine pairing," said Clyde walking out.

After dinner, Ankyer said: "I have to get an early start in the morning. Carl is showing up tomorrow morning with the mechanics to check out the Qatari F-18.

Want to come?"

"Nope. Remember the Emir said he wanted to go shopping. He's picking me up at 10:00 AM. While you're playing with your airplane, I'll be with my new best friend spending down part of the Qatar fortune."

SECRET MILITARY AIR BASE
Qatar

COLONEL CARL FRANKLIN HOPPED OUT OF A MILITARY JEEP just as Ankyer walked through the door of a camouflaged building next to a large airplane hangar.

"Carl!" Ankyer exclaimed. "Glad you could make it to the party!"

"Are you kidding? Word is you're a big-time sheikh living in a palace with your consort Honey Pi. Kind of an 'Ankyer of Arabia' deal! I can't wait to see your digs. How's Honey Pi holding up?"

"It's more like 'How's the Emir of Qatar holding up?' He's taking her on a shopping expedition today. The Qatar GDP is in for a major hit! Where's the equipment and the team?"

"They are unloading the Harpoon missiles from the plane. It was a tight fit, but we managed. Dr. Finkel must be really connected to score two Harpoons on such notice, or actually any notice."

"You have no idea," said Ankyer. "I'm constantly in awe of what he manages to pull off."

"Speaking of pulling things off, I understand Honey Pi has a pipeline into Wally burgers."

"She does. I've put on three pounds since we've been here. Chief Bell wants to go into business with her and open up a franchise operation."

"Sounds like a plan," replied Carl.

"Not a very good one," said Ankyer. The Chief would eat all the inventory."

"Let's check out the plane. Our usual ride is in pieces at the Abbey," said Carl.

"No problem," said Ankyer. "The mechanics will have it back together in no time."

"Not likely. All the mechanics are here," said Carl as a large man in fatigues approached them.

"All the mechanics?" asked Ankyer

"Yes, all of them. They didn't want to miss out on touring your palace."

"General Muhammid, meet Colonel Carl Franklin, chief flight officer for the Red Protocol Group."

"Nice to meet you Colonel."

"And you as well, General."

"Among other things, Colonel Franklin flies our F-18 Super Hornet," said Ankyer. He will be checking out your Hornet and supervising loading on the Harpoon missiles and the other instruments."

"And tailhook assembly," said Franklin.

"Tailhook assembly?" asked Muhammid.

"As I mentioned earlier, we'll be landing on a U.S. aircraft carrier to refuel on our trip across the Atlantic," said Ankyer.

"Our mechanics have also brought the conformal fuel tanks to attach to the F-18. We'll flight test your Hornet to make sure everything is working properly and, importantly, to ensure the aircraft weight and aerodynamics are in balance with the additional equipment, ordnance and fuel," said Franklin."

At that moment, the hangar doors opened, and the Qatar F-18 Super Hornet was rolled out attached to an aircraft tug.

"Excuse me gentlemen. I have to supervise installation of the Harpoons and other equipment," said Franklin as the Red Protocol Group mechanics exited three SUVs and a flatbed truck containing the missiles and other equipment pulled up. The Abbey mechanics shook hands with General Muhammid, and they immediately started unloading the equipment and working on the F-18.

"Jake, I sincerely hope all of you know what you're doing," said the General.

"General, I have 200 hours, mostly combat, in the F-18, and Carl has flown 50 combat missions in Iraq and 60 more in Afghanistan. You're in good hands."

"I should have known. Sorry."

"No problem. The mechanics should be finished in about an hour or so. Then Carl and I will take it for a test drive."

An hour and twenty minutes later Ankyer and Franklin were in the F-18 cockpit.

Ankyer yelled down to General Muhammid: "How many flight hours does this have?"

"We have not flown it," replied Muhammid as the Emir walked up. "Assume zero hours."

"I wouldn't have missed this for the world," said the Emir as Ankyer waved and gave him a 'thumbs-up'.

"You want to do this or shall I?" asked Ankyer over the cockpit communications.

"Go for it. Just don't break their toy," said Carl.

Ankyer taxied the Hornet over to the runway, turned right and opened the throttle. The Hornet rolled forward, rotated and was airborne as he pulled back on the control stick. A moment later Ankyer fired the after burners and the Hornet shot forward over the airfield at Mach 1.3 causing an explosion along with a cloud of vapor on the tail. As he pulled back further on the control stick, the Hornet achieved a climb angle of 90 degrees while accelerating to 37,000 feet. He leveled off, then descended to 200 feet and flew past the airfield decelerating to Mach .9 causing a second, sound barrier explosion. Ankyer then turned the Hornet, slowed to landing speed and touched down at the end of the airfield runway.

"Show off!" said Carl.

"Comments on the aerodynamics?" asked Ankyer.

"It accelerates ok but seems a little heavy. Probably due to the extra weight from the conformal fuel tanks and the Harpoons. One of our mechanics was not happy with the older, underwing Harpoon missile attachments. The attachment wiring is out of spec with the newer Harpoons. It's probably ok but I'd like more testing time with it. Time is of the essence, I gather."

"You're right there," answered Ankyer as he toggled the Harpoon arming switch. "It looks ok now" he said, pulling the F-18 back in front of the hangar where the Emir, the General and all the mechanics, both Qatari and U.S., were applauding. Ankyer opened the canopy and said: "Well, what do you think?"

"What an air show!" exclaimed the Emir.

"I've never seen anything like it!" echoed the General.

"I'm not surprised," added the Emir. "You should have seen him drive the Porsche Spyder in Germany!"

Ankyer and Franklin exited the cockpit and shook hands all around.

"We need to make a few adjustments, but on balance it's ok," said Franklin to his chief mechanic. "Let's take another look at the Harpoon launch system. The F-18 Harpoon attachment specs are out of date with the plane they have."

"Gentlemen," said the Emir addressing the Red Protocol mechanics. "I understand you would like to see Jake's residence, so I've ordered lunch to be delivered there. Wally chili cheeseburgers!" All the mechanics cheered.

"I'm going to have to get a bigger flight suit," said Ankyer.

"Maybe Chief Bell's idea for a franchise is not so bad after all," said Carl.

"With Dr. Finkel's retirement plan the Chief can buy the whole business," replied Ankyer.

After lunch, the mechanics were given a complete tour of the palace along with the nearby guest residence. A staff member conducted the tour and the Emir met them after they had seen the guest residence where Anker and Honey Pi would be staying while the palace floors were replaced with marble at the direction of the Emir. Carl thanked the Emir before the mechanics returned to the airfield to continue F-18 instrument upgrades. Carl told the Emir that he needed to speak with Jake and Honey Pi prior to returning to the airfield and was escorted by attendant back to the palace. He joined Ankyer and Honey Pi in the palace library.

"Does Dr. Finkel know what you guys are up to here?" asked Carl. "This place is incredible! I'm going to tell Dr. Finkel that the likelihood of you returning to the Abbey is between zero and zero."

"Dr. Finkel knows all about this. As a matter of fact, he encouraged the Emir to make me a sheikh. The Emir took it a little farther than we thought..."

"He wanted to make Jake the next Emir and me his consort," said Honey Pi. "Jake can do the sheikh thing but I'm way too busy to be consorting."

"You are something," replied Carl. "Anyway, one of our guys had a portable transceiver in his pocket to check for listening devices in this place and the guest palace as you requested. He said nothing registered in either location."

"Thanks. I figured a request for a tour would give us a chance to check for bugs. Looks like it worked," said Ankyer."

"You never know with technology, but I think we're ok for the moment," replied Carl. "On another subject, your colleagues at the Abbey are thrilled with Dr. Finkel's new pension plan, but the rumor is that Qatar is shoveling money to you guys. What do you do with all of it?"

"You know Carl, I've been thinking about that and have concluded that it's not much if you can't spend it."

"How so?" asked Carl.

"Well, the Emir is a nice guy and very generous, but the ton of money coming to Sheikh Ankyer is going directly to a royal account in a Qatar bank. It turns out that the Emir keeps his Qatar riyal's close to the vest."

"But you can move money around, right?" asked Carl.

"Sure. But if I move it to any place outside of Qatar, I get taxed at 45%. So, guess what? It doesn't get moved. As for the palaces, I can't sell them because there's no one to buy them. They are held in trust for me by the Crown and can't be sold."

"What about living expenses?" asked Carl.

"Well, you got me there. I haven't spent a riyal yet. I checked with the butler Claude and asked who keeps track of my expenses.

He said no one, since by order of the Emir I have no expenses to keep track of. By way of example, you were hanging out with the Emir. Right Honey Pi?"

"Glad you asked Jake. The Emir didn't want me to feel slighted since I'm an integral member of the Red Protocol team. We walked out in front to the circular drive and, you're not going to believe this. There was a pale purple Bentley Continental GT Speed convertible. I turned to the Emir, who was beaming, and he said, 'for you' and said that the car would be parked along with Jake's collection. The butler would retrieve it for me whenever I wanted. He then popped the trunk in which was an open case with two matched Peter Hofer 12 and 20 bore sidelock shotguns. He then said that Dr. Finkel told him I was very accomplished with a shotgun and asked if I would be willing to give a seminar to his senior protective guard. I of course agreed."

"So, there you have it, Carl. Honey Pi and I are in the lap of luxury. The 'yellow brick road' in Qatar may be gold but with an indeterminate destination. I think we will probably be taking advantage of Dr. Finkel's pension program along with the rest of you guys."

"Ok, I give up," said Carl. "What about the mission?"

"It's pretty straight forward," said Ankyer. "We take off from here with the Qatar F-18. We refuel on an aircraft carrier in the Atlantic. Make two more refueling stops in the air with MQ-25 Stingray jet refueling drones. Then fly on over to Moon's place in Colorado. Fire the Harpoons. Blow the place up. Then head to the Abbey and take the rest of the day off."

"The Harpoon's should do the trick, but we don't know exactly where the computers are housed. We could miss," said Carl.

"Enter the genius of Honey Pi, said Ankyer.

"I was wondering when I was going to get some credit," said Honey Pi.

"Honey Pi suggested we check out how Moon's compound generates energy. It turns out that all the systems are powered from four 30,000-gallon tanks of LPG gas strategically located around the compound. Between the Harpoons hitting the compound and the LPG gas tanks exploding, the entire area for a square mile will be converted to a slag heap, according to the science boys at the Abbey."

"Sounds promising," said Carl. "As we usually say on our missions, 'What could go wrong?'. I'll have another glass of this terrific, iced tea," said Carl. "This place is great!"

"As long as you don't leave," said Honey Pi.

LESTER'S PIT STOP
Washington D.C.

"WHERE DO YOU FIND THESE RESTAURANTS?" asked Finkel.

"They are all over the place," said Makin, speaking softly through his mastoid implant. *"It's a good way to have confidential conversations. The likelihood of running into other executive office staff who know you is less in a low-end eatery. Problem is that so many high-end staff are now using low-end places for high-end conversations, people are going to high-end places for low-end conversations."*

"You're kidding," said Finkel.

"Yes. It was a joke," replied Makin.

"Oh," said Finkel.

"Well, on to business," said Finkel. *"We have developed a plan to eliminate the sound weapon threat at Moon's estate in Colorado. It involves Jake and Carl flying an F-18 from Qatar to Colorado and incinerating Moon's estate where the communication facility is housed, while SLUG and Tensale are eating lunch in the private dining room at the White House."*

"Sounds promising," replied Makin. *"The timing is critical."*

"The snag is it only solves part of the problem," said Finkel. *"We have to decapitate the head of the snake in addition to destroying the body."*

"Tensale," said Makin.

"And SLUG," replied Finkel. *"Since you are at ground zero, so to speak, I have been discussing a way for you to help take care of that part of the problem."*

"And that is...?"

Finkel continued and described the idea.

"What an elegant solution," said Makin. *"You have outdone yourself Doctor."*

"Thank you, George. I always appreciate compliments from my colleagues."

"SLUG insists on having his lunch at exactly 11:45 AM every day. He has asked that I join him numerous times, so he has company when he ruminates about having his head carved on Mount Rushmore and being awarded the Nobel Peace Prize. His latest idea is having every high school student tested on his Presidential memoir prior to being allowed to graduate."

"What's a passing grade?"

"100," said Makin.

"Well, our plan should keep higher education intact in the U.S.," said Finkel.

"Indeed. He has advised me that Tensale will be joining him for lunch on the 15th. He wants me to station myself outside the private dining room in case he is attacked by Secret Service personnel. After lunch he intends to announce disbanding the Secret Service and appointing me the U.S. Security Czar. A high honor indeed."

"Let's hope our plan succeeds," said Finkel.

EAGLE RIVER RANCH
Eagle River Ranch Colorado
Burner Phone Conversation

ONE OF MOON'S BURNER PHONES BUZZED. Moon was getting tired of the burner phones for two reasons. First, the conversation usually upset her, and second, Mallory Tensale, who Moon increasingly disliked, was usually the one with whom she was conversing.

"Yes? What is it now?"

"Calm down Anastasia, we are almost there," replied Tensale. "All the computer tests have been completed and the sonic weapon software has been loaded. We ran a test in a lab with some monkeys by launching the weapon from your location. Everything worked as expected. The monkeys created a mess in their cages, what was left of them."

"The sound weapon did that?"

"We've increased the power of the weapon to the point that it super heats the brain causing a meltdown."

"And Gatling is going along with that?"

"Absolutely. He has really gotten into the program and doesn't want to take any chances on targets recovering and possibly being reinstated. Our friend Gatling is more than pissed off. He now wants revenge on anyone he thinks has conspired against him... which is just about everyone," said Tensale.

"That could turn out to be a problem," replied Moon. "If I'm going to be Vice President, the last thing I need is having a paranoid nut case over me."

"I take your point," Anastasia. "But he shouldn't be around for long."

"What are you talking about? He's going to declare martial law. He wants to set himself up as a fucking king!"

"Look. He can set himself up as anything he wants. But keep in mind he is going to get rid of the Secret Service. The only one protecting him as far as he's concerned is Winston White."

"Who we tried to kill twice," said Moon.

"I'm going to have a chat with Mr. White," said Tensale. "He will be able to get to Gatling any time he wants. With you as President, we could make White the Secretary of Defense or something equivalent. Everyone has his price."

"I'm not so sure of that in White's case."

"Ok. In any event, I wanted to let you know that everything is under control. The Chinese technicians are ready to activate the programs. The head technician is named Chu Bak and he will be coordinating the whole thing at your end."

"He's already introduced himself to me as Colonel Chu Bak," said Moon.

"He's also a senior scientist with the Chinese Secret Police. The Chinese are not taking any chances," replied Tensale.

"Well, he's not exactly a charming guy. He told me that once he and his friends start firing up the computers, that in his words, 'I should stay the hell out of the way.' A real sweetheart."

"Hang in there Anastasia," said Tensale hanging up.

ADMIRAL ANSELM HOLLOWAY'S OFFICE

Vice Chairman, Naval Operations
Pentagon
Washington, D.C.

ADMIRAL HOLLOWAY'S ADJUTANT, LT. COMMANDER ROGER BUNSEN, KNOCKED lightly on the door to Holloway's inner sanctum.

"Admiral. There's someone on one of your secure lines who won't identify himself but indicated it was a "code purple" matter and requested that you be put on the line. "Code Purple' is so high up the security chain I don't think we have ever had one come in. How would you like me to deal with this?"

Holloway opened a drawer on the side of his desk and removed a smart phone that had a red light blinking in the upper right-hand corner.

"Roger, I'll take the call. Post an armed guard outside the door to my office suite. Stay with the guard. No one is to be let in. Period. I'll come out when I've finished."

"Yes sir," replied Bunsen closing the door.

Holloway pulled out his wallet, removed a slip of paper and entered the numbers and special characters on the paper into the password field on his phone. The phone blinked, and crosshairs appeared on the screen. Optical recognition software on the phone confirmed the authentication. He set the phone down on his desk and pressed the speaker icon.

"Asher, how the hell are you?"

"I'm fine Anselm, but I need to ask a favor," said Finkel.

"What's up?"

"I have a situation which requires that an F-18 Super Hornet fly from Qatar to Colorado. The most direct route is over the Atlantic. The plane will be on afterburners all the way and will exhaust its fuel halfway across the Atlantic."

"And you need a gas station," said Holloway.

"Exactly. Do you have any around these coordinates?" reading the numbers off.

Holloway pulled up the U.S. fleet dispersion software and entered the coordinates. The computer screen displayed U.S. military vessel icons in the Atlantic in blue, along with NATO ship icons in the same area in red.

"It looks like the USS Chicago is your best bet. There is a British carrier a little closer..."

"Can't use the British carrier," said Finkel. This is too sensitive to let our 007 friends get involved."

"Ok. Let me see if I can get the Captain of the Chicago on the line. Wait one."

Three minutes later, Holloway said: "I have Captain Julius Berg on the line. Captain Berg, meet Dr. Asher Finkel."

"Nice to meet you Dr. Finkel. How can we be of assistance, Admiral?" asked Berg.

"Dr. Finkel has a mission that requires a Super Hornet to re-fuel halfway across the Atlantic. The USS Chicago is the closest carrier we have to the required refueling coordinates."

"We can handle that," said Berg. When will the Hornet be in the area?"

"Tomorrow morning around 2:00 AM Greenwich Mean Time," said Finkel.

"We may have a problem," said Berg. "We are currently ex-periencing heavy seas with 20-to-25-foot waves. The weather is forecast to worsen over the next two days. The pilot will have to be exceptionally skilled. Who's driving the Hornet?"

"His call sign is 'Death Dealer'," said Finkel.

"Death Dealer! I was in the Top Gun fighter pilot school with a pilot called Death Dealer, Admiral. He blew through every com-bat flight sortie the school could throw at him. They wanted to make him a senior instructor, but he disappeared. His name was Jake Ankyer. Is that your guy, Doctor?"

"Well….," hesitated Finkel.

"Tell him Asher. We're under code purple security," said Holloway.

"It is Jake Ankyer. He normally is involved in land-based opera-tions, but we have a unique situation here that requires his skills."

"He'll definitely need all his skills if our weather continues to deteriorate," said Berg.

"By the time he gets to your ship, Captain, according to our calculations, and even with his auxiliary tanks, he will be out of fuel. He will have to land."

"I understand," said Berg. "There is a risk that our stabilizers won't be able to compensate for the pitch and yaw of the back of the boat and the landing deck if the waves exceed 40 feet. Even more problematic, if we can't land Ankyer and he has to ditch, I won't be able to launch a copter to pull him out. Is there any way to delay this mission a few days?"

"Believe me, Captain, if there was a way to delay things I would do it. Unfortunately, there is not," said Finkel.

"Does the Hornet have weapons on board?" asked Berg.

"Two Harpoon missiles," replied Finkel.

"Game, set, match," said Berg. "If Ankyer hits the back of the boat trying to land and the Harpoons explode, the part of the boat that houses the nuclear reactors could be affected. We could have a nuclear event sinking a billion-dollar asset along with a crew of 5,200, just so we're clear here," replied Berg.

"Ok, Julius. Let me speak with Dr. Finkel and I will get back to you."

"Yes sir. Out."

"What if we don't do this Asher?"

"The United States will sink into anarchy and millions of people will die. The United States government will cease to exist in its current form."

"And that's your considered opinion and not hyperbole?" asked Holloway

"Absolutely," replied Finkel. "The United States will devolve back to what it was during the Civil War. Even worse if that's possible."

"Gatling is involved in this isn't he?" asked Holloway.

"Yes," said Finkel.

"Alright. Get Ankyer in the air. I'll talk to Captain Berg. God help us."

QATAR
Special Forces Emir Al Sallazon Airfield
F-18 Super Hornet Hangar
Crew Ready Room

ANKYER AND FRANKLIN HAD JUST FINISHED PUTTING ON PRESSURIZED FLIGHT SUITS with the assistance of the Red Protocol Group mechanics when Honey Pi and the Emir walked in.

"All dressed up and someplace to go," said Honey Pi.

"Dr. Pi and I wanted to see you off to what we sincerely hope will be a successful mission," said the Emir.

"We very much appreciate that your Highness," said Ankyer, as General Muhammid looked on. "General Muhammid and his men have been very helpful with our preflight checks. We are fueled up and ready to go. Time is now of the essence."

"Before you leave, I need a private word with you and Dr. Pi," said the Emir as the General opened a door to another room. Ankyer and Honey Pi followed the Emir into the room. The General closed the door behind them and remained outside.

"I'll be brief," said the Emir. "You both have been instrumental in helping my country, Jake. You have saved my grandson and protected the line of royal Qatar succession. Dr. Pi, you have clarified my medical condition and arranged for my treatment. As I mentioned before, prior to the oil and gas discoveries, Qatar was a poor country. Now, with our newfound wealth, the only thing we have to reward those who rescue our people as you have is money and titles. It occurred to me that with our gifts to you, you may think we may want something additional in return. I wanted to assure you that nothing is further from the truth. Any funds we have deposited in Qatar's Royal bank will be moved to any other bank at your request and protected by tax shelters. Your palace along with everything else we have given you will be duplicated in a location of your choosing should you decide not to remain in Qatar. I wanted to be sure that you are aware of my country's good intentions. It's important to me."

"Your Highness, your willingness to lend us your F-18 speaks volumes of your friendship to us and to our country. We could not ask for more," said Ankyer.

"My sentiments, exactly," said Honey Pi. The Emir hugged Honey Pi and shook Ankyer's hand and then exited.

Honey Pi turned to Ankyer and said: "The Emir and I will be flying to the Abbey so he can start his medical treatment. I'll be there keeping track of you with Dr. Finkel."

Carl Franklin walked into the Ready room.

"You ready to go, Carl?" asked Ankyer.

"Let's do it," replied Carl as he and Ankyer walked into the hangar, climbed into the Super Hornet and were moved out to the tarmac by an aircraft tug. The F-18 was moved to the runway. It taxied and was airborne. Ankyer made a pass over the airfield and pulled up into a ninety-degree climb. He engaged the afterburners, and a moment later a loud boom shook the buildings.

"What was that!" exclaimed the Emir.

"Sheikh Ankyer's speed just passed Mach 1, the sound barrier, your Highness," said the General.

"Welcome to the world of Jake Ankyer your Highness," said Honey Pi, as the fighter became a dot in the sky to those remaining on the ground.

"Will he be alright?" asked the Emir when the F-18 had disappeared.

"I don't know," said Honey Pi. "I'm not sure this time. He's had numerous dangerous missions. This is more complex and dangerous than usual. We had better get to our plane. The doctors at the Abbey are expecting you."

"Jake will come back," said the Emir. "I feel it."

The Emir and Honey Pi walked over to the Boeing 777. "Wait until you see the waterfall in the plane," said the Emir to Honey Pi. It's really something."

PART THREE

...And, lo, there was a great earthquake;
and the sun became black as sackcloth of hair,
and the moon became as blood.

SECURE RADIO COMMUNICATION.
Dr. Asher Finkel to Captain Julius Berg.

"CAPTAIN BERG, THIS IS DR. ASHER FINKEL. Death Dealer is in the air and headed in your direction."

"I spoke with Admiral Holloway, Doctor. We will do everything we can to assist. You should know that we are expecting hurricane force weather."

"Understand," said Finkel.

"I hope your man is as good as his reputation, Doctor."

"He's better. I'll contact you when he's inbound to your coordinates. Thank you. Over and out."

F-18 SUPER HORNET
Over the Atlantic Ocean,
Headed towards USS Chicago

ANKYER LEVELED THE F-18 OFF AT 48,000 FEET with afterburners at full thrust while communicating with Franklin over the intraplane com system.

"What's our ETA with the Chicago Carl?"

"We've got a tail wind which should help us somewhat. Considering a speed of 1.8 Mach we should be in the area in about 4.5 hours. The bad news is that at our current speed we'll be on fumes when we get there."

"Can't help that," said Ankyer. "Since this plane has less than one hour of flight time, we better run systems check."

"Our guys did that in Qatar but you're right. Operational systems check at Mach speed is in order. Ready?"

"Go ahead, Carl."

"Ok. Give me a minute...ok."

"Electrical systems...nominal

"Avionics systems...nominal

"Flight control systems...nominal

"Fuel system...nominal

"Hold on...ok. All other systems nominal," said Carl.

"That covers it, Jake. You can tell our guys have been all over this plane. It's highly unusual not to find a glitch somewhere. Especially right out of the box."

"Can't argue with you there," replied Ankyer. "Let's talk about landing this guy on the carrier."

"It will be a little tricky if the weather continues as reported," said Carl. "Actually, tricky is an understatement. If we encounter waves over 25 feet, it will be tough. Over 30 feet the back of the carrier will be going up and down like a yoyo."

"I agree. How's this for an idea..."

"Interesting," said Franklin. "I've never tried something like that."

"Neither have I," replied Ankyer. "A first time for everything."

"Seems like a lot of our missions are a 'first time for everything' kind of deal, now that I think about it," said Franklin. "Oops. Running into chop even at this altitude."

"Must be getting close to the edge of the storm. I'm climbing to 60,000 feet. That should cut us a little slack," said Ankyer.

"Agree," said Franklin. "Our forward-looking radar indicates high energy cloud formations even at 60,000. Get ready for maneuvering around these bad boys."

"Will do," replied Ankyer as the F-18 gained altitude.

ARNOLD'S PIZZA PALACE
Washington D.C.
Makin/Finkel Conversation

MAKIN'S MASTOID COMMUNICATIONS IMPLANT CLICKED.

"I must say George, you're going to gain weight. Every time we speak you are in a restaurant," said Finkel.

"As a matter of fact, Arnold's has excellent deep-dish pizza. The next time you're here we'll have lunch. My treat."

"You're a gentleman, George. The Abbey has come up with a plan for SLUG and his friend for September 15th."

"Sounds promising."

"It turns out that we've had a turn of good fortune. One of the presidential minor butlers was at a party last week where a person was infected with Covid. The butler has been sequestered and a butler with appropriate clearances has been assigned to replace him using the White House temporary staff agency. It turns out the same temporary butler that has been assigned to SLUG's lunch service on September 15th is our very own Jose Hernandez."

"Jose!" exclaimed Makin softly. *"He holds the record for Chief Bell's Wally Burger 'eat till you drop' contest two years running. He's unbeatable."*

"You never know. Former Navy SEALs have many tricks up their wet suit sleeves," said Finkel. *"In any event, you and Jose are now integral pieces of our plan. It goes like this..."*

After Finkel had finished, Makin said: *"You folks never cease to amaze me."*

"Thanks, George. I'll pass your compliment to the Abbey. When you leave Arnold's, Brother William will walk past you and surreptitiously hand off the material."

"How's Jake doing?" asked Makin.

"He's headed to his first refueling stop now. We are concerned about the weather which is getting worse by the hour. The timing for this entire plan is exceptionally delicate. You and Jose won't know if Jake succeeded, so it's critical that you implement your part irrespective of Jake's result."

"Count on it, Dr. Finkel," said Makin ending the conversation.

F-18 SUPER HORNET
Mid Atlantic Ocean
17 Nautical Miles from USS Chicago

THE F-18 WAS AT 62,000 FEET CRUISING AT MACH 1.2. Ankyer was constantly dodging thunder heads over 60,000 feet increasing the F-18's fuel consumption.

"We'll be on fumes by the time we reach the Chicago," said Carl.

"Roger that," replied Ankyer. "By my calculation, we will have enough fuel for one pass by the Chicago to assess the degrees of pitch and yaw on its runway and then then we have to land it. In one piece preferably."

"Can't argue with that," replied Carl.

"Time to contact our gas station," said Ankyer.

Using the secure frequency Captain Berg gave Finkel, Ankyer initiated contact with the carrier:

"Chicago this is tail number 2097 out of Qatar, over."

"Tail number 2097 this is the XO of the Chicago. What is your call sign, over?"

"Death Dealer. Over."

"And the call sign for your flight officer, over?"

"That would be "Crash". Over," said Carl.

"We were told you guys were really something. You just verified it. I'm passing you over to our senior Landing Signals Officer. Over."

"Death Dealer, this is Lt. Commander Arthur Bucholtz, your Landing Services Officer for tonight in the air traffic control center. We have you on our radar 16 miles out at 60,000 feet and a speed of Mach 1.2. Is that correct? Over."

"Roger that. Over."

"You gentlemen are landing in a hurricane with wind gusts of 110 miles per hour and sea swells with a peak of up to 85 feet. Do you have an alternative landing plan? Over?"

"Negative, Chicago. We will have ten minutes of fuel remaining when we intersect with you. Over."

"Understand Death Dealer. Be advised if you must ditch, we cannot launch sea rescue craft. Over."

"Roger that. Over."

"Do you have experience with the Fresnel Lens Optical Landing System? Over."

"Affirmative. Over."

"Excellent. We are increasing the intensity of the amber meatball light and the green lights to help you see the edge of the runway better if it's under water, which is a good possibility. Just to review, you have four arresting wires for your tailhook. Given the current conditions we expect you will probably hook on to the fourth wire. If you miss everything and bolt you can make a second pass, if necessary. Over."

"Bolting is not an option. We'll be out of fuel. We will have to land right the first time. I would like to make one pass by the ship to assess the pitch and yaw of the aft of the carrier and then come in for the landing. We will be coming in hot to counter wind currents. Over."

"Roger that Death Dealer. We calculate your intercept at five minutes given your current distance and speed. Good luck. Over."

"Thank you. Roger. Over and out."

During the conversation with the Landing Safety Officer, Ankyer reduced his altitude from 60,000 feet to 400 feet and his speed to 400 knots as he approached the Chicago.

"This is Death Dealer, Chicago. I have visual with you. I will make my first pass in 5 minutes. Over."

"Roger that, Death Dealer. We have you locked on our radar. Over."

"Jake, you know they don't think we are going to make it," said Carl.

"They don't know us very well, do they?" replied Ankyer as he decreased his altitude to 250 feet."

"Any lower and we'll hit a wave," said Carl.

"Ok. Here we go," said Ankyer.

The F-18 approached the Chicago off its port beam at 400 miles per hour. Ankyer and Carl observed the pitch of the Chicago's aft which appeared to be rising and sinking by about 65 feet. Its ship stabilizers were engaged but the carrier was still difficult to visualize given the driving rain. The F-18 shot by the control tower which was brightly lit and filled with people looking out the window. The jet executed a loop and came up behind the Chicago a mile back, dropping its altitude and aligning it with the amber 'meatball' light centered with the green lights on either side.

"Ok Carl. I'm timing the landing for when we are even with the plane of the aft. We will touch down when the aft is halfway up the wave and the meatball is centered. The second you feel touch down, hit the reverse thrusters. I will be reversing flaps and hitting the brakes, just like we practiced."

"Practiced!!" exclaimed Carl. "Practiced!?"

The F-18 looked like a bouncing cork as Ankyer locked onto the meatball. They followed the aft of the carrier exactly, maintaining perfect runway alignment with the carrier's up, down, and sideways attitude as it plowed through the monster waves.

The plane touched down at 350 knots exactly, when it was even with the back of the Chicago's runway as planned. Even with the deceleration, the tailhook caught the first wire and cut through it. It cut through the second wire and came to a halt when it caught the third one. A perfect landing, with the fuel gauge light blinking red, and the indicator dial reading empty. Ankyer rolled the F-18 over to several yellow shirt crew members waving light batons. When he stopped the plane, the crew attached chains to keep the F-18 secured to the deck.

"Nice landing, Jake," said Carl. "How many carrier landings does that make for you?"

"Three including this one, but don't tell them that. They might throw us overboard."

Ankyer opened the canopy, looked down at the runway crew and said: "Filler up boys!" as the crew applauded.

When Ankyer and Carl had climbed down from the F-18 cockpit, a crew member driving a plane tug hooked it up and moved it to an elevator hangar which promptly lowered the fighter down into the bowels of the carrier. Crew members wearing shirt colors for their specific jobs; purple for fueling, red for bombs and missiles crew, and brown for maintenance gathered. A lieutenant walked up to Ankyer and Carl and said: I've been ordered to escort you to the pilots' ready room. There are a few people who want to talk to you."

"Lead on, lieutenant," replied Ankyer. They followed her to a large room with teleprompter screens. More than 50 crew members were seen applauding on the teleprompter screens as Ankyer and Carl removed their flight helmets and were greeted by a Commander.

"Welcome to the USS Chicago. I'm Arthur Witherspoon, the Executive Officer. The pilots and I wanted to applaud you gentlemen on the finest carrier landing under extreme conditions we have ever witnessed."

"Luck had a lot to do with it," said Ankyer.

"I think not," replied Witherspoon. "In any event, we'd like to present you with USS Chicago "Killer Bees" tee shirts and our pilots would like a "Death Dealer" and "Crash" autograph on their flight helmets if that's ok with you."

"Our pleasure," replied Ankyer and Carl.

Fifteen minutes later, someone shouted "Attention. Captain on deck!" Everyone in the room came to attention as Captain Julius Berg walked in.

"As you were," said Berg. "Welcome Commander Ankyer and Colonel Franklin, or if you prefer, Death Dealer and Crash! It is not usually boring around here, but you gentlemen kicked everything up a notch with that landing. I'm going to rescue you from these pirates. Commander, please show our guests to my quarters."

"Attention on deck!" exclaimed a voice and Berg exited the room followed by Commander Witherspoon, Ankyer and Franklin.

Once inside Berg's quarters, which were decorated in very nice 'functional', Berg said "make yourselves comfortable, gentlemen. There are sandwiches and excellent navy coffee on the sideboard. We can sit around the conference table."

"Thank you, Captain. It's been a while since we ate," said Carl.

"Actually, I wanted to thank you guys for not crashing into my nuclear-powered ship and blowing us up. Everyone is breathing a collective sigh of relief. Our research shows that you Colonel Franklin, were awarded 'Ace' status for your tours in Iraq and Afghanistan; and that you, Commander Ankyer, hold the sortie record at the Top Gun flight school. Thank you for your service and rest assured gentlemen, that I would have never authorized landing on my carrier under these weather conditions without your credentials. Admiral Holloway left it up to me as Captain of this vessel."

"Thank you, Captain," said Ankyer. "We appreciate your confidence in us."

"Your F-18 should be refueled, and the systems check completed in about 30 more minutes. We haven't had an F-18 aboard with conformal fuel tanks so it's taking a little longer. Does that give you enough fuel to complete your mission?"

"We'll be on afterburners from here to the East coast. We're meeting up with a MQ-25 Stingray jet refueling drone, taking on 15,000 additional pounds of fuel, and will have one more drone refueling stop after that to get us to the objective."

"I'm assuming the two Harpoon missiles you have on board will be launched in U.S. territory," said Berg. "Don't answer that. I know it's classified. Admiral Holloway said that I wouldn't believe what's going on and that's good enough for me. Let's get to these sandwiches."

Twenty-five minutes later there was a knock on the door.

"Come," said Berg.

A Lieutenant in a yellow vest with "Shooter" on the back entered the room.

"Excuse me sir. We are ready for the F-18 launch."

Everyone in the room stood up.

"This is Lieutenant Adami, your Landing Safety Officer," said Berg. "He and his team will be responsible for your launch, which should also be exciting since the hurricane is increasing in intensity to a Category 5."

"We will be adjusting the catapult to maximum thrust sir," said Adami. "You will want to do an afterburner launch off the runway at the top of the wave. I will give you the launch signal and the catapult will immediately deploy. You should be good to go."

"Thank you, Lieutenant," said Ankyer. "And thank you Captain...for your assistance and for the coffee and sandwiches."

Ankyer and Franklin followed Lieutenant Adami down to the hangar. The F-18 was positioned in the front of the hangar bay with the canopy up and stairs to the cockpit in place. Ankyer and Franklin climbed into the Hornet and Ankyer initiated the electronic systems check sequences. The stairs were removed, and the Hornet was connected to the tug.

"Thanks again to you and your team, Lieutenant," said Ankyer.

"You're welcome, sir," replied Adami as he stepped back and saluted along with the launch team that had lined up next to him. "The wind gusts up on the flight deck are now around 70 knots so we have to get you moved to the runway and hooked up to the catapult as fast as possible. "We've warmed up your engines so you're ready to go. I'll give you the launch signal just before we get to the top of the wave, and we'll blast you out of here."

"Roger that," said Ankyer as he returned the salutes and lowered the cockpit canopy.

The elevator carried the Hornet, the tug, and the launch team to the deck. The elevator door opened, and everyone was greeted by howling hurricane winds. The tug moved the Hornet into position on the runway and disconnected. Two green shirted catapult crewmen secured with safety harnesses ran under the Hornet and attached it to the catapult coupling. The 'shooter', Lieutenant Adami, also hooked up to a safety harness, signaled to Ankyer that they were ready. Ankyer fired up the F-18's twin engines and increased the thrust.

"Ready Carl?" Ankyer asked.

"Ready," replied Carl.

Ankyer looked out the F-18 canopy and saluted the Shooter. The bow of the carrier headed down into the trough of a 70-foot wave and accelerated to just short of the top of the wave as Adami gave a signal with his lighted baton. The Green shirt catapult crew member hit the catapult launch control. A high-pitched steam whistle shrieked, the sound engulfing the deck and the Hornet shot forward with its after burners at full throttle. The Hornet lifted off at an 80-degree climb, exactly as the enormous wave reached its peak and the carrier went down into another trough.

"God almighty, where did that guy learn to fly!" exclaimed the Executive Officer to Captain Berg on the carrier's bridge as they watched the F-18 Hornet scream away elevating almost straight up, its engines emitting long tails of flame.

"When I spoke to Admiral Holloway, he said we should be ready to see something we've never seen before. It looks like he was right."

———————————

As the Hornet powered into its 80-degree climb, Ankyer said to Carl: "I'm going to see if I can get us above this turbulence. We can't take a chance on damage from these winds." Ankyer increased the speed to Mach 1.2 causing a sound barrier boom. At that moment, there was a blinding flash, a second much louder boom, and the plane shuttered. They immediately lost 2,000 feet of altitude.

"Goddamn it!" exclaimed Carl. "We got hit by lightning."

"I've got control," said Ankyer. "Have to get us out of this storm before we get hit again." Anker pulled back on the stick and increased the speed rocketing up to 50,000 feet. "The controls feel ok. Do the systems check out Carl?"

A few minutes later Carl said, "The tailhook deployment system indicator is red. So is the landing gear retraction system indicator. The landing gear was up since we got hit after we were aloft. But if we put it down again it'll stay down. Otherwise, it looks like we're ok. That was a direct lighting strike on the bottom of the aircraft."

"What about the Harpoons?"

"Weapons systems are showing green," said Carl. "It's a damn good thing they weren't armed," said Carl.

"We must be living right," said Ankyer as they passed 60,000 feet encountering semi clear air. I'm taking us up to 65,000. The afterburners will chew up fuel at that altitude. That refueling drone better show up at the coast."

"Our ETA at the refueling coordinates is currently 3.3 hours at Mach 1.2. If we stay at this speed, we should be ok," said Carl.

"Roger that," said Ankyer. "Better keep an eye on the systems' instruments though for any delayed effects from the lightning strike."

"Roger that," said Carl.

Ankyer brought the Hornet up to 65,000 feet; high enough to significantly reduce the turbulence from the hurricane below.

BUSTER'S DOWN HOME CHILI EMPORIUM
Washington D.C.

SITTING ACROSS A TABLE FROM JOSE HERNANDEZ, a Red Protocol Group senior operative, George Makin studied the six-page menu and said: "I strongly recommend the Chili Cheese Macaroni Bowl Supreme."

"If you are trying to get me sick so you have an edge for the Abbey's annual Wally Burger Festival, forget it. I won the last two years in a row and this year will be no different," said Jose.

"So you say," replied Makin. "There's a limit to your capacity and I came within one Wally burger of beating you last year. I've been in training this year eating at all these goofy restaurants to keep away from the prying White House eyes and ears when I talk with Dr. Finkel. You don't have a chance."

"We'll see," said Jose. "Dr. Walthour and the Abbey science guys are working on electronic stimulation to temporarily expand stomach size. Even Finkel is in on it. You can't trust any of these science guys. I'm going to demand everyone get a medical clearance this year. Either you enter the contest with the stomach God gave you, or you sit in the bleachers and watch."

"Fat chance of that with Dr. Finkel in the mix," said Makin.

"I'll appeal to his higher angels," said Jose, laughing.

A waitress came by, and Jose ordered the Chili Cheese Macaroni Bowl Supreme with Bull's Breath Hot Sauce, and Makin ordered the same.

"After eating here we'll be lucky to be alive to execute the mission," said Jose.

"Which brings us to the question, 'How do we do this?'"

"No problem," said Jose. "I'll meet you in the underground service corridor at 11:30 AM. You give me the material and I'll take it from there."

"It would be easier if I gave it to you before you got to work," said Makin.

"I agree, but I'm an underbutler, which is another way to spell 'scum', who just delivers stuff. All of us underbutler types get searched before reporting for service."

"Ok. I definitely don't have that problem," said Makin.

"Timing will be critical," replied Jose. "Maybe we should meet earlier, say 11:00 AM."

"I'd agree except if you're gone too long someone may be sent to check on you. It will take you ten minutes to make the delivery and ten more to get out of the White House."

"Ok. 11:30 AM it is. How's Jake doing?" asked Jose.

"Last I heard, he and Carl were going like a bat out of hell at Mach 1.2 over the Atlantic. They gassed up and took off from an aircraft carrier in the middle of a hurricane to the amazement of all present. Dr. Finkel said Jake's on time and should reach the coast as scheduled."

"Here comes the waitress with our chili bowls. My god, she's wearing mittens," said Jose.

"What's the matter, Jose? Second thoughts? And you actually think you're going to walk off with a prize this year?"

PART FOUR

For the great day of his wrath is come;
and who shall be able to stand?

ATLANTIC OCEAN
20.7 Miles From New York City.

ANKYER AND CARL PILOTED THE F-18 DOWN TO 42,000 FEET and reduced their speed to 400 knots.

"Time to check in," said Ankyer activating his mastoid implant while Carl did the same.

"*Dr. Finkel we are currently 20.7 miles from the U.S. East Coast at the required latitude and longitude with a speed of 400 knots. Over.*"

"*Roger that,*" replied Finkel in Ankyer's and Carl's ears. *We have you on our satellite radar. Continue your current speed and heading. The* MQ-25 refueling drone *will be on your starboard side in 4 minutes. Over and out.*"

The refueling drone appeared on the F-18 forward looking radar and 3 minutes later Ankyer and Franklin had a visual of the drone. The black drone was cigar shaped, roughly the size of the F-18 fuselage and three quarters as long. It had a straight stubby wing at its center and slightly elevated rear wings at its end. Red lights blinked at the tip of each wing and the end of its body. A flexible fuel line extended 40 feet from the MQ-25's mid-section with a male connection at the aft end. Ankyer swung around the back of the drone, opened the F-18's midair fuel receptacle, and matching the speed of the drone, connected. Five minutes later, 15,000 gallons of aviation fuel had been transferred to the F-18. The MQ-25 automatically disconnected the fuel line and Ankyer pulled away closing the F-18's fuel receptacle.

"*Refueling complete,*" said Ankyer.

"*Jake, I have Chief Jim Marshall who's flying the drone hooked into our com link. He wants to do a visual check under the fuselage of the Hornet. The lightning strike you experienced is of some concern,*" said Finkel. "*Over.*"

"*Roger that. Over,*" replied Ankyer

The drone flew under the Hornet and transmitted real-time images to the Abbey.

"*This is Jim Marshall. There is significant blackening around the midsection under the wing. Have you done systems checks since the lightning strike? Over.*"

"*Jim, this is Carl. I did a complete diagnostic systems check. The tailhook deployment system indicator is red. So is the landing gear retraction system indicator. All other systems seem ok. Over.*"

"*There appears to be blackening around the Harpoons. Over,*" said Marshall.

"*I checked the weapon's system. It came back 'green',* said Franklin. "*I haven't armed them yet, so I don't have operational confirmation. Over,*" he added.

"*Ok. Dr. Finkel, ordinarily with this kind of assessment I would recommend scrubbing the mission,*" said Marshall.

"*That's not an option, Jim,*" replied Finkel.

"*If one of the Harpoons fails to arm, we have a chance with the second. One Harpoon strike should be enough,*" said Ankyer "*Over.*"

"Agree," said Finkel. "We really have no choice considering what's at stake. Keep going gentlemen. Over."

"Roger that," said Ankyer. "Over and Out."

The MQ-25 pulled away from the F-18.

"Jake, you know what I'm worried about," said Carl.

"I know exactly what your worried about. If we arm a Harpoon and it shorts out we can blow ourselves up," replied Ankyer. "Ok then. We arm and launch one of the Harpoons instead of pressing our luck with two."

"My thought exactly," said Carl.

With that, Ankyer fired the afterburners and climbed to 65,000 feet, passing Mach 1 on the way.

EAGLE RIVER RANCH
Eagle River Ranch Colorado

ANASTASIA MOON HAD A TABLE IN THE GREAT ROOM SET UP with food and beverages. The Great Room was also used for the technicians' meals. She wanted to keep an eye on her Chinese 'guests' which is why she housed them in the guest wing of the compound. Each room had hidden audio and video technology so she would have a record of what they were up to when they were not fiddling around with the Quantum computers. If this thing went 'south' she would need to know exactly who was doing what. The Senior technician picked up a sandwich and approached Moon who was standing in the center of the room.

"Ms. Moon, we will be leaving tomorrow. On behalf of myself and my associates I want to thank you for your hospitality during our stay here."

"Well, Mr. ...I never did catch your name..."

"Chu Bak, Ms. Moon."

"Well, Mr. Chu Bak, let's be clear. The sooner you and your friends are out of here, the happier I'll be."

"I completely understand," replied Chu Bak. "However, I should tell you that I am a senior member of the Chinese security service. I'm also an emissary from my government with a message for you."

"And the message is?"

"This is a very complicated project. My government is of the opinion that any of several things could go wrong. On the other hand, if it's successful, Mr. Tensale and President Gatling could very well establish themselves as dictators and alter the governance of your country. We believe that President Gatling has, shall we say, a 'fragile mind' and that Mr. Tensale will be running the country with Gatling as a puppet. It is not clear to us what Mr. Tensale's agenda is for your country. What we do know is that the plan includes you being installed as Vice President. We have been impressed by your steady hand and believe that you would make a good partner for us."

"A partner to do what?" asked Moon.

"Oh, a number of things. Help us finally bring Taiwan into our orbit, for example. Help us establish clarity regarding the islands in the South China Sea. Work with us to make adjustments to the government in North Korea. The list is long."

"And why would I be inclined to help you?" asked Moon.

"The relations with your country and ours have turned sour with the trade war started by your former president. We would work with you to end the trade war and give you all the credit. We would also work to support all your world interests and help bring Iran, and most importantly Russia, into your foreign policy orbit. No one would be able to stand up to a strong China/U.S. alliance. You would be credited with bringing international enlightenment to the world!"

"Sounds like a plan," said Moon. "How do we do it?"

"I am just a messenger," said Chu Bak. "Once Tensale and Gatling are fully in charge with you as Vice President, you will be contacted as to how we might help make adjustments to the new administration."

"Ok. But first things first. We need to eliminate all the congressmen and others standing in the way."

"Believe me, Ms. Moon, that is the easiest part, starting on September 15th ... tomorrow."

SEPTEMBER 15TH
White House

JOSE HERNANDEZ WORKED HIS WAY THROUGH THE LABYRINTH of passageways under the White House. He turned the corner at the end of one corridor and almost ran into Makin.

"Shit. You startled the heck out of me George."

"Sorry Jose. You never know who you're going to run into down here," as Makin passed the container over to him."

"So, this is it. Doesn't seem like a lot," said Jose.

"It isn't," replied Makin. "You don't need much."

"Ok. I've got to get back."

"So do I. SLUG is really on edge and his paranoia is ramped up. Not surprising considering what's going on today."

"See you later," said Jose.

With that they each turned and headed down separate corridors.

The F-18 dropped down to 40,000 feet over Wichita, Kansas where Ankyer and Franklin made visual contact with a MQ-25 refueling drone as planned. Twenty minutes later the Hornet detached from the drone and ascended back up to 65,000 feet with Ankyer lighting the afterburners again.

"What's our ETA to Moon's compound coordinates, Carl?" asked Ankyer.

"We should get there about 11:40 AM Eastern Time," said Carl. "It's cutting it close, but better we're a little early than a little late."

"Moon's coordinates are programmed into the Harpoons. When we get there, I'll drop us down to 55,000 feet to the lower limit of the military air corridor. When we hear 'fire' from Dr. Finkel, you hit 'weapon release' and we'll head to the Abbey. Work for you Carl?"

"I'm with you. Buy you a drink when we get back," said Carl.

"Drinks are on me, pal. After all, I'm the Sheikh!"

Asher Finkel, MD, PhD, sat at a large round, highly polished, black cherry wood table in the Red Protocol Group's Abbey library. Around the table sat Brother Lester Arlot, PhD: Augustus Carter, PhD; Mike Blastow, Abbey Executive Chief; Command Master Chief Neil Groton, Martin Asbury, MD PhD; Brother William, with Varna curled at his feet; acoustics expert Dr. Juno Su; math and computer expert Dr. Wen Lee; and Dr. Honey Pi. Covering most of one wall across from the table were multiple, large TV monitors.

Turning to Honey Pi, Finkel asked: "How is the Emir doing?"

"He's fine. He tolerated the prostate procedure well and was informed that he should expect a complete recovery...for which he is most grateful."

"Excellent," replied Finkel. "

The monitors flickered and blank screens were replaced by real-time images.

One was a flight path with a yellow dot over Kansas moving rapidly towards a stationary red dot in Colorado. A second screen showed the F-18 'heads-up display' in real-time looking forward over the right shoulder of Ankyer. A third screen showed a live satellite image of Moon's compound and the surrounding area.

"As you can see, we have visual tracking of mission elements as they apply to Moon," said Finkel. George Makin will advise us regarding the outcome of the SLUG part of the mission."

"Jake, what is your arrival estimate to the target. Over?

"We will be on station at 11:40 AM Eastern Time, Dr. Finkel. "We will do final systems checks and await your command. Over," said Ankyer, his voice filling the Abby library.

"Confirmed. Over and Out," said Finkel.

At 11:50 Eastern Time there was a light knock on the polished hardwood door of the President's private dining room adjacent to the Oval Office of the White House.

"The lunch you ordered, Mr. President," said Winston White, now acting as the President's personal security person.

"Thank you, Winston. You know Mr. Tensale?"

"Yes sir. We have met on several occasions."

"After we're done here, I'd like to speak with you," said Tensale to White.

"Certainly sir. I'm available at your convenience, with the President's permission."

"Absolutely," said the President. Mr. Tensale and I have been discussing possible positions for you in the Administration."

"Thank you, sir," replied White.

An underbutler wheeled in a cart with silver place settings, covered dishes and beverages.

"The lunch you requested, Mr. President," said the underbutler dressed in white jacket, black trousers, and white gloves as he distributed the lunch items.

"Do I know you?" asked Gatling.

"No sir. I'm a temporary replacement for Morton whose roommate was exposed to COVID, and they are both quarantined for two weeks."

"Too bad. What's for lunch then?"

"Your favorite, sir," as he lifted the covers from the dishes. "Meatloaf au gratin, stuffed with sharp cheddar cheese and bacon, complemented by double baked mashed potatoes and steamed peas and corn liberally dusted with parmesan cheese."

The underbutler placed a small gravy boat with a ladle next to each plate.

"And this is?" asked Gatling.

"Rich port wine and beef marrow mushroom sauce for the meatloaf sir. Another of your favorites."

"Excellent!" exclaimed Gatling.

"You may leave now. Close the door after you, Winston."

After they left, Gatling said: "I'm starving. Dig in Tensale."

Once outside the dining room and having closed the door, Makin said: "You are as smooth as they come, Jose. I'm hungry listening to you."

"Trust me. You're better off with Wally Burgers," said Hernandez, as he moved quickly, disappearing into the service elevator.

Meanwhile, Gatling and Tensale were admiring the lunch display.

Tensale said: "I'm starving too. It's one minute to Noon. The Zoom call will be starting."

"They will be expecting me," said Gatling.

"Trust me," said Tensale. What they are expecting and what they will get will be quite different. We should make the call, then let's dig in."

"By the way, when we're finished with the congressmen, here's a memory stick with 2 million IP addresses of various movers and shakers and their organizations who opposed me in the last election. I want to take care of them as well." He handed the memory stick to Tensale, who placed it in his shirt's breast pocket.

"That's a lot of addresses but we are up to the challenge, sir. No problem. Here's the phone. Do the honors. Just press talk and say the word I gave you. Are you ready, Mr. President?"

"Yes! I'm ready!

Ankyer and Franklin were circling the F-18 Hornet at 40,000 feet over the residence of Anastasia Moon in Eagle River Ranch, Colorado. Carl had rechecked the flight systems.

"We're set," Jake.

"I'm arming the first Harpoon," said Ankyer. "Armed."

"We didn't blow up!" said Carl.

"What the hell, I'm arming the second one." "Armed."

"We are leading a charmed life my man!" said Carl.

"Dr. Finkel, we are ready. Over."

"Roger. On my command. Over."

THE INSURRECTION PROTOCOL

At exactly 12:00 Noon Eastern Standard Time on September 15th ....

President Stephen Louis Gatling pressed the burner phone 'talk' button and said:

"FIRE"

Asher Finkel, MD PhD said to Ankyer's and Franklin's mastoid implants:

"FIRE"

When Gatling said "Fire", Chu Bak who was standing next to Anastasia Moon in front of the massive Great Room picture window, turned to the technician standing in the doorway of the room open to the Great Room and nodded. The technician pressed an icon on a smart phone he was holding. Back in the room, lights on both quantum computers blinked and lights on the communications server started flashing. The technician looked up at Chu Bak and gave him a thumbs up.

"It's started," said Chu Bak to Moon.

When Finkel said *"Fire"*, Carl Franklin thumbed the controller on his weapons' joystick and said: "Harpoons fired." The "fired" indicator on the weapons panels in front of Ankyer and Franklin flashed green followed by the word "launched" on an LCD screen...And nothing happened.

"Looks like we have a problem," said Ankyer.

"The weapons system thinks the Harpoons are armed and fired. As far as its concerned, the Harpoons are on the way."

"Had to be the lightning strike. Must have damaged the housings holding the Harpoons but not the weapons system electronics. We got a false positive.

"No time for problem analysis, Carl. We have to act. The Quantum computers are probably activating the sound weapons.

"Are you thinking what I'm thinking?" asked Carl.

"Definitely," replied Ankyer as he started the dive from 40,000 feet.

"I'm locking the autopilot at 2,000 feet with a trajectory into Moon's compound. When we get to 2,000 feet, I'm blowing the canopy and we eject. The Hornet will continue and hit the target. It's the only option. When we eject, try to steer your parasail chute as far away from the glide path as possible. Things are going to get exciting down there."

"I'm definitely with you there," said Carl.

Ankyer nosed the Hornet down and lit the afterburners. The plane shot down at Mach 1, bleeding altitude. 15 seconds later, at 2000 feet, he blew the F-18's canopy and he and Franklin pulled their ejection handles. The ejection seats unclamped, and the ejectors fired, forcefully blowing the seats upward with trailing cones of fire.. Moments later, the Hornet hit the middle guest wing of the Eagle River Ranch main house, igniting its remaining fuel, and exploding the two Harpoon missiles.

Ankyer, Franklin and their parasails detached from the Hornet's ejection seats with the seats' thrusters going full throttle. Both Ankyer and Franklin temporarily lost consciousness. Ankyer regained consciousness just as a column of super-heated air from the explosion lifted him and his parasail 5,000 feet from the ejection point. He immediately started maneuvering away from the blast site. He saw Franklin's parachute a quarter mile away at about 7,000 feet. The portable oxygen canisters attached to their parasail harnesses would keep them from oxygen deprivation, but not for long. Ankyer started looking for a flat landing space to head towards.

He thought to himself that ejecting from a fighter jet at Mach 1 and surviving was rare. But he did it and was still alive, floating around. Worse things could happen he thought...

...And then...they did...

...The four, 30,000-gallon tanks providing energy to Anastasia Moon's Eagle River Ranch exploded. The resulting mushroom cloud rose several thousand feet. It passed Ankyer sending him bowling over, unconscious again, and headed towards various Colorado mountains. Carl Franklin was surrounded by dust, fumes and blinding smoke which didn't bother Carl as he also was knocked unconscious as well by the blast.

After Chu Bak gave the signal to the technician, Moon handed him a glass of wine and said: I've been thinking over your proposal, and I'm interested as long as I can link my various business interests into the new administration."

"I can assure you that you will get everything you deserve and more!" replied Chu Bak as he sipped his wine.

Gazing out the massive plate glass window of her Great Room, Moon looked up and noticed a dot in the sky rapidly headed in their direction. She pointed it out to Chu Bak.

"That's strange. It almost looks like a pla...," not finishing her sentence as the Hornet sped into Moon's compound.

The pressure wave from the explosion propelled both Moon and Chu Bak through the plate glass window. Moon's mouth formed an "O" and her eyes bulged as she was reduced to atoms along with Chu Bak and the Chinese technicians, the Quantum computers, and everything else within the center two square miles of the Eagle River Ranch's 130,000 acres.

The occupants of the library in the Abbey were stunned. All eyes were fixed on the monitors. They watched as Ankyer and Franklin ejected, and the Hornet exploded into the compound.

With the flames, smoke and the mushroom cloud filling the monitors, someone murmured: "No one could have lived through that."

"Honey Pi asked: "Have we heard from Jake or Carl?"

"No," said Finkel.

"They could still be alive," said Honey Pi, her voice wavering. "Maybe they're unconscious from the blast. We have to at least try."

"They could be unconscious," said Su. "We know they ejected. Maybe their parachutes carried them away from the blast. There may be a way to contact them...wake them up...if they are unconscious."

"I know what you're thinking, Dr. Su," said Dr. Lee. "A harmonic pulse."

"Exactly," said Su. Turning to Finkel he asked: is there a way to send a strong harmonic pulse to their mastoid implants.?"

"Of course!" exclaimed Finkel."

"Can we do it from here Brother Arlot?"

"Absolutely. I'll do it now and make it strong," as Arlot typed into a laptop. "Done."

"Jake or Carl, can you hear me?" asked Dr. Finkel

"Do it again!" exclaimed Honey Pi and Arlot sent another stronger harmonic pulse."

"*OUCH! Oh man! What was that?*" as Ankyer's booming voice filled the library.

"*Beats the shit out of me,*" boomed Carl's voice in the library. "*I'm hanging upside down in a scrub tree at the foot of some god-damned mountain.*"

"*Jake, give me a sit rep please,*" said Finkel.

"*I'm sitting in a field semi naked. The explosion blasted off most of my flight suit. Sounds like Carl is doing yoga in a tree somewhere.*"

"*Add that a bear tried to climb the tree and eat me for lunch. I put a couple rounds over his head with my 45 to dissuade it, for the moment anyway,*" said Carl."

"I have them located through their mastoid implants," said Brother Arlot. They are three miles away from each other. Two helicopters are on the way to pick them up, said Arlot."

"*Tell them to bring some clothes for me. It's cold up here!*" said Ankyer.

The soft woosh of the air conditioning in Stephen Louis Gatling's private, executive dining room kept the temperature at a perfect 74.5 degrees, Gatling's favorite temperature. He had a lot of favorite things, and the meatloaf served for his lunch was one of them.

"Tensale, when will we hear about our former congressmen and their seditious friends? Our meatloaf is getting cold."

"I imagine they're busy at Moon's ranch at the moment. It's now 12:15. We should hear something in ten minutes or so. In the meantime, I agree with you. Let's eat."

With that Tensale poured a generous amount of gravy onto his meatloaf, the gravy running down the sides and pooling around his double baked mashed potatoes. Gatling followed suit, forking a piece of meatloaf dripping with gravy into his mouth. Tensale heaped some mashed potatoes and peas on a large piece of meatloaf and gravy, chewed, and swallowed.

"This is absolutely spectacular," said Tensale as he loaded another helping of meatloaf and gravy into his mouth. This gravy is absolutely to die for. Where did your chefs get the recipe?"

"Beats me," said Gatling forking more meatloaf and gravy. "I just told them what I liked, and presto, this is what they came up with."

"You definitely should keep them in our, oops sorry, your new administration!" said Tensale.

As they continued to eat contentedly, Gatling started to look at Tensale curiously.

"Mallory are you alright? You seem to have some blood seeping from your eyes."

"Funny you should mention that. I was going to make the same comment about you," as Tensale suddenly stood up holding his stomach. "GAAAAK!" Projectile blood, meatloaf and gravy vomit hit Gatling in the chest. A second 'GAAAAK' issued forth from Tensale, followed by gray, partly dissolved viscous, fleshy chunks of stomach trailing distended veins. The grey pieces followed the meatloaf and other gore, landing in the middle of the table then sliding to the floor in a congealing, gelatinous mass. Gatling faired not much better, blood gushing from his mouth, eyes, and nose. He pushed back from the table falling over from his chair and hitting his head on the table on the way down to the floor.

Sitting outside the executive dining room, a Secret Service agent turned up his nose. "What's that godawful smell?" he asked Winston White as White walked into the anteroom.

"Wow, I don't know, but it does smell foul. Maybe you should go in and check."

"I was given specific instructions not to enter the room under any circumstances."

"I'll tell you what," said White. "I wasn't given any instructions like those. I'll go in and check. If he gets pissed it's on me, not you."

"Good idea. Thanks for that."

White opened the door and walked into the room. He encountered Tensale on the floor, parts of his stomach lying next to him in a brownish fluid along with undigested pieces of meatloaf and mashed potatoes. The Secret Service agent who had followed White into the room looked around and immediately vomited on Tensale adding to the mess.

"Call an ambulance and get the White House medical staff in here," said White as he moved over to Gatling. "The President's still alive. Hurry!" The agent turned and hurried out of the room. The moment he was gone, White removed the Red Protocol Group tracking watch still on Gatling's wrist and put it in his pocket. He also noticed a memory stick partially exposed in Tensale's shirt breast pocket, which Makin picked up and transferred to his pocket. A moment later, the room became over run with Doctors, nurses and more Secret Service agents. White went outside the room with a senior agent and gave him a summary of what had occurred.

"I thought you were supposed to protect Gatling? the senior agent said.

"Gatling's still alive," said White.

"Point taken," replied the senior Secret Service agent. Ok, I have to start processing this mess," said the agent as a gurney with Gatling was rushed by. "See you later."

"At your convenience, agent," replied White.

White/Makin left the White House and got into the back of a black Range Rover waiting outside.

"How'd it go, George?" said Jose Hernandez.

"It was definitely memorable," replied Makin as the car headed to the private jet parked at General Aviation in Reagan National Airport.

HOLY INNOCENTS
TRAPPIST MONASTERY

Gila National Forest
New Mexico
September 20th

THE ABBEY'S LIBRARY WAS OCCUPIED BY SEVERAL Red Protocol Group members. The meeting was chaired by Dr. Asher Finkel. As was their custom, a hearty buffet lunch was available from a long sideboard, the health-hearty selections sampled by all. Chief Bell entered with a cart filled with Wally chili cheese bacon burgers and made sure everyone got at least one. He said that it was the opening shot in his Wally Burger franchise program. Varna moved his 385-pound frame from table-to-table mooching protein bars and succeeding from everyone. Carl Franklin had been pushed into the room in a wheelchair by Dr. Margie Tallon, his leg in a cast. Master Chief Neal Groton was wriggling his eyebrows and smirking at Franklin, who was giving Groton a dirty look back.

Ankyer waved over to Franklin and said: "Hey Carl, how's the leg coming?"

Franklin replied, "Just fine no thanks to you!"

"What are you complaining about? Everyone has signed your cast including the Emir of Qatar! If you had more practice ejecting at Mach 1 maybe you wouldn't have broken your leg hanging from a tree limb waiting for a bear to eat you for lunch!"

"Oh yah. Flying with you should give me plenty of practice." He threw a protein bar towards Ankyer, and Varna reared up and snagged it in midair, as everyone in the room laughed including Ankyer and Carl.

"Ok, gentlemen. Time to get serious," said Finkel

"First of all, congratulations to everyone on a superb conclusion to the mission."

"Is the Emir still mad at us for crashing his F-18?" asked Ankyer.

"He was somewhat upset, until I informed him, we would be providing an upgraded replacement along with a second F-18 for his trouble. Both the Emir and Major General Muhammid are delighted. They are also delighted with the delivery of a significant number of Harpoon missiles. Seems that his new weapons capability has improved the arms parity between Qatar and the other countries in the region. Now, I would like to share a recent news broadcast with you."

Finkel pressed a button on a remote on his table. The large TV monitor on the far wall flickered to life.

(Music) A voice intoned: "This is World News Summary from New York with Lana Bumpers and Holcomb Farleigh."

Bumpers: Good evening. The United States is in chaos today. We are starting to receive information regarding the status of President Stephen Louis Gatling who is in intensive care at Walter Reed hospital. Gatling was taken ill with what was initially described as food poisoning. Gatling is now said to be unresponsive and in a coma. Doctors hold out little hope of recovery.

Malcolm Tensale, Gatling's former Chief of Staff, was pronounced dead upon arriving at Walter Reed. One physician who refused to go on the record said that parts of Tensale's stomach had been expelled through his mouth. The White House has announced that the 25th Amendment has been invoked and Aneal Mercastor, Gatling's recently named Vice President, was sworn in as President. After the swearing-in ceremony, Mercastor resigned the Presidency and was followed by the resignation of Gatling's entire Cabinet along with Gatling's Chief of Staff, Phillip Merklin.

Merklin was found to have ties with Tensale, was arrested, and is now being interrogated by the FBI. Melody Bunsen, Speaker of the House of Representatives, has been sworn in as President, immediately filling her cabinet with acting appointees. The White House announced that President Bunsen will address the nation this evening. And there's more on this incredible news day. Over to you Holcomb.

Farleigh: Thanks Lana. Just prior to Gatling's alleged food poisoning, Gatling was to join a large Zoom meeting consisting of all the senior committee heads of Congress as well as the members of the Supreme Court, members of the military Joint Chiefs of Staff, and other senior officials. The purpose of the call was secret and the people on the call were using government laptop computers. The call's agenda was murky, but one White House staffer, off the record, said he was advised that Gatling was intending to invoke martial law because of the earlier disabling of Gatling's first Cabinet at a meeting in which his Secretary of Education, Boopsie McNulty, died because of what appeared to be a sabotaged raspberry filled jelly donut.

As we understand it, a high-pitched sound came out of the secure congressional laptop computers. Fourteen congressmen were overcome and died, and the remaining Zoom attendees suffered dizziness and vomiting when the sound coming out of the government laptops suddenly stopped. This is reminiscent of the sickness suffered by State Department staff in Cuba and the U.S. Embassy in China, but there is little additional information available. But that's not all. Over to you Lana.

Bumpers: This news day is one for the history books, Holcomb. There has been a massive explosion at the Eagle River Ranch located in Colorado. Eagle River Ranch is the residence of Anastasia Moon, the wealthy owner of the Alfernon Corporation. The property is so big it has its own postal code. All the land around the ranch for two miles was completely obliterated.

It was reported that Moon was there at the time of the blast and is assumed to have been killed. You may recall that it was rumored that Moon was on the short list for Gatling's Vice President at one time. The cause of the blast is under review, but it is known that there were four 30,000-gallon LPG tanks supplying power to the property and the immediate suspicion is that they may have exploded. Finally, the Chinese government announced that they had loaned two incredibly expensive Quantum research computers to Moon's company and demanded their return which may be a problem since an Alfernon company spokesperson said the computers in question were located at the Eagle River Ranch.

The TV monitor flickered and went blank.

"There you have it, ladies and gentlemen," said Finkel. "The facts of the matter reported by the international news becoming the actual facts reported to the public. Your decision to crash the F-18 into Moon's ranch achieved N.S.A.'s deniability involving the fighter aircraft as well as the existence of the Quantum computers."

"But the Chinese remain in possession of the sound weapon," said Dr. Su."

"And the Quantum computers to deploy it," added Dr. Lee.

"Excellent points," gentlemen. However, one of our mission requirements from N.S.A. was, if possible, to obtain the sound weapon software. We accomplished that with Leonard, our computer specialist, who hacked the Quantum computer the software resided on and downloaded it prior to the computer being obliterated by Jake and Carl. Take a bow Leonard!" said Finkel. Leonard stood up, sartorially enhanced with a green and red polka dot bow tie, an Everleigh Brothers 'Rock On' tee shirt, and purple Bermuda shorts. Leonard clasped his hands over his head, waved, and sat down again. A standing ovation was led by Master Chief Bell. Varna padded over and gave Leonard an especially wet lick.

"But the Chinese still have the sound weapon," persisted Dr. Su."

"Correct, Dr. Su. So do we... And the Chinese know it." It's a MAD, mutual assured destruction, situation. They now know if they use it again, or for that matter give it to anyone else to use, they will be on the receiving end of an enhanced version of the weapon."

"I'm wondering why Tensale died and not Gatling?" asked Dr. Martin Asbury. "They both ingested the same 'destroying angel' and 'death cap' mushroom emulsion."

"Hard to say," responded Finkel. "Hold on," said Finkel as he touched his ear. "I just received a data note. SLUG has died. So, it worked the way it was designed. It's effects just took longer in SLUG than in Tensale."

"We'll have to look into that," said plant biologist Miles Zastovich. "We may have to make some adjustments."

"Agreed," said Finkel. "Before I forget, on the way out of Gatling's dining room, George picked a memory stick out of Tensale's shirt pocket. Turns out it had two million Internet Protocol addresses, including known enemies of Gatling...he had a lot... and millions of people no one knew about. If George hadn't been so observant and if Gatling had succeeded with his plan, millions of people might have been murdered. Well done George!" said Finkel as everyone applauded."

"Thank you, Dr. Finkel. I was pleased to contribute to the mission even though I put on 20 pounds from eating at all those Washington D.C. restaurants and barely avoided death by dismemberment thanks to Chief Bell, Brother William and Varna!" Everyone applauded again.

EPILOGUE
Qatar
Red Palace

SAND. A WHITE ribbon coursing and undulating through a forest of large, desert trees among boulders and artificial lakes and rivers.

"We knew that you and Jake liked to remain fit, so we wanted to provide you with a place to run," said the Emir of Qatar as he joined Honey Pi on a third story veranda of what was now referred to as the Red Palace. Since we are in the desert, we thought an arboreal setting with desert trees and streams would be nice along with a six-mile white sand running path. We imported the sand from Destin Florida which has the whitest sand in the world."

"It's beautiful," replied Honey Pi. "I haven't had a chance to run on it yet, but Jake is out there now," pointing to a distant figure coming around a bend at considerable speed with an exceptionally large animal running alongside him.

"Jake likes to exercise with Varna and the running path is perfect."

"I hope it's not too long," replied the Emir. We had one of our marathon runners try it out. The various elevations of the path had him winded after one circuit."

"Won't be a problem. This is the third circuit since they started."

"Why am I not surprised!" said the Emir "I see another figure down there."

"That would be your grandson," said Honey Pi. "He has formed a close attachment to Jake and likes to join Jake and Varna in the final circuit. They slow down for him, but they are gradually increasing his speed. It's great conditioning and he absolutely loves Varna."

"Speaking of which it seems that Varna is working overtime increasing our wolf pack population here."

"Yes. Since Jake and I are dividing our time between here and the Abbey, having a security wolf pack makes sense."

"By the way, I was pleased to hear that Dr. Finkel has appointed you and Jake as co-coordinators of the Red Protocol Group."

"Jake and I have different ways of looking at things, but we usually come to similar conclusions. Dr. Finkel is remaining highly involved as a consultant, but the operational aspect of the Group is being coordinated by me and Jake. The Group is very collegial, and the arrangement works out well. Plus, we have a lot to keep us busy."

"Well, I'm glad you are here in Qatar. We are major supporters of the United States and see ourselves as a bridge between the United States and the Middle East."

"It looks like our runners are coming here," as Ankyer waived. "Can you join us for lunch?"

"I wouldn't miss it!" said the Emir.

UNITED STATES

THE UNITED STATES CONGRESS, after a period of considerable disruption reconvened with newly appointed senators and representatives to replace those killed by what was now being called the 'Gatling Insurrection' since even right-wing voters and their representatives came to see Gatling's conspiracy as an assault on American democracy. Numerous members of Congress with associations with the late Stephen Louis Gatling announced their retirements to spend more time with their families. The new Congress wasted little time reverting to their divisiveness and backbiting. Asked by a reporter to explain the continued Congressional disfunction to the public, a newly minted congressman was quoted as saying: "Why should the public be surprised? They voted for us."

THE ABBEY

ASHER FINKEL'S PRIVATE PHONE BUZZED IN HIS STUDY AT THE ABBEY. It was the Emir of Qatar.

"Dr. Finkel, Salazar here," said the Emir. "I have some exciting news."

"Which is?" asked Finkel.

"You may recall that Jake mentioned that there is a three-panel painting called 'Three Seas' which many say is highly sought after by major art connoisseurs in the Middle East. An understatement if ever there was one," said the Emir. "The painting is priceless and is desired by many, including myself. Its possession would be a centerpiece in any country's art collection. It's a national treasure."

"What is it you would like me to do?" asked Finkel.

"I would like to request that the Red Protocol Group track it down," said the Emir. "There is an unconfirmed rumor that it may have surfaced in the United States. Possibly in Arizona or at least somewhere in the western part of the country. I realize that the Red Protocol Group is engaged in very high priority missions including matters of State. But the Group is so effective I would be in your debt if you could allocate some time for Qatar."

"Art investigation is outside our normal remit," said Finkel. "On the other hand, you have been more than kind to Jake and Honey Pi and to the entire Red Protocol Group for that matter. It would be the least that we could do to help. I'll look into it."

"Thank you, my friend," said the Emir.

Ankyer and Honey Pi were on one of their many palace verandas reviewing the details of a North Korean ballistic missile program when their mastoid implants activated.

"Dr. Finkel, good to hear from you!" said Ankyer.

"Hello Dr. Finkel. How's things at the Abbey?" asked Honey Pi.

"Everything is fine. World-wide chaos has seemingly abated, for the moment at least. Say you two, I just got off the phone with the Emir. We have an interesting situation..."

......But that's another story......

THE END

www.ingramcontent.com/pod-product-compliance
Lightning Source LLC
Chambersburg PA
CBHW060346260626
47160CB00006B/2213